The Travels of Dr. Rebecca Harper

Past and Present

Elizabeth Woolsey

Elizabeth Woolsey Horse Doctor Press

The Travels of Dr. Rebecca Harper Book 4

Past and Present

ISBN: 979-8-9869111-8-2

Copyright 2021 by Elizabeth Woolsey (Horse Doctor Press)

All rights reserved. No part of this book may be reproduced or used in any form or by Electronic or mechanical means, including information or Storage or retrieval systems—except in the case of brief quotations embodied in critical articles or reviews —without permission in writing from the author, Elizabeth Woolsey.

The Travels of Dr. Rebecca Harper Past and Present is a work of fiction.

Any similarities to places or persons, living or dead, are coincidental.

Cover design by David Blake

Edited by Marilyn Anderson

Published in the United States

elizabethwoolsey.com

To My Educators
Both professionals and
those that taught me how to survive
in a profession that could have ended differently.
To the clients whose horses provided me endless stories.
Thank you all!

Part 1

Reunion

CHAPTER 1

Rebecca

"Maggie, any letup in the rain yet?"

"I think I see some blue sky." Maggie Clayton, our clinic receptionist and head nurse, pointed as she peered out of the hospital window. She and I had just finished a marathon week. Alf Webber, my associate, would relieve me of my duties. He and John Harmon, my other associate, did the lion's share of the work at our clinic and town hospital in Virginia City. I typically worked a few days a week, and one whole week per month, during which I stayed in town and covered the after-hours. I still conducted most of the obstetrical work.

This last week had been difficult. Three delivering mothers experienced more complications than usual. I performed two caesareans and attended the delivery of a still-born. We knew the baby had died in utero and had not reached full-term. I was supposed to be off now. With the unusual autumn rain, though, I couldn't return home to my husband, Sam Buchanan, and daughter, Hanna.

The good news is that I have two adorable grandchildren from Sam's son, Dan. Lizzy is almost three years old, and Little Hank is nearly a year old. Hanna, our adopted daughter, was turning fifteen by our estimates. Indians had abducted and raised her and returned her to the cavalry when death and starvation followed a series of skirmishes and the relocation of many indigenous tribes. She was given to the Virginia City sheriff, who passed her on to me for care. Sam and I adopted Hanna nearly four years ago. She was growing tall and, in my eyes, beautiful.

The rain and ensuing flood had trapped me in Virginia City. I had to cross a creek to return to the Cattle Creek Ranch. Sam and Dan built a bridge over the stream several years before. However, this bridge was no match for the floods during the last few days, which stranded me in town. Our sturdy hospital had been constructed a few years earlier. The unusual storm caused a great deal of damage all over town. Flooding and leaky roofs brought destruction to many businesses and residences. All the available rooms at the hotel were filled due to the rain and flooding.

The boardinghouse where I stayed when I was in town had sustained significant water damage, and I'd been forced to sleep at the hospital. That meant I was getting up at all hours. We had employed other nurses now, as we were the leading hospital for a large area.

One nurse was exasperating because she would call me at a moment's notice. I could have throttled her. I probably hadn't slept more than two consecutive hours for the entire week, and now I was working overtime since there was no chance of going home to the Cattle Creek Ranch.

I met with my good friend, Ray Thompson, for lunch or dinner at least once daily. We met at the hotel or café to talk and even play checkers. He was also Sam's closest friend. He had arthritis and other typical infirmities of older men. Like Sam, he was in his late sixties. Sam was lucky that, despite his age, he did not show any signs of slowing down. I was fifteen years younger than Sam. He was not my first husband. Alas, I seem to have a penchant for older men. Sam was actually a few years younger than my first husband, Jeff.

That's a long story. In a nutshell, I'm a time traveler who came from the 1980s to the 1850s. I couldn't find a way back to Jeff or my daughter Lauren until almost twenty years after I initially time traveled. When I returned once, I discovered they had both moved on. By then, I'd fallen in love with Sam Buchanan of *Comstock*, my favorite television show. Who knew it really existed? Anyway, I now was living the dream, literally, in the 1870s as a mother, wife, town doctor, and veterinarian.

My present goal is simply returning to my *Comstock* family and getting some sleep. The obstacles were the flooding and another mother in active labor who wasn't quite full term, yet she was experiencing robust contractions. It's not as if we have all the drugs that have probably been discovered following the 1800s to calm her uterus or even the oxygen for a premature baby. It's "fly-by-the-seat-of-your-pants" medicine at best. I was lucky to have surgical skills I learned on animals before I time traveled.

I received further medical training when I first arrived in the 1800s from Dr. Thomas Walker, a prominent surgeon in San Francisco. He introduced me to anesthetics that could be used at this time. In addition, I worked as a surgeon both during the Civil War and at a progressive hospital in Baltimore before returning to Virginia City. I realized my limitations, and I often sent my associates, Alf and John, to meetings to upgrade our conjoined efforts to practice quality medicine.

When I was at home, I cared for the men, women, and children who lived and worked on my family's ranch. I additionally went up to our cabin in the beautiful little valley we call Hank Heaven. Sam built the cabin for me several years ago when I time traveled back to my modern-day family. I elected to return to be with Sam and his family and ride out my days on the Cattle Creek Ranch.

"Darn it, Maggie. I wish this woman would give birth or get off the bed. I want to go home."

"You and me both, Becky. I don't suppose we could make her ride a horse today?"

"Why not? There's no malpractice yet." *Now that was a rare slip. I hardly ever do that anymore.*

"What's malpractice? Becky, you have the darnedest ideas. What's that Oreo thing you used to mention?"

"Just things that were happening when I was in Baltimore. Never mind." *Please, do never mind.*

The sun was out, and I needed some fresh air. I walked to the stable to visit my beautiful mare, which I named Penny II for my beloved first mare that I rode when I arrived in the 1850s. Hanna found her running wild on the ranch and broke her in for me. She presented her to me on my birthday three years ago. I loved the original Penny, but this mare was something special. My daughter was a master at starting young horses under saddle. Sam was so proud of her and termed her the best breaker on the ranch. He would never let her ride a bronc, though, which was men's business. After the buck was out of the young stock, however, her father gave her several to finish. He was even riding a younger version of his old buckskin, Cash, that Hanna had started. The new one was called Cash as well. Even Dan had a younger paint named for his old horse. These men had no imaginations. *What am I saying—Penny II?*

When I returned to the hospital, Alf commented that the woman had begun to dilate. "Becky, I hate to ask, but can you hang around until this baby is born?"

"Do I have a choice? The creek is a raging river. I'm certainly not going home today."

In fact, I spent two more nights. We ended up performing a cesarean the next day and delivered a little girl. Sam eventually crossed the stream and arrived in Virginia City as I was going into surgery. He had errands in town. Sam had seen Ray and would have a meal with him while he waited for me. He was confident we could safely cross the creek later that day. He seemed excited, and I was so glad to see him. Our frequent separations kept our love young and exciting despite the years. He whispered that he wanted to try to be back by dinnertime. I knew my birthday was coming, and I guessed he and Gee Ling had planned a dinner with Dan, Jenny, and the kids. I was exhausted but attempted to finish early.

Well, that didn't happen. The surgery went well, and the baby was strong and healthy, but the mother had a bleed. As a result, I was required to go in a second time to remove her uterus to halt the bleeding. I didn't conduct transfusions then, and it was do-or-die in those days. For this reason, it was nine o'clock before I was done. Sam waited in the staff room and still wanted to go back to the Cattle Creek Ranch.

"I'm so tired, and I definitely don't want to face Gee Ling's wrath. Can't we wait until tomorrow?"

"I must get back, Bec."

"You're the boss."

"I'd like to think so."

He dreams, but how could I deny my husband anything? "Let's ride, cowboy." Sam didn't have his regular horse. He said Cash had been injured. Crossing the stream in the moonlight wasn't as difficult as I expected. As we approached the Cattle Creek Ranch, a sole lamp was lit. It must be midnight. Our dog, Skeeter, was outside and greeted me as though I was a hero.

I could tell Sam was more animated and nervous about something. I imagined a big present or a surprise party at the house. We unsaddled the horses and took them to the barn. Sam generally did this task, but he wanted my help. I was convinced there was something in the house, but I wasn't sure what it was.

Lauren

So much has happened that it's hard to explain. First, I'm at the Cattle Creek Ranch, and I think it's the 1870s. I was almost drowned trying to get here due to a massive flood. I guess I'm a time traveler now. I took stock of my current situation: I'm an unemployed horse vet at twenty-five who is engaged to the finest man alive. Jim Kennedy is a highly-skilled, small animal surgeon. *What am I saying? I'm currently with people who are dead. It's pretty confusing.*

Thanks to a history instructor, I'm in the exact location where I've lived, but more than a hundred twenty years earlier. I've left my time, my dog, my fiancé, and my family. My fiancé is in the Middle East, caring for bomb-sniffing dogs for our country. At least that's what he thought he would be doing, but it might be something else. He wasn't sure. The bad news is he was incommunicado for his deployment as a reservist in the army for six to twelve months.

My family believes I embarked on an overseas humanitarian-veterinary trip. I made sure everyone thought I was in a place other than where I actually am. I left a scary stalker, who has a fixation on Jim and has been threatening me for a few weeks, as well. Furthermore, I'm involved in a nasty situation with the local sheriff's department and two shady deputies, who would benefit from my being indisposed when their corruption trial is held.

I am waiting at the Cattle Creek Ranch for my stepfather, Sam Buchanan, to bring my mother home from Virginia City to meet me. The ranch cook, Gee Ling, planned a surprise dinner for her birthday with Dan Buchanan, his wife, Jenny, their two children, and his sister, Hanna. Of course, I'll be the big surprise. My mother was late getting back to the ranch, and everyone eventually went home to bed. I have tried to stay awake even though it seems that they are not coming tonight, after all. I think I'll nap for a few minutes on the couch in the great room in case they return tonight. I have only a few days until I should get back to the real world.

CHAPTER 2

Rebecca

As we approached the door of the house, Sam stopped me.

"What's going on, Sam?"

"Becky, I have a surprise for you. We have a guest. In case she's asleep, I think it's best if we try not to wake her."

I thought about several people I would love to see—my old friend Martha Tyler, a schoolteacher, married to our former minister, Earl Tyler. I hadn't seen her for a year or more. There were Hiram and Jeannette Merritt, who were my great-great-grandparents in real life, although only Sam and I realized that fact. She and her husband held agricultural interests all over California and Oregon. There were also several more women. I was so tired, I prayed our guest would be asleep, and we could visit after I had slept awhile myself.

Sam put his hand up, wanting me to wait until he scouted the house. When he emerged, he placed a finger on his lips and led me to the divan. A young girl was lying on the settee. It was dark, but I could just make out her face. I gasped quietly, sat down on the table in front of her, and simply stared. Sam sat down behind me and held my shoulders. I cried, and I could feel his hands trying to calm me. I don't know how long we were there, but it must have been an hour. Oh, how I wanted to touch her and stroke her hair.

Finally, she blinked and opened her eyes. I could tell she woke up in a strange place and was disoriented. She finally recognized me and smiled.

"Hi, Mom. Happy birthday."

Lauren

It was my mother. I wasn't sure about her reaction, and I reached out tentatively to take her hand and feel her touch. She immediately embraced me, and we both cried. Sam stood up, smiled at me, and mouthed, "thank you," in my direction. I returned the salutation. I don't know how long we hugged, after which my mother held me at arm's length and embraced me again.

"How?"

I interrupted her. "We have a mutual friend."

I believe she understood I meant Frank Lash.

She glanced at my engagement ring and inquired about my fiancé. I laughed and admitted it wasn't the one she thought.

"Mom, is it okay to call you that? I can say something else when others are here."

Sam smiled. "Lauren, I'm the only one who knows her history. 'Mother' or 'Ma' will work in public." Sam set the rules, and we would all follow them. I didn't mind because I recognized he had my mother's interest at heart.

I laughed. "Ma, I can tell you are tired. How about we all go to bed, and we can talk in the morning?"

My mother nodded and dabbed away at the tears with Sam's handkerchief. She handed it to me to do the same.

"I'll need to carry two handkerchiefs now." I could see Sam's eyes were filled.

We all laughed, and she hugged me again. "Pleasant dreams, Lauren." Sam put his hand around her waist and headed her upstairs. I could perceive the love they shared. I'd already witnessed this with my own parents, and that's what I wanted in a relationship.

Rebecca

I generally sleep longer the first morning after a long week at the hospital, but not this morning. I was up early and found Gee Ling making breakfast with Hanna.

"Ma, did you meet Lauren? I have a sister who knows all about horses and veterinary stuff. She's so smart, Ma, and she even made a shoe for Pa's horse. Lauren says Pa's horse broke his coffin bone. That's the bone inside his foot. The shoe makes Cash walk some, but he's still lame. She's so pretty, and she wants to talk to me about my life before I came to live with you and Pa. My sister thinks I need to write it down and even write a book. She's tall too. Did I tell you she talks like she's from the South? At least, that's what Pa says."

Hanna hugged me. "I missed you, Ma."

"I missed you, too, Hanna. We should be quiet until Lauren's awake."

"I am awake." I turned to see my beautiful daughter.

Lauren was dressed and ready for the day. She had on Jenny's riding outfit, which was a little short. I was so excited to talk to her, but I was wary that Hanna would not understand the many implications.

"Good morning, Lauren. Do you drink coffee or tea?"

Hanna and Gee Ling greeted her. They appeared to like Lauren. I couldn't take my eyes off her. She reminded me of Jeff. Except for my curly hair, she was still much more like him. Lauren was always daddy's girl.

"Coffee, thanks. May I help at all? I am the worst cook. I can barely boil water, but I'm willing to learn."

"Ma wants me to learn everything that Gee Ling knows, so when he's dead, she won't starve."

Gee Ling swatted Hanna. "You no talk about me dying, little missy. Gee Ling not dying until you old and have grandchildren."

"Ow, Ma, did you see him hit me?"

"You're lucky he got to you before I did. Set the table."

"I'll help you, Hanna. We sisters must stick together."

Sam entered the kitchen and asked about the delay. He was planning to take Hanna to Dan's.

"Oh, but Pa, I want to stay with Ma and Lauren today."

"Hanna, they haven't seen each other for a long time. You and I will give them time to catch up. Lauren won't leave for several days. You two can spend some time together later."

"But Pa." Sam gazed at Hanna, who realized she had no option but to obey. The consequences of disobedience might be painful. When I was young, in the 1950s, my father was a spanker. I can't remember ever being spanked beyond twelve years, yet I recognized these were different times. I wondered whether Jeff had ever spanked Lauren.

Lauren and I walked out to the barn to inspect Sam's horse, Cash. He'd improved even since yesterday when he had his rim shoe nailed onto his hoof. "I can't tell you how much this horse means to Sam. I can't thank you enough."

"My pleasure. He seems like a nice man."

Men were coming in and going out of the barn. "Maybe we should ride to a place where we can talk. We could ride down to the creek. Sam said you'd lost something when you emerged in the flooded waters. I can't believe you even survived."

"Yes, me too. My guess is it's reached the Pacific Ocean by now."

I saddled Penny while she saddled Pocket, and we were off after getting some food for lunch.

"Lauren, I just want to say that I'm so sorry about the way things turned out. I really did attempt to find you. I tried for years. I'd have done anything to return to our time, and you, and your father."

"Mom, I know. I realize how much you tried. Both Frank and Sam explained to me that you sought a way back to the 1900s for years. I don't have any bad feelings for you. I'm not here to admonish you, or fight with you, or anything like that. I'm here simply to see you, discover the way you live, and tell you how I live. Dad and I are fine. I've had a great life. I know I can say both Dad and I have led wonderful lives. Your sister, Sherry, is a terrific mom. She treats me as if I was her own. I have a few conflicts right now with my fiancé's deployment and lack of communication. I'm temporarily unemployed, but my life is and has been amazing. I have everything I want. Please don't worry or have any regrets. I only wish you could have found love sooner."

Lauren

That Hanna can sure talk. I don't think I've ever received such a grilling. Thankfully, Mom's husband could shut her down with a single look. Mom wanted to get away so we could talk. Only her husband knew her story. When she inquired about my life, I told her the basics. I left out any of the scary stuff and concentrated on my graduation, my work, and made sure I didn't make her regret the way our lives turned out.

Since I realized she felt terrible about not contacting me, I mentioned what dad said about loving two people simultaneously but committing to only one. I told her I believed, based on what my dad said, that she'd made the right decision not to contact us. I don't know whether that helped to ease her mind, but it was true. I wish I could have met her then, but I wouldn't hurt her with such words.

I described what I brought with me and my desperate attempts to hold on to it. We discussed the time-travel portal. We both knew how dangerous the creek flow might be on the other side of time and that this would be the only occasion I would do this. She confessed she was never going to time travel again. We agreed we had lived at different times, and I clarified I would soon return. I was worried the weather would change back in my time. What if the water rose, and I experienced a similar torrent when I returned? I was going to stay for a few more days and head back. Nothing she could say would dissuade me.

She took me up to the area of the rock slide. We decided to ride down from there to search for indications of the parcel I'd lost. I laughed as I described explaining transparent plastic bags to her husband, Sam. "How do you do it?"

"Do what?"

"Live in these times without the mod cons?"

"Mod cons?"

"Baggies, cellophane, you know, modern conveniences. Mom, have you been away that long?"

"That's nothing. Try living without Oreos and tampons."

I stared at her, and she realized what I was thinking.

"No, I don't need those anymore." My mother explained how women used rags and washed them.

"Totally primitive." Sheesh, not for me thanks.

Mom rolled her eyes, and we both laughed. It was so good to share this knowledge.

We arrived at the slide area. Of course, no evidence of it exists now because it will happen in the future. I told my mother about the plaque. She was embarrassed. "Oh, my God. For me? I'm no one. How ridiculous!"

"Mom, you're a legend in my time. Everyone in that region of Nevada knows about you. You're folklore."

We stared down into the creek, where the water had dropped significantly. It was still murky, but it was clearing. The course of the stream had changed. We both gasped. I was having problems orienting myself, but I was reasonably sure a colossal boulder had dropped from above into the portal pool below. Water swirled on both sides of the rock, but it split the stream in half. My heart sank. My mother rose in her saddle and peered down at the scene.

"I know it will be fine." My mother repeated herself several times, but I knew from her voice she wasn't convinced, and she was worried. I was apoplectic. No, my guess was it would not be all right. The boulder was almost the size of a car.

"That might change things somewhat." I thought about Jim and wondered how I could get back. I was sick, and I kept staring at the pool that last week barely flowed. I glanced at my mother, who understood my devastation. My thoughts ranged from panic to my modern-day friend, Rich, who was a teacher and—in the off-season—drove big machines that could move the boulder. Could we blow it up out of the water, or would that impact the portal? I just didn't know.

"Lauren, let's not jump to any conclusions. I'm sure there's a way back."

"Let's hope I find it in a shorter time than you did."

We rode in silence back to the ranch house. I went into my bedroom and asked to have a short nap. I didn't sleep. I just had a pity-party cry. My mother rode to Dan and Jenny's house to speak to Sam. When I emerged, Sam was back, sitting at his desk in the great room. Because Hanna was there, as well, nothing was mentioned. Dinner was cooking, and Dan and Jenny were scheduled to arrive at any time. I went into the kitchen, where the old Chinese cook was kneading dough.

"Mr. Ling, may I help you with anything?"

"Not Mr. Ling, Gee Ling. Talk to me. Your mother and Mr. Sam very happy you here. Gee Ling very happy too. Hanna very happy. Everybody happy. "

"Thank you, but I need to work. What can I do?"

"You do what I do, then we let it sit and get big once more." I knew he meant I could knead the dough and let it rise again.

"Missy, Gee Ling thinks you sad. What makes missy sad?"

"Homesick. Do you get homesick? Where's your home?"

"Home on Cattle Creek Ranch. No other home now. This my home."

I continued to knead the dough. Hanna came in to announce she was stealing me. She'd made a present for her mother and wanted to show it to me before our mother woke up. We climbed the steps to her room, which was the first time I had been upstairs. Hanna's room was simple and decorated with a mixture of Indian artifacts and American memorabilia. A copy of the Constitution, some Indian spears, and even a bow and arrow were on the walls.

There were no pictures of rock stars or television characters. I had to laugh at how sparse the decorations were, by contrast to my sister's and my room when we were that age. I'd been obsessed with horse pictures and famous racehorses. I had photographs of Olympic horses and a few bronc riders in their jeans and chaps. I'm sure my parents frowned at the men with provocative poses, but they never said anything. Hanna had written about and drawn several pictures of Indians and her life before she left them.

Her artwork was outstanding. It was all bound in a leather sheath and made a beautiful book, with etchings of images from her tribal days on the cover. I was jealous. I had nothing and could not compete. I'd brought my mother a picture of Jim and me, but that had been washed down the creek.

Chapter 3

Rebecca

When Lauren announced she would nap, I quickly rode over to Jenny and Dan's home. Hanna wanted to know if Lauren was at the house. "Yes, but she's taking a rest. Do not, I repeat, do not, wake her."

"Yes, ma'am. I'll help Gee Ling with dinner until she wakes up."

"Tell him we won't be late tonight. Run along."

I went in to find Sam holding Little Hank and Lizzy while sitting in Dan's stuffed chair. "Where are Dan and Jenny?"

"They went to look at the cattle. Jenny was getting cabin fever." He smiled. I had a feeling there was more to inspecting cattle than what was said.

"Hmm, I wouldn't mind another baby."

"Me, either."

"Sam, since we're almost alone, I need to tell you something."

He sat up and stared at me. "And?"

"You know how I've never explained the way I came here or could travel back if I wanted to?"

"I've wondered."

"I think we may have a problem. A huge problem."

"What did Lauren say to you?" He glanced angrily.

"She didn't say anything. I think she's in shock. We went up to the portal, and it was different. It may be gone. It's not for sure, but it looks as though a large boulder has blocked the portal."

"Am I going to see what you're talking about?"

"We won't have time before dinner, but I'd like to take you up there tomorrow."

"Can't we move the boulder?"

"I don't know. I'll let you inspect it tomorrow. Just be aware Lauren declared she's only staying here a few days. I wish she would stay forever, but I know she loves her fiancé. She thinks she's stuck in another time right now."

When the front door opened, a happy and relaxed Jenny came in and hugged me. "I guess you've seen her. What do you think?"

"Overwhelmed. I can't believe this has happened. I'm so blessed."

I picked up Lizzy. "When may I take her to work? We need another doctor in the family. It's time I started her training."

"She's going to be a teacher like her mama." Jenny took Little Hank as he was starting to fuss.

As Sam got up, we prepared to leave. "Six o'clock sharp unless you want the wrath of a Chinaman."

"It wasn't us who were late last night."

Sam and I needed some time alone. We led our horses back to the main house. I was still quite emotional. Never in any of my dreams or aspirations had I ever thought I would see my beautiful daughter again. I hoped she would stay here, although I knew it was selfish and unrealistic. I realized her heart was yearning for her betrothed. *How many times had I lost, or been separated from, the man I loved?* My heart ached for her. We stopped just for a moment as Sam told me he would move heaven and earth to clear a path for her to return to her time and the man she loved. "I won't like it, Becky, but I'll do it if that's what makes you happy." He took me in his arms and kissed me. "Maybe we need to check the cattle."

"Definitely."

When we returned to the house, dinner was almost ready. I greeted Lauren and Hanna. I could tell Lauren had cried. Hanna didn't know what had happened that afternoon. I took Hanna upstairs, where we dressed for a birthday dinner. I'd apologized to Lauren that we didn't have any formal clothes to fit her. She didn't seem to care.

Lauren

I knew I was expected to be the guest of honor at dinner, even though it was my mother's birthday. I had to suck it up for the evening and pretend everything was hunky-dory. I wondered if that phrase was used back then. I donned the one dress that seemed the most festive. There was a knock on the door. "Just a second."

"Lauren, it's Sam. May I come in?"

I quickly buttoned the dress and asked him to enter. He had a box. "I bought this in town yesterday, and one of the men brought it out today for me. I understand you're here simply for a short time, but I thought you might like to wear it."

I opened the box with a carefully folded, bright-green-satin dress. "Oh, Mr. Buchanan. You shouldn't have." It wasn't my style or anything I would have ever wanted to wear, but I knew it was fashionable for the times and must have cost a fortune. I could wear it, and then they could set it aside for Hanna. She would not be as tall as I was, but they could cut it down. "Thank you."

"Your mother told me about your dilemma. I'm going to check the creek tomorrow and determine what we need to resolve the problem. Can you bear with me and try to make her happy tonight?"

"Sir, you didn't have to ask me. I already planned to do that. I'd brought her things and a few pictures from home, but they were lost in the current, and now I have nothing to give her. I feel terrible."

"No one will be able to compete with your presence tonight. You are the best gift any of us could have ever imagined. I realize it took courage to come here, and I still don't understand how you did it, but I guess I'll learn tomorrow. Now, why don't you get that dress on and maybe freshen up a bit, and we'll see you in a few minutes."

"I'll be down shortly and don't worry. It will be my mother's night. Thank you, sir."

He smiled and left the room. Two minutes later, Hanna came in, jumped on the bed, and went on to tell me how to wear the dress and what to add to it to make it look nice.

"Lauren, would you please tell Pa I'm old enough to court?"

Court? Is that what they called dating? "How old are you?"

"I'm fifteen. We don't know for sure, but that's what Ma thinks. Pa will not let me court until I'm eighteen, but I know for a fact he allowed Dan to court a girl when he was fourteen."

"I guess that's your father's way of saying he loves you and wants to protect you. I know it doesn't seem fair, but that's how my father was, as well. You're his only daughter, and he wants you to stay little and young."

"He has you as a daughter too, now," Hanna commented while tying a bow for me.

"Kind of. Since I'm grown, and I am spoken for, your father isn't truly a father to me. I had a wonderful dad, and I'm not looking for another. That's not to say your father isn't a marvelous father, but I'm not searching."

"Could you still put in a good word for me?"

"I can try, but he and your mother know what's best for you. Are you interested in one specific person?"

"I kind of want to court a few fellas before I decide. However, right now, there's one called Caleb."

"How old is he?"

"He's nineteen."

"Nope, not gonna help you on that one."

"Pa believes he's too old, as well, but Pa's much older than Ma is, and I think he's not being fair."

"Sorry, I'm with your pa on that one. At your age, one year is equal to ten at your parents' age."

"Huh?"

"Never mind. I'm starving." I had no appetite ever since I saw that boulder, but I wouldn't want to spoil my mother's birthday for anything.

We emerged from the bedroom. The dining table was transformed into a table laden with roast and everything else imaginable. Chinese lanterns hung from the chandelier. Dan and Jenny were talking with my mother in the great room. Dan whistled at the modern, 1870s dress I was wearing. I could tell my mother was impressed.

That was the point. Entrance made, and now could I just go back to my life? I had planned to stay no more than a week. I'd already been there for five days. I liked these people, and I loved my mother, but we hadn't really talked about anything except our physical lives. I didn't feel I had gained any earthshaking guidance or insight into her or her life yet.

"Lauren, you're beautiful." Jenny touched the dress.

"Thank you." I was pleased they liked it. I glanced at Sam, who was beaming. He'd walked over to my mother and had his hand around her waist. I could see my mother was emotional. I wondered if she was always like that. I must take after my father in that respect. It took a great deal to make me cry—something like a boulder stranding me in the 1800s when my fiancé was in the 2000s. Now that's a reason to weep.

We were all given a glass of sparkling wine. We toasted my mother and my arrival. I'm not a wine lover, but it was delicious. The bottle had a label, and I inquired where it was from.

"It's from the Bordeaux region of France." Sam had ordered it for a special occasion. I was impressed.

We were summoned to the table, where I was asked to sit next to my mother. Hanna asked to sit next to me, and the rest all sat on the other side of the table. Lizzy sat in a handmade highchair next to Jenny.

Following grace, we began a magnificent meal. Dan and Jenny continued posing questions that my mother, Sam, and I answered or deflected as best we could. I decided that I would say I was from Virginia. I claimed I lived in New York during the Civil War with my father, now dead. I hated saying this. It seemed to me that I was betraying him. I was against all forms of slavery, but I understood that it was only one of the Civil War issues. Finally, when all the grilling was over, Sam produced a letter from his other son, Clint, who currently lived in Australia. He and his wife were parents to two young girls.

My mother said she would read it later. Hanna ran upstairs to retrieve her leather-bound collection of stories and pictures. My mother was so pleased and fussed over it. I was sure she could tell that Hanna was feeling second-rate in my presence. Dan and Jenny gave my mother some new fishing lines and some flies Dan had made at night. Neither of them lived for fishing, but they knew my mother enjoyed a break from her work by angling, especially up at Hank Heaven. Sam gave her a beautiful pendant that was like the one I wore. She put it on immediately. They genuinely loved each other.

I was embarrassed to have nothing. I could see they recognized my dilemma. Everyone expressed disappointment. They all hoped their present was my mother's favorite one but were outdone by my presence, which was the most fantastic present she had received in many years. Even Hanna agreed.

Gee Ling, who had moderated the dinner, signaled to Hanna to begin clearing the table. I jumped up to assist. I could tell this was not expected or even appreciated, but I piped up, "We sisters have to stick together." Hanna observed me, and the sting of her gift being second-rate was gone in a flash. The others realized the effort I had made and gratefully handed me their plates.

After the table was cleared, Gee Ling brought in the lemon cake from the previous night. My mother stood up following our slightly different rendition of "Happy Birthday."

"This has been the best birthday I've ever had. I want you all to remember this evening and cherish the moment. We're all here. Although Clint, Johnny, and even Hank aren't with us, we're blessed with our family and the addition of my daughter. Thank you, one and all." She sat down, and we quietly began to eat the tasty cake.

My mother went to the kitchen to bring Gee Ling back. "One more thing. We all need to thank our other family members for making this delicious meal and for helping to knit our family together. I realize Dan and Jenny would never come to dinner if they had to rely on me to cook." Everyone laughed, and Gee Ling beamed.

We all retired to the great room and were given brandy. Hanna could take a sip. My mother requested one more favor from us. "I would like to go up to Hank Heaven for a few days. I understand Hanna needs to start school. Jenny, if it's all right, may she stay with you all? I wish to take Lauren to church tomorrow to see the town and meet a few friends, but I want to head for the meadow after that. Sam, can you join us? I think you have a cattlemen's meeting?"

Hanna started to protest, but one look from Sam, and she knew better. My mother put her arm around Hanna. "Hanna, darling, you and I've had many trips up there, and we'll have many more when Lauren is gone."

Sam glanced at Dan. "Will you represent the Cattle Creek Ranch while I accompany these two beautiful women up to Hank Heaven? I want to ensure they don't steal the last fish out of the lake."

"Right, Pa." Dan appeared pleased, but my mother laughed.

I looked at her. "Nothing. I was thinking of something in my past." She later informed me that she remembered Dan always commenting, "Right, Pa," on *Comstock* when she was a child, watching the program on television.

"Is this dress appropriate for church?"

Jenny shook her head. "Stop by the house tomorrow, and we can all go together. I have another dress that will suit you better."

"Thank you. I'll be gone before you know it, and you won't have to raid your closet any longer."

They all stared at me with puzzled expressions.

My mother realized "raiding the closet" was a foreign expression. "I recall hearing 'raiding the closet' in Baltimore. It's an Eastern expression." *Saved again.*

Rebecca

After the men hitched the wagon the following morning, we all climbed in. Cassie, my long-term girlfriend, and her husband, the head stockman for the Cattle Creek Ranch-cattle enterprise, joined us. I introduced my daughter to them. "Lauren, this is Cassie and Merv." Maybe they had already met? "Have you met Lauren? Cassie and I are the thorns in the sides of the men on the ranch. Cassie teaches school on the Cattle Creek Ranch. She taught Hanna until this year. Hanna's going into Virginia City for some advanced studies, so she can move on to college, pursue more education, and have a career." I wanted her to have options. I knew Hanna would probably marry a local boy. The ability to care for herself and any future children would be something to fall back on.

Hanna was noticing the boys. I realized she was partial to an older boy, whom I knew was trouble. His mother was an old dance-hall girl who, despite her age, had maintained her looks and her job for several years in the local saloon, the Bucket o' Blood. Pam Wilkins practically ran the place. However, her son Caleb, who ran wild, was much too old for Hanna. I was sure he had experiences that Hanna found attractive—over my dead body. I understood she'd probably seen 'coupling' from her life with Indians, but this was a different time and society—not on my watch.

Lauren ran into Jenny's house and emerged, wearing a modest cotton-gingham dress. It was somewhat small but would suffice in the heat and still be appropriate for the church and meeting my friends in Virginia City. Sam drove the buckboard, and I sat in between Sam and Merv. Everyone else had seats in the back of the wagon, which Sam and Dan had constructed for the occasional hayride with church members. Even without the bridge, which had washed away, crossing the creek was easy because the water had returned to its seasonal level.

I might not have returned to Virginia City that Sunday if I didn't Lauren to show off. Despite my standing in the city, I knew most of the older townsfolk suspected I was not married before, never had a child, or she was dead, and I simply wouldn't accept it. Ha!

As we arrived, word spread that I might be bringing a special guest. Several ranch hands had come to town yesterday, and the story was out that my long-lost daughter had surfaced. Everyone was anxious to see her, and most people were genuinely happy for me. We all got out at the church and wandered over to the churchyard, where we gathered each Sunday. Sam and Merv drove the horses over to the tie rail and settled them in with feed and water. It was blazing hot, and the horses drank heartily, and after that, they ate with feed bags on their heads.

I took Lauren's arm, and Sam took the other one. He recognized that Lauren was not experienced in answering tricky questions. Sam had prepared answers for the 'where the heck have you been all these years' kinds of queries. The story was her father had recently died, and he and Lauren had been under the impression that I had been killed while traveling out West. Lauren had encountered a doctor who knew of me, and she made the journey to determine if I was still alive. Lauren was engaged and would be married in a few months. She wanted to visit—and reunite with—her long-lost mother before her wedding.

Ray was particularly pleased to meet Lauren. They chatted under Sam's watchful ears. "You're a lucky son of a gun, Sam. Now you have two beautiful daughters."

"Three, if you count Jenny." Sam beamed and suggested Ray come out for dinner before Lauren went back East again. He told Ray we would head up to Hank Heaven after church. "Apparently, she likes to fish too."

"Half your luck, Sam. Maybe you'll have some fishing grandchildren, who can carry you down to the lake when you're too old to ride there."

"That'll be the year after you're too old and arthritic, you old goat."

When we all went into the church, I had a happy surprise. My old friend, Martha Tyler's husband, Earl, was there with two of his boys. He was the guest minister for our church this week. He was still as handsome as ever. I saw Lauren look twice, and I thought she must recognize him. I hugged him and the boys. "Where's Martha?"

"Becky, Martha is still teaching. She can't come because her class begins tomorrow. She sends her warm greetings."

The next hurdle was the prying and intrusive Mrs. Gardiner. She never missed an opportunity to tell Sam what I was up to and make mischief. She walked directly over to us and introduced herself to Lauren. "I hear you're from the South. Strange that we've never met you before, Lauren."

"Yes, ma'am. Life can have its ups and downs. Pleased to meet you."

"Oh, that accent. Is it Mississippi or Alabama? Not exactly the cultured accent I'm accustomed to."

"Sorry, ma'am. I like to hang around the stables a bit too much—Virginia. I guess some of the manure is hard to get rid of. Hope to see more of you, ma'am." Lauren turned and whispered quietly to me, "Who the hell is she?"

"One of the more upstanding citizens, at least in her mind. I'll tell you about her later."

Dan witnessed the interaction and saved the day by taking Lauren to meet some of his and Jenny's friends. After that, we all took our places in the pews. Lauren and Hanna sat together. Lauren appeared as if she had seen a ghost. I would ask her about it later. Following Earl Tyler's rousing sermon, we sang some of my favorite hymns. Funny that we never sang "Amazing Grace." I wondered when it came out.

I saw Hanna point to the young man, Caleb, whom I didn't want to join the family. He sat with his mother, who was overdressed with her usual dyed hair. Pam Wilkins sat quietly and enthusiastically sang the hymns without having to read them in the Bible. It seemed she wanted to talk to me. I walked over to her. "Hi, Mrs. Wilkins."

"Hello, Dr. Buchanan. We have a mutual problem. I love my son, who is looking a little too much at your daughter. I disapprove."

Hanna had been the subject of harassment since she had lived with the Indians during her early years. I was amazed that someone like a barroom girl would even think along those lines. I was furious.

"I'm sorry you feel that way, Mrs. Wilkins. My daughter is a cultured, fine young woman. Simply because she lived with Indians...." Mrs. Wilkins cut me off.

"Dr. Buchanan, I don't care about her previous life. I am concerned about her age. Take it from me that she's much too young for my Caleb. He will easily lead her astray."

"May I call you Pam? I'm Becky to my friends. I believe we're on the same team."

"Not sure about the same team? Yes, for sure. I was worried you would make an exception due to Caleb's good looks. He gets them from his father, you know."

"He resembles you a lot, Pam."

"Thank you."

"How about you and I have coffee together the next time I come into town for work?"

"You do know what I do for a living?"

"Pam, my father used to say there's dignity in all work." I think I heard it on a Comstock episode, but I did hear it once. I returned to my family and quietly mentioned to Sam that we owed Pam Wilkins a favor someday.

We stayed only a short time for refreshments. I introduced Lauren to the minister, at whom she just kept staring. I was sure he wasn't a fellow time traveler. We hurried home to drop Hanna and Dan's family off at their house. Hanna was excited about her new school tomorrow. Hanna had prepared everything, including her clothes, making it easy to leave her with Jenny and Dan.

Hanna would stay with my associate, Alf, and his wife when snow prevented her return to the Cattle Creek Ranch during this upcoming school year. Hanna was planning to stay with Dan and Jenny unless the weather was too dangerous to ride home. I kissed her goodbye and commented how proud I was of her.

Sam, Lauren, and I rode down the trail and turned toward the rock cliff and Hank Heaven by midafternoon. Lauren suggested it might be too late to access the cabin since it was so late, and someone else might already be staying in it. Sam asked her who was going to get it. She glanced at him and laughed. "I forgot. I keep thinking about visiting when I'm in my time."

"Do other people come up here in your time?" Sam appeared perturbed.

"It's a national forest, and anyone can come up," Lauren started to explain.

I stared at Sam. "It's more than a hundred years from now. We'll all be dead."

He huffed. We approached the rock-slide area, and the water level had gone down even more than it had the previous day. The huge boulder, which had fallen from above, was in the middle of the pool. I was sure I had not seen it before. We could freely talk, as Sam knew most of what I learned. I asked Lauren if it was there when she came to this time, and she didn't remember it even being in the area.

For the first time, I described to Sam how time travel worked in this particular place. He merely stared and shook his head. He studied the creek and general canyon area. "I'll move heaven and earth to resolve this matter. Let's just enjoy the days we have together." I felt better hearing him say this, and I could tell Lauren relaxed somewhat, as well. We proceeded because the sky was threatening.

As we came to the top of the climb over the ridge, we gazed down into the meadow. It seemed the same as always. When I asked Lauren if it appeared any different from when she was here last, she replied it was the same. We slowly made our way down the trail. As we approached the valley floor, the ground was wet, and the rivulets were running, which was unusual for late summer. A small waterfall was descending from one of the cliff faces. Sam remarked that he had never seen it so wet for this time of year.

Chapter 4

Lauren

Home, sweet home. Well, minus the man of my dreams. If the famous Sam Buchanan believed he could fix it, I had reason to relax. And the bonus is getting the cabin no matter what. *What a score! Fishing and skinny-dipping, here I come.* I would have to work out something with the old folks, but at least I could explain my plan to my mother. It was a little late for that tonight.

After we unpacked, Mom and I headed straight for the lake. She had an old-fashioned bamboo fly rod. I used Sam's similar one. It was awkward, but I waded out to reach a sweet spot I had identified when fishing with Jim. My mom was reeling them in left and right. Sam watched from the lakeshore. Sheesh, I was making a mess of it. I even tangled my line twice.

Sam signaled with his finger for me to come into shore. He turned me around and took my arm, as my father did when we were up here a few weeks earlier. He cast the line by holding my arm. I finally got the feel of the unbending rod. He let go, and I directed the line as I generally did. He took my arm and redirected me again.

"Lauren, you need to relax and let the rod do the work. Sometimes it's best to allow others to carry the burden. The same goes for the rod. You might try to keep your wrist stiff and allow your arm and rod to do the casting. Fishing is like life. You don't have to do it all yourself. Others can carry some of the burdens."

"Thank you, sir."

"My pleasure. You've made Becky extremely happy, which makes me happy. Don't worry. We'll get you back to your betrothed. Let us have a short amount of time with you, and I know your mother will think this is the best time of her life. I can't help you with whatever you face on the other side, but I'll do anything I can to help you get there if that's what you want."

"All right. I'll try."

Right then, a nice fish hit the fly and took off. I spent several minutes taking control. By the time I landed it, my mother had enough for dinner. I walked back to the makeshift privy. When I returned to the cabin, Sam was embracing my mother, who appeared to be crying.

She stared at me while she was simultaneously laughing and crying. "Don't worry, Lauren. They're tears of joy." I hugged her as she clung to me fiercely. "I'm so happy. Thank you for coming."

"That's because you outfished your daughter, Bec. When I am done teaching her, you'll be hard-pressed to compete."

"I doubt that, sir, but I certainly will try tomorrow."

We cooked the meal together while Sam read the Bible near his son's grave in the fading light.

"Mom, do they sing 'Amazing Grace' here now?"

"Funny that you should ask. I was thinking the same thing in the church today. By the way, what made you stare at Reverend Tyler?"

"You wouldn't believe what I know! I know his great- or great-great-grandson, who is a minister in Virginia City. The same good-looking face with dimples in which you could hide the moon. I met him just before I left, and his last name is Tyler too."

"Lauren, remember to be careful about what you know. Sam isn't familiar with the *Comstock* television series."

"You're kidding? What else am I not supposed to say?"

"I try to not change history too much. I was present at the Gettysburg Address. I wanted to tell Mr. Lincoln not to go to the theatre, but I didn't."

"You saw Abraham Lincoln? Who else did you see?"

"I'll tell you more tomorrow. Do you recall the words of 'Amazing Grace'?"

I began to sing it, and my mother joined in. Sam listened from the porch. I popped my head out to announce dinner was ready. He smiled and said the song was beautiful. He wanted me to teach him the lyrics. After dinner, we sang some melodies from the 1900s. Sam, who had a beautiful voice, liked the John Denver songs. My mother wasn't a bad singer, but I'm not buying the album. I had so much fun that I forgot about the portal. We retired early, and I slept well into the morning. Who would have thought that merely sitting around singing could be entertaining?

When I woke up, my mother was sitting on the porch. Sam returned to the portal pool early to examine it from ground level. "He's a nice man, Mom. I'm glad you two are together. How did you meet him?"

She recounted the rock slide, as well as finding herself alone and unarmed in the creek bed. She explained walking into town, thinking it was a place where they were filming a television show, only to discover it was the real deal. She described meeting Sam and Gee Ling, how nice they were to her, and how—for only a modest amount of work—they lent her the beautiful mare, Penny. She recounted traveling to Sacramento, meeting Tom Walker in San Francisco, and basically the entire story until Sam relocated my mom in Baltimore. She mentioned meeting many famous historical figures, such as Samuel Clemens and Clara Barton.

Sam returned after lunchtime. My mother had finished her story, and we all shared a small meal. I glanced at my mother and Sam and asked them if they minded if I bathed down at the lake by myself. My mother got the drift, but I think Sam was oblivious to my real intentions. He was going to take a nap, and I headed down to the lake.

Down at the lake, I stripped off and waded into the shallow warm water I had remembered from a previous trip with Jim. It was pure luxury. After sitting and some swimming, I walked out onto the grass. With a long table cloth my mother had given me, I lay in the sun to dry. I needed to shave. The national forest was sprouting. Good thing Jim wasn't nearby. I fell asleep for only a few minutes.

Since I could see and feel the start of a sunburn, I dressed and returned to the cabin.

I'm convinced more than just sleeping had occurred while I was gone, but I pretended not to notice. I can't think of anything I would rather not think about than my parents 'doing it.' I know my dad and mom occasionally did it. Still, we kids whispered and made gagging noises if we suspected anything like that was taking place. I wondered how long it would be before Jim and I decided enough was enough. Sam and I wanted to further explore the valley while my mother could fit in a nap and read her new medical book. Sam discovered an arrowhead at the edge of the cliffs. I was impressed.

"Wow, very cool."

He laughed. "Is cool an expression you use frequently?"

"Definitely."

"Tell me more about your fiancé, if you don't mind my asking."

"He's about as tall as you are and maybe taller. His hair is sandy brown, but that's a little short-lived." I laughed.

"I'm thinking about what he does that attracts you to him. Looks don't last, you realize. We all grow old."

"Yes, sir. That's true. He's truly kind. I watched Jim talk with a little boy about the child's rabbit at our veterinary clinic. For that moment, the only thing in the world that Jim focused on was that kid. I watched the relief on the boy's face when Jim described the problem with the rabbit and how the boy could care for his pet. When he talks to you, it's as if the entire world goes past, and it's only you and him. He makes you feel important. You kind of remind me of him in an older way."

Sam laughed. "I suppose I should take that as a compliment."

"I didn't mean to be disrespectful, sir."

"None taken. I hope you don't mind my inquiry?"

"No, sir. Jim's certainly my number-one favorite topic."

"Let's hope it continues to be."

"Do you mind my asking what attracted you to my mother?"

Sam paused. "Spirit, intelligence, determination, loyalty, and her ability to cast a fly." He laughed. "When I met your mother, she was wet, cold, and bruised, but her sole concern was compensating me for her stay. She didn't want anything to do with me. She was trying to get back to you and your father. I'm sorry for all Becky had to suffer during the early years, but she finally gave up and settled for me. I understood I was her second choice initially. When Becky returned from your time after she heard your voice and rescued your grandfather, though, I realized I had become her first choice."

Sam glanced off thoughtfully. "It was the happiest day of my life. As you may know, I've had three wives before your mother. However, at some point, you must put the memories behind you. I hope you don't ever have to do that, but life isn't fair. We attempt to make it fair, but it isn't always. Anyway, I would do whatever it takes to make your mother happy. If that's moving the boulder, so you can return to your other life, of course, I'll move it."

Our subsequent search for more artifacts uncovered a few more broken arrowhead pieces. When we returned to the cabin, Mom had everything ready for dinner, except the meat, which we grilled on an open fire. I walked to the gravestone at the edge of the clearing. I thought about telling them that I knew that more headstones were under the huge tree that had fallen in the storm when I had visited this same place with my father. Such a revelation might change history, though. My mother told me a little about Hank and his sudden death.

"It's such a beautiful place. Sam and I hope to be buried here after we die. When you return, this is where you can come if you want to visit my gravesite." I swallowed hard. I didn't say that I already had.

Rebecca

We spent two more days up in Hank Heaven. On the last day, the heavens opened, and torrential rain fell once again. It was not the kind of rain that flooded the area, but it raised the creek level enough that moving the rock would be dangerous. I would never let Lauren go in the water at that level, boulder or not.

As we returned to the Cattle Creek Ranch, I remembered my first encounter with Sam and Gee Ling on a rainy night when I initially arrived in the 1800s. I was desperate in so many ways. Cold, hungry, bruised, and battered, I was in no position to decline the offer of accommodation.

"Remind you of an earlier time, Becky?" Sam gazed fondly in my direction.

"You had me over a barrel, and you took advantage of my indisposition if I remember correctly. Having Gee Ling was a great ploy to persuade me to accept your offer."

"I think that was a fortunate coincidence, don't you, Lauren?"

"Huh, sorry, yes, of course." Lauren was studying the creek.

I could tell she was worried again. The creek was not survivable in high water. How she made it out was a miracle. It was evident to Sam and me that Lauren would need to spend several more days than she planned before attempting a return to her previous life. I comprehended her pain all too well.

Chapter 5

Lauren

We were soaked when we arrived back at the ranch. It was cold again. Sam and I took the horses into the barn while my mother went in to dry off. Sam's horse, Cash, was recovering from a fractured pedal bone. He was now fully weight-bearing. I'd suggested the use of a unique rim shoe to minimize movement within the hoof. I was confident he would eventually make a full recovery. I could read the relief on Sam's face when he saw how much progress his beloved gelding had made in such a short time. Sam was bent over, feeling his leg, when he glanced up and smiled. "You are sure your mother's daughter."

"Thanks, sir. All in a day's work." Internally, I was elated. It's difficult enough to make a diagnosis even with modern technology, but doing it without a radiograph is part skill with a great deal of luck thrown in. "My guess is you'll be riding him again in six months."

Sam stood up, and I could tell he wanted to hug me. It was awkward for me, and I stepped back. He understood, and together we slipped under a tarp to run from the barn to the house. "Did Becky tell you about our snow one year?"

"Oh no. Not the *S*-word. I don't want to hear that."

"Don't worry because it's never snowed this time of year here."

When I woke the following morning, the ground was covered with a fine layer of snow. I was sick with worry. This was becoming a nightmare. Could it be any worse? Hanna was happy to be excused from going to school. I didn't have anything even remotely warm enough to wear. My mother rummaged through their old clothes for some of Dan's cast-off outfits.

The only good thing about this for me was wearing pants again. I don't know how my mother endured wearing dresses all day long. Snow in Kentucky was a once-or-twice-a-year event. I was all for it, but I recognized it was a pain for many. I longed for my Alabama weather. Maybe an ice storm might occur in the odd year, but it wasn't as cold as Kentucky was in the winter. I must say the first snow is always pretty. We were situated at a lower elevation. I realized the snow would be much deeper and heavier near the portal.

Despite the snow, Sam took a few men up to the creek to assess any easy removal of the boulder. Dan wouldn't go along. "Why change the flow now? It's been changing all my life, Pa."

Sam declared something to the effect that it was the start of a significant change in the stream's course. It could jeopardize several paddocks and even Dan's house. Of course, no one believed him. Some people might think he was losing his marbles at his age. He smiled, winked at me, and rode out to inspect the rock with the men.

Hanna listened while my mother and I talked nonstop. She hadn't heard all the stories about my mother's early days. We could talk without divulging information we didn't want Hanna to have. Hanna and I played checkers, after which we went up to her room to work on her Indian stories. By evening, I had written outlines for her adventures, which she would have to fill in. The snow was gone the following morning. By the time I came into the dining area, Hanna was gone, as well. Since the weather had reverted to normal, she went to school.

Sam returned from the creek and remarked that moving the boulder would be difficult. He believed he could do it, but it would take several days to transfer it from its current position to the next pool. Mom asked him to move it without damaging the base under the rock.

"I'll ask this only once. Is that definitely the pool, and could another hole work?"

"Maybe, but I doubt it." My mother then informed Sam she had gone back one other time when he was in Cuba and feared dead.

"Why?"

"I wanted to check for a death certificate, so I knew you were still alive."

"And?"

"Nope. The county records were all lost in a fire."

"So, you don't know when we're going to die?"
"No."
"Is that a strong no, or an 'I know, but I'm not going to discuss it' kind of no?"
"I don't know. Be careful today. You're no good to me dead."

Sam had a man at the rock now drilling holes where dynamite could be inserted. He planned to reduce the size of the boulder by blowing its top off. The two men who oversaw the preparations for blasting had worked in mines. Apparently, Sam Buchanan had fought in the cavalry and gained extensive knowledge of dynamite.

Mom asked me to come to her little infirmary to see some of the cases she attended that day. The women were more than happy to share their infirmities with a woman, but the men were another proposition. I was amazed at my mother's ability to treat men and women and maintain such a warm, caring relationship.

A couple of indigenous women consulted with my mother about their arthritis. One may have had tuberculosis. She advised me to stay away, covered her mouth, and disinfected the area as best she could.

Dan came by to ask Mom to look at a colicky horse. The younger gelding had been pawing and stretching out for an hour. When he'd been ridden earlier in the morning, he demonstrated no apparent problems. We both examined him and decided he must have twisted his intestine. Dan seemed puzzled when Mom kept deferring to my suggestions. I said such things as "Father would suggest we do such and such...."

"Becky, what do you recommend?" Dan was worried that my mother was simply being nice to me at the expense of the horse's welfare.

"Dan, Lauren's father, who was my first husband, was obviously a good vet. It appears he's thankfully taught Lauren how to treat horses. She might not have a degree, but she obviously picked up enough knowledge to be a veterinarian. We would do well to respect her opinion."

Dan seemed satisfied with her reply. "Yes, ma'am. Lauren, what do you think?"

"I'm sorry, Dan. It doesn't look good. I'm convinced this horse is not going to make it. Never say never, but I believe he requires surgery, and that's just not performed on these kinds of cases." I really stuck my foot in it by even suggesting surgery. *What was I thinking?* My mother saved the day.

"Yes, I read a report about this a while back. Too bad we don't have the anesthetics and instruments."

"Should I shoot him?" My mom and I stared at each other and nodded. Dan was devastated, but he took him behind the barn, and I heard a loud report before silence. The gelding was dead. A few minutes later, Dan returned and asked us to open him up and make sure we were correct, which we were. My mother showed Dan the twist. A large part of his small intestine was black and necrotic. That had to be going on longer than we all thought. Mom said he must have been quite a stoic horse to have been ridden in the morning and not shown anything unusual.

After that, Dan asked me all types of questions. I felt terrible for stealing my mother's limelight. She told me she'd never been so proud, although Mom confessed she had nothing to do with raising and educating me. I quietly thanked her. I thought about how many times my future mother and father had commented about how proud I would have made my 'deceased' mother. We never thought of her as anything but long gone.

Rebecca

As Sam and I lay in bed that evening, I recounted the activities of the day. It became challenging to explain Lauren's knowledge without admitting she had gone to college and was educated as a veterinarian. He felt it was too much of a burden for Dan to keep a secret from Jenny, and where would that lead?

"How long do you think it will take to get her home?"

"Darling, with this erratic weather, I'm thinking spring."

"Oh, Sam. That would be horrible. Not that I'd mind having her here longer, but do you remember after you left Baltimore when you had to wait until I joined you? We weren't even engaged."

"Longest time in my life, Becky. I understand how she feels. Believe me, I'm trying."

The weather was back to its autumnal best the following day. Lauren wanted to go for a ride. She and I rode together up to the top of the mountain, where we enjoyed a view of Lake Tahoe. Lauren mentioned she regularly rode up to this spot. She brought Jim up here and introduced him to back tickling. I remembered tickling her back when she was little. I often tickled Hanna's back, as well.

Lauren told me that Jim's mother was distant. Despite that, he was an incredibly loving man who realized his mother was different, and Jim was strongly inclined not to repeat that with his children. He wanted to have a baby as soon as possible.

"How do you feel about having children so early in your career?"

Lauren cocked her head and pursed her lips in a faint smile. "You tell me."

I laughed, remembering being pregnant soon after Jeff and I were married while still in school. "Oh yeah, there is that. I wouldn't change a thing. I felt I had it all. I loved your father, and I was excited about beginning my career. Your father had already practiced for a long time and was willing to allow me to concentrate on my studies and work, and he would take care of you. Do you mind my asking how he is?"

"Mom, he's getting older like Sam. He's healthy and preparing for retirement. He and Mom, I mean Aunt Sherry, are considering moving closer to the Smoky Mountains to fish and hike from their house. Jane is the youngest, who will leave for college soon. Andy's starting his second year. I think he might study vet medicine too, but he plays baseball and is fairly good, so who knows? Aunt Sherry has quite a good group of friends, but she's willing to move as long as there's a nearby golf course."

"Wow, what a life!"

"Mom, I think you can tell your life is more exciting and probably far more fulfilling than ours is. I'm so glad I can see what you do and the way you live. I realize you didn't have a choice initially. When you did have a choice, however, you made the right decision. This is a wonderful life. It would be nice to have rectal sleeves and a stomach tube for drenching horses. Aside from that, though, you do the best you can. I can see that."

"And Oreos." We sat for some time, gazing at Lake Tahoe from the mountain.

"This is the place Sam proposed to me."

"Really. Jim proposed down at the lake in Miner's Meadow, I mean Hank Heaven." Lauren told me about her proposal and how she didn't accept it until later that night when Jim wouldn't let her into the tent until she agreed to marry him.

"There was none of that with us. This is the 1800s. I know a lot of premarital sex goes on. Babies are born short of nine months and out of wedlock, but that wasn't going to happen with Sam—not that pregnancy was an issue by the time we were together."

Lauren plugged her ears with her fingers. "Mom, the last thing a daughter wants to hear is anything about her parents doing it."

"Hopefully, you still can when you are as old and decrepit as we are."

"Mom, please," and then she laughed.

"I'd like to say we'll revisit that when you are my age, but I'll be dead."

"In case you've forgotten, you're dead already." That thought was not lost on either one of us.

"We'd better get you back home."

"Which home?"

"Yes, there is that." We tightened the girths and remounted. I usually used a log or stump, but I could easily mount my mare without any aid. To show Lauren I was still fit, I climbed on with a quick hop and took off, cantering in the direction of home—my home. She followed and soon was level with me. It was such a thrill to be loping alongside this beautiful daughter of mine. Oh, for a camera.

We soon slowed the horses down for the descent back to the house. We heard a massive boom, and Lauren turned toward the creek.

"Fingers crossed, Lauren." We both smiled.

"Mom, I hope I'm as lucky as you were when you married that man."

"Sounds like you will be, darling."

Chapter 6

Lauren

Mom wanted to buy me something from town to wear if it was cold again. We rode in early and dropped Hanna off for school. She planned for me to meet more of the hospital staff members. My mother was acquainted with an artist who had done a painting for Sam.

Mom wanted to find out whether he would paint a picture of me, so she could have a memory. I didn't tell her I had a photograph of her. I'd left it at my friend Rich's house, where I had stashed my belongings before coming to the 1800s. I couldn't risk my father seeing it.

Hanna took us to meet her teacher. She was an older woman, who appeared as if she could inflict serious harm on the students, but I could tell she was a bit of a bluff. She was a college graduate who had studied English literature.

Hanna could be somewhat of a renegade, but this woman had her measure. I met a few of Hanna's schoolmates. She was the youngest, yet it was apparent she was learning to cope with the older kids' scorn and abuse. They called her 'Indian Girl.'

My mother was distraught, but she'd been in such a small school when she was young that she was probably at the top of the pecking order. Hanna didn't want any interference from her mother. On the other hand, I was influential in convincing some older girls to treat Hanna better. If I was there the next week, God forbid, I promised I would watch the class and maybe report some of my experiences as a 'mature' woman. The one older boy was Alexander Thistlewaite, who was gangly and studious. His name was familiar to me. I smiled at him, and he shyly looked at me.

We went to the hospital. Alf Weber was out on rounds, but I met John Harmon. He oversaw the removal of porcupine quills from the dog that belonged to the hospital receptionist, Mrs. Clayton. The poor dog was thrashing and trying to escape. My mother took over and soon administered the anesthesia, and I removed the quills. Mrs. Clayton was relieved my mother was there. I know the dog certainly was. Thirty-two quills later, it was resting in a small room off the reception area. I met another nurse, and my mother saw a woman who had delivered her infant by cesarean a few weeks earlier. Her sutures needed to be removed. They were of crude material. "Catgut?"

"Something such as that." We didn't discuss it further because the woman was present. I held her baby while the woman lay on the table.

When we left the hospital, we ran into Ray Thompson, my mom's good friend. He was heading home but decided to meet us at the diner for a cup of coffee. "So, Lauren, how are you getting on?"

"Fine, sir. I've seen some beautiful places. I really am enjoying my stay."

Mr. Thompson noticed my engagement ring. "When do you leave? I'll bet there's a fella who is anxious to have you back home. Didn't you say, Virginia?"

"Yes, sir." I could see my mother was nervous.

"What's his name? What line of work is he in?"

"Jim Kennedy, sir. He's a vet, as was my father."

"Keeping it in the family?" Mr. Thompson sipped his coffee, but I could tell he was eyeing me suspiciously.

My mother decided to stop the grilling by asking Ray about the Wilkins boy, Caleb.

"He's kind of a larrikin, Becky, but his mother keeps him on a tight line. Is he bothering you?"

"No, Ray. Hanna's infatuated with him."

"I can speak to Pam. She's a good woman once you look past the face paint and the satin dresses. I'd be happy to talk to her for you."

"No, thanks, Ray. She and I had a conversation already. It's probably more Hanna than him, anyway."

"I'm looking for Mr. Forbiger. I want him to paint a picture of Lauren before she leaves."

"I think he's out of town with his wife, Becky. He left a week ago."

"Well, that's out the window."

"You and your expressions."

After we left Ray, I asked my mother about her cabin. She didn't own it anymore, but she was sure it was not currently being used. My mother mentioned she and Sam had a disagreement many years ago when she first arrived, and that's when she headed to the East Coast for medical school. She explained that Sam sold the house after she left and gave the money to the town doctor, who had sent it to her. "I made a smart profit on the sale too. I was paid two hundred dollars."

"Really, in those days? Who bought it?"

"Hmm, I never asked. I believe it was rented out for a while."

"Mom, is there any chance it wasn't sold?"

"No, I received the money."

"I saw the deed, and it appears to be in your name until several years from now."

"How did you see the deed?"

"Long story, but I was interested in buying it, which was before I located your letters."

"What letters?"

"Some were from Dr. Thomas Walker, and one was from Jeannette Merritt."

"You're joking."

"Nope."

"I want to see them."

"Mom, if you take the letters, and they aren't there anymore, how would I discover them? Also, how would I even have tried to find out if you lived during this time? You know how you claim you don't like to change too many things? This is one you shouldn't change."

"I guess you're right, but I don't own it now. That's for sure."

"I don't think it will hurt to go to the land office to check out the register. Is there one in the town?"

"Excellent idea, Della."

"Who's Della?"

"Perry Mason's secretary."

I stared blankly at my mother, who shook her head. "How about *Ironsides*?"

"Raymond Burr?"

"Finally, a sign of culture. Your dad raised you in a vacuum."

"Probably." I laughed, recalling all the television programs I watched as a kid.

We arrived at the land office, where the agent quickly retrieved the deed for the cabin where my mother lived for a short time.

"Here it is, Becky. You're still the owner."

"But I sold it years ago, George. I haven't paid any taxes, and I received two hundred dollars for the sale. It's got to be a mistake."

"No, your taxes have been paid every year since you bought it." The land agent showed me the receipts. The initials next to each payment were the initials 'SB.' Sam had paid the taxes and left it in my mother's name. I suspected the two hundred dollars was not for the property sale but as a gift. *Could he have given her that exorbitant amount of money to help her get through medical school?*

"He gave you the money, Mom. It's pretty obvious, isn't it?" I could see a mixture of emotions flit across her face.

"That old bastard." My mother laughed heartily.

"I'm telling." She had warned me that women didn't swear at this time.

"Don't you dare!"

I would not reveal that I remembered the following names on the deed were Hanna and Alexander Thistlewaite, but that was many years from now. And, of course, the cabin burned down a few days ago. I could hardly wait for my mother to confront Sam. This confrontation could be ugly, or it could be quite heartwarming. I was betting on the latter.

Rebecca

We purchased warmer riding clothes for Lauren. I would have loved to buy Lauren a wetsuit for the transition back to her time, but that wasn't going to happen. We ran a few errands for Sam and picked up some cloth for Jenny. Little Hank was growing out of his everyday clothes. Jenny prided herself on making most of his outfits. I suspected there might be another baby on the way, but I wasn't sure. It had not been a long time since the birth of Little Hank. I had described how she could at least attempt birth control, but I don't think either one of them cared. She and Dan were so in love and were wonderful parents. I hope Lauren noticed how they took turns with the care of my two beautiful grandchildren.

We picked up Hanna and rode home together. Since Hanna did not have to go to school the following day, she and Lauren planned a girl's day out. They were going to hunt for gooseberries, so Gee Ling could make gooseberry jam. It was a favorite, but Lauren had never tasted any. As usual, Hanna never stopped talking. She had an assignment due the following week. I suggested she head up to her room to start on it before dinner. "I want to see that you have done at least part of it before you go out tomorrow."

"Yes, Ma."

Lauren glanced at me. "May I help?"

"Let her begin it first, then you could read it after she's done. What's it about, Hanna?"

"I need to write a story about going back in time. I must pretend I'm in the Revolutionary War."

Both Lauren and I choked, trying to stifle a laugh.

Lauren replied, "Ask your father."

"Is he that old?"

Lauren giggled. "I dare you to ask him."

Sam was still out. He'd ridden up to where some timber was being harvested. He arrived back home just before dinner. He got the look from me.

"What did I do?"

"We'll discuss it later, darling."

"Am I in trouble?"

"Possibly."

Sam looked at Lauren, who smiled and turned away. "I think I'll find out if Gee Ling needs some help."

Dinner was ready, and Lauren helped set the table and bring out the food. We called Hanna down from her room. She told Sam about her assignment and asked why we wanted her to request his help. "Did you serve in the Revolutionary War, Pa?"

Both Lauren and I got the giggles. Sam did not think it was funny, which made our mirth even harder to control.

THE TRAVELS OF DR. REBECCA HARPER

All I had to do was look at Lauren, hiding her face in her napkin, and I broke out in more laughter. Hanna had no idea what this was about, but it was contagious, and soon she was laughing too. Sam pretended he was not amused. However, I detected the tiniest crack in his demeanor.

When the girls went upstairs to work on Hanna's assignment, Sam and I were left downstairs alone. "What have I done?" He used his authoritative voice that made everyone sit up straight. It wasn't going to work on me that evening. Well, maybe a little.

"So much trouble, mister. So much trouble."

"Do you want to tell me what this is about?" I think he sensed Lauren had taken Hanna upstairs so we could be alone. We could hear them laughing uproariously. Lauren would not tell Hanna anything. However, whatever it was must have been hysterical. I was glad Lauren wasn't fretting about returning to her time, at least for one night.

"I went to the land office this afternoon."

"And?" I could tell Sam had no idea about where this was going.

"Did I tell you Lauren was living in my old cabin? She found some letters in the attic from Tom and the Merritts, which is the reason she's here. That clue persuaded her to believe Frank Lash's story."

"And?"

"Sam, because she wanted to buy the cabin, she investigated its history of ownership. Lauren was renting it, but she didn't know who owned the cabin."

At last, I attracted his attention. A smile came over his face since he understood where this was going.

"I see." He lit his pipe before he sat down in front of the fireplace.

"Two hundred dollars, Sam. You sent me two hundred dollars and maintained the cabin in my name. There was no sale, was there?"

"That was a long time ago, darling." I could see the lines on his face relax.

"It's still in my name, yet you've paid the taxes all along, haven't you?"

He smiled broadly. "The taxes are simply a few dollars per year. I wanted you to have options. I realized I had misbehaved when you told me about yourself. I'd have done anything to make it up to you. I knew you were as stubborn as I am. Frankly, I think you're far worse than I am in that respect. It was one small way to set things right. I was extremely sorry I had driven you away. Becky, I was in love with you, and all you wanted was to find your husband and Lauren."

Once again, I felt as though I was falling in love for the first time. "Should we have an early night?"

He peered upstairs. "Full moon, and the bunkhouse is empty."

"I'll tell the girls we're taking a moonlight walk."

During breakfast the following day, Hanna inquired about how our moonlight stroll was. Sam and I replied simultaneously. He responded "brisk," and I answered "slow."

Lauren stared down at her plate and tried to stifle a laugh. Oblivious to what might have happened, Hanna replied, "Ma, you should walk faster and not slow Pa down."

At this, Lauren got up, placed her napkin over her mouth, and excused herself to the kitchen. Sam put the newspaper up, pretending to read, while I remained at the table with our innocent young daughter. "I'll try." I somehow managed to retain a straight face.

Chapter 7

Lauren

That was funny! I scared Gee Ling, who thought I was choking. Thankfully, he didn't know what had happened. Ah, young love. My assumption was the evening's activity resulted from the exposure of the cabin's actual ownership. It was a nice thing to do. I hope Jim is like Sam in that respect. I was convinced he was.

Gee Ling prepared a picnic lunch for Hanna and me. Hanna knew where the gooseberries grew. We took Pocket, and Hanna had her new horse, which she was breaking in. Hanna wasn't allowed to take this horse to school, but she rode him on the Cattle Creek Ranch. She had a verbal contract with Sam and Dan. They assigned a value to each horse. If Hanna increased the dollar sale, she could keep half the money for which the horse sold above its stated value. She was a clever little businesswoman.

Sam instructed us to stay away from the place he was once again blasting on the creek. Sam handed me a rifle, as well. He queried whether I knew the way to load and shoot it. Since it was somewhat different from the ones I had used, I received a quick lesson in 1800s riflery. Hanna had already been taught how to clean, load, and shoot all the rifles in Sam's gun rack.

"Sister, this will be Lauren and Hanna's excellent adventure." I mounted Pocket, Sam handed me the rifle, and I placed it in the sheath attached to my saddle.

"Huh?" Hanna didn't understand my reference.

"Never mind." Hanna would never know what she missed with movies and general modern culture. She and I said goodbye to our mother and Sam, and we headed in a new direction for me. I couldn't orient myself from my modern recollection. We stopped at a pond, where Hanna described her mother's mule, Spit, and his fatal encounter with a rattlesnake. She informed me we needed to be careful of snakes, which is how my mother's beloved mule had died. A small cross designated his burial site. We eventually identified a shady spot near a new creek with gooseberries. I couldn't imagine the tart gooseberries making good jam, but the entire family seemed to delight in their taste.

When our sacks were full of berries, we removed our shoes to wade in the creek, which was too small for fish but still cold. We discussed her favorite topic, men, during lunch. She asked me about my fiancé, what he was like, and what attracted me to him.

Hanna claimed she wanted to experience adventure and travel. She understood all about sex and reproduction and talked freely about the topic, which surprised me. My stepsister confided in me the extent of her knowledge, which was far more than I understood at her age. She wouldn't dare let her father know.

Still, Hanna had lived a different life with the Indians. Our mother made sure she learned the ins and outs of pregnancy prevention and how bearing a child early in life would limit her prospects. Hanna possessed no bad feelings toward her parents and acknowledged they kept a tight rein on her activities. She'd attended a single church dance, during which her father kept an eye on her all night.

She talked about the horses and her role in fine-tuning them after they were settled. Hanna was proud that she had trained the horse our mother rode. She and our mother frequently worked on horses together. Hanna realized she had a way with horses but claimed most Indian children were good horsemen in the village where she'd been raised.

"Lauren, you haven't answered me."

"Hanna, you should stop talking long enough for someone to respond." I was about to go on when we heard a rustling in the bushes behind us. We sat up and gazed around, and I reached for the rifle next to me. I was too slow. An Indian grabbed the gun from my hands, and a second one snatched Hanna. They were young, strong men whom we had no hope of resisting.

Hanna spoke in a native tongue that I did not recognize. They understood her and replied. The larger of the two men tried to carry me to a secluded area. I fought, but I had no chance of withstanding his strength or desire. Hanna shouted something to the man. He stopped, examined me, turned me, and bound my hands. Hanna, who was already tied up, didn't say anything to me. I could only hope she told them I had a disease or something to repulse them.

They placed us on horses and took us farther into the woods. We arrived in a clearing with huts that were a cross between a teepee and a lean-to. It was primitive. Sweat and body odor in the 1800s was more than in my time, but these Indians took smells to an entirely new level. They were clean but had something in their hair that I guessed caused it to shine. I'll never again complain about Jim and his male-body odor. *Was I going to see him once more?* I'll admit that I was scared to death. One overriding detail was these people seemed to be starving. Even the children appeared like the pictures I had seen in television ads for charitable organizations that aid developing nations.

Hanna conversed with them. As usual, she never stopped talking. I was sure they were arguing, and she was losing the argument. Hanna was separated from me, and I didn't see her for several hours. She was finally brought out of a hut late in the afternoon. I was so relieved when Hanna signaled to me that she was okay. I feared the men would want more from us both, but she shook her head when I shot her an inquiring look without saying anything. We both knew the question.

I was taken into a hut and tied to a tree immediately outside the hut's interior. I tried to talk to the people, but they didn't demonstrate any recognition of my questions. They presented me with some grass-like broth and left me alone with a single older woman, who ignored anything I did. She hit me with a stick when I yelled for Hanna, who did not reply to me. I was desperate to reach her to ensure she was all right.

After what seemed like hours, I was getting cold, the woman threw a hide over me, and she went to bed. I watched her until I was convinced she was asleep. I observed her sleeping as I attempted to work on my bindings. At some point, a man entered and hit me, as well. I understood he was telling me to sit still. He sat down to watch me. Did he want more than to watch? I had no idea. I must have dozed after several more hours.

The next thing I noticed, it was much lighter, and there was more noise outside. I smelled something cooking at daybreak. The old woman sat up. I tried to indicate my need to relieve myself, but she shook her head. I was going to have to wet myself. I begged her to untie at least one hand. She finally relented and handed me some grass to wipe myself. The urine was simply allowed to dry in the dirt. It was humiliating, but my overriding concern was for Hanna. My mother and Sam would kill me if she was injured or became pregnant. I realized they would be looking for us by now.

"Hanna?" I asked the older woman where she was. I made the shape of a woman by showing curves and pointing to my breasts. I believe the woman understood what I wanted to know. She laughed and didn't respond. I was given more grass broth. I was eventually led outside, where the meat cooking was that of a rat. I was not offered any as the rat fed the children. I was appalled. I searched around for Hanna but didn't see her.

I was tethered to another tree in the sun. The warmth was so lovely that I almost dozed off again. It must have been hours. I could tell that rain clouds were gathering. I was hopeful that I might survive this kidnapping. The Indians showed no inclination to kill me yet, which gave me hope that I might endure the ordeal. My mind drifted until I was nearly delusional. I wondered where Jim was, and if anyone had figured out I was not in Honduras.

When the rain started, I was left outside. I was soaked and felt a chill. I also became seriously hypothermic when the temperature soon plummeted. Someone would occasionally look out at me and return into a hut. Many of the men appeared to be missing. I had no idea where Hanna was. I prayed she was safe, but I was sick with worry, as well as feverish.

An older woman untied me, led me to a makeshift latrine, and stood while I took care of my visceral needs. She pointed to a new lean-to and, with a stick, hit me to force me inside. After I was bound to a different tree, another hide was thrown over me. My throat was sore, and I was finding it difficult to swallow. I knew I was getting sick.

What happened next was a blur. I wasn't aware of how many hours or days passed, but finally, someone with an American accent called my name. I couldn't focus, but it sounded like Dan Buchanan. I was too sick and weak to respond. I lay there for what seemed like hours. I tried to sit up to answer, but I was shaking too much. I felt a hand on my shoulder and glanced up to see a man with a hat, whom I didn't recognize.

I thought I was dying and had gone back to my home in Kentucky. LB was licking my face with her soft tongue. I went back to sleep and dreamt someone was carrying me and placing me on a horse. My next recollection was that I was in a buckboard under a dark shroud. Somebody was driving the horses while someone else was keeping me warm and sponging my face.

It was dark when the buckboard stopped. Now I could hear women talking, and I was carried into a house. I was confused. I thought I was in Kentucky with my mother and father. My sister was by my side at home. I fell asleep once again. When I woke up several hours later, I was in the guest bed at the Cattle Creek Ranch. Sam Buchanan was in a chair next to my bed, while Gee Ling was on the other side. I realized I had survived, and I could feel my fever breaking, but I wanted Jim. I attempted to hide my disappointment.

"Hello, darling. I'll get your mother," and with that, Sam was gone. My mother took his place. Apparently, she'd been by my side for ages and rested for a few hours before I woke up. Gee Ling made some broth. When he left, my mother handed me some tablets and told me to swallow them quickly when no one was around. I knew they were some of her precious antibiotics. She told me that I had pneumonia. I drank some water and broth and slept for several more hours. I needed to relieve myself, and my mother assisted me, after which she sent me straight back to bed.

I dreaded asking this, but no one was forthcoming. "What happened to Hanna?"

"She's fine. We didn't want to take a chance, so she's staying over at Dan and Jenny's. She saved you."

I smiled and nodded. I was not strong enough to sit up and eat until the next day. Sam informed me the starving Indians traded beef and flour for my life. "The darn fools didn't need to do that. I would have given them the food, anyway. You were a hostage. Hanna brokered the deal. She told them I would kill them all if you both had not returned."

"Thank her for me, I think."

Chapter 8

Rebecca

It was several days before Lauren felt strong enough to get up and even leave her room. To make it easier, we moved her upstairs next to our bedroom. Either Sam or I would check her periodically throughout the night. After three days, we allowed Hanna to come home. She slept in a trundle bed below Lauren and monitored her breathing. Once Lauren felt well enough, Hanna moved back into her own bedroom.

I'm incredibly proud of Hanna. She's such a clever girl. Sam brags she gets it from his side of the family. Knowing she's our adopted daughter, we both assume claims wherever we can. Hanna's no fool when she hears us squabble over from which side of the family she inherits one trait or the other. She always says she receives it from Gee Ling. Three guesses who is Gee Ling's favorite Buchanan.

Sam and Dan had already been out searching for the girls when they hadn't returned. They discovered Hanna running toward home. Hanna told them about the abduction as soon as she saw her father and Dan. Because the Indians wouldn't let her have her horse, she swung up behind Dan, and they returned for supplies and a wagon. Sam had six steers and a milk cow ready by morning. He and Dan took a wagon as far as they could and drove the cattle on horseback. Hanna was permitted to come for translating. She was not allowed into the village, but she explained to the Indians that her father would bring more food later.

When Lauren was located, she was feverish and semiconscious. Dan put her on his horse, and they took her to the buckboard. They put her in the wagon bed to bring her home. It required only one look to realize Lauren was terribly ill. I had Sam get the antibiotics I had locked up for so many years in the safe. When Gee Ling was getting her some liquids, I put some in her mouth. Sam and I got her to swallow them with great difficulty. After three days, she began to recover. I was not confident how the antibiotics would work since they were several years out of date, but they did seem to help.

Lauren kept ranting about returning to her time. On a couple of occasions, Gee Ling heard her and commented about how feverish she was. Something told me Gee Ling knew more than he was saying. I didn't ask. He was quite attentive and caring, just as he had been with me when I broke my leg so many years ago. He never complained, and he always was there with broth or tea when she stirred.

Sam had begun to work on moving the rock again. Progress was slow, but he, at last, had a harness made to encompass the rock. It was hitched to two of the plow horses, and the boulder was moved in two days. I felt the time was coming that Lauren would return. I was devastated, but I knew it was the right thing to do. I could not figure out how to explain it to Hanna, who wished to go to Virginia to see Lauren, where she lived. She wanted to attend the wedding. Lauren was right to discourage her, but it's tough to get Hanna to move on once she sets her mind to something.

Sam thought that Lauren would have a clear passage through the water by Monday. At night in bed, he held me and let me grieve about the pending parting. It was quite common in these times for a young woman to marry, leave her family, and not return. I tried diligently to let go. I would never allow her to know just how sad I was to lose her for the second time. I could tell she experienced similar feelings.

When we woke up on Sunday, expecting to go to church, a cold wind began to blow. Since Lauren had not fully recovered from her pneumonia, I decided to stay at home with her. The rest of the family went into Virginia City for a church service. Hanna wanted to see Caleb.

Sam had everyone in the buckboard. He glanced at Hanna and mouthed, "Not going to happen." I was relieved. Sam visited Virginia City and had alerted the church of the need to help this tribe of Indians with donations of both food and clothing. Sam realized what would happen to these tribes who valiantly tried to hold out and stay in the area. We had discussed this many times, and he believed me, despite my appalling lack of historical education.

After the family left for Virginia City, Lauren and I decided to take a short ride to search once again for the material she'd lost when she arrived. Sam had traded two horses each for Lauren and Hanna's horses, taken when the girls were abducted. We saddled Penny and Pocket and took off toward the creek. Despite the initial cold wind, the air had warmed, but the rain was threatening, and I didn't want Lauren to get sick again. I knew she would try to leave in the next few days.

Lauren told me she could have delayed her return for several weeks, and no one would notice. Her family and friends thought she was in a foreign country, and only my old friend Frank Lash knew otherwise. Her fiancé wasn't due back for months. Her new job at the veterinary clinic wasn't going to start until after Christmas.

The sole reason for the rush was the weather. She had already experienced an unusual occurrence with the flash flooding, which nearly killed her. I would be happier to see her go sooner. I understood she wouldn't wait until next summer. By then, anyone who knew her would think the worst. I realized Frank wouldn't say anything and expose himself to the world.

For such reasons, I said nothing to dissuade her plans to travel in the next few days to return to her real life. As sad as it was for me, I could tell she had made the same decision to be in the time of her lover. *How could I blame her?*

We took off for an area we had not really examined, which was below the washed-out bridge. I would have killed for more antibiotics. I also would have loved to look at pictures my daughter said she brought. We rode to the creek to follow it downstream for a mile or two. We saw no signs of the bridge or what Lauren lost on her perilous introduction to the 1800s. We stopped along the creek and ate some lunch that Gee Ling packed for us.

I was still convinced there was more that she was not revealing to me. I thought, now that she was going home, maybe she would share her troubles with me.

"Lauren, are you sure there isn't more going on than you're telling me?"

"Why do you ask?"

"I can see you glance away and become quiet when you discuss your return. Is there something you're not telling me, so I don't worry?"

"No, ma'am. I'm just anxious about Jim. I hope he's okay. Since he couldn't tell me what he was doing, I'm afraid it's something dangerous. I may be wrong, and God, I hope I am, but I just pray he's all right."

"I see. I don't blame you. Lauren, when I left Sam to find you, we both understood that if there was a compelling reason to stay, I would. Because your grandfather was so desperate to get out of the hospital, I realized my return would be delayed. All I thought about was whether Sam would be alive or even want me when, and if, I returned. I felt the way you feel now. My only advice is that if he really loves you, he'll be there when you come back."

Lauren nodded and walked down to the water. "I'm not sure he believes in time travel, but he knows I've considered coming here as a possibility."

"In your father's case, he could only think that I was dead. At least, Jim can suspect you might be in another time."

Lauren peered down into the water. She continued to stare.

"What?" I got up to look.

Lauren pointed into the creek. A bright-yellow rock was lodged in the base of tree roots. To get it out, one of us would have to get wet.

"I'm not taking any chances, Lauren. I'm going in."

I waded into the cold water. Despite the mild current, my boots slipped on the rocks, and I went completely under. I grabbed the stone, which was very heavy. I resurfaced, and Lauren laughed. "Guess the whole creek isn't a portal." Lauren reached for my arm and nearly went in with me when I slipped again. I handed her the rock and clutched nearby tree roots to climb out. I was freezing and shaking, and I stripped off and placed my clothes on a branch to dry. Despite the increasing clouds, they dried quickly. I stared again at what seemed to be a massive gold nugget. "Lauren, if that's real, it's worth a fortune."

"It's on Cattle Creek Ranch property, so I guess it belongs to you."

"No, you found it. It's yours."

"Mom, in a million years, it's yours and Sam's."

I laughed. "Do you know that I don't own anything? If Sam dies, everything goes to his boys. Women don't inherit anything unless no male heirs exist. I own the hospital or at least part of it."

"What? You're kidding?"

"No, really. The Cattle Creek Ranch goes to Sam's boys. I have a generous provision, but I could be kicked off the land according to the current laws."

"That's not fair."

"Lauren, in case you've forgotten, we can't even vote."

"Neanderthal."

"Yes, but I still wouldn't change a thing. I returned with the knowledge that life would not be fair, but we all make sacrifices. How much do you think it weighs?"

"It's got to be a pound, at least." Lauren felt it and tossed it from one hand to another. She went back to search the area again. "I wish I could find another."

"This nugget would probably buy a house in these times." Lauren kept lifting the nugget up and down, feeling the weight.

"It would possibly buy a car in modern times."

I decided it was best to show Sam the nugget privately. We returned to the house at the same time Sam and Hanna arrived. She jumped off the wagon, ran straight to Lauren, buried her head, and cried. I stared at Sam, who shook his head and winked. He yelled at Gee Ling to set another place at the table for dinner tonight. He turned to me to say Ray was bringing a date.

Sunday dinner was usually a family affair. Dan and his family would be down this evening. Ray Thompson was coming too, and we were all planning on a delicious roast dinner. Gee Ling was in his element. Controlled chaos. Hanna was enlisted to help with the preparations.

"Gee Ling, make those two places." That set him off, and he broke into his native tongue, raving about who knew what.

I turned back to Sam. "Are you serious?"

"Serious as can be."

"Well, that two-timing ba..." Fortunately, I caught myself. "So-and-so."

Sam laughed and grabbed me around the waist. "I knew I had reason to be jealous of him. Just wait until you see her."

"It isn't Mrs. Gardiner, is it?"

"They'll be here in a few hours, my jealous wife. You must really wait."

There was a bit of news from town. The orphanage had lost the matron, who had run away with the bank manager. An inquiry commenced into the pair, who had absconded with untold orphanage funds. That led to a run on the bank by depositors wanting their money. When the stockholders calmed the townsfolk, a significant run was averted. Even Sam was told he couldn't receive any of his assets until the situation was resolved and the manager was caught. Glenn Frasier headed the posse seeking the hapless couple.

The church regulars had gone all out to fill the buckboard with supplies for the Indians. Sam and Hanna would take them tomorrow. She would translate for Sam. A teary-eyed Hanna eventually told me Caleb had moved to the other side of the Sierras, near Georgetown, to become a logger. His uncle oversaw a logging camp.

"I know how it feels. It takes a while, but you'll eventually get over it. I'm so sorry, darling."

"I know you and Pa are happy he's gone, but it really hurts right now. Lauren understands."

"I never want you to be sad, Hanna. Whether we thought he was right for you or not, we understand you were in love."

"I am in love, Ma, not was."

"Give it a year or two."

"A year or two? Is that how long it takes?" Hanna appeared horrified.

"With any luck."

I saw Lauren laugh to herself.

I'd hidden the nugget in my saddlebag. I showed it to Sam when he and I were alone. He let out a long whistle. "Where'd you find it?"

"Lauren found it in the creek. We'd stopped to eat. She was probably looking for trout, and she spotted it among the tree roots."

"If anyone finds out about this, there'll be an invasion on the Cattle Creek Ranch, which we won't be able to stop. It's crucial to hide this, and we must let Lauren know how dangerous it is. You understand, don't you, Becky?"

"Yes, I do. That's the reason I showed it only to you. Lauren understands." I realized Sam was appalled by the destruction that mining had caused in the area. He wasn't opposed to mining. He had mines in other areas, but he didn't want the environmental damage on his land. He was quite the conservationist for his time. I could hardly wait for Ray to come with his date.

Lauren

I was still not over pneumonia and was taking it easy at my mother's insistence. I hoped to travel back this week to my true home. I was doing everything in my power to be well enough, even if it was cold and wet when I got there. As long as I arrived in my time, I knew I would be fine if I could get to the hospital with the help of Cary and Mel, my two emergency-doctor friends.

I'd been permanently moved upstairs into Hank's old bedroom. They had not changed it since he died so many years ago. I could tell how badly this had affected Sam.

He still grieved. My mother was enormously supportive of anything that would help her husband to ease the pain. They loved each other deeply, and I think their mutual grief for both Hank and me, until I arrived here, was touching. I prayed Jim and I would never experience the loss of a child. I thought that I might not wait to start a family. My father wasn't getting any younger, and I wanted him to share the joy of a grandchild. I also wanted him to have some time to start the baby on fly-fishing lessons as he did with me.

I must have fallen asleep. Hanna came bounding in to announce that Mr. Thompson had arrived with a dance-hall girl, and it seemed our mother was in a state of shock. "You need to come downstairs to see this, Lauren. It's Caleb's ma."

"I need a minute to freshen up. Get back down there and be ready to report to me. I'll be down as quick as I can. Are Dan and Jenny here yet?"

"No, but they won't be long. Dan knows not to be late for Gee Ling's cooking."

"Go on, then."

I put on one of the dresses Sam had bought me and headed down to see the spectacle. I was introduced to Pam Wilkins, the barmaid, who apparently ran the main saloon in town. I awkwardly shook her hand. I don't think hand-shaking among women was the 'done thing' at that day and time. Mr. Thompson kissed me and insisted I call him Ray. Hanna wanted to know why she couldn't address him by his first name, but Sam just frowned at her because the answer was obvious.

My mother served drinks, which Mrs. Wilkins declined. "I drink only for work and not pleasure." When I laughed, everyone stared at me as though I was crazy until they realized what she had said and joined in. "Actually, I don't drink at all. When one of the boys offers me a drink, I have Cosmo make a cider that appears and smells alcoholic, but it isn't. We split the money. Hence, I stay sober and make more than my salary in tips."

"And that's why Pam can help with the orphanage." Ray gazed at Pam and smiled. "How long have we known each other, Pam? It must be fifteen years, at least. You were one of the reasons I survived being the town sheriff. Becky, no one else could stop a fight as Pam can."

"Well, it's cheaper to furnish a free round of beer than it is to repair the Bucket o' Blood. So, in the long run, the offer pays off."

Pam Wilkins was no fool. She may have dressed as a barroom hussy at work, but her dress was plain, and her makeup was toned down considerably that evening. Her hair was still far blonder and probably less gray than that of anyone her age, but I could tell the method to her persona.

Ray started to exhibit the effects of the alcohol and looked fondly at Pam. I noticed my mother eyeing him suspiciously while Sam watched my mother. I began to feel the spirits too. I was close to getting the giggles as a witness of this interaction.

Ray stared at his empty glass. My mother realized she was neglecting her duties and poured some more. "What's the plan for the orphanage?"

"Pam has assets that aren't in the bank in town. What am I doing? You explain it, Pam." Ray affectionately gazed at Pam once again, much to my mother's consternation.

"Ray's right. You understand I have the advantage of knowing a great deal more than the average citizen of Virginia City knows. Alcohol is a great loosener of lips. I realized the bank manager and the orphanage matron were, shall we say, meeting more frequently and in places that might suggest more than a casual relationship." She stopped and observed Hanna.

Sam grasped the situation and sent Hanna to the kitchen to assist Gee Ling. Of course, she was onto the subject and started to protest but thought better of it when her father gazed at her.

"If the bank manager and the matron were in cahoots, I worried the bank was not a safe place to keep the money. Since I didn't want to scare anyone if I was wrong, I just moved my savings to the Carson City bank.

"Pam," Sam interjected, "you and I should be better friends."

Right then, Dan, Jenny, and the children arrived. I took Little Hank, who was already asleep, while Lizzy went straight to the kitchen, where I could hear Gee Ling and Hanna greet her. I could tell Dan and Jenny were surprised to encounter Pam Wilkins, but they were quickly caught up in the entire saga.

"Anyway, I was an orphan myself. However, despite that, I've had a great life. My son is now employed, and it seems as if he will be a good lumberjack. My needs are simple. I have more money than I can use. I want to sponsor the orphanage until it's back on its feet. The Buchanans can't do all the philanthropy. My only request is no one is to know it comes from me. I have a reputation to uphold."

At that, everyone laughed, and dinner was announced. As usual, it was a feast. I was particularly aware that this would be my last big family meal with my 1800s family. My mother and Sam were aware, as well, and both doted on me. Following dinner, when everyone was gone, they gave me the present of a beautiful gold bracelet with the Cattle Creek Ranch brand etched in the design. It brought tears to my eyes, and I hugged and thanked them both.

I had feet in two worlds. I was never going to be completely happy living in one world. It was my cross to bear to constantly long for the family in another time. We discussed my return to the 2000s. The plan was to be unexpectedly called away while Sam and Hanna delivered the supplies to the Indians. My mother and I would go to the creek, where I would take the plunge to my final destiny.

"I can't thank you enough for making my visit so rewarding. I'll love and think of you and your entire family until I die. I have the best father in the world, but I'll consider you like another father now too." I knew I would go home to Kentucky to watch the *Comstock* series with my other mother. I wondered what she might think about my renewed interest in the series and my probable *Comstock* binging.

When I was in bed and about to turn off the lamp, someone knocked on the door.

"Lauren, may I come in?" It was Sam.

"Of course."

"I want to thank you for not disclosing the problems you'll face when you return. If I could protect you, I would do anything to do so."

"Thank you, sir."

"Well, I have done something that might help. When we were doing all the blasting, I buried a gun in the rocks that might survive until you get back. I want you to examine this map with me and make certain you understand where it is located."

He opened a paper, which I studied. The gun was buried not far from the creek, in a place I believed had not been disturbed by any of the machinery my friend Rich had used to change the course of the stream and shore up the rock-slide area. He pointed to the X on the paper and told me to pace off from a large tree. He inquired if there had been any logging or fires. I didn't know, but I thought not. I hugged and thanked him once again.

"I assume one more plea to stay would land on deaf ears?"

"What did you say? I didn't hear you."

"Pleasant dreams, Lauren."

"Thanks, Pa. I guess I could say that once. Please make sure my mother is safe."

"You really made an old man happy." He laughed, kissed me on the forehead, and returned to my mother. *Yep, America's favorite television father.*

I lay quietly, but I hardly slept that night. I didn't let my mother know I was awake when I heard her at one stage come in to replace a blanket on me.

Our plan would commence the following day, but I could hear a light rain outside. It would not affect the water level. I was out of here in the morning—home, sweet home.

Chapter 9

Rebecca

Failure to launch. This was what Lauren called it, but it was much more than that.

The morning I was supposed to accompany Lauren to the portal pool, as we called it now, was one of the worst days in my life. I woke up early, as did Lauren. We wanted a few more hours together. We spoke of our mutual love and pride. Each of us had achieved her goals, and our ambitions had resulted in such success. I was convinced something was in the back of her mind, but I couldn't persuade her to divulge her secrets.

We started the oven fire for Gee Ling and prepared his tea and our coffee even before he was awake. Lauren's plan was to surface from the creek, dry off and walk out of the area. With luck, she would catch a ride to her friend Rich's house and a plane to Kentucky. Once there, she could lie on the couch and watch *Comstock* programs with my sister, Sherry. I was kind of jealous. At least, she could see what Hank was like.

Gee Ling shooed us out of the kitchen. He was fixing extra food for Sam and Hanna to take to the Indians. We went out to the barn and noticed the horses hadn't been fed. We both fed and watered the stock. By the time we were done, breakfast would be made, and Sam and Hanna would be wondering where we were. We were laughing and doing anything to make us forget what was coming. When we entered the house, it was eerily silent, except for Gee Ling yelling for us to get to the table.

I climbed the stairs to open Hanna's door to tell her it was time for breakfast. She rarely slept in, and there was no school today since she would take the supplies to the Indians. "Rise and shine, darling."

I proceeded to our bedroom, where Sam hadn't moved since I left him. I bent down to kiss him, touched his forehead, and instantly realized he had a fever. He was burning up. I went back to Hanna's room, but she hadn't moved, either. Hanna was feverish, as well.

"Ma, my throat is so sore. I want to sleep some more. I'm sorry, but can Pa go without me?"

"Hanna, stay in bed. I'll be back with something in a minute."

I returned to our bedroom, where Sam was barely stirring. He'd risen but nearly fell over. I caught him and helped him back into bed. I shouted for Gee Ling. He came up, complaining about his breakfast growing cold. When he realized Sam was sick, though, he immediately asked what he could do.

"I'm not sure yet. Hanna's sick too. Probably best if you bring some tea for them both. I'll get something from my bag to decrease their fever. Tell Lauren not to enter either room." I peered down into the barn area, where there was no activity. I tried to remember who'd gone into town over the weekend and who had not. I suspected influenza. Sam, Hanna, and anyone else who went to church would probably fall ill. I had to keep Lauren away. She needed to get to the portal.

I stayed upstairs and had her come to the edge of the steps. I explained the situation. I instructed her to eat quickly, head to the creek, and leave this time by herself. I asked her to take Pocket and turn her loose when she left because the horse would come back. I told Lauren how much I loved her and wished her all the best in the world. From downstairs, she inquired if I had aspirin. I didn't know of any remedy to lower fevers, except for cold-water baths. We weren't there yet. Fevers helped the body fight infections in some ways until the vital organs were too overwhelmed with toxins. Fevers were then more harmful than helpful, which was the pervasive thought when I was in vet school. Phlebotomies were still used in the 1870s. Thankfully, my associates, John and Alf, were aware bloodletting would not help, though. The problem was there was nothing to reduce the fever, and aspirin was simply an unrealized dream.

"I love you." I glimpsed around and knew we were alone. "Now, get the hell out of Dodge." I smiled and turned, so she wouldn't see my tears.

"I love you, too, Mama." She turned and left. I returned to Hanna's bedroom, and Gee Ling brought my bag and some warm tea.

Everyone from the Cattle Creek Ranch who had gone to the church was sick. Whatever the virus, it was highly contagious. I needed to do whatever I could before I was struck down with it. From what I recalled, later today—or even the next day—I would most likely have the symptoms. I remembered Jenny and Dan. I told Sam I was going down to their house. I saddled Penny and, on the way, Cassie stuck her head out of her cabin and let me know both she and her husband, Merv, were sick. "Just stay inside and take care. I'll feed the stock later. I'm headed down to Dan and his family. Sam and Hanna are also sick."

"You okay, Becky? How about Lauren?"

"No, we're all fine." I thought I'd better wait to be sure she could get away before announcing her departure. This would be easy. I would say I told her to go home before she got sick.

I rode down to Jenny and Dan's and knocked on the door. I could hear Little Hank crying. No one answered. I was alarmed and entered without hearing any noise. Little Hank was his beautiful, boisterous self, but the rest were in bed sick. I did what I could for them and took Little Hank with me. He was going to have his first taste of cow's milk. I took him back to my house, and Gee Ling assumed charge. He would warm some milk and feed and change Little Hank. Gee Ling, who claimed he felt great so far, had taken broth up for Hanna and Sam.

"Both Mr. Sam and little missy sleeping. Very hot but sleeping. I tell them I am now the boss of Cattle Creek

Ranch, and they do what I say. Mr. Sam say he not argue with me about that today. Food need to get to Indians. Gee Ling will take them supplies if you show Gee Ling place to take it."

"Oh, I forgot. When Sam wakes up, I'll find out where to go." I left Gee Ling with Little Hank, and he seemed to be settling. God, I love those two men.

I went back up to Sam and Hanna. She was asleep, but Sam had just returned from the water closet. He smiled weakly. I quietly announced that Lauren had gone. He was so delirious that he lost control of his emotions. I could see tears in his eyes. He took my hand and said he loved me and how sorry he was that she was gone. I figured that if I were to contract the virus, I would already be infected, so I kissed his forehead. I informed him about Dan, Jenny, and Lizzy. He laughed when I told him about Little Hank downstairs. "Thank God for Gee Ling."

"Amen to that, my sick, sorry husband. Luckily, I have two husbands."

Sam fell asleep after drinking some tea. Hanna entered our room on her way to the water closet. She was almost staggering. I assisted her and put her back to bed. I asked her for directions to the Indian tribe. She told me to travel about a mile past Spit's grave, along the creek and valley and to the gooseberry patch near the smaller stream, and to leave the buckboard there. "Ma, the Indians will find it. Just leave it there. I'll go with you." However, she was asleep again in a minute.

I explained the drop-off location to Gee Ling. I recognized the place she was talking about, but he was unfamiliar with it. Little Hank was asleep, so Gee Ling and I harnessed the horses, and I took off with the food and clothing. Gee Ling remained with Little Hank and the rest of the family. It was an hour to Spit's grave and an hour to the end of the road. I started to unload the crates, and two Indians took the food and clothing and indicated for me to go. I turned the wagon around, but the wheel jammed. It took more than an hour to free the wheel, even with the aid of the Indians.

I would not be back home until after dark. It was cold and beginning to rain. I hadn't brought anything to keep dry. It was dark by the time I passed Dan's house. I stopped in to perform assessments on the patients. I made them all some broth and changed poor Lizzy, who was now vomiting. I decided to take her with me. I wrapped her in a blanket and carried her to the wagon. I stoked the fire and left poor Jenny and Dan in bed.

As I arrived home, Gee Ling helped me unhitch the horses and told me to go into the house. I understood this kind of effort was painful for him with his arthritis. I hugged and kissed him. I clutched Lizzy, who had vomited once again, and rushed her into the warmth of the house.

Lauren was seated in Sam's chair, holding Little Hank, feeding him warm milk with a soaked cloth. She handed me a large, unlabeled plastic bottle. "Aspirin."

My jaw dropped, and I let out a small shriek. "Mom, it's not a gold nugget. It's only plain aspirin." Little Hank stirred, and I got the look from Lauren. "I just got him nursing on this primitive contraption. Quiet in the peanut gallery, please."

It appeared Lizzy was going to vomit again. I took her into the bathing room off the kitchen. She vomited into a bowl, glanced up, and smiled.

"Oh, Lizzy, are you feeling better? Grandma's going to take care of you now. There, there. You're going to feel better soon." I stripped and sponged her clean. I always had clothes for her at our house, and I put her into a sleeping gown after she was dry. Lizzy clung to me, and I could feel she was starting to relax. I put one of Lauren's precious aspirin into a cup with some sugar water. With patience, I got her to sip it, and she began to settle. I took her upstairs to lay her in a small cot in Hanna's room. Hanna smiled and wanted the cot moved beside her bed. I returned down to the great room, where Lauren was still holding a currently sleeping baby.

"Does Sam know you're back?"

"Just Gee Ling and Little Hank. I assume you didn't tell Gee Ling. He only wanted to know where I'd been."

"I wanted to make sure you made it. What happened? Why are you here?"

"I didn't go. I thought about the way you stayed for Grandpa Jack, and I simply couldn't leave you like this. I can go later. When I walked from the portal pool downstream, I discovered a few things along the way."

"You brought a bottle of aspirin?"

"That was mainly for me. I have a few other items." While she reached into the cloth bag, Gee Ling came in.

"Later, Ma." We both smiled. Little Hank had drunk himself into a stupor. Gee Ling laid him in a cot we had made for Lizzy when she was an infant, which he set close to the fire. We went upstairs to Lauren's room, where she emptied her bag on the bed. There were several trays of antibiotics. The boxes had disintegrated, but the capsules were still sealed. She reached into her jacket for a small plastic bag with several pictures. The first waterlogged photograph was of Jim, yet I could see him. He wasn't movie-star handsome, but he had a gentle look about him. "How tall did you say he is?"

"I don't think I ever asked. Jim's taller than Sam is."

"I can tell why you're attracted to him."

"Oh, can you? I wasn't attracted at all when I met him, but I wish you could see him. It's his manner that I love."

We heard Hanna getting up. Lauren put away the photos and medicine as I went to tend to her and Sam. Both were coughing, and their fevers felt as though they were increasing. I administered some aspirin to them. Hanna appeared to settle, but Sam was still extremely sick. I decided an ice bath was in order. Gee Ling, Lauren, and I brought a tub up to his room while he slept. We carried up buckets of water, and Gee Ling provided the ice. Lauren left as we stripped Sam and assisted him into the bath. He still was unaware that Lauren was back.

After the bath, I sat all night with him as Sam would rouse for a few minutes and cough until he was too tired. I gave him antibiotics and doubled his dose of the aspirin. His breathing became more regular since his fever was reduced. Sam soaked his sleeping gown and the bed with sweat. I replaced his nightgown and laid towels on the bed after changing the linen. I instructed Lauren to take the pills down to Dan and Jenny and gave her directions about how frequently they should take them. By the third morning, I was confident that the worst was over. Sam and Hanna seemed to be on the mend. Lizzy had stopped vomiting, but she started to cough, as well. *Could this be whooping cough? It would make sense that Lauren and I were immune as we both had been vaccinated.*

The people living on the Cattle Creek Ranch were emerging from their cabins. Fortunately, several men were away, either logging or tending cattle. Those living at the Cattle Creek Ranch were all sick. Two pensioners continued to live with us despite retirement. They'd worked for Sam for many years. The oldest, Smokey Bill, passed away. In addition, his brother, Willard, was quite sick, but he survived.

When I was convinced everyone was improving, I left Lauren and headed into town to help the people there. I arrived at a community on its knees. The hospital was bursting with patients, and tents had been erected nearby to care for the overflow. Alf had contracted the virus and was home in bed. John was doing the best he could. Except for Maggie Clayton, the nurses had all become ill during the initial two days. Thank God for Maggie. She could do the work of three nurses. Our problem was that the hospital required at least six Maggies.

"I'm so sorry, Maggie. Almost everyone at the Cattle Creek Ranch is also sick. Has anyone died?"

Maggie pointed to a tent far down the main street. "Eleven people so far. It's mostly the older folks. This illness has nearly wiped out the population at the rest home."

"We lost Smokey Bill. I think the worst is over for us. Any idea how it started?"

"No, just that a wagon train came through, and a few of the travelers came into town a couple of days before the outbreak. I certainly am glad you're here, Becky. John's exhausted."

"Where is he? I'll relieve him now. Have you heard anything about Ray Thompson?"

"Sick, but he's not the worst. Pam's been helping him. What a woman. She's incredible, a total workhorse, and a quick learner."

"Pam Wilkins?"

"None other."

"How are you feeling?" Maggie's hair was loose and greasy. Her eyes were swollen, and she was dressed in clothes that may not have been washed for days.

"I have a touch, but nothing like the rest of them."

"I can take over. When did you last sleep?"

"Got a calendar?"

"That bad, huh? Go home, and that's an order."

"Yes, ma'am. Gladly."

I went into the hospital, where John was sitting in a chair with his eyes closed. I felt his forehead and knew he had a fever. "John, it's me. Go home. I'm taking over."

John glanced up and smiled. "Ah, God answered my prayers with an angel."

"I'll turn into a devil if you don't get the hell out of here now."

"Damn, Becky, no need for profanity." He got up, smiled, and left.

I gazed around. A great deal needed to be done. Individuals were in various stages of distress. I started in one room to assess and assist with removing bodily fluids and the patient's grievances. Most of them were respectful, but some wanted more than we could deliver. I brought all freshwater from the communal watering pump. I ordered them to drink it, despite their reluctance to rehydrate themselves. Along the way, in between rooms, I encountered Pam Wilkins. "Had a change of profession?"

"The saloon is nearly empty. You know how I like to keep the boys drinking. According to John, liquid consumption is the key to their well-being, and I thought that's something I could certainly help with. If the men don't survive, there won't be anyone to have a drink with me."

"Becky Buchanan is reporting for duty, ma'am. Where can I help?"

"I think you have the roles reversed, but I'm simply going from room to room and from tent to tent. I give them water, give a little beer to a few, and take away the results in the piss pots." Pam seemed exhausted.

"How's Ray?"

"He'll live. He's at home."

"Okay. I'll begin in the tents, and we can meet up in a few hours. If anyone appears to be critical, come and get me. Thanks, Pam."

"No problem, Doc."

Following three exhausting days and nine additional deaths, the worst of it was over. Sadly, two of the dead were infants. When Pam recruited two other barmaids, who seemed to be improving, the load lightened considerably. Alf also was able to help. I longed for a moment when I didn't hear a cough from somewhere.

I hoped Lauren had immunity like mine. I hadn't received any news from home, but I thought that was probably a good thing. I'd given strict instructions for Lauren to use the antibiotics only if a second fever started for a family member. I had her grind the aspirin and make it into a drink for the workers. I hoped she was coping. In a few days, I planned to return to the Cattle Creek Ranch.

I understood Lauren would depart for her home and life in the future. I wished we could have spent our lives together, but I realized many people lived lives separated from their loved ones. I knew Sam wished Clint had not gone to Australia, yet we received letters every year from him, and someday we might be reunited. There would be no communication from Lauren again. If she died early or had children and grandchildren, I would never know.

I pondered this while I was closing some tents. The sick who survived were returning to their shacks, mining camps, and houses. Maggie Clayton was back on duty. Since John was still too sick to work, though, she and Pam Wilkins provided my primary support. Pam was phenomenal. She was one of the few people in town who had not been hit with this virus. I would not have survived without her. We sat down on the last afternoon before I left for home.

"Of course, you're my new best friend, Pam."

"Bullshit, Becky. You've got a whole family and a husband."

Bullshit? I guess working in a saloon could be liberating. "That's family. I'm stuck with them. How about you? Heard from Caleb? Does he have a father?"

"Long story, Becky. Not going there. No word from Caleb, and I wouldn't expect to hear from him, anyway. He's a boy. When's your girl returning to her fiancé?"

"In a few days, I expect. Lauren delayed her return when everyone got sick. Hard to let go, isn't it?"

"A few months ago, I would have paid someone to take Caleb. But after watching so many sick people die, I wish he was here."

"He'll be fine. I'd better go. Thanks again, Pam. I really appreciate your help."

A young boy came up to us with a telegram for Sam. He wanted me to deliver it to him urgently. It was sealed and had a return-to-sender notation from the United States Army.

I saddled Penny and took off for home. I deviated and went up to check out the portal pool. The water was fast, but I believed it was survivable. I prayed the other side was safe. Thankfully, everyone was recovering when I returned, but still quite sick. I think Sam would have died without the antibiotics in the early phase. As it was, he was still quite ill. Jenny and Dan were not much better. Poor Lauren and Gee Ling had carried the burden of caring for the entire family. Little Hank had hardly slept due to a new cough, but Lizzy was running around, seeking attention, and wanting to be with her parents.

As I entered the house, Lauren greeted me as if I were the Second Coming. "I'm cured."

"Of what?"

"Kids and marriage. Not gonna have it no way, no how. If Jim says he won't marry me, then I'll die a happy, barren woman. Sick old men, sick teenagers, sick toddlers, and a sick baby. Not gonna happen."

"I'll give it a week on the other side, and I guess that proclamation will be out the window."

Hanna came downstairs. "The other side of what?"

Lauren replied quickly, "The Great Divide. I'm going home soon."

"Oh, Lauren, please don't go. At least, let me go with you." Hanna had a coughing fit. I felt her forehead.

"You're still feverish. Go back upstairs now."

"But Ma." About then, Sam came down the stairs. With one look from her father, Hanna headed up the steps past him.

I looked at Sam, and we embraced. "I've missed you so much." I kissed him and felt his forehead. "You, too, Mr. Buchanan. Back to bed. I can tell you still have a fever, as well."

He hugged me. "Missed you, too, Becky. Anything happening in town?"

"Oh, I forgot." I reached into my satchel to hand him the telegram.

Sam opened it and reached for the glasses he needed periodically. He read and reread it. He seemed extremely upset.

"Is Merv here? I must see him. Lauren, can you see how he is?"

As Lauren left, I motioned for Sam to give me the telegram.

"We have a problem." He handed me the paper.

I read it.

Dear Sir,

Confirming you can send two hundred head of cattle and thirty horses to Santa Fe immediately, per our agreement. While this is just the initial lot, it will satisfy our Commander that you are a trusted supplier to the proposed complete agreement of nine hundred cattle and ninety horses.

Col. Malcolm Hurt

United States Army

"Oh, Sam. This couldn't have happened at a worse time." The wranglers who were away and safe from the virus received a visitor from the ranch who had infected them, and currently, they were all sick. Lauren and I were the only ones who were truly not sick. Even Sam was too ill to take on a cattle drive.

"Let me see how Dan's coping."

I rode down to his house. Although he was still quite sick, he had improved enough to come immediately back to the house. Lizzy raced to his arms, and even Little Hank began excitedly babbling when he heard his voice.

Dan read the telegram. "Pa, we have to do this. If we don't, we'll lose the entire contract, and that would be the end for us."

"Daniel, who's going to help us? The men are all ill. I realize they would help, but I don't want anyone else dying on the trail. Maybe we could ask for a week's extension."

"Pa, this is a test. If we don't do it, they won't contract with us ever again, and you know it."

Lauren returned, listening to Sam and Dan discussing the problem while they sat at Sam's desk. Sam glanced at her, waiting for a report.

"Not good, sir. Merv agreed to go, but he doubts he has enough men to get the job done."

I listened and asked for the number of men required to drive the cattle and thirty horses to Santa Fe. They would catch a cattle car up from there to Denver. Otherwise, they would have to cross the Rockies, which would cause losses.

Sam and Dan seemed desperate. I took Sam by the arm. "I can go. I think I have someone who can assist us, as well."

"Who?"

"You're going to have to trust me on this one, Sam."

"I'll go too. I need another adventure before I settle down." Lauren had a look of determination I had not witnessed previously.

"No, you need to get home." What a nice gesture, but no thanks.

Sam gazed at her, and I could see his admiration grow. "Lauren, you've sacrificed far too much. I can't let you do it."

"Sir, with all respect, I believe you aren't in a position to object."

He looked at me with the look that meant *not over my dead body*. Lauren stared hard at me. "Ma, are you coming with Dan and me?"

"Definitely. No one's going to defeat us Buchanans."

"But, Lauren, you won't get home until spring then." Sam was exasperated, I was elated, and Dan was confused.

"Anyone want to explain what's going on?" Dan's brow had that expression of confusion that was so endearing on *Comstock*.

Sometimes you must take a stand. I yelled, "Dan, it's time you accepted some orders from your mother. Go home and pack. Sam, get your sorry"—I was going to say ass but caught myself—"self back up to bed. If you die, I'll never forgive you. You and Hanna aren't going anywhere until I say you can."

I don't think I ever raised my voice to them like that before. Everyone was shocked. Lauren stared at me and smiled but understood not to say anything. Time was of the essence. Enough cattle had been brought down from the high country to fill this order. The horses weren't far away, either. We would start in the morning. Gee Ling couldn't come on horseback, but he could drive a chuck wagon. He and I would go into town for another cousin. I also hoped to persuade a friend to join us.

Lauren

You could have heard a pin drop after my mother informed everyone what she planned to do with her motley crew of Dan, Gee Ling, me, and someone from town. I wondered whether Ray Thompson could ride all day.

I questioned if Sam had been addressed like that in years. I went out with Dan, who recommended which horses we should take. We would ride our regular horses and trade out the ones we were selling. They would acquire some miles under saddle and be ready for the army by the time we arrived. We would take extras to sell if they weren't needed to trade out at the end of the cattle drive.

"I dare your ma to come within reach of my pa before we go."

"Not gonna happen, bro."

"Lauren, where are you from, really? You and your ma have the strangest way of talking."

"You can't get there from here, Dan. You'd better take those children home. Ma will recruit them for the drive. However, if it's just your pa and Hanna without Gee Ling, they'll be cleaning pens, washing dishes, and chopping wood before we get back."

"I'll retrieve them now. If I survive my father's wrath, I'll see you in the morning."

I fed up, cleaned in the barn, and oiled the saddles. I set out halters, harnesses, and buckets for the next two months. Fortunately, we would be away from snow on the trip because we were headed south. Feed for the animals could be a problem this time of year, but I guess they took this into account. The Buchanans, who had made this trip numerous times, would have contingency plans in place for feeding the stock along the way. All I had to do was learn to drive cattle. My short career at showing reining cow horses at quarter-horse shows wasn't probably going to be of much use. Learn, and you earn. I think Sam mentioned the ranch hands were paid forty dollars on a cattle drive. I thought that meant a day, but he explained that was for the entire cattle drive. How cheap can you get?

I overheard my mother and Sam arguing until late in the night. I couldn't make out the words, but it seemed to me that my mother was holding her own. I couldn't be sure, but I think I heard them laughing as the evening progressed.

The following day, my mother and Gee Ling left for town. Dan was heavily layered in clothes and coughing up a storm. Two wranglers and I headed up to the mountain meadow to bring the cattle to the corrals near the main house. The horses were fitted with halters that were tied to a lead horse. We practiced leading fifteen from one horse. We required more men but would make do as best we could. Maybe we would pick up some drovers along the way.

Oh, I was going on a real cattle drive! I needed a camera. I required a few other supplies, as well. The monthly rag thing was a pain, but the alternative was ugly. That was something I would happily forget when I got home. I am the best daughter a mother could want. I wasn't convinced how this was going to go down back at home. I hated to consider that my family would look for me and think I was dead. They would possibly believe that the nutcase stalker had killed me. What if Jim returned early? I was seriously beginning to regret my decision.

I was sitting on the divan, staring into the fire, when Sam came down in this ridiculous bathrobe he wore at night. He sat down in his chair and didn't say anything for several minutes. I could tell Sam was laboring to breathe. If he died, I wondered whether I could talk my mother into coming back with me. She didn't have to live with my dad or anything. I didn't know for certain if she was buried up at Hank Heaven. I was sure more than one person was buried there. Still, the fallen tree covered the tombstones making it impossible to read the grave markers. I clasped my hands in front of my knees. My feet rested on the divan.

"Want to talk?" America's favorite dad was doing his thing. It wouldn't work now. I totally screwed up. Why did I agree to do this?

"No, thanks." Short and sweet. Well, short, at least.

"Having second thoughts?"

"No. Not at all."

"Really?"

"Well, maybe a little."

"Possibly more than a little?"

"Maybe."

"If we lost the contract, we would lose the Cattle Creek Ranch. Do you know what would happen?"

"No, sir." I glanced at him.

"We'd move and rebuild. We'd be all right. Dan, his family, your mother, and I would be fine. The people who would be hurt are those who work for us. Do you know how many employees we have, Lauren?"

"No, sir."

"Have a guess."

"Fifty?"

"Try one hundred. More than two hundred people work for us in the busy season, but one hundred of them are full-time. They live in other areas, and some are in other states. Winter aside, however, we employ over two hundred men. Most of these individuals have families. I've never let them down." He broke into yet another paroxysmal coughing fit. I poured him some brandy and found the aspirin.

"Thank you." He took a sip. "Someday, I know I'm going to die. We all do, you know, but I'm trying to hang on until Dan's children are old enough to help Dan as he, Clint, and Hank helped me. The fact that you and your mother are doing this for our family means the world to me. I would tell your other family, in your future time, that you are alive and safe if there was some way I could."

"I understand, sir. I accept responsibility for my actions. In the morning, I'll go on the cattle drive, and I'll do my best to assist my mother and her chosen family." Sam walked over to hug me. I stepped back, and I could tell he was hurt. He only meant well. He was such a kind man. I walked toward him and opened my arms. "You can count on me, as well, Pa."

Chapter 10

Rebecca
Gee Ling and I arrived in a town that was so much the same as I had left. I instructed Gee Ling to stay away from everyone. I would have preferred for him to wear a bandana, but he might be shot. The town was empty. We bought out the general goods store. You name the provision, and we took it. We weren't going to starve, and I observed Gee Ling becoming anxious. He limped as he stepped off the buckboard. I should find a cook to replace him. I walked over to the hospital, where both Alf and John had returned to work. I described our problem with getting the stock to Santa Fe. "Sorry, gentlemen, but I require a leave of absence. A long one. I'm going to be gone for two months, at least."

John crossed his arms and laughed, which sent him into a paroxysm of coughing. "After this last week, you can have the rest of the year off. We don't know how you do it."

"Me, either, but I had help. Got to go, gentlemen."

I headed to the Bucket o' Blood to see Pam Wilkins. I peered into the empty place, where the bartender, Cosmo, was playing solitaire.

"Hey, Cosmo."

"Hey, Becky."

"Is Pam around?"

"She's at the orphanage."

"Thanks. Mind if I borrow Pam for a couple of weeks?"

"Look around, Becky. We're plumb empty."

"It won't be long. Hang in there. Thanks."

"You too." Cosmo returned to his cards.

I went to the orphanage, where Alexander Thistlewaite, who was in Hanna's class, and two new orphans were added to the roster. The new matron had arrived. The bank manager and the old matron were still missing. Glenn Frasier failed to find them during his investigation. Pam was in a backroom, perusing the books. She made certain things were accounted for, and her money was spent wisely. No one, except for a few people, knew she was the current benefactor. I stuck my head through the door to greet her.

"Hey, Becky, what brings you here?"

"An adventure, Pam. I want to steal you for an adventure."

Alexander, seated next to Pam, added the columns in the accounting ledger on the desk. I'll bet Pam was good at counting, but Alexander lost his only parent in the latest plague. She was trying to help him with his grief and loneliness.

"What kind of adventure?"

I needed to ease Pam into this idea. "Can you cook, Pam?"

"What kind of adventure, Becky?"

"Can you ride a horse?"

"What kind of adventure, Becky?" Pam wasn't going to go down easily.

"Ever dream of sleeping out under the stars, Pam?"

"No to all."

"No, really, Pam. It'll be fun."

"I don't like cooking, riding, or sleeping rough. What kind of adventure, Becky?"

"A cattle drive."

"Why didn't you say that in the first place? Where are we going?"

"Santa Fe. It will be a short, quick trip of sixty days, max."

"Max?"

"Yes."

Alexander glanced at Pam. "Dr. Buchanan?"

"Yes, Alexander?"

"I want to go."

"Really? Have you done much with cattle?"

"We had cows at home. Only a few, but I can ride a horse."

"Hmm, would having Alexander there sweeten the pot for you, Pam?"

"I'm thinking. Two whole months. Which dresses would I take? I'm partial to the red satins, but what color are the cows? I figure blue is usually a good contrast. Then there's the hair, Becky. I need to, you know, maintain my youthful color. I don't know. How long until I must commit?" She coughed.

"One minute, Pam. One minute. You aren't feeling sick, are you?"

Pam tapped her foot. She gazed up, then at Alexander, and finally down at her well-manicured nails. "Oh, hell, I'm in. If I don't have to rope a cow, I'll do my best. Not sick at all. Simply a persistent cough. Too much smoke in the saloon. Be good to get away."

"Okay, cowgirl, you have one hour before we leave. Alexander, what do you have to keep warm?" I approached the new matron, who was laughing so hard she had to cross her legs. "One less mouth to feed for a while. Don't worry. I'll bring him back before Christmas."

Gee Ling was going to stay. God help us, Pam would cook. Alexander was going to help her drive the chuck wagon. Two more ranch hands were fit enough to accompany us.

Rough and undermanned as we were, we were ready. *Rawhide,* here we come.

Lauren

"Where's Ray?" My mother returned with the barroom lady and the young boy from Hanna's class. What the heck?

"Ray? Ray Thompson? Did you think I would ruin my reputation by taking along a single handsome man like Ray and leaving your stepfather to worry for two months?"

"Yes, I did."

"Nope. I brought along some real help."

"Have you lost your marbles? Are they the only live bodies you could persuade to come?"

"Actually, yes. Don't worry. It'll be fun."

Dan was in the barn. His jaw dropped when he spied a fifteen-year-old boy and a fifty-something barmaid. I was with Dan on this one.

"Dan, I know what you and Lauren are thinking."

I thought, no, you have no idea, Mom.

"Becky, this isn't going to work. What can she do on a cattle drive?"

"She says she can't cook, but maybe she can clean. You'll have to take a chance on this woman."

Dan took us into the barn. "If Gee Ling doesn't go, we'll all starve."

"Dan, have you observed Gee Ling lately? He can barely walk. It will be too much for him."

"This is foolish. We won't make it down the road."

"Dan, I have one thing to say to you—Spirit of Woodland. I went along with your crazy ideas. Now you should go along with mine."

Mom turned to me. "Spirit of Woodland, better known as Spit to those of us who knew and loved him, was a racing mule we bought many years ago. Sadly, he ran solely with a woman jockey. He was a marvelous mount for me, much to the embarrassment of your stepfather, who thought it was below the dignity of a Buchanan to ride a mule."

"Yeah, but Pa has a beautiful trophy from Spit." Dan was proud.

"And we'll bring back the honor of the Buchanan name and save the Cattle Creek Ranch. Somewhat more is at stake this time, Dan. We leave at dawn, so sharpen your spurs and kiss those beautiful children goodbye for me." My mom was on a roll. I detected the spirit she had in her step. I then took Mrs. Wilkins into the house. Alexander went home with Dan. Hanna was furious that she could not accompany us now that a classmate was coming along. Sam was shaking his head and coughing up a storm. I hoped the change in antibiotics kicked in soon. He was an extremely sick man.

Gee Ling was relieved that he wasn't required on the cattle drive. He assumed commando mode and welcomed Mrs. Wilkins into his kitchen, and they started their assault on the chuck wagon. Apparently, she could cook, but cooking simply wasn't her favorite thing to do. The chuck wagon was ready to go by late evening.

A little arguing still took place in the marital bedroom that night. My dad and my aunt certainly had their disagreements over the years. Still, this approach appeared to be unusual for my mother. I could tell it upset Hanna. I tried to comfort her, but she was yet quite sick, and her spasmodic cough was alarming. Our mother decided to give her the same antibiotic she had administered to Sam. We wouldn't know if it worked until we returned.

"Trouble in paradise, Mom?" We had settled Hanna, who was asleep. My mom was radiant. I recognized she was excited to be on an adventure with me and to play a part in saving the family's fortunes. I realized this disagreement bothered her, but she was carrying a cross, which she wasn't laying down for anyone.

"Lauren, you'll have a few of these in your marriage too. Hiccups, really. Don't let them interfere with the big picture. I love Sam, and I believe I'm the luckiest woman in the world. I would do anything to please him, even if he thinks it doesn't please him. It is a man's world in the 1800s. Sometimes you must cross the line to ensure life stays on track. He'll get over it. He's not used to people rescuing him. I think you can understand that fact. He's struggling to accept help."

"Mom, I'm glad I met you again. I know everything will be okay, but we need to figure out how to explain the distress this will cause my other family. I hope it doesn't kill Dad." She could tell how I was torn between my two lives.

"We'll get through this, and I am convinced you'll laugh about this year from now. Are you going to share this adventure with Jim?"

"I don't know. Probably."

"All right. Get some sleep, darling. We'll get those dogies rollin' at the crack of dawn."

"Rawhide?" Mom nodded.

We started those dogies rolling. We had the team pulling the wagon hitched and all prepared to go by the time Dan was up at the ranch house. Sam came to the door in the maroon dressing gown and weakly waved goodbye. I was seriously worried he might not be alive when we got back. Hanna coughed all night and didn't wake up when my mother went in, checked on her, and kissed her goodbye.

I was confident at least one of us was going to live. Alexander Thistlewaite's name was on the deed, indicating he bought the cabin from my mother years from now. He had to live. I had to think he and Hanna eventually married because the other name on the deed was hers. If such a greenhorn as Alexander would survive, surely, I was going to endure, as well.

Dan was feeling better and assumed command of the entire operation. We headed out to the corrals, where the men gathered and held the horses. My mom rode Penny, and I was on Pocket. Pocket was fresh, and even crow hopped when leaving the barn area. Alexander laughed and appeared to be enjoying himself. I considered him a shy, studious kid when I saw him in school, but I believed he might be quite handy on the trail.

The real surprise was Mrs. Wilkins. This was not her first rodeo. She was an accomplished muleskinner. She gave me a straight-faced nod of "I told you so" as she took the reins and started the horses off, and I returned her look with a smile. My mother and Pam seemed to be partners in crime. Since I think we were the only three people in all the vicinity who had not been ill, we had much more energy than the rest. Alexander still coughed and wheezed somewhat, but he was probably the least sick out of the crew. I noticed Pam also coughed. I hoped she was all right.

The beginning was difficult because we had to condition the cattle and horses into a routine. One horse seemed to test the tethering by lunging forward and backward all day. The cattle were inclined to try to turn around toward the ranch. My mother and I worked our horses almost to exhaustion in keeping the cows moving forward. Dan had done this many times, and he took over from me when one ornery cow was testing us. He and his mount soon had her sorted.

I was exhausted, dirty, and hungry by the end of the day. I smelled like sweat and probably body odors I had never experienced. Was it me or someone else? We didn't reach quite the distance for which we had hoped, but there was feed and water where we stopped, and we would attempt to make it up the following day.

My mother and Mrs. Wilkins got straight to the supper. Of course, it wasn't Gee Ling's masterpiece, but it was filling and hot. No complaints. Alexander and I took the first watch on the cattle. I recalled the television stampede scenes I'd viewed from television. I'd watched Lonesome Dove once, and possibly it was due to that, but I was nervous. We stayed up until my mother and one of the ranch hands relieved us. Since Dan was still sick, we decided to let him sleep the first few nights.

Thankfully, the night was quiet and without incidents. The cattle were likely as exhausted as we wranglers were from our initial day of travel. The horses had been hobbled, let out to graze for a few hours, and brought in and tied to long ropes strung between trees. The horse that had given the wranglers grief all day was still pulling back and creating havoc.

My mother was determined to ride that horse the following day. Dan wasn't happy, but he relented in the end. The gelding was a roan, and his first inclination was going anywhere but forward. My mother masterfully straightened him out, though, and he was toeing the line by lunchtime.

I considered bandanas as a fashion statement until the second day. My mother handed me one, which covered my face. I had dust and dirt in every orifice imaginable. I inhaled and ate dust all day long. My teeth crunched dirt when I chewed. My one bra, which I wore daily since arriving in the 1800s, was full of dirt at the end of the day. My fingernails also came up dirty when I scratched my head. I had weeks of this with which to contend. Kill me now.

I heard my mother humming the song "Strawberry Roan," which my grandfather sang. When was that song published? I knew Frank Lash and my mother used music to find each other. They hummed tunes from the 1900s as a signal to fellow time travelers to establish contact. She hummed or sang modern tunes when she and Sam were alone. This song sounded old-fashioned, and maybe it was from this time. I laughed and hummed with her. She smiled, and we hummed the Rawhide theme song, which we realized was not written until the 1900s. We were far from anyone, so we knew no one could hear us.

The second day went much better. We made up for the miles we lost on the first day. Dan again took us to pastures with feed, and we maintained the same lookouts. The wranglers were worn out from riding soon after their illness. Mrs. Wilkins went ahead at Dan's direction, and supper was well underway upon our arrival. I must say that Mom was correct. Mrs. Wilkins was a hand. Her food was filling, and salt always added some flavor. Because the meat would not last, we would eat jerky for the next few days. A town was coming up where we could be supplied with eggs and more meat, but we feasted that night.

This went on for several days. The horses and cattle settled in, and we were able to get ahead of schedule, according to Dan. He was now enjoying himself. He was feeling better, and I even did night watch with him, so Alexander could sleep. We sat with our horses saddled and ready to go, but we were by the campfire drinking coffee.

"Lauren, I understand you made a huge sacrifice to help us. I guess your fiancé is waiting for you to return. Possibly you could leave from Santa Fe?"

"Yeah, maybe."

"I've got to tell you, there's nothing better than sharing your life with the person you love. The good times and the bad times are much easier when you have someone to share them with. Don't abandon him for us, will you?"

"Ha! No chance of that, Dan, not in a hundred years." I laughed to myself about changing a million to a hundred. Dan told me the way he met Jenny. "She made me wait a whole month just to dance with her." He went on that she left him when a crazy woman pretended her son was his son. Dan discussed that his wedding was held at her parents' home instead of the Cattle Creek Ranch. He commented that the party his father and my mother threw for them was one of the best nights of his life. He mentioned a little about his first wife and child, who were killed, and how long it took him to get over it.

"Your mother surely helped when she returned to Virginia City. My pa was as nervous as a polecat when he waited for her to move back from Baltimore. When she was delayed, he was unbearable to be around. I know you don't remember her, but she's the reason my father is so happy, and that makes us all glad. I'm aware you couldn't have known she was alive, and I understand you were the loser in all this, but her life has meaning to so many in our town. I think you can see that. I just hope when you go back, you bring meaning to your home and family in Virginia, or New York, or wherever you end up."

"Dan, if you could bring back your mother, realizing all you know now, I still figure you would do it."

"Not if it meant losing Jenny and the kids. Just like you, I had to move on. Of course, I was a baby, as well. My life is wonderful, and I guess I have to say I wouldn't change a thing, except for this awful, cold coffee. Why don't you go to bed, and I'll wait up until the next guards come on? Pleasant dreams, Lauren."

"You, too, Dan."

The next few days were the same. I was saddle sore for the first few days on the trail. Spending ten hours in the saddle was challenging. I gradually became accustomed to it and didn't really think much about it anymore. The food tasted better every day. Well, maybe my expectations decreased, and anything warm and filling was pleasant. My mother went from strength to strength. Despite being about twenty years older than anyone else here, except for Mrs. Wilkins, Mom held her own for any of the work. She and Mrs. Wilkins always talked and shared the tasks of washing dishes and packing the chuck wagon. They both slept under the wagon. I could hear them laughing until one of them fell asleep. Mrs. Wilkins wore regular clothes. Except for her dyed blonde hair, overdone war paint, and those ridiculous fingernails, you would never guess her usual trade. Almost.

Toward the end of the second week, our first accident occurred. We had hired a drover from the previous town to help us out during the rest of the trip. He was capable, but his horse, which he insisted on riding, was a mongrel. When the man unsaddled him one night, the horse kicked him in the ribs and stomped on him. His injuries were significant. My mother said he'd broken a bone in his foot and might have sustained fractured ribs. The injured drover would drive the chuck wagon while Mrs. Wilkins was going to ride with the herd.

Dan was worried. "Are you sure you'll be okay, Mrs. Wilkins?"

"Dan, one thing's for sure. If I hear any of you call me Mrs. Wilkins again, I won't feed any of you. I'm Pam. Just plain Pam." She stared hard at Dan and me.

"Yes, ma'am," was the immediate reply from everyone.

I believe we all noticed she coughed persistently and was losing weight. Mom talked to her, but she said it must be the dust and hard work. I heard her tell my mom she was fighting fit. I wasn't persuaded my mother bought it, but Pam worked as hard as anyone.

It was easy to tell Pam knew her way around a horse. She rode Mom's horse, Penny, the first day. She mounted with ease and kept up all day. Her cattle-herding skills were average, but she did a day's work. At the end of the day, she still cooked supper for us. Mom was correct that she was certainly good value. I understood why Ray Thompson liked her. Mom had reason to be jealous.

The following week, we realized we had surpassed the halfway mark. We celebrated with beer, which was purchased from the local saloon we passed that day. Pam made sure no one drank more than their fair share, and everyone would be able to work the next day. We decided to keep the injured man. He could drive the chuck wagon, and he would always take part in the night shift, guarding the cattle, although he didn't ride at all.

I was the only one to notice a steer circle out and go into the scrub at the back of the herd one day. I peeled off to round him back into the herd. I took my time looking for him, and I heard Pam singing. I thought it was sort of funny because she wasn't good at carrying a tune. I listened for a while and tried to recognize the melody from her voice. It was familiar. With that voice, though, who could tell.

I located the steer to drive him up to the back of the herd. As I emerged from the bushes, I heard Pam singing the words to the Rawhide television song. When the steer ran into the herd, Pam turned and saw me. We stared long and hard at each other. It was a look that might betray my mother and me.

"Nice lyrics, Pam."

"Yes, someone taught me those last year."

"Hmm, if you say so."

Her face was red, and I could tell she was nervous. Extremely nervous. There was no doubt in my mind she was a fellow time traveler. I wasn't going to betray our origins.

"Gee, you're a bit of a surprise. Who would have thunk you knew how to ride so well?"

"Yeah, who'd a thunk it." She trotted up to the front of the herd.

Chapter 11

Rebecca

Leaving Sam was difficult. Asking a man to stand back to let his wife do a man's work in the 1800s is about as bad as it can get. Our last night together before we left was tense. Sam was ropable and still extremely sick. I bounced between wanting to stay to make sure he got better and wishing to throttle him. We quietly fumed with each other. In the end, he reluctantly relented. He recognized how vital this cattle drive was to a great many people. He really had no say in the matter, not that he didn't try.

My other concern was the probable long delay in Lauren's return to her home and fiancé. There was no way she would safely traverse the water portal until spring and probably late spring at best. Even if the water was low on our end, one couldn't predict its level in the 2000s.

I could detect the stress on her face. She claimed she wanted to help. I believe she and Sam discussed how important it was, not just to us but to our workers and other creditors. We needed to get these cattle to the army. She's a tough woman, but so was I, and it almost killed me to not return to my former life. I didn't know how to comfort her. She was much more stoic than I was. If she was crying, she was doing it alone.

Dan and I had a rare moment to talk. "I told you so. Pam's a great addition to our team. Dan, I realize how hard it is, but we're ahead of schedule so far. The cattle are maintaining their weight, and the horses are so much nicer with some miles on them. Even that crazy bay horse is behaving now."

"I have to hand it to you, Bec. It could be a lot worse."

"We'll be in Santa Fe in two weeks. I'll book a bath first thing." The thought made it all worthwhile. *Well, almost.*

"I'm having a cold beer myself. Boy, I can hardly wait to get home to Jenny and the children. I'll bet Little Hank can walk by the time I get back."

"Haven't you seen him walk yet?" I saw Little Hank walking during the week I cared for him. Because I didn't want to spoil it for Jenny and Dan, I didn't say anything at that time.

We had to get there first, though, and that was when our troubles began. We experienced three days without water. The cattle were getting weak, and two horses got colic. We decided to hold up while Dan searched for water. He was gone for a day. Keeping the cattle together with little to eat and without water was torturous. We took turns day and night, but they were trying to push on.

We lost two steers. However, we brought ten additional steers in case this happened. The men were becoming anxious, as well. The two colicky horses responded to extra water. Still, we rationed the water that we drank and allowed the horses much more of our reserve. Finally, Dan returned and informed us the water was a day away but in the wrong direction. We drove the cattle at night, so they wouldn't get too dehydrated. We stayed an extra day to make it through the desert, which paid off. When clouds formed and the rain came, though, the going was treacherous.

We were still ahead of the plan. If we didn't make it to higher ground, however, we would need to abandon the chuck wagon. We made it through, but two more horses got an allergic condition called greasy heel or mud fever, which made them too sore to move. Their legs were swollen and crusting. Such a painful condition can get out of hand. It starts as dermatitis on the back of the pasterns. Alexander and Lauren worked on them all day long, using salves I made to calm the swollen legs and reduce the swelling. I didn't know if they would pass the inspection. We wrapped them in rolls of cotton linen with grease and some herbs, which an old Indian woman had told me about.

This remedy didn't help, but the horses weren't any worse the following day. We had to cross a large river, which, according to Dan, was usually a dry creek bed. We were all getting chilled from working in the rain and sleeping under the chuck wagon. Pam's cough was somewhat worse. We were able to off-load the man with the fractures. Getting rid of his horse was the best part of the deal.

Alexander and Pam worked better than did our own men who were experiencing a resurgence of their viruses. Lauren was staying steady, but she had lost a considerable amount of weight, as had I. Dan was getting the shakes, and I feared he was contracting something far worse than the bacterial infection that frequently follows influenza. I remembered his bout of yellow fever or something like that when we looked for Sam in Cuba a few years earlier.

"Dan, you're taking the day off to ride in the chuck wagon. Alexander, you can drive it. The rest of us will be with the cows." No one complained, except for Dan, of course, who thought he should guide us. I suggested that Alexander drive the horses and wagon, and Dan could occasionally direct him and sleep in between points. We would follow with the cattle and horses.

Indians liked to scout out this area and occasionally raid the cattle drives, primarily for firearms and the occasional steer. We loaded our guns and had them ready to fire. If I'd known about this situation, I would never have allowed Lauren to come. I regretted bringing her. I would never forgive myself if she were injured. I ensured all the rifles were clean, dry, and prepared.

We headed out and watched the hills for any signs of an attack. Toward the end of the day, we began to relax. We caught up with the chuck wagon at a watering hole. Dan and three men were on guard that night. He was better due to his day of rest. Pam, Lauren, and I slept inside the chuck wagon, where it was cramped and uncomfortable, but we felt safe.

It rained and was almost monsoonal the following day, which Dan seemed to think would lessen the chances of any Indian raids. We decided to stay another night. We were still several days ahead of schedule and could afford to rest the stock and ourselves. Lauren and I stood guard during the day. Our slickers were no match for the rain. Although it wasn't too cold, by afternoon, we were feeling the effects of being wet through and through. Lauren was shivering and couldn't seem to control it. Pam wasn't much better. We were relieved of guarding the cattle when it was time to cook. Starting a fire in the continual rain was impossible. We shared jerky, hardtack, and cold beans. There was no place to get out of the rain except under or inside the wagon. Pam and Lauren elected to stay inside. I was wary of possible lightning and a stampede.

Consequently, I saddled Penny and, despite the wet and cold, rode all night. Dan had the same idea. The lightning arrived, and the cattle were spooky, but no stampede occurred. The sun broke through, and the clouds receded by morning. Pam was back on wagon duty.

I noticed that Lauren kept staring at Pam. She didn't seem hostile, but I could tell she was interested in what Pam talked about. I wondered what triggered this unusual awareness. When Lauren and I were alone, I asked her what was going on between Pam and her.

"Mom, you know how Pam, you, and I were the only ones who didn't get sick back in Virginia City?"

"Yes, thankfully. And?"

"A while ago, I was chasing a steer that had entered the scrub. While I was bringing the steer back up, I heard Pam singing. Man, she can't carry a tune to save her life."

"I'm not getting this. What's so riveting about Pam's inability to sing?"

"The cadence attracted my attention. She didn't hear me because the cows were bellowing. She was singing the words from the *Rawhide* song. I realize that song is before my time, but it sure as heck is later than this time. Mom, I think she's a fellow time traveler."

I considered what she said. Some things made me think it could be true, but there was probably an explanation. Pam knew Frank Lash. They didn't work at the same saloon, but she mentioned him. Pam remembered I disappeared when Frank did and, like everyone in town, had wondered if I had gone off with him.

"My guess is she learned the words from Frank or from someone who knew Frank."

"Maybe, Mom. However, when I approached her and inquired about the singing, she got pretty embarrassed."

"If she isn't a time traveler, I don't want her realizing we are. I believe it's best if we don't explore that possibility."

"What if she is aware of a safer way to return to the future? What if there is a way to come and go, and we could see each other again? What if I could bring you some grandchildren?

"Lauren, let me think about it."

Lauren

I finally told my mother what I suspected. I might be wrong, and she thinks I am. She believes a logical explanation exists for Pam knowing lyrics to music that hasn't been written yet. Is she kidding? Logical? None of this is rational—none, nada, zero. I agreed to leave it in her hands. I don't want to jeopardize her life and standing in her world. Still, I made a significant sacrifice to aid her and her adopted family. Possibly Pam has a different portal that's safe. *I won't interfere, but what if I can go home during winter, and what if I can come back?*

We attempted to go to the upcoming town because the rain had stopped, and the sun was out. I don't know whether the mud or the dust is worse. I knew in the future that people paid money to go on cattle drives, and I had seen the *City Slickers* movie with Billy Crystal. The 1800s version wasn't so romantic.

We still had a long valley that was known for Indian ambushes. We were all on the lookout. Dan was feeling much better, and his cough was nearly gone. He'd lost a lot of weight, which was concerning my mother. Dan's fever and shaking had resolved, and he was laughing about something with the men. We all sensed he believed the worst was over. We had sixty more miles to go, according to his reckoning. Bath, sweet bath. Portal pool, precious portal pool. I decided if the water level were down, I would go for it and take my chances on the other side since no one would be the wiser.

About midday, we planned to stop, and three of us would switch horses. The rain appeared to cause saddle dermatitis. In my time, it would be termed rain rot, but that was a specific bacterium, and this disease seemed like little fungi to me. It was spreading rapidly on most of the horses. One of the horses we hadn't used much was a fiery palomino gelding that my mother had named Trigger. He stood out with his color, but that didn't mean he was a good horse for riding. I saddled him and circled him around me at the end of the rein. A short, small circle was a great way to detect lameness that might be subtle. He moved well. Too well. He kicked me out and caught me in the thigh. I went flying. Fortunately, no one witnessed it, but I could barely walk. My thigh was on fire, yet it was simply a bruise. I remembered the young high school girl whom I had briefly mentored. She, like many girls her age, often swore. Not that I didn't swear, but I suggested that swearing was perfectly acceptable sometimes. I called that horse many different words. None of them were accepted at this time. Again, thankfully, no one heard them. *Or did they?*

"Have a problem, Lauren?" Pam Wilkins appeared from around a boulder, where she must have taken a nature break.

I smiled weakly. "Trigger and I are having a difference of opinion."

"I have not heard a few of those descriptions around these parts."

"Yeah, it's a *back-East* thing."

I got the look. "Must be."

Trigger must have sensed the error of his ways and settled down straight away. I hopped on and trotted off back to the herd. I wondered if some of the swear words I had used were modern. I sure as heck wasn't going to ask anyone.

We decided to make camp toward the evening. A small creek to be crossed could wait until morning. We hadn't seen any Indians, but the men were taking no chances. We guarded the cattle in teams of three: one woman and two men for each shift. Even Pam assumed duty these nights. We would be near a small town where we could relax the following day.

During my shift, I thought I heard a birdcall that didn't sound right for the dead of night. I listened carefully, and it was repeated. I alerted Dan, who was watching with me.

He rode over to eavesdrop. The call came once more, he woke up all who were sleeping, and they clutched their rifles and stood by the wagon for protection. The cattle became restless, and we moved out and circled them. Dan, Alexander, and I were mounted. The remainder walked on foot around the horses and herd.

We all stayed awake until dawn. When we returned to the chuck wagon, we realized that much of the food had been stolen. We felt foolish, and Pam was incredibly remorseful. "Damn it to hell." She stared at Alexander and me. "Oh, sorry, son. I hope I didn't offend you?"

"No, ma'am. That's worthy of a cuss word."

I didn't say anything. I understood Pam was making a point with me. I listened as she and Dan discussed purchasing supplies at the next town. We still needed to cross the river. It was slow-moving. After several attempts, though, Dan identified a shallow spot to move all the stock and the wagon safely across. As we were about to traverse the river, we heard a wagon approach us. Four women were riding in this uncovered wagon. They wore the typical bonnets and long dresses of traditional pioneer women. They were tight-lipped, and one woman held a shotgun on her lap. These women, who were not surprised to locate us, explained they had been following our trail for several days. They each had a small trunk. Dan and my mother approached them on horseback.

"Ladies." Dan tipped his hat to them.

My mother rode up to their wagon to quietly ask if they needed anything. She discovered they did not have any provisions.

"We're from Idaho, traveling to Albuquerque to join the minister in the Mormon faith. May we join you until we arrive there?"

My mother glanced at Dan, who shrugged. "When did you last eat? I don't see any food. We're only going to Santa Fe."

"We ate two days ago. The Indians stole our second wagon and all but two of our horses."

The two remaining horses were old and arthritic. They could make it to Santa Fe, but it was doubtful they could go any further.

"You can come with us, but we were robbed too. I'm sorry to say we have a little hardtack, but that's all."

One of the women was in advanced pregnancy. My mother laid her down in our chuck wagon. I talked with the other three ladies about how they lost their husbands.

"Husband, not husbands."

I could tell that Alexander became quite fascinated with this story. I led him away, and we rounded the cattle and drove them down to the river for the crossing. Alexander wanted to know about the marital situation.

"As they say, where I come from, different strokes for different folks. According to their religion, it's all right for a man to have more than one wife."

"Can a woman have more than one husband?"

"I am not sure, but my guess is it's forbidden because men make the rules."

"I might become Mormon then."

"I kind of think you might marry just one woman, and she may be more than you can handle."

"No, ma'am. I'll handle her and then some."

"Maybe." *In your dreams, my friend.* I was sure the subsequent owners of my old cabin were Alexander and Hanna Thistlewaite. If he marries my stepsister, Hanna, he'll be lucky to survive that marriage. I should look in the county records to determine whether there are any survivors from that line when I return. I would not share any of this with my mother.

We got the cattle across the river, followed by the wagons. The pregnant widow went into labor. While the other women seemed like they were in their late thirties or forties, she had to be in her early twenties. My mother had us continue driving the wagon toward the town while this young girl grunted and howled the entire time. One of her fellow wives stayed with her to assist her.

While my mother took a break from her birthing duties, I inquired about the other women. "Where are their children?"

"I don't know. Maybe they've grown up?"

"Seems somewhat strange, don't you think?"

"Yes, it does."

"Do you think they're telling the truth?"

"What do you think they're hiding?"

"Maybe they ran away from their family or group or their husband."

"Possibly. I am convinced this isn't the first baby for this woman."

"Really?"

"I'd better get back up to try to help her."

Dan asked what was going on.

"Dan, she's hours away from giving birth. Let's keep going to see if we can make it to the next town. Maybe a doctor or midwife will be able to take over."

"Will she make it?"

"She should, but I'll stand by just in case." Mom rode off toward their wagon.

We started up again, and I heard wailing coming from the chuck wagon all afternoon long. We arrived in the town, where there was a doctor, but he was drunk. My mother moved her into his house and spent the entire night with the inconsolable woman. Her sister-wives all stood by her, rubbed her back, and positioned her as the pain began and waned.

Finally, at daybreak, my mother called me to let me watch as a dark-haired boy emerged from the woman's womb. That group would not travel for a few more days. The town took up a collection and helped the woman and baby. There were several eligible bachelors in town. My mother and I thought the chains of slavery might be broken. I hoped no one was following them. We figured they broke away from their family and church and had to leave their children. We suspected, due to the age of the older women, that the children were closer to adults. These women did not confess to anything.

Chapter 12

Rebecca

End of the trail and praise the Lord that we made it with several days to spare. The procurement officer for the army was surprised to see us. He had a bet we wouldn't make it or wouldn't have all the horses or cattle agreed upon. Dan smiled and thanked the crew for such an effort. There was a nice hotel for the women. Pam, Lauren, and I all bought time in the bathhouse. There was only one room, but we didn't care about modesty after almost two months on the trail. The three tubs were filled with piping-hot water, and we each removed our clothes and eased ourselves into the tubs.

Heaven on earth. We soaked for an hour. A woman came in to add hot water as needed. I have to say I can't remember feeling this good in months. I laughed, looking at Lauren's sleek body, so white with a farmer's tan. Too bad we couldn't return to Hank Heaven, so she could skinny-dip and lie in the sun. For me, just getting the dirt off was enough. I glanced at Pam, who had her eyes closed when something caught my eye. She had a smallpox vaccine scar. I don't think I had seen one since I had touched Lauren's dad's arm more than twenty years ago. My suspicions were increasing, but I wasn't willing to sacrifice my or Lauren's life over the issue. *Or was I?*

"Rollin', rollin', rollin', keep those dogies moving." I could say I learned those words from Frank, as well. I watched Pam's reaction.

Pam replied, without looking at me, "Don't try to understand them. Just rope, throw, and brand 'em."

Lauren was right. Pam couldn't carry a tune to save her life. Luckily, Lauren didn't join the singing. Pam and I could use the excuse that we heard the song from Frank, but Lauren hadn't met Frank.

"Becky, did you ever hear anything about what happened to Frank Lash? You know, I saw him riding out that last night with a woman."

"No, I've never heard anything." She knew it was me, and I was being tested. However, I resisted any temptation to continue the conversation.

The following day, the men were somewhat worse for the wear. Lauren and I drank wine that night, but Pam didn't join us. I wondered if the reason for abstaining was that she was afraid of talking about what she didn't want to be known. The cough seemed a little better. Maybe it was the dust. Having noticed how much weight she had lost while we were bathing, I had my suspicions.

We received a telegram from Sam. He and the family had all survived, and he was waiting for our return. The snow had begun in the high country, which was a covert message for Lauren and me. I could interpret the disappointment on Lauren's face as she read the telegram. She handed it back and simply stared away.

We stayed long enough for Dan to negotiate with the army regarding the large shipment, now expected by June of the following year. The contract was signed, and the Cattle Creek Ranch was saved from ruin once again. I hadn't thought about the closing of the television episodes for years, but this would be a good ending for one of them. I absentmindedly hummed the *Comstock* tune as I walked down the main boardwalk. Pam was inside one of the shops, stepped out, and heard me.

"Want to talk, Becky?"

I gazed at her and smiled.

"Maybe. What about?"

"Our mutual past lives?"

"Not sure what you're talking about, Pam."

"I sort of think you do. I assume we have more in common than just the last few months."

I glanced around and nodded. "We might."

"Does Lauren know?"

"Well, at this stage, I want to leave her out of it. Does anyone know about you, Pam?"

"Not even Caleb."

"Maybe we should go someplace private."

We walked to a grassy spot near a creek. It was currently December, but it was still warm down here. My heart was beating so hard I could almost hear it. We sat down on two logs near each other. We were in plain sight of the town but far enough away that no one could overhear us.

Pam asked me straight-out, "When did you get here?"

"More than twenty years ago. How about you?"

"I was pregnant with Caleb, so just at twenty years."

"What year did you leave when you came here? I figure I want to know if we came from the same time or different times?"

"I don't know. I was born in 1955. And you?"

"1949. Where are you from? Where did you come in?"

"I'm not certain. My husband was an alcoholic who liked to hit me when he was drunk. He beat me soon after we were married, and he hit me when we realized I was pregnant. It was never going to end. I had to get out of there. He hit me one night, and the next thing, I was in Chicago in the 1850s. I don't understand how I got here. I just know I would never go back. Never."

"Do you have family back there?"

"No, and it wouldn't be worth it if I did. I live here and now. I don't want another life."

"Who's the uncle for whom Caleb is working?"

"Not really an uncle, more like a friend. We came out West together before Caleb was born. It didn't last, and we parted company. No animosity, we merely didn't see eye to eye."

Here was the dicey question. I glanced away from Pam. "What do you know about the Buchanans?"

"They aren't time travelers. I know that."

"That's all?" How could she not recognize the family from her youth.

"Am I supposed to know them?"

"Didn't you watch television?"

"No, I lived in an orphanage. I never watched television."

"Pam, how did you know the *Rawhide* song?"

"From the radio."

"Is that why you're keen to aid the town orphanage?"

"Pretty much. Orphans usually have a tough life. I don't know many who thrive in an institution. Do you?"

"No, we just have to hope they are adopted."

"Not convinced how successful that goes, either. Any chance you have a place for Alexander on the Cattle Creek Ranch when we get back?"

"Yes, he's a bright young man. I'll talk to Sam when we get back. I know Dan thinks the world of him."

"That would be wonderful. Thanks, Becky."

"Pam, I believe it should be our little secret. Don't you?"

"Becky, we never had this discussion."

Chapter 13

Lauren

We started back for my mother's home two days after we finished the transaction and sold the extra few horses and cattle to the army, as well. I wasn't sorry to see Trigger go, that's for sure. I wasn't his sole victim; he kicked one of the soldiers too.

I was back on Pocket. She was a great ride. She was tough and conditioned for long-distance travel. The Buchanans could not have selected a better mount for me. I wondered if I could get her through the time portal. Maybe not. She was Hanna's horse, which I'll bet Hanna missed.

We made excellent time. Traveling through the area inhabited by the greedy Indians was still scary. Still, this time we did not experience any problems. Two men kept guard, and we could keep a better eye out for any raids since we did not have cattle to contend with.

We stopped in the town where we left the Mormon ladies. They had refused to consider marrying the local men because they were not Mormons. They planned to stay for a few more weeks, after which they would head down to meet their new husband—to each his own. My mother was satisfied with the progress and health of the newborn.

Pam and my mother were getting on well. They chatted privately about things. My mother explained she would be of no help in identifying a safer portal. Mom never said whether Pam was a fellow time traveler.

Dan was happy with our progress. He hadn't taken any chances and wired the money back to Virginia City. If we were robbed, it would not be for much. He was a bit of a slave driver. He was as anxious to return as we were. The December days were short, and the nights were growing colder. Pam, my mother, and I slept in the wagon some nights for warmth. We huddled up near a big fire on other nights. It was funny that sleeping bags had not really been invented yet. Pam's cough was increasing once again. My mom described it as asthma. I believed she might be protecting Pam's privacy. I didn't question it.

I thought about Jim constantly and wondered whether he was safe. I didn't know if Frank had survived the crazy-stalker lady. I was still contemplating a trip home, even though it would be dangerous. I would check on the creek when we got back to the Cattle Creek Ranch.

The weather was good for most of the return trip, and river crossings and mud were not issues. I watched Alexander Thistlewaite develop and improve his horsemanship skills during our journey. He had become a chatterbox and conversed easily with the men. I wondered if he was going to be sent back to the orphanage after we returned. I was confident he would be able to live on his own if he wanted to do so.

At fifteen, he was considered old enough to be treated as an adult. Pam mentioned all his family's assets had been sold to cover debts. He would have some money from this trip, but not enough to do much more than paying his board. I think any further education was going to end. I wondered how he and Hanna would be united. Maybe it was another girl named Hanna.

When we were a week away from Virginia City, Pam became ill. Her cough progressed to a severe respiratory infection, which sapped the life out of her. She finally relented and allowed my mother to examine her. They were in the wagon forever as we anticipated the verdict. My teary-eyed mother finally emerged. I knew this diagnosis was terrible. I expected her to say something to our group. We'd all gathered outside the wagon, waiting for the end. It was dusk, and Alexander and I had prepared dinner for the men.

My mother only shook her head. We didn't need to hear any details and realized that Pam was dying. My mother's new best friend was not going to be around much longer. Mom took some stew back into the wagon, and the two spent the night together. We heard Pam coughing and gasping for air most of the night. My mother attended to her all night long. Finally, in the morning, she came out and said it was over. Pam had passed away.

After many hours, my mother informed me that Pam had advanced cancer, which had spread rapidly to the lungs. She had palpated large abdominal masses and suspected it was either bowel or uterine cancer. Pam had lost weight during the previous few weeks but had hidden her condition by wearing more clothes, which we all thought was an attempt to stay warm. We buried her in one of the bright-red-satin dresses that she'd loved so much—a floozy with a heart of gold. My mother was distraught. She was reticent for the remainder of the trip home.

We arrived at the Cattle Creek Ranch late at night. Sam, Hanna, and Gee Ling were all asleep in the house. Dan dropped off my mother and me while the men, including Alexander, helped put the horses away and retired to the bunkhouse. Dan proceeded to his house. A storm had been brewing, and the wind had allowed us to arrive without detection. We went to our rooms without waking Hanna or Gee Ling. In the warmth of the house, I was asleep within minutes.

Rebecca

Bed, sweet bed. Husband, sweet husband. I couldn't believe I entered the room without waking him up. When Sam finally realized his space had been invaded, he shot up, probably thinking he was being robbed. Sam saw me undressing in the low glow of the fireplace. He jumped up and enveloped me.

"Thank God, you're home, darling. I've missed you."

"Me too. Are you sure you're back to normal? No residual cough? I've been terribly worried. Is Hanna all right?"

"No, we're all fine. Are you okay? You look tired."

I told him about the trip and Pam's death. I began to say more but was interrupted by sleep, from which I didn't wake until late in the morning. Sam kept Hanna out of our room. She wanted to just get in bed with me. He reminded Hanna that she would have plenty of time later. She sat outside my bedroom, waiting for me to emerge. We had a tearful reunion, and I listened to her chest with my ear and pronounced her fit. She updated me about school and everything occurring around the ranch. She wouldn't leave my side until Lauren got up even later than me. Once Lauren appeared, I was no longer the flavor of the morning.

Dan, Jenny, and the children were already at the house. It was apparent Jenny was expecting again. Gee Ling was cooking up a storm, and my late-morning breakfast was ready when I emerged. Because we'd run out of coffee a week or so earlier on the trail, my initial request was strong, black coffee. After that, the usual eggs, ham, and pancakes were consumed. We'd all lost weight on the trip. Lauren was incredibly gaunt. She was anxious to try to get to the portal pool. The wind was still howling, and the first significant snow was imminent. Christmas was a week away. She, Hanna, and Dan were going to ride up into the forest scouting for a Christmas tree. Sam suggested a grove near the portal pool, so Lauren could look without anyone being the wiser.

When everyone left for home or Christmas tree hunting, Sam and I sat down in front of the fireplace in the great room. I described what I knew about Pam and her passing. He held me and comforted me while I cried.

"She was quite a woman. I want to hold a service for her next week."

"Yeah, she'd love that. I'll head into town tomorrow and organize it. Are you going to begin work at the hospital again soon?" Sam stroked the back of my neck.

"I thought I'd wait until after Christmas. I believe Lauren will attempt to leave."

"The creek is low on this end, but that's unusual. You can't predict what will happen on the other side. I'll try to talk her out of it. I understand she's torn, but if she dies from the cold or gets swept away. Well, you know."

Gee Ling announced the water was prepared for my bath. He added he was going into Virginia City for supplies if the snow set in, and we couldn't get out.

He would be back later to cook a celebratory dinner. I went upstairs for clean clothes. When I returned, Sam was stoking the fire. "Becky, are you aware it's just you and me at the house?" He was grinning.

"Oh, really?" I was smiling and watching him.

"Really."

"I can't remember when we had the place to ourselves in months."

"Possibly we can do some cleaning?"

"I know where I'm starting." I walked toward the bathing room.

"Happy to help."

"How soon do you think anyone will be back?"

"Hours, darling. Hours."

We grinned at each other like teenagers.

"Time's a-wasting."

CHAPTER 14

Lauren

Light snow was falling when we made it to the grove that Sam had recommended for the Christmas tree. Several trees were suitable for us. Dan and Hanna argued about which one would go to the main house and which would go to Dan's. While they were sawing down the two chosen trees, I checked out the creek and portal pool.

The big rock was gone, the water was low, and the pool seemed safe despite the cold. What I wouldn't give for a wet suit! I understood the water temperature was going to be close to freezing. It would be similar in the future. I needed to take a change of clothes. I expected to do it tomorrow, and I wouldn't even tell my mother my plans. Mom would be upset, but she knew this time would come.

We would hold a celebration that night since the Cattle Creek Ranch had been safeguarded from financial disaster. I realized it would not last forever, but if the dynasty lasted until my mother died, I would be glad I assisted somehow. Gee Ling asked what I wanted for dinner, and I knew my mother wanted a roast, so that's what I proposed. He was going into town. I was sure my mother and Sam would be alone in the house. Despite my feigned disgust at older people *doing it*, I ensured we would take our time getting the trees back down the mountain.

As we tethered the trees to the horses, the snowfall increased. Dan glanced up and pointed to the trees swaying in the wind. "Best we get back down. Seems as if a real storm is coming in."

"Dan, may we help you put yours up before we go home?"

Dan was on to my suggestion. "You know, with Jenny back in a family way, she isn't much help. That would be good."

Hanna was oblivious. "I want to go back to see ma."

"Hanna, let's help Dan and Jenny. I'll be leaving soon, and I want to spend as much time as I can with everyone."

"My ma will definitely miss you. So will I, but I know why you want to stay away from the house. Why don't you just tell me what ma got me for Christmas?"

Dan and I stared at each other and grinned. "Nope, not spoiling that secret. You're just going to have to wait." For such a worldly girl, sometimes her innocence amazed me.

The snowfall was almost a blizzard. "Ladies, let's get off this mountain before we're disoriented and lost. Lauren, you should have seen the snowfall one time when your mother stayed with us before she left to become a doctor. We were stuck in the house for days. The entire town discussed how Becky remained alone with four men up here."

"Scandalous." I grinned.

"We had a grand time. Several mares were ready to foal, and we could hardly get to the barn. Your ma was a trouper. I wish you could have heard Becky describe it to Mrs. Gardiner, our town gossip. Hank and I laughed so hard we embarrassed your ma." Dan became quiet and glanced away. I recalled some of the fun times I had with my brother and sister. I was anxious to get back to my real home. I realized they would be distraught by now.

The snow was sticking even at the lower elevations, and I understood my plan for the following day would not happen. I was getting that homesick feeling. I pretended all was well. We put Dan's tree up, and I played with the children. Little Hank was almost running. He was a happy, smiling baby, which made me want one of my own. I thought about Jim, which made me even more depressed and homesick.

We finally returned to the main house, where my mother and Sam were upstairs. Hanna was immediately suspicious. "You don't think...."

"No," I stopped her. "Don't even think."

Dan interrupted me. "Can you two help me with this tree?"

We all stared upstairs. Hanna began to head upstairs.

"Hanna." Dan was exasperated. "Don't even think of it. Get over here and hold the tree while I put on the base."

Sam came down and was just as we had left him. "Your mother is sleeping. If anyone wakes her, you will have me to deal with."

"Yes, sir," we all responded.

The tree was up, and Gee Ling returned with supplies to last for weeks. The weather was looking grim. Dan went home and would return for dinner later. Hanna was finally allowed to see her mother. "If she's asleep, don't go into her room. Am I clear?"

"Yes, sir."

Sam and I were left alone with the blazing fire and the tree ready to be decked. He had brought down some of the decorations and wanted me to help him get a few prepared to place on the tree when everyone was here.

"Lauren, I want to thank you for helping our family these last few months. I hope you understand how much your mother and I appreciate the sacrifice you made." Sam gazed out the window by the dining-room table. I joined him, where we could watch the snow coming down and the thick accumulation on the trees around the house in the fading light.

"Sam, I'm homesick. Don't get me wrong. I've loved being here at your ranch with my mother. It's true, but my biggest concerns are my family and my father. If what Jim said is true, he probably doesn't even realize I'm missing, but they would. They must be frantic. I feel terrible for putting them through this."

"I can't promise you anything, but I have a plan if you can be patient."

"Huh?"

"Simply give me a few days. Could you do that?" He placed his hand on my shoulder. For once, I didn't resist, and he hugged me. I may have sobbed for a mere second. I hoped he didn't hear it. He pretended not to.

"Let's get everything ready for tonight, shall we? I want your mother to have the best night possible. Becky's been through so much with the town, the cattle drive, and the loss of her friend. You're going to be the next loss. I need to protect her."

"Thanks for taking care of her. I want her to have the best life she can too."

My mother appeared with Hanna an hour later. She was dressed in a beautiful red dress with a white collar. Hanna was attired in a green dress of a similar design. Sam gazed at them and beamed. So much love in this family. So much.

Rebecca

We had a beautiful dinner, after which we all decorated the tree. Little Lizzy was lifted onto Dan's shoulders and placed the angel on the top of the tree. I could tell that Lauren was trying to join in and look happy, but this was probably her first Christmas spent without her family. I realized her prospects for returning were poor. Unless there was a miracle, she was having a Comstock Christmas.

The following morning, Sam, who wanted to pick up something in town, was ropable when he knew he couldn't get there. It must be a present, but he wasn't talking. Sam walked around the house and out to the barn. He went down to Dan's and back to the barn. I was a little frantic, as well. I don't think any of us had planned for Christmas. We still gave one another a single gift, and I had not done anything in preparation. Sam said not to worry this year due to the circumstances. If we had a small present for Hanna and Lizzy, no one would notice or care. He had something for Jenny.

"Your present is saving us from financial ruin." He hugged me and went back to looking at the weather.

All I cared about was a day not spent in the saddle. I treated several of the ranch hands and their families for various ailments. A few still hadn't resolved their respiratory infections. They tended to be smokers, which were increasing in number. I tried to caution them, but I was competing with the folklore that smoking was beneficial. As if.

I spent several hours talking with Lauren, who wanted additional details about my life in the 1800s. I asked for more descriptions about her life, short as it was, and her plans. She discussed Jim and described some of the surgeries he performed.

"We could use his skills here, you know. No one would be the wiser."

"I'm convinced he would do it too, but let's not go there." She glanced around. "Where's Hanna?"

"She went out to help in the barn. I think she's expecting to ride Pocket to and from school when you're gone."

"Are you sure she isn't becoming interested in Alexander?"

"No, he's a wonderful young man, but Hanna has her sights set only on the fancy boys. She could do worse, but poor Alexander doesn't stand a chance." I laughed.

"Mom, we all go for the fancy boys at first. I certainly did, but I went for substance when I got wiser."

I looked over at Sam, who was perusing figures at his desk. I nodded. "Yep, substance trumps flash any day, but sometimes you are lucky enough to have both."

Lauren rolled her eyes. "If you say so."

"I heard that." Sam didn't glance up, but I could tell he was attempting not to laugh.

"Sorry. I'm sure you were quite dashing in your day." Lauren quickly realized how that sounded and winced.

"In my day?" Sam looked up, and Lauren's face reddened.

"I think he's extremely handsome now. I wouldn't trade him for anyone." I smiled as I gazed over at him working at his desk.

"Not even Robert Redford or James Garner?" Lauren and I had discussed the movie stars when we were alone on the cattle drive.

"He recognizes they are always on the table."

Sam reached for his pipe. "Thankfully, they aren't even a twinkle in their grandparents' eyes."

Lauren gave Sam 'the look.' "You know that stuff will kill you. I'm counting on you to take care of my mother for years to come."

Sam gazed at his pipe. "We're all going to die someday. I might as well enjoy a few pleasures. Your mother's somewhat of a taskmaster, you know. She's not easy to keep up with."

"Speaking of which, Sam, can I get you to see what Hanna's up to? It's so cold outside, and she's been gone a long time."

Sam stared up at Lauren. "See what I mean?"

Lauren laughed. "My mother has taught you well. I hope I can learn some of her husband-training tips before I leave."

Lauren

The snow ceased falling during the night, but too much covered the ground for travel to town. Mom and I went to the barn to recheck Sam's horse, Cash. His lameness was decreasing rapidly. It appeared he would be good enough to ride in another month. "Sam's so happy you examined Cash and suggested the rim shoe."

"I wish I had a Christmas present for you and him. I don't even have one for Hanna. I hate this."

"Sam says not to worry. He got her something, and he says it will be from everyone."

"I understand he says things like that, but I'm not used to this situation. I feel like a child who just receives and doesn't give."

"You mustn't feel like that. Your gift was coming here and staying to help us when we needed it so much. We're the ones who should be grateful, Lauren. Not the other way around."

When we rounded the corner in the barn, Hanna was kissing Alexander Thistlewaite. Well, I saw her. Fortunately for Hanna, my mother didn't see it before they realized anyone was nearby. Poor Alexander was so upset he ran from the barn. I pretended I hadn't noticed anything, but Hanna was aware I'd seen them.

Oblivious to what I had just seen, mom turned to her. "Hanna, it's too cold out here. Finish with the horses and go back inside. According to your father, you have a project fto complete for school. I want to see it this afternoon, and it should be well on its way to completion, or you will be in your room for the rest of the Christmas holiday."

"Yes, ma'am." Hanna stared at me, and I knew she was silently pleading with me not to tell. I remember how many times my sister and I had the opportunity to snitch on each other. We didn't, and I wouldn't, but she and I needed to have a conversation for sure.

Mom and I returned to the house. Sam was upstairs, and Hanna was in her room. I tried not to think about how homesick I was. I was seated in front of the fire and just gazed into the flames. My mother sat next to me. She quite tentatively put her hand around my shoulder, and we leaned against each other. At some point, I fell asleep and woke up with my head in her lap. Sam was back downstairs, simply watching us.

I was a little embarrassed. I shouldn't have felt guilty, but I did. I had attempted to maintain an emotional distance out of loyalty to my other family. It was difficult. I'm sure children in families of divorce feel like this. There was no reason to feel guilty, but I did. My number-one loyalty was to my father. It wasn't my mother's fault, but he was my rock. This visit was but a dream. It could hardly be real, and it was time to wake up.

The snow was melting by the following day. My mother, Sam, and I drove into town. We took Alexander with us at my insistence. Hanna wasn't allowed to go because her project wasn't even started. After Sam gave me some money, I went to a few shops for some small presents. I wanted to buy Hanna, Dan's children, and Gee Ling something. If I found anything else, that would be a bonus.

My mom and Sam went to see Ray Thompson and the minister. The Christmas Eve celebration would also be a time to honor Pam Wilkins. Ray was going to deliver the eulogy, and the orphanage was being renamed for her. Caleb, her son, had been informed by telegraph. However, since the passage over the grade was impossible, he couldn't come. Ray was planning to sell Pam's house and place any personal items in storage for Caleb.

I bought some little hard candy and a few small things for my Christmas presents. My mother had suggested items that were not expensive but held meaning for her family. I purchased paper and some colored paints for Hanna, handkerchiefs for Gee Ling, and, against my better judgment, pipe tobacco for Sam. In the back of the store were a few books, including a collection of poems by Oliver Wendell Holmes, which was partially hidden on a shelf. My mother mentioned meeting him. I found a children's picture book for Dan and his family.

We returned to the Cattle Creek Ranch, where my mother gave me plain paper and colored ribbon to wrap them. Hanna was sulking, but she was happy when Alexander returned with all his possessions. He was going to live with Cassie and Merv at their insistence. Cassie would keep an eye on him and make sure the boy continued his studies. He would ride with Hanna into town when school resumed and earn his keep with chores around the Cattle Creek Ranch and protecting Hanna during her trips back and forth to school.

"Isn't that the fox guarding the henhouse?" I was curious that neither Sam nor my mother noticed the obvious.

"He's a good boy, and he and Hanna are only good friends." My mother was going through her medical bag.

"If you insist." I rolled my eyes. While my mom was clueless, I may have planted a seed of doubt in Sam.

I went up to Hanna's room. "We need to talk, little sister."

"It was just a kiss."

"I get that, but that's how it starts. If it goes further, the next thing you know, you'll be pushing a buggy and up to your eyeballs in diapers. There won't be any more freedom or choices, Hanna. You'll spend the rest of your life worrying about the baby, and you won't ever go anywhere or see any sights."

"I would like to visit you, Lauren. I want to come to your wedding. I promise I won't do it again."

"Pinkie promise?"

"What's that?"

I showed her how to lock our little fingers and said, "Swear on a stack of Bibles." I felt guilty, knowing she would not come to see me or attend my wedding. I wondered how Mom and Sam would tell her.

"I swear."

The following afternoon was Christmas Eve, which was cold, but the sky was clear. The snow had not melted, but the road was passable. Sam, Dan, and Alexander harnessed up the big wagon. Our family and several others rode together into town for the church service. Gee Ling stayed at the Cattle Creek Ranch with one of his many cousins to fix a late dinner that night and prepare for Christmas dinner.

My mother and Hanna wore their red and green dresses. I wore one of the dresses Sam had bought for me several months ago. It was not a fashion statement, but I was warm and festive. I was always carrying a lump in my throat. I tried to hide the melancholy, as they put it, but I believe they noticed.

The new minister was the son of Earl and Martha Tyler. He was as good-looking as was his father. Ray Thompson's eulogy for Pam Wilkins was perfect. He described Pam as a woman who could sort out drunks, pour beer, enliven the saloon, cheer a despondent patron, and literally amass a fortune often used to prop up the community chest.

During the years, she'd donated money to the library, the school, and numerous events, including the town races. She'd aided many families who had fallen on hard times. At her request, this benevolence had all been conducted anonymously through Ray. She loved Virginia City, which had become her adopted town. Even though she was buried out on the trail, the city would erect a monument in her name at the watering trough and nearby public bench.

The service ended with traditional 1800s Christmas carols. They were the same tunes and different words or different tunes to familiar lyrics. We drank some eggnog, after which our entourage and the sleeping children were bundled into the wagon to return to the Cattle Creek Ranch.

I could tell my mother was sad. She'd only begun her friendship with Pam just a few months ago, but she was already mourning her passing. Sam was incredibly attentive to her and kept his arm around her all the way home. I hoped and prayed Jim was all right and enjoying some Christmas cheer with his fellow army buddies.

Jenny and Dan came over with the children the following day. We opened presents. Even though there were only two small presents, the same delight was felt as if there were ten. We had a beautiful breakfast, during which Gee Ling was presented with gifts and feted like the most honored guest in the family. He walked with a limp, but he was happy, and he recognized he was a respected member of this family. I'd asked my mother if Gee Ling ever sat down at the main table with them. Mom answered that she had tried many years ago, but he didn't want to and was adamant he liked his place in the family as it was. It still made me uncomfortable.

We sang Christmas carols and lit candles for Hank, Johnny, and Clint, representing family members absent from the Cattle Creek Ranch this Christmas. My mother observed she'd lit a candle for me every year. At least for this one Christmas, though, it was not necessary.

We ate turkey and stuffing. The turkey was somewhat gamey, compared with modern turkeys, and the breast was small, but Gee Ling cooked three, so there was plenty of meat. I peered around this table and, for a while, rejoiced in the moment. I let my homesickness take a back seat to the joy of spending one Christmas with my mother and her family.

When all the guests had gone, Hanna, my mother, and I sat in front of the fire together. My mom tickled Hanna's back. I recalled how my aunt tickled my back even as an adult. I was jealous, but I didn't say anything.

Sam went upstairs and returned with three small boxes, which we opened. Each contained a gold pendant with the Cattle Creek Ranch brand almost hidden in the design. It matched my bracelet perfectly. We were all quite surprised, and my mother was teary. We all hugged and thanked him. He had them made when we were out on the trail. I was genuinely touched by this man's thoughtfulness. My mother was truly blessed. We all went upstairs, and someone knocked at the door right before I blew out my lamp.

"Lauren, it's Sam. May I come in?"

"Yes, sir."

"I'd like to talk to you for a moment." He hesitated. "I have another gift for you, but it isn't here yet. I hope it will help you. I recognize what a sacrifice you've made. Your mother and I want you to know how much we love you, and we want you to have the same joy we have in our lives with your fiancé. None of this has ever been your fault. Some mysterious act of God tore your family apart. It's been to my advantage, and I just want you to understand that if I could keep you here, and if I could have raised you, I probably would not have done any better a job than your father has done. I don't know how you can thank him for sharing you, but I would have liked to meet him and thank him personally."

"Thank you, sir. We all know that isn't going to happen, but I appreciate your thoughts. Despite my desire to go home, I've had a wonderful adventure here. I'm glad I came, and who knows? Maybe we'll all meet up in heaven someday." Hank Heaven came to mind.

As if reading my thoughts, he replied, "Wouldn't it be great if it was Hank Heaven?"

I nodded, and he kissed my forehead and left. He would have been such a good father—a little strict—but a lovely, caring man for his time.

Chapter 15

Rebecca

Sam left early for Virginia City. I was going to go back to work following the new year. That was soon enough for me. Lauren had quietly given me the pictures she'd lost in the river when she arrived several months ago. I placed them in the secret compartment of my dresser with the photographs of Lauren from my return several years ago.

I wondered how Frank Lash was. Lauren admitted he had been helpful to her, although it took some pressure from her, and I asked her to thank him. She stared away and appeared worried when I mentioned his name. I was convinced something had happened that I didn't know about. She would not explain, but I was sure she would face problems when she went back to her time in the future.

Sam returned from town late in the afternoon. He said nothing, but I could tell he was disappointed about something. The following morning was brisk yet clear. Sam seemed to be watching all the signs of the weather. He was planning something, but I had no idea. He and Dan had gone back into town, and he said he might spend the night. Dan was planning to return. Hanna and I prepared a small New Year's Day celebration, for which Gee Ling always supplied Chinese fireworks.

Lauren and Hanna decided to ride their horses as a remedy for their cabin fever. I suspected Lauren was taking her to the portal pool in the creek. I stayed to see a few ranch women who were expecting. We enjoyed a small tea party. I made some suggestions to help them during childbirth and with the immediate care of their newborns. Gee Ling served scones, and the women were lots of fun. Cassie joined us for support.

I asked Cassie about Alexander, and she mentioned he was an excellent addition to the ranch and to Merv and her, as well. She loved the attention he gave her. He cleaned and washed the dishes every night. She went over what he knew and where his schooling had ended. Cassie described him as astute and thought he would make an excellent mining engineer. She would help him as much as possible to procure the funds to go to a mining college. I was confident Sam would help, as well. Now that would be a great first boyfriend for Hanna. Too bad she wasn't interested.

Sam returned the next day, smiling from ear to ear, with a large box. He was excited to share it with Lauren, but he commented that it had to be done privately with only us adults. After dinner, we sent Hanna to bed early. Sam went upstairs for the box. He inquired about the portal pool.

Lauren appeared hopeful. "It was calm, and the flow was moderate. If the weather was warmer, I would go today."

"Let's say you could arrive there, get in and out of the water, and be dry. How would you make it to a safe shelter? Would you go to the cabin or walk all the way to town?"

"Town."

"What if it was snowing, or there was a blizzard? Do you believe you could make it to town safely if you were dry?"

"I think so. If I was dry, but we know that can't happen. Even if I had clothes on the other side, changing in these temperatures and with me all wet, I'm not sure I could do it. I'd like to try, though."

Sam opened the box. "This is a Mackintosh diving suit. I ordered it from Scotland. It's a canvas suit covered with rubber. It seals and keeps divers dry in the ocean. I had to decide if this suit or one from France was better, but I chose the Mackintosh. I think we need to test it. Lauren can get in a bathing tub filled with water to determine whether she can go under. If she stays dry, she might just make it."

Lauren and I stared at him and laughed. He was upset initially. When Sam realized the humor in it, however, he laughed with us. Lauren was clearly impressed, yet I wanted her to stay longer. "Where did you hatch this idea?"

"I wrote to one of my maritime friends, who retired from his ship recently. He described the suit to me, after which I sent a telegram. It eventually reached Mr. Mackintosh himself in Scotland. I wired the money to him the first week you left for Santa Fe. I've been waiting forever. I wanted to give it to you for Christmas, but it didn't arrive until today. If it works and the water level isn't too high, the sole risk is being swept downstream if the creek is flooding. Since it appears that you won't have much ability to move around, we must count on the creek not flowing too much. I studied the history of rain. Despite the snowfall, melting snow increases the flow in the spring."

I simply stared at the suit and at Sam. I was torn. I recognized this suit as the key to her return to the future. Sadly, Lauren was thrilled and wanted to try it out immediately. She hugged and kissed Sam, who replaced the suit in the box and returned it to our bedroom. Lauren grinned and hugged me. I attempted to be happy for her, but I just couldn't fake it that night.

Upstairs in bed, Sam and I discussed the entire idea. I could understand the reason my husband didn't tell me. His loyalty was to me, but he realized I would have objected. He thought the best plan was for me to take Hanna into town the following day while he and Lauren tested the suit.

Gee Ling was going into town for a New Year's celebration and would not be back for several days. Dan would take Jenny and the children to see their friends in Carson City for their annual New Year's Eve party and would not be back for three days. If the suit worked and the weather held, Lauren could leave on New Year's Eve. I wasn't sure how I would handle this situation with Hanna and everyone, but Sam seemed confident that it would work out.

Lauren

I would see Hanna once more, but I hated leaving Gee Ling without saying goodbye. The same would happen with Jenny, Dan, and the children. My excitement was tempered by this knowledge. After my mother, Hanna, and Gee Ling left for town, Sam filled the tub with ice water. It was filled close to the top, but we needed it to be deep enough that the helmet would be submerged.

I wanted to wear what I planned for my return to the future. I was wearing Sam's long underwear, two shirts, a sweater, and pants that Dan had left. Such attire made getting into the suit rather tricky, but I eventually had it on up to my neck. The helmet was secured to the bodysuit. I would have to cover the breathing tube with my hand. We didn't dare stick anything into it if I couldn't open it and suffocate as a result.

I would carry a knife to cut a hole in the suit on the other side if necessary. My time in the water would be seconds unless there was a snag or I was carried underwater.

As Sam picked me up to lift me into the tub, he said something about I needed to lose weight. I couldn't hear this under the hood because the knitted cap I was wearing muffled the sound. He shouted while repeating himself, and I laughed. His grip on me slipped, and I fell into the water, which splashed all over and soaked him. I thought my mother claimed he had a great sense of humor and never swore. She was mistaken on both counts. I could see through glass goggles that he was wet head to toe from the splashing of the icy water.

I stood up in the water, and he pointed to me to get down into the water to attempt submersion. It wasn't as easy as we thought. The air in the suit made me very buoyant.

Several tries were required before we believed I had tested the bodysuit enough. Since it was impossible to remove the helmet with gloves, I needed to wield a knife and free my hands. So, this suit would be used only once. I was dry and not cold at all, unlike Sam, who was saturated and chilled. He took off the helmet, undid the suit, and left to change into dry clothing. If I ever returned to this time, which was highly unlikely, I could do it in a wet suit. I could, of course, bring one for my mother if she wanted to come back with me.

Several minutes later, Sam returned while I carried the water back outside and mopped the floor. He was embarrassed, and I stared at him and shook my head.

He pointed his finger at me. "If your mother hears about this before you leave, you can guess that you will go home with a sore backside. Am I clear?"

"I'm not the one who swore." I was going to say more, but I received the look, and we both laughed. "Yes, sir," but I couldn't stop laughing. He realized I found it very funny and not a social faux pas. "Sam, everyone in my time swears."

"What does your father say about that?"

"We were spanked when we were little, but now he simply asks me not to swear when he hears me do it."

"At least he has some sense of civility."

"A great deal, actually. Assuming Dad hasn't died of worry or grief, I'll see him in a few days."

"I'm sorry that I won't meet him."

"Yes, me too."

While time travel for my mother was always a possibility, a journey for Sam or my father was just not even considered.

I thought about the real Sam Buchanan, showing up in modern times, looking like the actor who played him. It would be interesting, to say the least. He still had no idea that he was a television star and the subject of one of the most popular programs in television history. I wondered if my mother would ever tell him.

CHAPER 16

Rebecca

Hanna and I returned from town. Sam and Lauren heated the dinner that Gee Ling had left for us. We ate in silence, but Hanna filled in the gaps. She thought she might go see Cassie about some stitching with which she was having problems. Sam observed her thoughtfully. I wished it were Alexander whom she wanted to see. I saw Lauren give her a stern look.

Again, I was missing something, but I had more immediate concerns. "How was your day?"

Sam gazed at me and smiled. "Greatly successful." Lauren smiled, as well. She laughed, and I noticed Lauren and Sam exchange looks that told me they had a secret.

"I'll probably leave for home soon."

Hanna pleaded, "No, don't go, Lauren. Please stay. I know we can get you a better fiancé here."

Sam observed her and smiled. "Hanna, some people spend their entire lives looking for someone and never find them. If your sister believes Jim is the right person, we will dishonor her to change her mind. You're going to feel the same way someday. When you're eighteen, we'll respect your decision. Before that, heaven help you if you try anything that might be considered out of line with your age. Am I clear about that?"

"Yes, Pa."

I was sure our daughter would test us during the next few years. "Hanna, you may be excused. Would you take those extra muffins over to Cassie's and return within the hour, darling?"

"Yes, Ma." Hanna kissed me. She took some material, thread, and muffins to visit Cassie. When Hanna was out of earshot, I turned to Sam and Lauren. "So, the suit worked?"

"Perfectly. I was dry and warm, and we used extremely icy cold water. You can ask Sam."

Lauren stared at Sam and giggled. He shot her a stern look, which made her laugh even more. I could tell he was trying not to laugh but was barely holding himself together.

"We're set for launch." Lauren was obviously happy.

"Modern expression?" Sam gave us a quizzical look.

"Man to the moon expression."

"I would definitely love to see that."

I glanced down. This was not a happy day for me. I kept thinking that I would be ecstatic if I came home to my fiancé and my father. I needed to share her joy, but what if something went wrong? I would never know. I wouldn't ever hear anything again. I wouldn't know if her fiancé was alive and home from the army, whether her father was all right, and if Lauren had children. I made my choice years ago. For me, it was still the right one, but it was challenging, nonetheless.

Hanna returned and, after pleading one more time with Lauren not to leave, went straight to bed. We moved to the couch in front of the fire. Sam sat in his chair, drank a glass of brandy with us, and then left us alone. We quietly sat and gazed into the fire.

"Last chance to tell me anything. Anything at all."

"Mom, I'll be fine. I'm going home. I'm marrying Jim, we will have lots of children, and we will both practice as vets. We'll take turns with the parenting. I have a job, and I will remain in the area until Jim returns. After that, we may move. I'll take care of Dad and Aunt Sherry until they die. I'll think about you and love you until I die. I will have a wonderful long life, and you shouldn't worry about me."

We sat for a little longer until we yawned and agreed it was time to go to bed. Sam wished to go over the plan for the next day with Lauren one more time. I assumed there was more to the visit, but I had to let it go. I trusted Sam. Possibly he would try to talk her out of leaving once more. I waited until he returned.

"Well, she's going." Sam changed into his sleeping gown.

"Can we both go up to the pool?" I wanted to be with her until the last minute. I understood Sam had to be there to help with the diving suit.

"What about Hanna?"

"Do you think we could ask Cassie to watch her for a few hours?"

"Becky, have you noticed that she's going over there several times a day? Why do you think that is?"

"I think she and Cassie have a rapport."

"You know, for a modern woman, you're a bit naïve."

Knowing what was to come in the morning, Sam held me until I fell asleep. *Who would comfort Lauren tomorrow night?* I realized she had a hard and lonely time coming up. I grieved for her as much as I did for myself.

The following morning brought clear skies and a cold wind. Snow was still collected in the shaded areas. Lauren and I drank coffee, but neither one of us was hungry. Sam walked Hanna over to Cassie and Merv's place. He needed to have a quiet word with Merv. He saddled the horses and left some chores for the few men who were still at the ranch.

Lauren, dressed in several layers of clothing, hugged Pocket and mounted her for the ride to the portal pool and the future. Barely having survived her entrance to our time, Lauren was nervous. We all understood it could be the same when she returned to the future. Sam had the diving suit wrapped in a blanket tied onto his saddle.

We started off as if going for simply another ride. Lauren wasn't talking. Sam spoke to her and assured her it was still okay to change her mind. These words were falling on deaf ears. She is such a strong, determined woman. I was so proud of her and yet sick at heart for the parting.

When we reached the pool, Sam stepped away to give us a few minutes of private time. "I'm so sorry, Lauren. I love you so much. I want only the best for you."

"Mom, I have the greatest life. I have nothing but respect and love for you. Please have a wonderful life. You are an inspiration to me. I just hope I can be half the woman you are. I'm so blessed to have met you again to see how you and your Buchanan family live. I don't want to change a thing. This has been one of the best times of my life. Thank you."

Sam came back with the diving suit and helped Lauren dress while I watched and wiped away the tears. After she had the diving suit on, he held the helmet, and he and I kissed her one more time. She was crying but smiling too.

"Thanks again to both of you. I love you very much."

Sam placed the helmet on and sealed it. It was tough for her to manipulate. I was frightened that the weight would impair her ability to maneuver and emerge from the suit on the other side. Sam had strapped a knife to her waist and gave her one to hold in her hand. She would hold her other hand over the air vent in the helmet. Sam helped her walk to the edge of the pool. He steadied her as she walked into the water, he patted her head, and she walked into the center of the stream. The suit made it difficult for Lauren to submerge herself. She tried, would come up to take deep breaths, and make another attempt. At last, Sam walked out a short distance into the water and held her head down.

"Safe travels, darling." He pushed her head down forcefully. The swirling water made the sand stir. We gazed deeply into the water, but she was gone. He came out of the water, and we held each other, overcome with grief.

Lauren

The last night at the Cattle Creek Ranch was so sad. The house was not filled with the joy that this family had presented so many months ago. I would miss all the

Buchanans, but I realized this time would be tough for my mother. She'd told me so frequently that I was making the right decision, but it was still painful. I would never see her again.

When I returned to my bedroom for the last time, Sam knocked at the door, said goodbye, and thanked me for making my mother so happy. He went over the map where the gun would be buried, and he instructed me to retrieve it at all costs when I emerged. He was convinced it was in a container to keep it clean and ready to use a hundred or more years from now.

"One last thing. I'm not expecting anything, but I studied my journals. It's never flooded in July since I've owned the Cattle Creek Ranch. If there's ever a time you might come back, that is the month. I know it's dangerous, and I understand it will be impossible if you have children. However, maybe just once, if you thought you or you and Jim might return, I think that would be the best month to come."

He squeezed my hand. "I won't tell your mother, but I plan to take her to Hank Heaven each July until we are unable to come. I won't tell her the reason, but I will have her in Hank Heaven the first weeks of July. If you decide to return, simply come on up to join us for a short visit. Will you consider it?"

"I can't promise that, but I'll think about it. Thank you for the idea and for all you've done to assist me. Take care of my mother. I realize she'll suffer for a while."

"You know I will. Pleasant dreams, Lauren."

We rode up to the creek the following morning. I hugged Pocket one last time. I was strapped into this antiquated diving suit and prepared to take the plunge back to my real life. Was it all a dream? Would I come out of the water, and Frank and I would be ducking for cover from the maniacal stalker? Would my father have died of grief due to losing yet another family member? I would find out soon enough.

Sam maneuvered me toward the water and held my arms as I walked into the pool. He attempted to help me immerse myself in the water. When it was evident that once again, the air in the suit was not allowing me to submerge, Sam pushed me down into the water. For a brief second, I was underwater, and he released me, yet I didn't stay down long. I was almost propelled to the surface with the air locked in my diving suit. This wasn't going to work.

PART 2

RETURN NORMAL

Chapter 17

Lauren

I rose and was able to stand on a sandy surface. I turned around to see whether my mother or Sam had any other ideas. They were gone, and I was alone. The diving-suit glass mask was foggy with condensation, obscuring my vision. I couldn't clear it. I still held the knife, and I had the other knife strapped to my waist. My fingers were useless due to the gloves with the thick material. I yelled. While my shout was muffled, I was certain no one responded. I was in the water up to my waist, and the flow was slower than when I went in.

I had to get out of the water before I would start to remove the suit. I needed to cut the sleeve on one side and free one hand to begin to undress. I had to do it blindly. I waded to a shallow spot in the pool. When it was low enough, I got down on my hands and knees and crawled out of the water. I was dry and quite warm, despite what must be a winter day. I could see white that must be snow, but it was still blurry. I stuck my tongue out to tell if I could clear the mask, but my tongue wouldn't reach the glass.

I crawled out of the water and thought I was on the far side of the stream, on the side where Sam explained he left the gun. I considered simply wading across the creek with the protection of the suit to stay dry. I was confident the stalker would be long gone. The bears would be hibernating, and mountain lions would be rare. I decided to follow his direction to acquire the gun before leaving.

I slowly used the knife in my hand to cut away one arm and sleeve as close as possible to my hand to take off the helmet. It took several minutes, and I did nick myself once. I was able to remove the helmet when my hand was free. I gazed around and could make out landmarks that were familiar to me. I saw the rail that had been constructed from the rock-slide repairs. I was on the opposite side of the creek and away from the trail. The water was surprisingly low, so I could detect a place to cross the creek without getting wet by hopping from rock to rock.

I searched behind me, locating a group of trees that Sam had shown me on a map. I removed the rest of the suit and bundled it up. The diving suit would be hidden in the trees until I could come later to remove it. The tree that Sam described had changed in the years since he had buried the gun. This was my last connection to my mother and her family. I hoped I had located the correct tree. An old, rusty, metal pickax was leaning against the tree. I could tell its handle had been gone for a long time. I used the pick to dig in the frozen ground. It was hard work, and I was sweating in the layers of clothes my mother had given to me.

After digging to the depth Sam had estimated would be a box, I felt the pick hit a hard object. I furiously dug around the site and, with great effort, cleared the top of the metal box of dirt. The box had rusted over time but still seemed solid. The elements had not ruined the structure, but getting the lid off would be difficult. I wanted to leave it in the ground and remove the gun, but I needed to clear more around the top to hit the rusted edges and free the lid.

After several minutes, I was able to loosen the lid. Employing the pick and tapping on the sides of the box, I finally felt it move. With more tapping, I could pry open the box. The gun was wrapped in an oilcloth. It was dry and appeared new. According to Sam, it was not loaded, and I would have to load it with bullets, which were wrapped separately in another oiled cloth. Before loading the gun, I cocked the hammer and pulled the trigger. It moved flawlessly. The bullets seemed as though they had recently been purchased. I took six out of the small tin to place them in the chambers. I considered shooting the gun one time to ensure it worked, but I could not be sure there were no hunters or anyone out looking for me in the area. I decided to just keep it without testing it.

Another object inside the box was wrapped in paper. I pulled out a well-preserved leather pouch. Reaching inside, I nearly fainted when I realized it was the gold nugget my mother and I found in this creek a few weeks ago. *Enough to buy a house in her time.*

A small note in the pouch read:
Hope to see you in July one year soon.

With all our love,
Sam and your mother.

It was in Sam's handwriting. When I thought about them, I realized that they were both dead and buried in Miner's Meadow. I cried for a few seconds, but I believed I heard voices. I walked toward the creek where I saw two men in winter clothes on the trail, coming from Miner's Meadow. If I hurried, I might be able to catch a ride to Rich's house.

I managed to catch up with them. The men gazed at my outfit and inquired if I was lost. I laughed. "You wouldn't believe me if I told you." I didn't ask any questions, and they didn't mention a missing person. Maybe no one was looking. Could I be that lucky? They dropped me off at Rich's place. As luck would have it, he was out riding because it was Saturday. The nosy neighbor greeted me. According to her, the police had come by several times, looking for me.

"Are you wanted?"

"I hope not. I had to go away for a while, but I'm back. I don't suppose you have a key to the house?"

"No. I'll bet you're cold. Do you want to come in?"

"Sure, thanks. I'm Lauren. I don't think we've been formally introduced."

"No, we haven't. I'm Helen."

She made me a cup of coffee and offered me a sweet roll.

"Yes, please." I was starving.

It was so nice to have running water, heating, and all the mod cons again. I love my mom, but no man is worth giving up what I have. Well, maybe one man is. I felt the gun and the gold nugget hidden in the bag under my coat.

"Has anyone suspicious been hanging around lately?"

"Do you mean that crazy lady? No, she was around for a few weeks after you left, but she finally went away. Rich claimed you went on a mission to provide veterinary care to people in Honduras. How did that go?"

"Really well."

"I lived down there for a time. How did you find it?"

Gulp. "Rural. When were you there?"

"1973. My church went there on a mission."

"Oh, that sounds interesting. What did you actually do?" I thought I might deflect any questions by encouraging her to talk about herself. It worked like a charm! I heard all about her life for the next hour. When she was about to tell me about her other missions, a car pulled up.

"Sounds as if Rich is back." She peeked through the window curtain. "Yep, it has been great fun talking to you. I hope we can talk more."

"Sure thing, Helen. Thanks for the coffee and sweet roll." I loved sweet rolls, but I had already missed Gee Ling's cooking. I doubt I will ever eat as well as I did in the 1800s, but I'll drink modern coffee any day.

We walked out as Rich was getting out of his car. He was on the phone, and he grinned when he saw me. He came over, hugged me, and even kissed me. I whispered, "Still in the closet?"

He whispered back, "Emerging as we speak. Later."

When we entered the house, he hugged me again. "I thought you were dead."

"Yeah, does anyone else think I'm dead?"

"Your father calls every week and asks if I've heard from you. You can thank me now. I lied my ass off for you. I said you had contacted me, and you were still in Honduras. At one point, the sheriff came over, and I was afraid I might be charged with your murder."

"Oh, heck." I laughed to myself, remembering that in August, I would have said, *oh, shit*. I wondered how long my piety would last. "How about my friendly stalker?"

"Lauren, you wouldn't believe it. She took a shot at your friend, the professor, and was arrested for having an unlicensed gun and attempted murder. She's on bail! Can you believe it? On bail."

"Is she around?"

"I have no idea. That nutcase stopped coming around here. Hey, you have mail."

"Anything from Jim?" My heart was racing.

"Yes, ma'am." He went to his desk to pull out three letters.

I wanted to read them, but I reconsidered that I'd better shower, put on some deodorant, and—most importantly—call my parents.

Chapter 18

Rebecca

My grief was palpable. I rode home from the creek with Sam, went up to our room, and climbed into bed. Our bedroom was cold, and I got under the sheets fully dressed and cried. Sam left me for a while and later came up to our room, sat, held my hand, and stroked my back.

"Did you tell Hanna?"

"Yes, she's still at Cassie's. She was mad that we didn't let her come. I told her that you and Lauren may never see each other again, and she would probably be with us until we died."

"How did that go over?"

"She said as soon as she was old enough, she was going to move to Virginia to be with Lauren."

"We do have two daughters, while some people have none. I guess we should count our blessings."

"Three, including Jenny. My blessing is you, Bec."

"And you're mine." I sat up, and we held each other for several minutes.

"Sam, do you think she'll ever come back? I mean, she could."

"I'm not counting on it. We all make choices in life. Time travel is not without its danger."

"She's really a wonderful woman, isn't she? I realize I didn't raise her, but I am so proud to be her mother."

"Becky, she's a card to draw to. You should be so proud. I'd better get something going in the kitchen. You want to stay up here for a while?"

"Maybe for a few minutes more until Hanna returns. We have a second daughter to raise. Sam, how did you cope when your wives died, and you had children to raise?"

"It was hell, but I needed to get up the next day to take care of the boys each time. You painfully get on with life. You learn how to cope."

He left me, and soon Hanna was lying on the bed beside me, crying. "It's not fair."

"No, we try to make life fair, but we're all individuals, and someday you're going to do the same thing. It's the way of nature, and I wouldn't have it any other way."

"I'm never leaving, Ma."

"We'll revisit that in a few years, darling. Go on down to help your father, and I'll be down in a few minutes."

Despite the pending new year, which would arrive in less than a few hours, dinner was a somber affair. Sam and Hanna ate without comment. I stirred my food and attempted to eat, but I was not hungry. We all sat in the great room in front of the fire while Sam read *Little Women* to us. It was a happy section, thankfully. After Hanna went to bed, Sam and I sat together on the divan, and he read another book with my head in his lap.

I considered how diligently Sam had worked to help Lauren get back to her time. It reminded me of something in my youth—Father's Day.

"Did I ever tell you about Mother's and Father's Day?"

"No, I don't recall."

"I don't know when it started, but we first celebrated Mother's Day, a designated day every year, and Father's Day the following month. In our family, my sister and I gave my mother a card, and we tried to cook dinner for her. She would usually have to rescue us since we were hopeless cooks."

"Nothing's changed much there."

I reached over and socked him in the arm. "Anyway, you're the best father in the universe." I sat up to kiss him. "Call me a bad mother, but I love you so much. I still choose to stay with you."

"You're the best mother we could ask for. Dan, Hanna, and the little ones are lucky to have you. I'm lucky to have you too. Want to stay up and greet the new year?"

"Not a chance, cowboy."

"Good, I'm ready for bed. It's been one of the strangest days of my life. I want to return to the real world."

I thought about what the "real world" was. "I don't think that's possible."

Someone knocked on the door right then. As Sam approached the locked door, we heard one of the ranch hands holler for me. "We're going to have a New Year's baby."

I would welcome in the new year with a delivery. Sam kissed me and said he was going to bed. "Send for me if I can be of any help."

"If I need to take her into town for a cesarean, I'll call you. Happy New Year, darling." I kissed him good night and left with the nervous, soon-to-be new father.

I didn't return until mid-morning the next day. Hanna was already out in the barn with Alexander, cleaning the stables. I only wished she would show an interest in him because he was such a hardworking young man. Cassie was so impressed with his intelligence and efforts to please her. I'm sure he's motivated to do well because the alternative is the orphanage. Knowing my husband as I do, the money would be forthcoming in a couple of years if the boy desired further education.

As I walked in the door, I smelled breakfast. "Happy New Year." Sam kissed me. "Have something to eat and go to bed."

"That sounds delicious. We have a new ranch hand. Samuel Lloyd Marker was born this morning. He's named for you."

Sam smiled. "I don't understand why I didn't name one of the boys after me."

"Maybe Dan will name the next child Sam. Shouldn't they be getting back today?"

"Everyone will be back today." He glanced at me and noticed me falter. "Well, almost everyone."

Chapter 19

Lauren

The hot water running from the showerhead was a wonderful invention. I marveled at a great many things. The bathroom heater, the toilet, disposable razors—the list went on and on. When I came out of the bathroom, Rich had made lunch for me. "You'd better call your folks right now. I'm not covering for you anymore. What did Jim say?"

"I haven't opened his letters. What if it's bad news? Not to change the subject, but what's happened with you and lover boy down South?"

Rich smiled. "All systems go. My new principal is gay. She's out and proud—job security. The love of my life is moving up in a few months. He's not a snow bunny, and he wants to wait until the temperatures warm up."

"That's love for you. He loves you only when it's warm?"

"We all have our limits."

I remembered everything that occurred in the last few months. I thought about how hard my mother and Sam tried and worked to make my trip memorable. I recalled how my mother and I went on the cattle drive and risked our lives to aid Sam. Was love different now, or was this not the great romance of a lifetime for Rich? Would Jim do what Sam had done for my mother to help me get home? I wasn't convinced that even my real father could meet my new benchmark. Speaking of which...

I'd better make the call. I dreaded opening the letters. What if Jim didn't love me anymore, was injured, or was not returning for an extended time?

Because the latest letter was dated two weeks earlier, I figured he was still alive. I decided to call the Virginia City vets to learn my start time. Good news. I was lucky that one of the owners answered. While these vets had agreed to take me on in January, they would prefer February. They would honor their agreement, but they tried to reach me and knew I was out of the country. I had changed numbers, so the stalker wouldn't be able to contact me. I probably forgot to give them the new number. I explained about the different contact numbers but had not given the reason I had switched. I agreed to the February start date, which gave me time to adjust. I planned to travel to Kentucky to visit my parents and get my dog Ladybug or, as I called her, LB.

I kept staring at the letters. Rich was perplexed. "Why haven't you opened them? Are you afraid of bad news?"

"A little." I couldn't explain it, but I think I was concerned that his letters might not match my expectations. I now had two men who exemplified what I wanted in a man.

I thought Jim was the man, but what if he wasn't? I knew it was crazy, but time away from someone might make me realize he wasn't who I thought he was.

We ate lunch, after which I turned on my telephone. The missed calls began to signal on my phone. Most of the forty-three missed calls were from my mother, or aunt, and father. Still, eleven calls originated from an unlisted number, and three of them hailed from a number I didn't recognize. There were several messages, and my emails even started to come through. I believed it was best to work backward.

The last message was from my dad, pleading with me to answer my phone or send him a text message or an email. He sounded worried but not frantic. Phew, that might go better than expected. Some hang-ups came from North Carolina, which may be a new number from my vet-school friend, Lisa. Eleven calls were all silent numbers. The first few were just hang-ups, but the last few were threats from a masked voice. It was the stalker.

I went into my bedroom to make the calls. Rich was going back for more food since I would be there for dinner. My first call was to Frank Lash, who had shown me how to time travel and who knew my mother through time travel. I got an away message. Without using my name, I left a simple greeting and mentioned I was back in town and would call later.

I made the dreaded call to my mom and dad. Thankfully, my sister answered. "Hey, Janie."

"Oh, my God, you aren't dead."

"Nope."

"Enjoy the rest of the few days you have left. Dad's gonna kill you."

"Are they home?"

"They're trying to get someone interested in your disappearance. We all believed you were in Central America. Since no entries are on your passport, they thought you'd been abducted. Wait until I tell them."

"I'll catch the first flight I can get home. It's a long story."

"There's no story that's going to fix this. You are done like dinner."

"I'm sorry."

"Not sorry enough. Dad would like to throttle you. Want me to hide the hairbrushes?"

"And any heavy objects, including the tennis-table paddles."

"I can hardly wait. Lauren, you're toast."

"I'll call mom's phone. Don't say anything. How's LB?"

"LB, who? Oh, the dog dad sold to the pet shop last month. Could you wait for an hour, so I can see their faces?"

"One hour?"

"Hey, Lauren?"

"Yeah?"

"Glad you're alive. Sucks to be you, though. I guess Santa will not forget, and your presents for this year will be given to charities. LB's fine, but she's probably pissed too."

"Thanks. One hour, but not a minute more." I hung up, dreading the next call home. I stared at the letters and called Frank one more time just in case. Once again, no answer. I didn't leave a message.

Well, I'm alive. The stalker hasn't been around lately. In one hour, my parents will be relieved that the number-one daughter is still alive, breathing, and preparing for severe punishment. I touched the letters. The time had arrived.

I began with the initial one, which was dated soon after he left.

Dear Lauren,
This letter officially tells you that I am holding
you to the contractual agreement we made
two weeks ago at Miner's Meadow. Any deviation
from the contract will not be allowed. I am yours
forever—well, as soon as the army releases me.
I think about you day and night, and I will die
protecting you. I miss my fishing lessons and
need to practice.
Practice, practice, practice.
Forever,
Jim

The following letter was dated October 16.
Dear Lauren,
I am safe and well, and I hope you are the same.
Because my letters are scanned and censored, I must
be careful about what I say. Re: the fishing lessons.
Well, you know what I mean. I don't think I can talk
about things like back tickling, so I won't talk about
that at all. I am fairly sure it will be censored if I talk
about the other things I like about you, but I know it's
okay to say I miss your accent and the extra syllables you
add to words. I miss seeing you pull a foal out of the
mare and miss seeing you sitting in the lake at
Miner's Meadow. Counting the days
and want you to know I am safe and will be back soon.
Your fishing partner for life,

Jim

Finally, one was postmarked two weeks ago.

Dear Lauren,

Merry Christmas, darling. Please say hi to Rich for me. I'm so sorry I haven't organized a Christmas gift for you. Things have not gone well here. I will tell you about it when I get back, but the date for my return may be longer than I anticipated. I am safe, but I can't say any more than that. I am counting the days, which looks good only if I divide the numbers by four. I think of you day and night. It will be a while. I'll send you an address at which you can write to me. A letter from you will

eventually get to me. Please tell me you are safe.
With all my love,
Jim
P.S. The men here all call me Hank Buchanan. They say I look like him. I don't, do I?
Give LB a scratch for me and tell her Daddy's coming home.
JK

That was it. I lost it. In one day, I had left my mother and my second family forever. I discovered my mother and dad were sick with worry, which would soon translate into fury. I read an extremely concerning letter from my fiancé that things weren't going well. His release from the army would be delayed. The stalker somehow had my number and was out on bail. I couldn't reach Frank, and was he even alive? I still didn't know anything about the police corruption case. I cried for a half-hour, and then my sister texted me to call home. *How did she have my number?*

I pulled myself together and dialed the home number. My mother answered. "Hi, Mom. It's Lauren." There was silence on the phone. The next voice I heard was my father's.

"Where the hell are you?"

"Nevada, Dad. I can explain it."

"I don't think you can. There's no explanation for what you've put your mother and me through."

"Dad, I'm sorry."

"Lauren, I'm so mad I could throw this phone across the room right now."

"I know. May I come home? I've missed you, Dad."

He finally responded after a long pause. "I want you home as soon as possible, but don't think it's going to be a bed of roses, young lady. Right now, I am so mad I'm not convinced I'll ever forgive you. The FBI and the sheriff's office are both looking for you too."

"I'm at Rich's house, and he doesn't know what's going on."

"It's been kept out of the news for your safety. Your stalker is out on bail, and she's gone missing, as well."

"I'll call everyone today, Dad. I'm sorry. I'll start driving home tomorrow."

"No, absolutely not. I'll fly out, and I'll drive back with you."

"Dad, I'll be fine. You don't need to come."

"Lauren, I'm not negotiating."

"Okay, let me know when you'll be here, and I'll come to the airport."

"What's the address where you're staying? No, don't say it aloud. Have one of your friends text me the address. You never know who's listening." He hung up without allowing me to say another word. A minute later, my mom was on the phone. "We love you. Hurry home, honey."

"I missed you, too, Mom."

I attempted to contact Frank, but there was still no answer. After Rich returned from shopping, I used his phone to text my father the address. An hour later, I received a reply that my father would come in two days and for me not to leave the house.

I then called the FBI. I was transferred straight to the agent handling the corruption case. All the men were on parole, but they had monitors on their legs and had to remain in their homes. When I asked how reliable they were, the agent answered he would not stake his life on the system. "They know they're under surveillance, but the odd guy, Kenny, is a problem. He's living in a rented apartment, and there's no telling who visits him. They all know you have been gone. By the way, where have you been? You scared the shit out of your parents."

"Hiding out. If I am required to, I'll go back there, so that's a secret. I'm heading home to Kentucky in two days."

"Is that your parents' home?"

"Yes, my cabin was burned down, which reminds me. Do you know about a woman who is stalking me?"

"I think I heard about her. Man, you are really in trouble with her. Maybe you should go back to wherever you've been hiding. She's a nutcase. How she made bail is beyond me."

"Do you know her name?"

"Give me a second." I could hear the agent typing on a keyboard during a pause.

"It's not my case. Jasmine MacArthur has a pending trial for carrying a weapon and the attempted murder of a Frank Lash."

"So, Frank is still alive?"

"You are out of the loop. Mr. Lash chased Jasmine down after she shot at him and a woman up in the national forest."

I didn't ask about the woman. I would retrieve that information from Frank. "Are any of the trials set with a court date?"

"The corruption trial is set for late February, and Kenny's trial is coming up. That's a local-level trial for which I don't have the date. The attempted murder is not scheduled until May. That's our trial since it occurred on federal land. What are your plans in case we need you again?"

"Not sure. You realize this stalker lady, Jasmine, is after me?"

"Yes, Frank explained that. We can offer you protection, and we can get an order barring her from approaching you."

"Does it help? I thought those orders were a waste of time, and she would know I'm back in the real world."

"Have you considered returning to wherever you were? You fooled us for sure."

"No, that isn't possible. I should get on with my life." I thought about my real mother and her family and the feeling that despite the wild West, I felt protected on the Cattle Creek Ranch. "I'll let you know where I am. I'll change the phones again because I already have messages from the stalker."

"How'd she find that number?"

"I don't understand, but she has it."

"Listen, you would probably qualify for witness protection."

"No, if I really need to go away, I have a place. If I was gone, what would happen to the trials?"

"We have plenty on the cops, and Kenny is going down, but his sentence might not be much. Jasmine MacArthur is not about you. Because there was another witness besides Frank Lash, we feel confident that she will do time. Frank took a bullet for you, so to speak."

"So, to speak, but not really. Tell me Mr. Lash didn't get hit."

"No, but he said he helped you disappear."

"Okay, when I have a new number, I'll notify you."

"Since I might put a tap on the current phone, please provide me the number to save me the trouble of looking it up."

I furnished him with the number and hung up. *Whom do you trust? Where was that woman?* I tried Frank again. Because it was New Year's Eve, I was fortunate to reach the FBI guy. I wanted to call my friends Lisa, Mary, and Ted but determined it was best to lie low until my father arrived. Rich had plans to go out and invited me to accompany him, but I was exhausted. I felt that time travel really knocks you out. I laughed inwardly. I dreaded the reaction of my father when we would be reunited, but how I wanted him to take me in his arms and protect me the way Sam Buchanan had done.

I wrote a letter to Jim but tore it up. I attempted to compose several other letters. Nothing expressed my feelings. Rich and I shared dinner, after which he left for his party. I simply wanted to sleep, so I did.

Chapter 20

Rebecca

Sam and I tried to get on with our lives. Dan and Jenny were disappointed they could not say goodbye to Lauren. Still, they understood she needed to get back to her fiancé. Jenny wanted to write her a letter as soon as we had an address. I explained that Lauren was moving, and she would send us a new address soon. Hanna, Sam, and I continued to grieve.

I went back to work at the hospital for a week and then returned. Hanna and I stayed at the boardinghouse so she could attend school even with bad weather. Alexander Thistlewaite rode in and out of the Cattle Creek Ranch. He was such a nice boy, and it saddened me that he and Hanna weren't closer. She was performing well in school. I detected no other possible suitors, which was probably good since

I wanted her to concentrate on her studies. Alexander was a great help in that respect. He and Hanna studied together whenever they were both at home.

A church social was coming up. I had not attended one in a long time. I was sorry that Lauren never had that experience. Since she was already spoken for, I don't think she minded. I recalled my first few dances in the 1850s. I remembered dancing with the young Buchanan boys and finally their father. Despite my desperation to locate my husband in those early days, I liked dancing with the real Sam Buchanan.

I still did love dancing, of course. Sam and I danced together a few times, after which Ray Thompson asked me to dance. He was such a good dancer. It was so much fun to dance with him. Pam Wilkins never attended the socials. She would have been working in the saloon at night. I could tell Ray was a bit down. He told me several days beforehand that he and Pam were only good friends. Still, he had relied on her as a dinner companion and someone who kept him informed about aspects of the town that were vital to reduce potential crime. Because Ray had already retired, Glenn Frasier was in charge. Ray continued advising and assisting Glenn to maintain peace. We endured a rather nasty period when the mines were slow due to the winter, and men had a great deal of time on their hands. Pam wasn't there anymore to keep the peace in her saloon, and the other tavern was never under control. Poor Glenn had his hands full.

Ray, Sam, and I ate a box dinner that Gee Ling had prepared. Sam and Ray reminisced about the old days, recounting one event that happened even before I came on the scene. They had spent many days chasing some cattle thieves. After several days of tracking them, the posse was about to give up. Ray hatched a plan to circle miles around them to force the wrestlers into a canyon. Their standoff with the wrestlers lasted for days. At last, they decided to come at them from the side of the mountain they would have never considered possible. It worked because of the element of surprise.

I commented, "Kind of like a Hail Mary." Sam and Ray stared at me. I immediately realized this was a modern expression.

Ray gazed up thoughtfully. "Sam, where have we heard that 'Hail Mary' term before?"

Sam recognized it as a mistake on my part. "It must be one of her Eastern expressions." He squeezed my hand under the table.

"Yeah, but I've heard it before."

"Ray, want to dance? The band is starting."

"No. I'm going outside for some fresh air. You two lovebirds can have this one."

Sam grabbed my hand, and we went out on the dance floor. "You know, Ray's correct. You aren't the first person to say that. I can't recall who, but someone used that term."

"Really?"

We danced several more times. I finally persuaded Sam to dance with Mrs. Gardiner, which usually kept her in check for a few weeks on the gossip front.

I danced with Ray once more while he repeated, "Hail Mary, Hail Mary." As we packed up and Sam harnessed the buggy, Ray came over. "Sam, I remember. It was that funny guy, Alex, who used to visit the town every summer. I can't recall his last name. Do you remember?"

Sam stared away for a minute and then smiled. "Conrad, Alex Conrad."

"I know his name. Did I ever meet him, Sam?"

"Becky, he was long gone when you arrived. That was many years ago, wasn't it, Ray? I wonder what happened to him. He simply left and never returned."

"What did he look like? His name's kind of familiar."

Ray described him, which didn't ring a bell. I was sure I had met him back East. On the way home, I fell asleep. It was freezing, but I was warm and comfortable, leaning on Sam under the blankets. When we climbed into bed, I remembered Alex Conrad and shot up. "Sam, he's a time traveler. I met him in the future when I went to rescue my father from the nursing home. He's a television producer who created Western television shows."

"Interesting." Two seconds later, Sam was asleep. So, that was the way Alex Conrad created *Comstock*. He developed the concept when he visited this area as a historian, as Frank Lash did.

For once, my life and the Buchanans all made sense. I laughed to myself. These people existed, and this life is not a dream. My mother and sister would have been excited to uncover this fact. The mystery of my current life was solved. I wish I had realized it when Lauren was here.

Sam inquired about Alex Conrad the following day. "What did you say about him?"

"I'm fairly convinced he's a time traveler. I believe he came here and got ideas for Western television shows."

"Ridiculous. Who would want to watch stories about people like us?"

Millions of people, I thought.

Chapter 21

Lauren

New Year's Day with no hangover. I'm slipping. I wondered how my real mother was. It was technically ridiculous. She was long dead and buried. I missed her and all the Buchanans. I went through my possessions and packed a bag to take back to Kentucky with my dad. I wrote two additional letters to Jim, which I crumpled up. I wanted him so much, but I didn't have a clue when he would return. It sounded as if it could be a long time. *It couldn't be more than a year? Could it?*

Rich woke up around noon. I watched him stir. "Big night, cowboy?" I asked sternly.

He closed his eyes and grimaced. "Don't shout."

"You know, I'm barely whispering."

"Whisper in a softer voice."

"Hydration is the key to salvation. Have some water and coffee." I shook my head. "Pathetic—at your age as well."

"Have you eaten breakfast yet? Want to go to the Coffee Café?"

"Must lie low. Too many bad guys out there. Daddy's orders. Maybe the FBI's order as well."

"Wow, already hobnobbing with the big guns. Want to tell me where you've been?"

"Sorry, cowboy, it's a state secret."

"If you insist. I understand you can't go out, but I could invite a few friends over later if you'd like."

"Rich, I'm leaving for Kentucky tomorrow. As much as I want to see everyone, it's a bit too raw right now. I'd love to see Mary, though."

"Mary Knox?"

"Yeah, have you heard anything from her?"

"I saw her with her son shopping a few weeks back. She wanted to know whether I'd heard from you. I told her what I told everyone, that you were in Honduras. You were, weren't you?"

"Certainly was."

"Good. I would hate to mislead anyone."

"Nope. I wouldn't want you to lie. No siree, Bob!"

"How about we wear a costume, and I take you out to Mary's as soon as I stop puking?"

"Water, Rich, water."

Rich had a great costume, including a mustache and beard. I resembled a guy. We drove out to Mary's ranch, where the snow wasn't too deep. Good enough for Ted to teach skiing, and not too bad for those of us who live with it.

I climbed out of the car and removed the costume. Mary screamed when she saw me.

"Lauren, I thought I'd lost you. Am I glad to see you! Hi, Rich. Thanks for bringing her out. Where's Ladybug?"

"In Kentucky with my family. I'm heading there tomorrow. How are you, Mary?"

I studied the terrain and tried to match it up with the 1800s. This house was close to the Cattle Creek Ranch-homestead location. I wondered whether Mary was aware of this. She made some coffee and served us homemade cookies.

"How was your trip, Lauren?"

I stared at Rich without blinking. "I definitely learned a great deal, but mostly it was an eye-opener. Hard to believe people live without electricity." Well, kind of—.

"I'm so glad you're here. Could either one of you assist me with this Social Security form?"

"Of course, Mary," we responded in unison.

"More like Social Insecurity if you ask me," she replied.

"What's the issue? How do you need help?"

"With the whole darn thing. I can't even tell what the government wants. The print is minuscule."

"Okay, let's get it done." The print was tiny. Even I had to squint. "Mary, they want your maiden name."

"Darling."

"Mary Darling. Get a lot of teasing about that?" Rich poked her.

"Now, don't you two start."

"All right, father's name and mother's maiden name?"

"Carl Darling. Cassandra Thistlewaite."

Both Rich and I recognized the Thistlewaite name. We smiled at each other as though we had heard the last click of tumblers on a lock. Rich was unaware I had met Alexander Thistlewaite. Still, he must have remembered that the Thistlewaites once owned my old cabin. There couldn't be that many of them.

"Mary, is your family tree recorded anywhere?"

"No, but I'm familiar with it. My great-great-grandparents are Hanna and Alexander Thistlewaite. Rich, do you know anything about them?"

"Simply that they owned the cabin where Lauren was living."

"I believe I knew that. My grandfather may have been born in that cabin."

Mary and I must be related by adoption. *Cue the "Twilight Zone" music.*

We left for home after finishing her paperwork. I was not looking forward to the following day. I'd observed my father when he was mad, and it wasn't pretty. Luckily, I wasn't the object of his anger on that occasion. Still, the entire family experienced the brunt of his rage one time when my brother and sister took the family station wagon. They crashed it after a drinking party with several friends. No one was hurt, but the car was totaled. Fortunately, I was away at college, but I "heard" the yelling two states away. I was going to receive his wrath the next day. The worst of it was that I had decided not to offer him any explanation.

Rich was still feeling the effects of his New Year's party. I cooked him some chops and potatoes. Gee Ling had taught me how to flavor the potatoes, impressing Rich. Gee Ling could have made a fortune with a cookbook now. Maybe one exists. I wondered if the actor who played him was still alive. I assumed most of the cast had passed away. I planned to watch them at home.

I finally figured out what to write to Jim in my letter:

Dear Jim,

I have so much to tell you about my last few months,
but it will have to wait until we are together.
I have witnessed what genuine love looks like and the sacrifices
we must make for each other. If I must wait twenty
years for your return, I will. I love you and want you to
know that I will love you forever. Fishing lessons can wait.
Love,
Lauren

I sealed and addressed the letter and turned on the television. Because Rich didn't have cable, the selection was limited. I watched a few minutes of a sitcom before bed. Sleep was elusive, and I dreamed of the Cattle Creek Ranch and the mare Pocket.

The following day, I had my bag packed and was ready to drive to Kentucky. My father was at the door sooner than I expected. Rich had decided the best plan for him was not to be present when our confrontation occurred. I made the *brock, brock, brock* chicken sound when he told me that.

"Chicken through and through. I'm living to fight another day."

When I opened the door, my dad walked in, hugged me, and didn't let me go. I heard him gasp, which sounded like a sob. That started me, and we continued hugging each other. At last, he let me go with a firm whack on my backside. "If you ever do something like that again, I swear I will take you over my knee."

"Yes, sir." We were laughing and crying simultaneously. The hard part was telling him that I had been gone, but I wouldn't discuss it, and he would have to accept that. For the first time ever, I was not going to share parts of my life.

Rich had brought my car into the driveway before he left. My dad placed my suitcase in the car, along with his small traveling bag. He drove and wanted me to keep my head down until we were out of town. When we were away from the city limits, he let me take over, and he slept for several hours until we had to stop for gas and food. This would be a marathon. Dad planned to drive straight through to Kentucky. He needed to return for work, and I was anxious to see more of my family and LB.

Chapter 22

Rebecca

We gradually began to experience some joy in our lives. We celebrated birthdays and the passage of time with the return of spring. The accumulation of snow in the mountains had been tolerable. The runoff from the melting snow was somewhat lower than it was during previous years. The days grew warmer and longer. By March, new buds in the foliage were emerging. Spring was imminent.

Hanna rode in and out of town regularly with Alexander. I still hoped perhaps she would eventually understand the qualities this young man possessed, which were required for a good marriage. Hanna never talked about other boys, and I wished she would put more effort into her studies. She was smart and could do whatever she wanted. Another doctor in the family would be excellent, but having a loving, caring daughter and more grandchildren would also be nice.

Dan's wife, Jenny, was getting bigger by the day. She was due in the summer, and I expected to attend the birth as I had done with the other two children. I worked more than usual for the last few months due to an increase in the population of Virginia City. Sam and Dan were busy with the ranch and finishing the army consignment. The cattle had lost a small amount of weight during the winter, and the new grass would help restore what was lost.

The horses were another matter entirely. They had been neglected, and the crews had been reassigned to other duties. In the past few weeks, the horses had been turned out. Currently, they were coming back in with varied issues, ranging from ringworm, a fungal infection, to hoof abscesses. These consequences resulted from the wet spring and muddy conditions.

These were not life-threatening ailments, but they slowed down the breaking and training of the young stock destined for the army. The following cattle drive would involve more than one thousand head of cattle and a hundred horses.

Once the horses had the buck taken out of them, several were given to Hanna and me to put on the finishing touches. Alexander helped us as well. He was a quick learner, and he and Hanna constituted a team. They each worked on several horses until late in the evenings and on the weekends. I did a few on the days I wasn't doctoring. I could tell how proud Sam was of Hanna, and he even discussed Alexander with admiration. Life was good until it wasn't.

I attended Mrs. Gardiner's niece for abdominal pain at Mrs. Gardiner's home. The niece had come to live with her the previous month. The woman—in her late thirties—was not married. She'd moved from Carson City to take care of Mrs. Gardiner, who had fallen and broken her arm. Lila Crompton presented with the classic symptoms of appendicitis. Her pain was in the right-lower quadrant of the abdomen. She required surgery to remove her infected appendix before it burst, causing peritonitis and death.

Mrs. Gardiner, who did not believe me, refused to allow me to take her niece to the hospital. I explained the serious nature of the condition. I offered a second opinion from one of my associates, but Mrs. Gardiner objected. While Lila was an adult, she lacked the mental capacity to make her own decisions. She depended on others to guide her in life. Her parents recently passed during our influenza episode. Mrs. Gardiner became her legal guardian since Lila's sister married and moved away several years ago.

I talked to them both for more than an hour. Because the pain was increasing in the poor woman's abdomen, Mrs. Gardiner finally relented. With the aid of the sheriff's deputies and my associates, we transported the rotund woman to the hospital.

My diagnosis was incorrect. Lila was suffering from an ectopic pregnancy. I decided to keep that information to myself. The staff assisting me in the surgery were well-schooled in professional discretion. The surgery had gone well, and soon the woman was in a bed, recovering from her surgery. I was sitting by her side when a man came in to demand patient visitation, claiming he was her paramour and had the right to see her. Mrs. Gardiner was consulted since she lived only a short distance from the hospital. She had no idea who this man was. I didn't mention the pregnancy.

I stayed in the room, where I observed the man berating Lila. He was furious that she had left Carson City to care for her aunt and that she'd permitted a woman to perform surgery on her. It was late when I was alone with her and the man. I asked him to leave as it was past visiting hours, and Lila needed her sleep. He first refused, yet he left after I threatened to get Sheriff Frasier.

Since I was wary, I stayed in the room with her. I got my small revolver to be safe. I fell asleep but was awakened by a gurgling noise. I thought I was dreaming when I saw the man from earlier in the night on top of Lila in a compromising position. His hand covered her mouth. I yelled at him to get off and get out. He jumped off the bed and approached me. I shot him. Instantly, I realized it was a fatal shot. Lila, who was awake, screamed.

Because she was the only patient in the hospital that evening, I'd sent the duty nurse home for the night. Lila was hysterical, and I was worried she would burst open her stitches. I administered some laudanum to her and waited for it to take effect. I waited until she calmed down to notify anyone. I then ran out to the house behind the hospital to alert Alf. We picked up the dead man to move him to another room. The sheriff's office was closed, so I had to go to Glenn's home, which was at the end of town. By the time I reached his house, heavy rain had soaked clear through my coat. I was shaking from the cold and recent confrontation.

Glenn came immediately. I related what happened and showed him the now-sleeping woman. I described the man on top of my patient with his hand over Lila's mouth. I was convinced he was going to rape her or kill her by strangulation. I explained that I had been sleeping in the bed across the room, but I shot the man when he lunged for me.

I was shaken, and Alf took over for me while Glenn and I wrote out a statement. By then, it was morning. Glenn could not locate any identification on him. We would have to wait for Lila to wake up. After the undertaker was called, he and another man removed the body. I was still the primary coroner, but an outside opinion was necessary due to my involvement in the man's death. With all the coming and going from the hospital, Mrs. Gardiner watched from her house through the window. When she noticed the stretcher emerge with its shrouded corpse, she was out the door and into the hospital, screaming that I'd killed her niece.

Alf took her into the room with her sleeping niece to recount what took place. Mrs. Gardiner didn't believe a word: her niece did not know this man, and the entire story must be fabricated. Lila stirred when she heard her aunt and glanced around frantically. "Where's Danny? I want Danny. She killed my Danny."

And that is when life became unfathomably difficult. Danny was Daniel Moore, whose father was a Carson City lawyer and a silver mine owner. Danny was the town wastrel. He was a hopeless alcoholic and would have been an itinerant if his father had not supported and rescued him on numerous occasions. This only son of Millard Moore could do no wrong in his father's eyes. This was going to be a difficult situation. Glenn suggested I ride back to the Cattle Creek Ranch and stay there until he could inform Mr. Moore and obtain a reasonable statement from Lila.

I left town to return to the Cattle Creek Ranch. Sam was out with the cattle, and Gee Ling was in his room. I ate a biscuit and went to bed. When I awoke after lunch, Sam had come home but allowed me to sleep. My husband had no idea about my ordeal of the previous evening. He smiled and greeted me as always. We were alone, and I hugged him and began to cry. It took a few minutes for me to calm myself and recount the story of the last twenty-four hours. Sam kept saying how sorry he was that he wasn't there to protect me. He was confident that the circumstances would show my action as self-defense. Sam knew Millard Moore and understood the man was a bully and a sharp lawyer, but it was evident that the son attacked me. He continued telling me I did the right thing. It was difficult to believe I would eventually get over the tragedy of killing a man.

Hanna had stayed at our boarding room that night and went to school without finding out what had happened. She returned late in the afternoon with Sam, who had gone into town. "Ma, are you going to jail?" She was concerned, as was Sam.

"Your mother isn't going to jail. She was defending herself."

"Pa, even the teacher said it might be murder." Hanna hugged me.

"Hanna, I don't want to hear any more talk about that. Do you hear me?"

"Yes, sir."

"Go on up to your room and start your homework. I need to talk with your mother."

Hanna began to protest, but she thought better of it with one look from him.

I watched Sam and waited. He put his hands around me. "Becky, I won't let anyone take you to jail, so help me. Many people are riled up, but they don't know the circumstances."

I was now worried. "How could I be accused of murder? The man charged toward me."

"Apparently, the lady you operated on says he simply turned and looked at you. He was visiting her. She says you repeatedly attempted to keep him out, and all he did was ask if he could stay."

"Bullshit." Sam raised his eyebrows and glanced at me. He realized that chastising me for swearing would not go down well. "You know that's not true."

"I know because I realize how honest you are. Is there anything you might have forgotten or that you haven't told me or anyone?"

"One fact. It wasn't appendicitis. It was an ectopic pregnancy." Sam recognized that from previous discussions.

"That could change things."

"Lila asked me not to tell anyone after she woke up and before the man arrived. I can't tell Glenn or anyone else. You understand, don't you?"

Following dinner, Hanna and I went out to work on some of the horses we were training. We worked until dark. After I sent her straight to bed, Sam and I discussed the possibility of my being charged with murder. In a committal hearing, when it was my word against that of an intellectually disabled woman who had just woken up from anesthesia, how could I lose?

We sent Hanna off to school with Alexander the following day. Sam went out to check on how the young horses

THE TRAVELS OF DR. REBECCA HARPER 211

were progressing, while I tended to a few individuals on the Cattle Creek Ranch who required medical attention. We ate lunch after Sam returned from the breakers.

As we were finishing and cleaning up, someone knocked at the door. Glenn had come to the house, and Ray rode along for company. "I think you know why I'm here. Becky, it pains me to do this, but you're going to have to go back to town with me. I have a warrant."

Ray came along to comfort me. "Now, Becky, we know you didn't do anything wrong. We only need to make sure that everything is conducted legally."

Sam stood next to me and put his hand on my shoulder. "Glenn, how could this happen? What's the evidence? You know she's innocent."

"The Moore boy was taken to the Carson City doctor, who claimed that Danny Moore was shot in the back."

"Bullshit." Both Glenn and Ray were surprised by my response. Sam simply smiled and shrugged.

"Becky, I'll get our lawyer, and you'll be out on bail in an hour."

We saddled our two horses, and the four of us rode together to Virginia City. The circuit judge was not in town until the following week. Our lawyer, Mr. Jonas, was away, as well. When we arrived, Millard Moore was at the sheriff's office with an order for me to appear the following morning in the Carson City court, where the committal trial was scheduled to be heard.

Glenn received a telegram from the judge, reading that due to my connections, I would not receive a fair trial in Virginia City. Glenn stated he would bring me over the next day. Despite Millard Moore's insistence that I should be housed in Carson City, there were no instructions from the presiding judge. I would spend the night in the Virginia City jail and be taken to Carson City tomorrow for a preliminary hearing.

I stared at Sam, who planned to organize bail. I was put in a cell while he left to locate a lawyer. I sat on a bed and considered the last two days. How could things go so horribly wrong?

Lauren

Please, earth swallow me now and spare me any more of my father's lectures concerning my failure as a daughter. He didn't put me through school, so I could just run off and not show him the simple courtesy of letting him know I was alive. He ranted for the entire trip to Kentucky.

Occasionally, he would stop to tell me how thankful he was that I was alive, after which he would remind me about the hell that I'd put him and my mother through. "And you can't even tell me where you were? I just don't understand you these days. What happened to my most responsible child?"

"Sorry, Daddy." I reverted to my former name for him in the hopes he would forgive me.

"Don't 'Daddy' me, Lauren. It won't work. I'll never comprehend what you did and the way you completely disregarded your family. Wait until your mother gets ahold of you. I guess the worst part, now that we know you're alive, is my disappointment in you. It was such a selfish act. Tell me you'll never do anything like that again."

I hesitated a little too long. Dad glared at me and really got mad. "Lauren Jeanne Harper, if you ever do something like this again, I swear, I will...." He stopped. I don't remember him using my middle name in years. I needed to take something for a headache.

"No, sir."

The cycle then started again—what was I thinking? Why did I do it? Did I realize the stress I had placed on my mother and him? On and on.

It all stopped when we crossed the Kentucky state line. I was driving, and he was going to have a quick sleep. He slept for about an hour, woke up, and calmly inquired whether I had a good time and if whatever I did was worth it.

"It was until I got in the car with you. I may be reevaluating that, though."

He laughed and warned me again not to do whatever it was I did.

"Dad, I have no reason to ever do what I did, but I can't say for certain."

"Okay. Well, prepare yourself. If you think I'm mad, wait until your mother gets ahold of you."

When I got home, however, she simply hugged me and asked if I was all right.

"Yes, ma'am."

"I assume your father probably ripped strips off you. All I can say is welcome home, you can tell me anything, and I won't judge you."

"Thanks, Mom."

My sole salvation was a reunion with my beautiful, sweet dog. LB curled her lips and made her way in and out of my legs. She wouldn't leave my side, with no yelling and no guilt-tripping, but just pure joy at seeing me. I love that dog.

"Any problems with Ladybug?"

"She's a wonderful dog, Lauren. We'd be happy to keep her, but I can tell she's bonded to you."

"Thanks, Mom."

"Have you heard about your difficulties with the lady stalker or the sheriff's men?" My mother paused and stared at me. "Were you under witness protection? Is that why you couldn't contact us?" Extremely tempting...

"No, but you can believe that was the reason if it helps. May I please take a shower and get some sleep?"

"Of course, honey. Do you want anything?"

"I'll be fine. I just need some sleep. Mom and Dad, I'm sorry. I didn't plan what would happen. It simply did."

Dad lifted my bag. "Do you have a lead weight in here? It weighs a ton."

"No, just a gold bar." That was close to the truth.

"Dinner's at six. Do you want me to wake you up?"

"Yes, please." I was starving. "Where's Jane?"

"She's practicing soccer with her friends. She'll be home later."

"Are we expecting snow tonight? It's freezing."

"Snow or ice. It's supposed to start early tomorrow."

"You haven't sold my clothes, have you? Is my good red jacket in my closet?"

"Sent it to Goodwill last week, along with your Christmas presents."

When Mom woke me up later, the three of us ate dinner. After supper, Dad picked up Janie from soccer practice while Mom and I washed and dried the dishes.

"Mom, is Comstock still on television?"

"That show was on in the afternoon the last time I watched the program. Want to see it with me tomorrow?"

"Will you tickle my back?"

"I'll tickle it now."

"No, I'll call Lisa now."

"Good idea. Lisa's been worried too. Does Jim know where you've been?"

"No one knows. I'm sorry for what I put you and Dad through. I can't discuss it."

"I hope it was worth all the torment you've given us."

I didn't respond to that. "May I use your home phone to call Lisa?"

Mom handed me her cell phone. "It's more private. I hope you haven't been unfaithful to your fiancé through all this."

"No, Mom. Never."

In my bedroom, I dialed Lisa's number. I knew she wouldn't answer. "Lisa, it's me. I'm home with Mom and Dad. Would you call me on the old home number? Not much is new, but I want to hear your voice, sista."

She didn't return my call that night, but the following morning she rang as my father and I were headed to meet with the local police. I agreed to call her back that evening.

The cops couldn't believe that my stalker, whom I now knew as Jasmine MacArthur, was out on bail. Her case was a federal offense since the crime occurred in a national forest. All the charges, lawyers, and even judges were not the same as the local corruption case, which reminded me to call Frank once more.

We changed the phone again and the number, but I emailed it to the Nevada branch of the FBI. If she could track it, this might bring her to an agent, which would assist with her prosecution. I contacted the vet clinic where I was to start work the following month. I mentioned I had to change phones and gave them the new number but asked them to keep it private. In addition, I called Rich, who was back teaching school, and left a similar message for him.

I waited until I was alone at the house to contact Frank. He answered this time around. "Hey, Frank. It's Lauren. Boy, am I glad to hear your voice!"

"I received your message from the other day, but today is my first day back—all good. I survived. Obviously, you did, as well. How's your mom?"

"Alive and still the same. I now understand what you meant when you inquired whether I had watched Comstock."

"Hard to believe. You would swear someone traveled back in time, met the townsfolk and the Buchanans, and created a television series about them by using the actual family as the characters. Did your mom end up marrying Sam Buchanan?"

"Yes, sir. She's still in love and happy."

"How does that make you feel?"

"We all wish our parents stayed together and lived happily ever after, but I'm glad for her. Both of my parents are satisfied with their lives. My dad was apoplectic when I went missing. He was worried, but he's nearly over it. Almost, anyway. Sir, why did the shooter make bail?"

"Good question. It was on some technicality. No one was happy about it, except for Jasmine's lawyer. I recently received a message that the trial date is currently March twenty-third. Lauren, you've got to be careful. She's certifiable and quite dangerous. She would violate her bail conditions in a heartbeat to get rid of you."

"I get that. How about if I stop by when I return to tell you more about my journey?"

"Sounds interesting. I'll have the grilled cheese ready at Meg's Diner."

"Thank you again for all you did. My real mother appreciates it too."

My present-day mother returned from a yoga class. It was too cold for golf.

"Hey, Lauren."

"Hey, Mom."

"Grilled cheese?"

"Sounds good, thanks. Want to watch Comstock after that?"

"Lauren, I'm shocked. I thought it was too unrealistic and boring for you."

"I'd like to see it, anyway."

After lunch, we sat down on the couch. Mom patted her lap, and I shook my head. "Your turn, Mom." She turned on the television. Following a few ads was a story about a racehorse that the Buchanan boys wanted to buy but had no money. I gazed at the actors, and I really couldn't tell much difference. Clint wasn't at the Cattle Creek Ranch when I was there. Hank had been dead for many years, but Sam and Dan appeared much the same, except younger.

Watching them on television was surreal. The more I examined the actor portraying Hank, the more I saw Jim. His army friends were correct that he resembled the television actor who played Hank Buchanan. I tickled my mother's back as she fell asleep. The commercials were so annoying because I wanted to see more. The Cattle Creek Ranch's great room was almost like the real one in which I had been many times. I noticed Sam called the couch a settee in the program, but my real mother termed it a divan. I should look that up. When the show ended, I had tears in my eyes. I was homesick for the Cattle Creek Ranch. No one saw, and I quickly wiped away the tears. I experienced the same feeling in my belly when I was at the Cattle Creek Ranch, thinking about my Kentucky home. Would I be happy in my own place with Jim?

I called Lisa that night on my new phone. She didn't answer. It was a silent number, and I figured she was careful. I texted her a warning that I was trying to call. She picked up on the first ring afterward.

We talked for a while, and I got the update. Lisa had moved on and currently was dating a schoolteacher with no kids. "This is definitely the one."

"How many times have I heard that? I'm doing the eye roll in case you can't see through the airwaves."

"Roll your eyes all you want, big sista, but this is the one. This guy loves cats, and he's a real go-getter."

"Does he start the fire in the morning and light the lamp?"

"Huh? What are you smoking?"

"Just an expression." I smiled to myself. The bar had been raised.

"Do you want to tell me where in the world you have been?"

"Nope."

"Okay, what else is happening? Where's the army man? Any word on when he's coming back?"

"Sadly, no."

"I'm glad you called. Could you put your mother on the phone, so I can have an actual conversation?"

"I start work the first week of February. How's your work?"

"Not as stimulating as I'd hoped, but tolerable."

"You going to stay at the Nevada clinic when Jim Bob gets out?"

"I have a one-year contract. Who knows after that? I assume it will depend on Jim."

"Hey, big sista, got to go. Let's talk in a few days."

"See ya."

The next week consisted of my parents looking at me as though I was an alien. Finally, my mother asked, "What's going on? All you do is watch Comstock and get teary. You couldn't stand it before. Your father and I are worried about you. You never go out, and you aren't even talking to your friends. I'll bet you talked with Lisa only once. Want to talk?"

"I guess it's Jim. I'm sorry. The weather is crap, anyway." I lied like a rug. I missed my mother and her family. I was scared to death about what was happening back in Nevada, and I missed Jim. "I think the Comstock Hank reminds me of Jim, which is why I watch it."

"Lauren, you'll experience plenty of disappointments in life. You can't simply mope around. Consider how much your father suffered when Becky died. He didn't just sit around."

Is she kidding? He was a basket case. She was there only after a time. Doesn't she remember? Sheesh. The same thing was happening to me, but I couldn't say anything about it. I had to grieve in private from now on. I would head back to Nevada in a week, anyway. I needed to get ready for the new job. Because I was going to board at Rich's place, I wouldn't be alone, fortunately. I wasn't sure whether I would ever tell anyone about the last few months. Only sixteen more hours before I can watch another Comstock episode.

Rebecca

Things were getting worse. Sam wasn't allowed to post bail. The trial would be conducted in Carson City, where Danny was known and loved as a larrikin, and I would be housed in the Carson City jail. The committal hearing was scheduled in two days, and Sam was convinced that this would be the end. A buggy transported me to my new facility the following day. Sam was with me, but the Carson City sheriff's deputy was under orders to keep me handcuffed. Sam attempted to shield me from being seen, but a crowd had formed outside the Virginia City jail. Most were supporters, but not all of them. A few people called me a murderer as I emerged from the jail en route to Carson City.

Sam was not permitted to touch me, and he could watch only from a distance. He rode along to keep an eye out for any individuals who wished to harass me or possibly take the law into their own hands. Ray came too, and he talked with the Carson City deputy about fishing and the general lay of the land. I could tell he was assessing the situation without arousing the deputy's suspicions.

I arrived near a mob of angry townspeople, many of whom loved the victim. I only knew that he was a wastrel. The lawyer Sam hired was a nervous young man who clearly lacked the necessary experience to defend me. Sam seemed shocked and even recommended a delay of the initial hearing. The judge, who would not hear of this, refused to consider bail. The judge repeatedly called Millard Moore, Danny's father, by his first name, while he addressed my attorney by his last name.

The initial hearing was conducted that afternoon. Because the single eyewitness was unable to attend, her aunt—Mrs. Gardiner—was instructed to recount what her niece said to her. I turned to my attorney to suggest he should object to hearsay evidence. Still, he simply stared at the judge and stated nothing. The doctor who examined the body noted, for the record, that the bullet hole indicated the man had been shot in the back. I demanded that my lawyer have the doctor describe the wounds and question him about his medical training. He didn't and sat silently in his chair.

Sam sat behind us and tapped him on the shoulder, but the young man was frozen and wouldn't respond to Sam's attempts to attract his attention. The initial hearing required no longer than thirty minutes, and neither the prosecution, defense, nor Carson City sheriff called me to testify. Glenn tried to talk but was told to sit down, or he would be in contempt of court.

The judge dismissed us all and announced he would hand down his decision the following day. I was returned to a new cell in Carson City, in an individual section, yet the other prisoners could see me. Two of them made hanging noises and repeatedly told me I would swing in the breeze.

Sam wasn't allowed in the cell and could speak to me for only a few minutes before the door to the cell was shut. I glared at the men who were in various states of drunkenness and turned away. I pretended to sleep. The sole salvation was that the food was good. I wasn't allowed to talk with anyone who was not in jail. In addition, I didn't receive any communication from the attorney. I listened to the men making grotesque noises and lewd comments all night.

The nights spent in the San Francisco jail were much more manageable than what I was experiencing this time. I wondered if my jailer, Raymond O'Keefe, was still alive. This incarceration was terrible, but I understood I would soon have the best lawyer money could buy. I waited for the dawn and prayed that Sam was able to identify a worthy advocate. I was appalled that the dead man's father was serving as the prosecuting attorney. I had no idea whether appeals existed in these days.

At mid-morning, I was shackled and brought into court. I wasn't allowed to talk to anyone. Sam, Dan, and Jenny were there. I didn't see Ray Thompson or Glenn Frasier from the Virginia City sheriff's department. Both of my colleagues, John Harmon and Alf Webber, were present, as well. They nodded when I glanced at them. I wondered who was running the hospital.

The young lawyer who was supposed to represent me entered with Mr. Moore from the judge's chambers. My attorney wouldn't look at me. When I said good morning, he replied I was not allowed to speak at a committal hearing.

The judge proceeded to summate the evidence against me. I stood up, and my attorney attempted to make me sit down. He had little chance. I was enraged and lost no time describing this trial as a farce and saying I wanted to speak on my own behalf. Several of my friends rose, but the judge told us all to sit down, or he would lock everyone in jail for contempt. "Mrs. Buchanan, this is not the place for you to speak. You may have your say during the trial that will take place in two weeks." He stated that he would try this case.

"Judge, Your Honor, my name is Dr. Buchanan, I have medical knowledge, and I can..."

Hammering his gavel, the judge cut me off, and I was directed to sit down. "Just because you have some remedial medical training does not allow you to question what is presented as facts by our town doctor and this establishment. You may instruct your lawyer to speak for you in any future dealings when your trial starts."

I was still shackled and led out. Sam tried to touch me, but the second deputy blocked him. "Bec, don't worry. I have a lawyer who'll straighten out this situation, and I've contacted the governor. I won't let anything happen to you, darling."

I smiled and mouthed, "Thank you." I was sent back to my cell and to my new friends, who yelled abuse at me. In the afternoon, only one person was permitted to visit me. Sam had gone to secure the lawyer, and Dan and Jenny had to return home. Gee Ling and Hanna were at the Cattle Creek Ranch, babysitting the children. They had their hands full. Ray Thompson entered the room in which we were all locked up.

"Becky, I'm so sorry about this. Don't worry. Sam's doing all he can, and you'll be fine. We know you're innocent. I'll stake my life on it."

"Thanks, Ray." The catcalling and abuse from the other prisoners continued during our visit. Ray peered at the men and shook his head.

"Let me try to sort this out."

An hour later, I was escorted to the basement, where the solitary-confinement prisoners were kept. While it was dark, cold, and isolated, it was peaceful, and I could do my bodily functions and sleep for the first time in two days.

Sam arrived the next day with a friend of a friend, who was organizing yet another friend to run the case. Mr. Jonas explained his expertise was not criminal law and suggested several men, who were not able to come on such short notice. Sam didn't know the lawyer's name. However, this lawyer was in California, He was headed back East, and would come to assist us. Sam had been assured he was an excellent lawyer. I was dubious, but I didn't have any options.

I was confident that Hanna and the rest of my family members were as good as they could be. The hospital was back running, and all was well at the Cattle Creek Ranch. Sam provided some food, which Gee Ling had prepared. The jailers, who examined it, would bring it down later.

Sam brought me some reading material, but it was dark. The single lamp that hung away from my cell made reading difficult. I was furnished with paper, ink, and a pen to record everything I could recall concerning the entire incident. I couldn't write down the surgical findings of the pregnancy, which were key to me. The woman was a liar through and through. If we could get her on the stand to question her, I think she would break down and confess that she lied about what happened that evening.

My most significant concern was the lawyer's ability to vigorously represent my story. I entertained severe doubts since everyone had failed to stand up to these corrupt men. I needed to meet the lawyer to talk with him before the trial, which was currently only a few days away.

I was finally allowed a short visit with my husband. I couldn't believe what was happening. "Sam, for goodness' sake, who is this guy?"

"Becky, I'm trying to find out. All I know is that, according to several lawyers, if the judge from Sacramento approved of him, he would be more than adequate. We must keep the faith."

"I can't leave this up to a friend of a friend. This is my life here. Please get Mr. Jonas to be there. If not, I'll do it myself." We held hands through the bar. I could tell the strain was taking its toll on us both. "Please tell Hanna how much I love her and everyone else. Do you have any word about who chooses the jury yet?"

"Just some Carson City citizens, which may not be a good thing."

"Oh, hell. Everyone in town seems to be behind this Moore lawyer. If there is one person who isn't, I have yet to meet him."

"Don't swear, Becky."

I laughed and gazed at Sam, astounded. "I will go to the gallows to swing in a few days, and you're worrying about swearing?" I might have expressed a few more expletives after that, which did make Sam laugh.

Sam was asked to leave. He had my papers, and he promised that if the lawyer came that day, he would give them to him. He was also digging around to some extent. We kissed through the bars. My heart sank, and I lay down on the cot, turned away, and cried silently. I thought about Hanna, Lauren, and the grandchildren, but my sadness was more for the loss of my husband.

Even Hanna could see me the following day. I talked with everyone and stared at Sam, who shook his head. The lawyer had not shown up. "Can we delay this trial?"

"I've already requested that. The judge wants to go fishing and will not postpone it."

"Fishing? Well, at least that's a reasonable excuse. In the remote chance that I survive, I want to go to Hank Heaven as soon as possible. Come to think of it, I figure I'm going up there either way." We both wanted to be buried in the valley next to each other. I certainly didn't plan on being first and having it happen so soon.

I was permitted to clean myself the following morning. Sam brought a green-velvet dress, which was sent down to me. I dressed and did my hair as best as I could. I was taken upstairs and escorted to the courtroom down the street while the entire town witnessed me in handcuffs. I entered the room where Dan, Jenny, Ray, and Glenn were present, but not Sam. The courtroom was filled, the jury was seated, and the only people missing were Sam, a lawyer, and the judge. My heart sank. The jurors would not look at me. *Bastards.*

Chapter 23

Lauren

I had to wait for a few days to leave Kentucky. Because the weather was brutal, my father banned me from going. My dad, the new vet clinic, and the FBI had my phone number. If the stalker, Jasmine, could acquire this number, I knew where the leak was coming from. Since I didn't want to blow my chances with the vet clinic, I didn't mention any of my troubles.

LB and I arrived back in Nevada after three days on the road. I was glad to be back home. No new letters had come from Jim, but I received messages from the clinic that an earlier start would be appreciated as several individuals fell ill.

Mary called to leave a message with Rich that we were expected for dinner as soon as I returned. Rocky's friends,

Phoebe and Brad Lay, had invited us for dinner and a winter ride. The trail to Miner's Meadow, which I secretly called Hank Heaven, was too icy and treacherous. We would ride down in the desert, where the footpath was flat and the snow was minimal.

I left a message for Ted, a fellow worker from my old vet practice. I gave Rich's number to everyone. I hoped he didn't mind. I hadn't seen him yet. I used Rich's home phone to call the facility where Rosa, my former intellectually disabled co-worker at my old clinic, was living. She was eating dinner, and the staff requested that I call back in an hour. I showered and marveled once again at the fantastic invention of hot running water, which I would think about forever. I decided to go to town only if Rich was with me for the first few days. After that, I would become the carefree, independent woman I had been just a few months ago.

Rosa was able to come to the telephone when I called her home again. She was happy I phoned. No baseball games were being shown on television. Thanks to her boyfriend, though, she had become enamored with basketball. They watched it every night, and things were going well in the romance department. Rosa reminded me that I should not bring LB if I visited her. The boyfriend doesn't like dogs. I assured her that I would not take a dog.

Snow was predicted over the weekend, and I believed it was prudent not to raise her expectations. I would probably not be there for about a month. I explained I was beginning a new job and had to be on call frequently. She instructed me to call in the morning or early afternoon as she watched basketball in the evening. I think I was kicked to the curb.

I told her to take care and give the boyfriend a kiss for me, to which she replied that kissing was out of the question. It was against the rules, and she wasn't going to be kicked out of her new home for anything. "No kissing, Lauren, not even from you."

Rich returned later in the day and inquired whether I wished to accompany him to the gym. "No, thanks." I was still feeling buff from my time in the 1800s. I would be joining him for a bit of body upkeep soon, but nothing needed tweaking yet. I had to keep myself in shape for the return of my fiancé, but that might not be for months. No sense in worrying too much about that issue.

Rich flexed his gorgeous muscles. "Since I'm expecting lover boy next week, I gotta keep myself fit and trim."

"Half your luck, roomie. Want me to find another place to live for a time?"

"No way. Jim and I arrived at an agreement about your upkeep. I would hate to tangle with him if I didn't maintain my end of the bargain."

"What kind of agreement?"

"I'm supposed to lay down my life for you and generally make sure you're alive and healthy when he gets back. He offered me a bonus if you're still interested in him, but I declined."

"Was any actual money involved?"

"He offered, but not beside the rent. I also have my standards. I need you too much if my horse is sick."

"Don't I pay the rent?"

"No, you're paid up for twelve months. Too bad Jim isn't gay. I could go for him."

I was confused. I loved Rich and appreciated his care for me. Still, I was somewhat put out that I wasn't informed about this 'agreement.' I was forfeiting my independence. I decided not to stir the pot yet. "Thanks, I guess. Is there anything else I should know?"

"Your birthday is coming up, which he has covered, as well, but I can't tell you about that yet."

"Nope, all good." I'm totally in love. Sam Buchanan and my dad have met their equal and then some. "May I cook for dinner?"

"I don't know, can you now? I saw no evidence of that a few months ago."

I retrieved a knife and walked toward him. "No more of that kind of talk, cowboy. I have a man to impress."

"Okay, wait until I get back, and we'll have some cooking lessons for the culinarily impaired."

"Be still my beating heart. I might just watch some DVDs I brought back with me."

"Anything I might want to watch?"

"Old *Comstock* episodes."

"Never mind. I have homework to grade. *Comstock*? To each her own."

I watched part of a *Comstock* episode and once again cried. This was a sad one, but it wasn't sad due to the plot. It was depressing for me to watch characters from the series. I had to remember that they were all dead now. That really sent me over the edge. I turned it off, went to my room, lay down on the bed, and hugged LB. If only my mother had been in any of the episodes, I could have been happy.

When Rich came back, he commented he encountered my emergency docs, Cary and Mel. "We'll go to the Coffee

Café first thing in the morning. You have some *splaining* to do."

Rich and I drove down for the morning ritual of coffee and sweet rolls the next day. Mel was there early. She was scheduled to work in an hour. Cary was just coming off work. "Your offsider was in last night." I was puzzled. "Ted twisted his ankle. Not bad, but he remarked he received a phone call from you and missed the number."

"Is he still in the hospital?"

"No, long gone. Ted wanted a certificate to get out of work, but I encouraged him to 'man up' to care for the little cats and doggies."

Cary arrived and gave me a hug. "Long time, no see. Where in the world have you been?"

"Sorry, can't tell, a state secret, or something like that." I guessed they assumed the cop case had driven me away.

"Want to come over for a party next weekend? We're both off duty at the same time for once. I'll even introduce you to my new partner." Mel was beaming, but Cary rolled her eyes.

"This weekend or next weekend?"

"Next weekend. It's a three-day weekend."

"All right. What can Rich and I bring?" We discussed options. Rich mentioned his friend was going to be in town and would be coming too.

"Oh, interesting!"

"Don't give him too much of a hard time 'cause he may be the one."

I figured Rich had told Cary and Mel about his life choices.

Rich drove me back to his place. I was alone in the house when a rock sailed through the living-room window. I called the police, who searched the premises and checked the surveillance cameras Rich had installed. The camera view showed the rock coming through, but not who threw it. They were barely out of sight. I was shaken and left a message for Rich. I called a glazier and waited for him. I moved my car to the secure garage at the back of the property. Nothing more happened that day. Was it the stalker or Kenny, the dope grower, or the corrupt cops?

At last, Ted called me through Rich. He was hobbling around at work. He liked the new owners and vets at our old clinic. I told him I'd talked to Rosa, who was happy in her new facility, which was a relief to both of us. We planned to meet for lunch as soon as I had a schedule. I gave him my number and made him aware the stalker was still around, and he cautioned me to be careful.

I had a lunch date with my time-traveling friend, Frank Lash, at Meg's Diner. Rich wanted to accompany me for protection, but I needed to talk to Frank alone. I arrived, and he was already there in a booth away from the rest of the patrons. He hugged me and asked if I wanted the grilled cheese.

"That depends on who's paying."

"My treat?"

"No. I believe I owe you one. I'll have soup and salad."

"I'd advise against it."

"Okay, grilled cheese it is."

"So?" Frank folded his hands and stared at the menu.

I told Frank about my arrival and the flooding. I then explained how I lost most of the items I took to give to my mother. I described meeting the Buchanans and, eventually, my mother and stepsister. In addition, I outlined my adventures with the Indians and the cattle drive. I inquired if he knew Pam Wilkins, which he did.

"Did you know she was also a time traveler?"

"Not a clue. Are you certain?"

"Yep. The bad news is Pam passed away."

Frank stared at me curiously. "Lauren, they're all dead now."

When I considered this fact, my previous sorrow returned. "Yeah, I guess they are." We ate in silence. I related my return with the diving suit, how Sam had buried a gun, and that I had left the wetsuit after I emerged. "You know, wearing a wetsuit would make it fairly safe to go back and forth, flooding aside."

"Have you considered going back?"

"No, not really. My mother understood I had a life here. I'm waiting for my fiancé to return from his deployment."

"I'm not going back, either."

We kept eating in silence. When we finished, I thanked Frank again for all his assistance. I will never forget his efforts to reunite me with my mother and her family. He warned me not to attend Jasmine's trial. "You never know. Knowing this jurisdiction, the way I do, she might just receive a suspended sentence." I hugged him and left. In two days, I was going to start my new job. I had the adventure of my life, thanks to that man. I would be forever grateful to him.

Rebecca

The onlookers were becoming restless since they were there for a hangin'. The jailer explained that when, and not if, I was judged guilty, I would be hung a day or two after the verdict. I was sure I remembered a *Comstock* episode in which the Buchanans and their ranch hands broke one of the sons out of jail in a similar circumstance. I believed this would be my only chance. Possibly this action is what spelled the end of the Buchanan dynasty. Perhaps either we all were shot or went into hiding. I saw no other way out.

Finally, the judge exited his chambers. The judge appeared flustered when he noticed the state governor seated in the gallery behind me. He stared at the prosecutor, Millard Moore, and smiled weakly. He would not look at me directly. He banged his gavel several times to quiet the gallery of onlookers. "It seems that Mrs. Buchanan's followers are so convinced of her guilt that they did not even hire anyone to represent her. However, this court does not ascertain anyone's guilt or innocence without conducting a fair trial. Mrs. Buchanan, do you want to proceed to represent yourself?"

As I stood up to reply, my knees were nearly buckling. Despite the bitter cold of the room, I was sweating profusely. How could Sam abandon me? He must be planning to break me out of jail. "Your Honor, I..." Right at that time, though, a door at the back of the court opened, and in strode Sam and a lean, good-looking man with an exceedingly pronounced mustache.

It had been more than ten years, but I recognized the gentleman from my time in New York. I almost cried out when he smiled and hugged me as he joined me at the table. He had a folder full of papers, and he whispered in my ear. "Hello, Becky. You have no need to worry anymore. I'm here." I glanced toward Sam, who grinned from ear to ear as he sat down next to Dan and Ray.

"Oliver, I can't believe you're here." Oliver Wendell Holmes Jr., who would serve as the head of the Supreme Court in future years, was my counsel. I now stood a chance of acquittal. "But how did you? How's your father? I can't believe you're here." My heart was racing, and my sense of hope was returning.

"Becky, I wouldn't have passed this up for the world. When I heard the circumstances and learned it was you, I just had to come. My father's fine."

The judge was unaware of this man's ability to know and interpret the law and handle himself in court. Oliver outmaneuvered him at every turn. It was a spectacle of beauty. Oliver had me released from the handcuffs. I reached back to touch Sam's hand, which was so comforting. I turned around to notice all my friends smiling for the first time. Alf was present, but John stayed back at the hospital for a delivery, which advanced more slowly than anticipated.

The prosecutor's opening statement was short and incoherent. An upstanding citizen of Carson City was visiting a dear friend in the Virginia City hospital when a crazed woman pretending to be a doctor shot him in the back. He went on for a minute to describe his son as a hardworking, caring, and friendly lad in his prime.

He added that the deceased had an ongoing relationship with the young woman. He simply tried to protect her and ensure that she was adequately cared for following an operation to remove her infected appendix. He was shot in the back while safeguarding her from any unnecessary surgery.

I turned toward Mrs. Gardiner, who was seated in the first row of the gallery, directly behind Mr. Moore. She occasionally dabbed at her eyes with a folded handkerchief. I scribbled notes, quickly wrote the words ectopic pregnancy on a piece of paper, and handed it to Oliver, who smiled. I indicated to him that the finding could not be shared due to client-patient confidentiality. He nodded and smiled once again. I glanced at him and shrugged, but he put his hand on mine and squeezed it. I turned back toward Sam, who nodded. I assumed he and Oliver had already discussed this information.

In Oliver's opening statement, he described a totally different scenario. He provided my medical training and the history of my work in the prominent Baltimore hospital. He read a telegram from Dr. Benjamin Meyers, who headed the hospital, and confirmed I was a well-qualified surgeon.

He suggested that the deceased was not the hardworking, caring man a grieving father portrayed. In fact, Danny was anything but that. Millard Moore objected, but Oliver continued recounting the events of the evening, the autopsy results, and the jump to conclusions. He claimed he would prove that the man was not shot in the back. Oliver spent a few sentences detailing the autopsy doctor's lack of knowledge, compared with the extent of my formal training. The

Carson City doctor had been trained purely by apprenticeship from a veterinarian.

I turned around, and Sam had his arms crossed. He leaned back in his chair and smiled. I returned the smile because I was still unsure of the outcome, but things were looking up. Jenny reached forward and touched my hand, which was a great comfort.

The prosecution presented its evidence. The primary evidence was the eyewitness account of Mrs. Gardiner's niece, Lila Crompton, who wasn't in the courtroom. There was a murmur when she was brought in. As she was called to the stand, two deputies escorted her and held her upright. Lila was sworn in and took a seat next to the judge. The judge glanced at her, smiled, and even patted her hand while the prosecutor asked her questions.

She described the day from the time she woke up to the moment when I shot Danny Moore. Lila was an incredibly compelling witness, and I could tell the jury was sympathetic to her testimony—that is until Oliver got a hold of her.

"Miss, or is it Mrs. Crompton?"

"Miss," she replied with a sweet smile.

"Ah, excellent. Miss Crompton, we're glad you received such excellent care from the surgical skills of Dr. Buchanan, which allows you to keep enjoying good health." He paused. "Are you aware that the type of abdominal pain you experienced that fateful day could have many causes? An inflamed appendix is not the sole condition accompanied by such horrific pain."

"No, sir. I have no medical knowledge."

"Other causes exist. In fact, the condition of an ectopic pregnancy would be far more common in a young woman of childbearing age, such as yourself."

"I am not aware."

"Am not, or was not, Miss Crompton? Didn't this topic emerge while discussing the possible scenarios after your operation? I'm not suggesting that was your cause of abdominal pain. I'm simply suggesting that you were informed of the causes in general."

Lila appeared agitated. Millard Moore objected to this line of inquiry. The judge sustained the question and asked Oliver what questions about the type of surgery spoke to the case of Mrs. Buchanan's guilt or innocence.

"I'm establishing witness credibility, Your Honor."

Oliver turned to Lila and paused. She was confused. Without anyone asking, she concurred that an ectopic pregnancy was mentioned. Still, she didn't know what it meant. Her answer was to be ignored by the jury members, but they heard it.

"Now, Miss Crompton, would you say you were a close friend of Danny Moore?"

"Yes, I would say I was a close friend."

"Miss Crompton, do you have many friends or friends who were as close to you as Danny was?"

"No, he is my closest friend."

"If you knew that Danny had impregnated many women, would you be surprised?" Before Mr. Moore could object, the look on her face said it all. She was shocked and furious. Millard Moore opposed the line of questioning, which was discontinued.

"Miss Crompton, if you were pregnant at the time of surgery, and we aren't saying you were, could anyone else have been responsible for that?"

Again, Mr. Moore objected to the question, and Lila was ordered not to answer that one. She was instructed to describe her recollection of the night following the surgery. She explained in detail the evening and subsequent confrontation on the second appearance of the deceased. Her explanation was exact, and her description of the entire scenario was recalled in a precise manner.

"Miss Crompton, thankfully, your memory is extraordinary, considering you were waking up from anesthesia. Most people would not be able to remember such detail at a time like that. Can you tell me which deputy came in after Dr. Buchanan left for help?"

"I cannot, sir."

"Well, maybe you can tell me where the body was lying when he fell?"

"I don't recall."

"Can you tell me the reason Danny was on top of you when Dr. Buchanan woke up?"

"I don't remember."

"Can you tell me if Danny's pants were on when he was shot?"

Lila just stared ahead. The gallery was silent, and the jurors were looking at her. "Miss Crompton, I can tell I have exhausted you. Do you mind closing your eyes for a moment?" She did and seemed puzzled. "Can you tell me the color of Dr. Buchanan's dress?"

"Green," Lila announced. She peeked once and afterward closed her eyes.

"And what color is my tie?" She didn't answer. "Maybe you can tell me the color of Mr. Moore's tie." Again, no answer was forthcoming. "You see, Miss Crompton, it can be quite difficult to recall detail under a stressful situation, such as speaking at a trial or recovering from life-saving surgery. We are done with this witness, Your Honor."

Mr. Moore didn't pose any further questions. I was pleased. We got the idea across that perhaps Lila had an ectopic pregnancy without admitting it. The possible father was Carson City's well-loved citizen, Danny Moore. Sam tapped me on the shoulder and gave me a squeeze.

The next witness was the doctor who'd performed the autopsy on Danny Moore. His handwritten report had been submitted to the court. Oliver studied the paper but had a hard time deciphering the writing. He examined other filings and smiled.

Millard Moore asked that the doctor inform the jury about his training. The doctor explained that he earned his medical education by following a doctor for several years. Oliver inquired how the doctor who trained him was trained. Was it formal education or by the method he had learned? The Carson City doctor responded it was in the same manner he had himself trained.

Oliver noted that this way was legal, and this educational method had produced some outstanding doctors in some cases. He asked the young doctor whether he could name the prominent muscle in the forearm below the elbow. Oliver removed his jacket and rolled his sleeve to show the man where he was pointing. The doctor couldn't name the muscle.

"It is difficult to read your report about the autopsy of Danny Moore. Do you mind reading it for me?" Oliver handed the paper to him, and the young doctor stared at it with pursed lips. He was profusely sweating and dabbed his forehead several times with a handkerchief.

The doctor attempted to read the paper, but it was clear he could not make out his own handwriting. Oliver handed him another piece of paper, and the doctor read it effortlessly.

"You can read this piece of paper, but not your own?"

"That second paper you gave me is my paper."

"Yes, it came from your office. What isn't in your handwriting is the autopsy report."

"No, sir, that is not my handwriting."

"Do you know whose handwriting it is?"

"No, sir."

"If you will indulge me." Oliver came out from behind the table and took two papers to the jury. They studied them and nodded. I figured many of them could not read or write, but the similarity of the writing would not be lost on them. "This is Millard Moore's handwriting."

The doctor seemed uncomfortable. Mr. Moore objected, and the judge again sustained the objection. Damage done, and point established. Oliver instructed the doctor to describe Danny's wounds. The doctor mentioned a bullet hole in Danny's abdomen, with black speckles and a similar lesion on the back. He described the entry and exit holes as comparable in size, which did not make sense, but then the jury was not aware of the science of forensics.

"While Miss Crompton stated Dr. Buchanan shot him in the back from the position of the bed, the wounds would line up only if she had fired from above him. The other curious thing is that no one ever found the bullet that exited the body. How could that be?"

The doctor stared at Mr. Moore. "I'm not sure, sir."

"To prove this, we will need to exhume the body to check for the bullet."

The crowd murmured. The judge called for order and recommended lunchtime adjournment. He called both Oliver and Mr. Moore into his office behind the podium.

I was handcuffed and taken into a small room off to the side of the courtroom. Sam could come in for a minute. We just gazed at each other, and he held my hand. The deputy stayed in the room, and we didn't discuss the case. After a few minutes, I was brought a small bowl of soup, and Sam was asked to consult with Oliver. I was left alone with the deputy. He was a friendly but simple man. He observed it was too bad I was going through all this when it was plain the jury had been selected to ensure I would lose.

I was shocked but tried to remain calm. Some motion had been made to delay any further testimony while the body was exhumed. That should settle it. I was escorted back to jail. What had to be a solid case in favor of my innocence was now looking like a debacle. Ray visited me, and I told him what the deputy said. We had to whisper since the guard stood a few feet away. He said he would pass all this on to Sam and Oliver.

"Becky, you've definitely lived an interesting life. You've met some fascinating people in your travels."

"Ray, *have lived*? I'm not dead yet."

"Sorry, I just can't understand why Millard wants to punish you so much. He knows his son was a rounder. I almost have the feeling he has another motive."

I considered what Ray said. "You know, you may be right. Could you inform Sam about what you said to me? Maybe there is another motive." Ray left, and I was alone once again. I was convinced I was doomed this morning, but I thought I had a good chance when Oliver Wendell Holmes walked into the courtroom. When the deputy told me the jury was stacked, though, my hopes plummeted. I was back to where I was at the start of the day. Once again, my hopes were dashed.

CHATER 24

Lauren

Big day. I was going to start my new job, and Rich's friend, Dirk, would arrive later today. With two big hunky blokes, how could I get hurt? When I got up, Rich had packed a lunch pail, including homemade chocolate-chip cookies and some cheese and crackers for a snack. He sent me off early and wished me well before heading off to school. Rich would come straight home to greet Dirk when he got there. I guessed I would be late, but it was winter, and the work tended to be slow.

When I arrived at the clinic, I parked my car out of sight behind the main building. I walked inside and discovered flowers and balloons. I thanked the receptionists, but they laughed. "Not us. Look in the envelope. We want to know too."

I opened the card, which was from Jim. I was assured he had arranged it with Rich. I texted Rich to thank him. He sent back a heart to say he was supporting the troops the only way he could. I explained to an older woman, who seemed to be the practice manager, that my fiancé was deployed. He had arranged for the flowers through my roommate. She took me into her office, where I completed paperwork and was furnished with a scrub top with the company logo on it. I had several horse calls for my initial day. Many of the clients from the old clinic had waited for me to begin working again. It was cold, yet the sky was clear. Snow was forecast for later, but I could get through the day and be home by dinnertime if I worked efficiently. "Don't expect that luxury in the summer."

"Yes, ma'am."

"I'm Dot. We're all first-name people, but we refer to the vets as doctors when speaking with the clients. You should update both your medical notes and billing before you go home. The money comes out of your salary if you don't collect it. You'll receive a bonus if you exceed our expectations. Your contract is for a year. Any suggestion of a raise in that time is highly frowned upon.

"We'll send a technician with you the first week, but you will be on your own after that. You'll be on call two nights a week and every third weekend. We don't mind if you trade or swap your after-hours, but you need to anticipate doing the minimum. The boss will ask you to take his after-hours regularly. I recommend that you accept maybe one night per week, but don't let him coerce you into any more than that. He wants you to go with him on the first call of the morning to talk with you and give you the lowdown on how we like things to work. Any questions?"

"May I have a raise?"

Dot stared at me and burst out laughing. "Ah, no. I think you'll fit in well."

"Here is an important question. Where is the boss?"

She glanced over my shoulder to point to a stocky, gray-haired man, who was about my height. He appeared to be in his fifties. He wore old green coveralls, and he was looking at my flowers. Dot introduced me to him.

"Lauren Harper?"

"Yes, sir."

"Doug. Doug Colfax. Pleased to meet you and thank you for coming when we needed you. It seems you have somewhat of a following around this area. You already have a clientele who wants your services. So sorry about Rocky. He was a top guy. Well, let's ride."

I followed him out to one of the three trucks, all outfitted with vet-pack inserts in the truck bed. "Nice. Where are we going, sir?"

"Call me Doug, not sir. We're headed up to Brad and Phoebe Lay's property. I believe you know them. Anyway, they think the sun shines out of your ear." I laughed at that. "I sutured a laceration on their colt last week. We'll check on how it's doing, then we're scheduled to radiograph a bull's leg. That should be fun. If we have time, we may see some of your other clients before lunch. After that, I'll drive you back to the clinic, and you can take Sara to head off for a few other calls."

"Sounds good." I was thrilled to be back at work. I was eager to try the new digital X-ray machine, which was all automated. It should take some beautiful radiographs if we kept it warm in the truck.

Phoebe hugged me as soon as we arrived. The boss stood back while I sedated the horse and changed the wrap. I quietly proposed a change of the topical dressing and a thicker, tighter bandage because the wound was breaking down in parts.

Doug observed me and smiled. "It's your case now. Do whatever you feel is best."

"Yes, sir."

"Jeez, will you stop calling me 'sir'? I'm Doug when we aren't in front of clients. New clients, anyway."

"Sorry, sir. I'm from the South. It's just what we do there."

"The South, huh? I would never have guessed." He used an exaggerated Southern accent that made me laugh.

"Relax. This isn't an interview. We're desperate for a vet, and any warm body would do. You'd be hard-pressed to break the contract and leave us. Isn't your father a vet, as well?"

"Yes, sir. I mean Doug. It's hard to break twenty-five years of conditioning in a single day."

"Work on it. It makes me feel old to be called 'sir.'"

When Phoebe returned with her credit card, I billed her and ran the card. All that remained was the medical record, which had to be done on the computer. As we left, I promised to come for dinner as soon as I could. Doug cautioned me not to get too close to the clients. "There are limits to what you will do for people. You could kill yourself in this business, Lauren. Take time for yourself."

"Thanks for the advice." I think this guy might be alright. He's younger than my father, but I could see they seem to have similar values. I wondered how he would react if his daughter vanished for several months. Ugly.

We next drove to a feedlot, where the cattle numbers were low as it was winter. We stepped inside a large shed. The first pen held a bull carrying his front leg. Other than setting up the X-ray machine, Doug stood back to let me assess the bull. He was three-legged-lame and had a large puncture wound. We sedated him and carefully slid the plate under his forearm—three guesses who got the honors of holding the X-ray plate!

Oh, my God. I've been through a time warp, captured by Indians, and on a harrowing cattle drive, and now a bull will kill me, and I will never see Jim again. The trick was to get in quickly and get out. We set up the machine and had the bull restrained, but it wasn't working. We knocked him down with some half hitches around his chest, and at least he was down on the ground. He was awake. It appeared the sedation had only dulled his responses. Still, the most he could do was paddle, which made getting the radiograph difficult, but I wouldn't be killed.

The radiograph was a shocker. Having a digital system was quite exciting. When the picture came up on a computer screen, we all tried to see it by hovering around the display. Inside the lesion on the leg was a long wire wrapped around the pastern.

Doug emitted a slow whistle. The wire had to come out. This wasn't going to happen with the bull awake. The plan was to take him off food, so he wouldn't regurgitate when anesthetized, after which there would be an attempt to remove the wire. The strategy was for Doug and his associate to come back in two days. I wasn't going to be invited, which was particularly disappointing. When we returned to the truck, Doug noticed my discontent.

"Lauren, he's a valuable bull, which is vital to their operation. I need the best and most experienced vets I can offer."

"I understand. I would simply like to be a fly on the wall."

"Your day will come. You have the next forty years to experience fun procedures like this."

"Yes, sir. I mean, Doug." If this were Rocky's practice, I would be present. The trade-off was I was part of a team, and they would only allow me to do what they believed I could do well. I wouldn't be thrown to the lions, and I had access to some superior equipment. We returned to the clinic, where another bunch of flowers had been delivered to me. The card read, *Loren, don't screw up, Jimmy.* The spelling was the first key.

I was shocked. These flowers had to come from Jasmine. *How was she even aware that I was working here?* I didn't want to alarm the staff on my first day. I don't think they would hire a vet with a crazy lady stalking her. During my lunch, I stepped outside to call the FBI. I was patched straight through to the agent handling the case. I offered the name of the florist and details. They agreed to follow up on this lead.

The rest of the day went well. No unauthorized deaths. Phew. Sara was fantastic to work with. She was a good horsewoman who raised Arabians. She knew where all the drugs were, and we breezed through the afternoon. At the end of the day, Doug asked whether I wanted to answer and accept his after-hours calls tonight and later in the week.

"Certainly, but I'll expect a night off in return if Brad Pitt asks me out."

"I thought you were engaged?"

"Oh, we each have an out clause. Mine is Brad Pitt, and Jim's is Scarlett Johansson."

"Just remember that it's foaling season. Have you had a dystocia yet?"

"Kind of. It was an abortion, but it was nearly a full-term pregnancy. I did foal watch at Auburn, where I witnessed numerous foalings and a couple of dystocias. I performed one last year for your client, if you recall."

"Oh, yeah. Call me if you have one. I think it's always best if we use a tag-team approach for those."

Doug gave me his personal number, and I took the truck and went home. I would park it in the garage since I was taking no chances. I called on my way home and was told to hurry because they wanted to eat. I arrived, took the truck to the back, and locked it in the garage. Rich was wary that my possessions were at risk. He gave me the best of everything, including the garage, to keep the stalker from any more vandalism.

Dirk was everything I expected and then some—good-looking, charming, and quite well educated. He read the classics and didn't watch television at all. Dirk was funny and not overly sensitive. I would never have guessed that either he or Rich was gay. I was in love. He cooked, sang, and cleaned as though we were going to have an army inspection.

I can't remember when I laughed so much. Rich and Dirk were hysterical together. Dirk planned to stay for a month. He was a firefighter in trade with another local firefighter. The Nevada station sent a man down to Arizona while Dirk replaced him up here. He was not excited about the snow. According to him, however, sometimes one must make sacrifices for love.

I feigned disgust. "Oh, please."

I learned about Dirk's history. He was raised in Arizona and attended the University of Arizona. He played baseball. He didn't come out until after graduation. Dirk has a large family, and there were not any issues with his choices. He was loved and happy in his life. He was enamored with Rich, and I already realized how Rich felt. It was fun to be part of it.

"I hate to spoil the party with bad news, but I received two floral arrangements from Jim today."

Rich was immediately upset. "What do you mean? I only sent one bouquet under army orders."

I left the flowers at the clinic but brought both cards home. Rich recognized which one he sent. A different florist sent the second arrangement.

"When will this bitch get her dues?"

Dirk seemed alarmed. "Tell me more, Lauren." I only recounted the basics for him, including the rock sailing through the window. I immediately acquired a new ally. "Okay, partner." Dirk turned to Rich. "We'll take turns going on emergencies with our little sister. She doesn't ever go alone."

"Move over, Rich, because I have a new 'favorite Brosky.'" I put my arm inside Dirks and smirked at Rich.

"I figured this would happen. I'm moved to second place after only one meal."

"There's more to it than that. But that's enough for tonight." Rich probably realized that I was referring to the corruption case, as well.

"Yeah, we don't want to scare him off on the first night. Does anyone want dessert?"

My business phone rang. A dog had been hit by a car. Dirk did the honors, and we went to the clinic together. When I evaluated the dog, I recognized it had a severed spine in the lumbar area. I explained this diagnosis to the owners, who already suspected it was hopeless. I did the deed, and the grieving owners left the dog for cremation. I had brought LB, who had cabin fever from being locked up all day at home. I dreaded the day that might be her.

Following our return, I went straight to bed. *I had the first day-on-the-job headache.* I understood this clinic would be an excellent place to learn, but I didn't think it was a "to-die-for" job. Early days—maybe I would grow to love it.

I was invited to accompany my boss with the bull with wire wrapped and buried around his lower limb. It had been snowing for the last two days, and the appointments had slowed down. The anesthesia was performed by an intramuscular drug with a profound effect on cattle. My boss and his associate worked on the wound and probed it, searching for the buried metal. The wire was located with great difficulty, and my boss was able to remove it. The area was flushed with antibiotics, the bull was administered some penicillin, and we left. I was glad to see how difficult it was to remove the wire and not be responsible. Lesson learned.

My coworkers were both respectful and helpful. The vets were, for the most part, tolerant of a new grad. I still did not have a solid year under my belt. I had not experienced a foaling or breeding season when things get busy. One of the vets was not very pleasant or approachable. He was not happy that the clinic had hired a large animal vet instead of a small animal clinician. I tried to help in the small animal clinic as much as possible, but there was no pleasing the man. I was told not to bother. He was always like that. Unfortunately, he was a partner, and there was no getting rid of him to solve the issue. I simply steered clear of him.

I was not on call that first weekend, but I was in reserve. I had to be on standby if I was needed to pass gas or help in any way. The second was rarely called, but I hung around the area just in case. We canceled the ride for the weekend due to the snow, but we went to Brad and Phoebe's for dinner Saturday night. I asked Phoebe if it was all right for me to bring Mary. "She's already been invited. So are Grace and Dan Hughes. It's a kind of welcome back for you."

"Great. What can I bring?"

"You and the boys. I heard Mister Hunkalicious is in town."

"Yep, *water, water everywhere and not a drop to drink*. It's so painful." We both laughed. "I'm not on call, but I may have to assist, so I'll have to limit myself."

"Who would want to be a vet?"

"Me."

When we all arrived at the Lays' place, introductions were made. Grace and Dan both hugged me. Everyone inquired about what I had been doing. Oh, I went home to Kentucky. You know, I just went places.

This was not lost on Rich. "We'd have to kill you if we told you. State secret."

I looked at Rich, smiled, and mouthed, "Thanks."

Dinner was great, but my phone rang. It was the grumpy vet who required a hand. He had a horse with colic, and he was not excited about treating it. I agreed to do it. He instantly changed from grumpy to thankful. I announced I had to leave. Rich and Dirk glanced at each other. Rich got the nod. "Guys, I'll be fine."

"No way." Rich and I left and headed to a farm not far from the Lays. It was a straightforward colic. I gave it pain meds and passed a tube to administer the oral fluids. We returned to a marvelous dinner. I hoped this would make things easier for everyone at the clinic the following week. The stalker and cop-corruption topic came up, but the missing mother was taboo. I didn't care anymore. I knew that one, and I was satisfied. I was happy to be among friends once again.

Dr. Crabby, as some called him, or Max Schulman offered me a donut at the office on Monday. He thanked me for taking the colic and said he would trade any hairy small animal cases I might have when I was on call for other large animal cases. "Sure thing, Dr. Schulman."

"Max."

I smiled. "It's a deal, Max." This place was beginning to grow on me. I worked for another lovely week with no threats. The FBI couldn't trace the second flowers to anyone. A woman came in wearing a ski outfit, but only her nose and mouth could be seen, and the girl who took the order couldn't identify my stalker from a picture lineup.

My week went well. I worked three nights of after-hours, but I declined any extra nights that week because I could tell it was not fair to Rich and Dirk. I was excited to hear that Ted was coming to the party at Mel and Cary's. I was going to be so glad to see him. There was a frenzy at the house with the guys cooking and preparing for Dirk's entrance. I hated to be the third wheel. I offered to take my own car in case they wanted to 'party on.' "Nope, you are under our protection until Jim comes back."

The party was fantastic. The softball team and a few other doctors from the emergency clinic attended. All was going well until one of the emergency doctors came in with his new girlfriend. Rich, Ted, and I intuitively knew it was Jasmine MacArthur, my stalker. My heart sank. I attempted to remove my engagement ring, but she saw it. Mel and Cary had no idea who she was. *How was Jasmine able to go to a party when she was on bail?* She immediately shot me daggers. I didn't flinch. I was with safe company. I walked up to her and extended my hand. Jasmine didn't reciprocate at first, but I left my extended hand out until she had to take it or look like a rude idiot. "Hi, I'm Lauren. I believe we have a friend in common."

Rebecca

I had no idea what was happening as usual. One thing in my favor was that burying a body in the freezing cold was difficult, if not impossible. A deceased person was often stored in a room next to the undertakers. Funerals were conducted in the spring when the ground thawed sufficiently for digging. I didn't know if that was the case or not. Unless he'd been cremated, Danny Moore's body would more likely be frozen, and it would take a while to thaw him out, but he would be preserved.

I assumed that Alf would have the honors, but I knew Sam and Oliver would attend. I didn't know whether Millard Moore would be up to the task of viewing his deceased son. He might just have the sheriff do so, or even the judge might observe the second autopsy. I could only wait and pray that the truth would prevail.

No word came until late at night when the guard notified me Danny's body had just been examined. Because it had to be close to midnight, he didn't know the results. I would have to wait until morning to learn if the court resumed or if it would be delayed.

A new dress was sent down for me the next day. I washed, changed clothes, and was ready to be escorted to the court by midmorning. No one came, and I sat waiting alone. I was sick with worry about the findings. I knew what I reported and did was the truth. Did the body reflect that? Did someone put a bullet in the man after he was dead to make it appear that I had shot him in the back? I had to wait.

Finally, a guard escorted me to court. Sam was present, and he smiled and held me for a moment. "It'll all be fine, darling. I won't let anything happen to you. I promise," he whispered.

"Are you and Hanna all right?"

"She's okay, and so am I. You'll have the wrath of a Chinaman if you don't get home and eat some home-cooked food soon."

Oliver left the judge's chambers and didn't show any emotion. We sat down together, and he whispered to me that the autopsy had been informative. I started to ask, but the judge came in, and we all rose and then sat down in silence. Oliver quietly leaned over to inquire about the prevalence of venereal disease in the area.

"It's not common, but it has been a problem with the local brothel women. Some men frequent the brothels. Did he have?" but Oliver placed his hand on mine, indicating I shouldn't talk.

I stared back at Mrs. Gardiner and her niece. I might hang, but Lila Crompton most likely would suffer a slow, painful death due to venereal disease, which should have brought me comfort. It didn't.

The judge announced that the trial would recommence. The first order of business was the new autopsy report, which the Carson City doctor, who performed the previous autopsy, would read. He seemed decidedly embarrassed. He read notes from the paper that had been submitted that morning. It included little that was new. He found the hole in the back was not from a bullet. He located the bullet entry point that would support my account that I shot him from the front. That was all he mentioned.

Instead of further questions, Oliver wanted Alf to present his report. Alf exchanged places with the Carson City doctor. He was then asked to read a second report on the latest examination of Danny Moore. Alf concluded that the entry had been from the front. The bullet severed the aorta, and Danny bled to death almost at once from that damage. "Thank you, Dr. Webber. Oh, just so the jury is informed, you received your training through a university medical school, did you not?"

"Yes, I did."

"Did your examination identify other findings, which might be important if Mr. Moore had lived, such as a contagious disease?"

"Yes, sir."

Millard Moore glanced up, surprised. "Objection."

The judge sustained his objection, but the point was taken.

Oliver smiled, and I turned to Sam, who also had a poorly hidden grin. I stared back at Lila Crompton, who was clearly upset. I felt terrible for her. Curing a venereal disease in the 1800s was difficult, if not impossible. Alf grinned broadly at me. He set the report on the judge's desk, patted my shoulder on the way to his seat, and shook hands with Dan and Sam.

The case was done. I was not allowed to testify. I was disappointed, but Oliver was taking no chances. He masterfully summed up the case and conclusions to the jury, as did a contrite Millard Moore. The jury was sent to a deliberation room. I was permitted to consult with both Oliver and Sam in a private room. I explained I'd heard the jury was a setup and that, despite the evidence, it would convict me.

Since Ray Thompson had already informed them, they were prepared for such an eventuality. The autopsy demonstrated that Danny Moore had a significant case of gonorrhea and advanced cirrhosis of the liver from his drinking. Alf and Ray went to see Lila Crompton. Sam was called out of the room. Oliver and I sat together for an hour, reminiscing about the past and his father's contribution to the medical community. By now, physicians were implementing many of his suggestions about preventing the transmission of disease by the simple act of washing their hands between treating patients.

"Becky, he always remembered you and believed you were way ahead of the standards for doctors and science in general." If they only knew.

Sam returned, and he appeared upset. He didn't say anything, but I recognized his distress. After two hours, we were called back into the court. I was almost weak-kneed and needed to be supported. Everyone who was there on the first day, except the governor, was in the courtroom.

The judge said that before the jury read its verdict, Millard Moore had an announcement. I stared at Sam, who would not look at me. Mr. Moore began to talk. However, before he could say anything, Lila Crompton shouted that she had lied, and Danny Moore had attacked her. She added that when I confronted Danny, he turned to go after me. My fatal shot was an act of self-defense. She withdrew her testimony and declared her aunt made her do it. She turned to her aunt, who was weeping, and mouthed that she was sorry.

The court audience broke out into yelling and cheering. Most of the townsfolk were not happy, but my supporters were joyful. Millard Moore was furious and started to move toward Lila and her aunt, who was still crying, with her face buried in her hands.

I glanced at Oliver, who was confused but relieved and happy. Sam was observing Millard Moore and grinning. He turned to Dan and shook hands. "That was close." I looked at them, and they smiled broadly at me. I cocked my head in a questioning way. Sam shook his head. The judge had been trying to restore order all this time. He finally attracted the attention of everyone and was able to speak.

"While this turn of events is most unexpected, and despite my sincere reservations, I reluctantly declare this case as a mistrial. The defendant is free to go."

The jury appeared surprised and disappointed. The jurists stared at Millard Moore, from whom they anticipated a response. He was alone, gazing down at his desk and away from the jury.

Oliver and I hugged, following which I turned to my family. Dan and Jenny hugged me first. I was at last in the arms of my husband. For once, I was able to contain my demeanor and didn't cry. "I love you. Thank you. I'm not certain what happened, but I'm grateful."

"I'll probably test you someday. You should thank Ray and Alf. I don't exactly know what took place, but we almost came to ruin."

I glanced over at Ray and Alf, who stood side by side, awaiting Sam and me. I walked over to Alf, who hugged me. I spied Lila as she tried to leave the building. The deputies attempted to talk with her, but she and Mrs. Gardiner kept walking.

We all returned to the Cattle Creek Ranch, where the entire story came out after dinner. Hanna was out in the barn, helping Alexander with the horses. How I longed for the two of them to find each other.

The autopsy showed severe cirrhosis, indicating advanced deterioration because of alcohol consumption. Danny additionally had advanced gonorrhea or the 'clap' as it was called in those times. Knowing that Lila had been pregnant, and the father had to be Danny, it would come out that she might also have it in an early stage, which was more treatable than later.

Alf was able to get her alone after his testimony. She sought him out without Mrs. Gardiner in attendance. Lila wanted to know what disease she might have. While she was not intelligent, she understood the ramifications of her problem. If Mrs. Gardiner realized that her niece was not the pure, chaste woman she pretended to be, Lila might be kicked out of the Gardiner home.

Consequently, Alf and Ray told Lila if she confessed that her testimony was false, she would receive preferential treatment and most likely live to a ripe old age. Of course, they had neglected to admit that even if she hadn't changed her testimony, they were bound to give her treatment, anyway. Ray and Glenn suspected that Millard had established some deal with Mrs. Gardiner. As a result, there was one more piece to the puzzle. Dan, Jenny, and the children had left. I'd observed Dan and Sam quietly talking and smiling earlier in the evening.

When Hanna had returned and the guests, including Oliver Wendell Holmes, either had been given rooms or had returned to Virginia City, Sam and I went up to our room. I could not deny his amorous feelings, which I admit might be mutual. "Not so quick, cowboy. I think we need to discuss something else."

"I have no idea what you're talking about." Sam continued to unlace my corset.

"I think you might. What were you and Dan so happy about?"

"Oh, that, but you don't have to worry about it now."
"I kind of believe I do."
"We almost sold the Cattle Creek Ranch."
"What?"
"I couldn't take a chance about the outcome. Millard Moore knew it, and he thought that a good gesture in offering a sale of the Cattle Creek Ranch at a reduced rate might sway the jury."
"What rate?"
"Free."
"And Dan went along with it?"
"Both Dan and Jenny."
"I'm not worth a tenth of the Cattle Creek Ranch."
"If you don't get into bed right now, I'll be inclined to agree with you."

Lauren

I was furious that such a situation could even happen, but I would reclaim my life. She was not going to intimidate me anymore. Rich was by my side immediately. He put his arm around me and introduced himself, after which Dirk stood on my other side. Again, introductions were made. I think we were all in shock that she was out socializing while she was out on bail for attempted murder. Her upcoming trial was scheduled in a few weeks. Finally, her date came over while we all stared at her. He seemed pleased that she was making friends. I realized he had no idea whom he was dating.

"Hey, Jazz, who are your friends?" He smiled as he stared at us.

She could barely speak. "I just met them. I'm sorry. I forgot your names."

"I'm fairly sure you know me. I'm the one you sent flowers to last week." The young doctor appeared perplexed. "I'm Lauren Harper. Perhaps Jazz has mentioned me. These two guys are my roommates." I didn't say their names, but the doctor was impressed.

"Half your luck."

"I think so." I smiled as I squeezed Dirk and Rich, who still had their arms around me.

The young doctor put his arm around Jasmine. "Hey, babe. I want you to meet the hosts." He took her over to Cary, and I could see he leaned down and whispered something to her. I could tell she was not reacting well to whatever he said to her. Cary and Mel were oblivious to the whole interaction. They greeted her warmly and offered her a drink. She drank a glass of wine. I wondered if the consumption of alcohol was a violation of her bail conditions.

Ted finally arrived with his partner. Ted and I hugged, and his gorgeous partner joked it was good she wasn't the jealous type, or I would have been in trouble. In most circumstances, I would have laughed it off, but I was somewhat sensitive.

"Yeah, some of that seems to be going on."

Ted returned with drinks and gave me a second hug. He understood what was going down, and he wanted to convince Jasmine that I had support from other friends. Rich quietly informed Cary that the woman we were all looking at was on bail for attempted murder. I noticed from across the room that she appeared stunned. Her mouth was open, and she stared at Jasmine.

Jasmine seemed to be aware that she was being talked about. She went over to her date, who probably had no clue that she was on bail. She apparently whispered in his ear that she wanted to leave. He glanced around and set their drinks down. He waved to Cary and said goodbye to Mel, who was in the kitchen, getting the food ready with her new girlfriend.

"Why so soon? We haven't even talked yet." Mel was clueless, as well.

"I'm sorry, but I have a ripping headache." Jasmine rubbed her forehead.

"Jazz, it was nice to meet you. Maybe you could join us for breakfast. We all hang out at the Coffee Café most mornings." Mel hugged her.

"Oh, that's nice to know. Thanks. Sorry to be a party pooper." She and her clueless date left.

I witnessed the entire scenario. I was fuming that this female dog could roam around town at will. I didn't blame Cary or Mel because they had no idea. Rich talked with them, and my guess was, by their demeanors, they had the whole story.

Ted got something to eat and returned. I quietly told him about the rock through the window and the flowers. He suspected that she had burned down the cabin. Only Frank and I knew I was there when she fired the gun at the creek. Even the FBI didn't think I was present. I should possibly have that awkward conversation with them.

This complication and two encounters with FBI cases were so improbable that Frank and I decided my involvement in the shooting could simply be better kept to ourselves. There'd been news in the local paper, but not much had been published when she made bail and was out in public. I would testify, if necessary, but Frank believed my testimony could be avoided. Jasmine would receive some serious jail time. All the FBI knew was that she was stalking me, and they were also concerned she was friends with the corrupt deputies. I doubted that.

Cary and Mel expressed how sorry they were that she attended the party. They were going to inform their colleague about her the next day. "He needs to know the woman he's dating is a nut job."

"I hope she doesn't do to him what she did to Jim. She never dated Jim, and yet she's made his life miserable for years. Of course, now she knows about breakfast and the Coffee Café."

"Jeez, that's the worst part of it."

"I guess someone can bring my coffee and sweet roll to the vet clinic now, huh, Cary?"

"Your wish is my command."

"You couldn't have known. I decided not to tell people about my stalker. I thought my problems were over when she tried to kill a friend, but maybe not."

"Why are you still even living here? You should have moved."

"She learned my family lives in Kentucky, and I didn't want her to harass them. She's dangerous through and through. Jim kept moving because of her. I refuse to move. We thought she was gone when he left for the army. Jim would die if he realized she was back. He and Rich made a pact to protect me in any case. Either Rich or Dirk accompanies me on calls at night. I rarely go to the store alone. "

"What about your job?"

"I haven't said anything to them. I believe the clinic might fire me if the vets heard I had a stalker."

"You need to tell them. If the stalker tried to kill your friend, she might attempt to do the same to one of the employees. Lauren, are you certain Jim's worth it?"

"Oh, yeah. Totally worth it." This conversation reminded me about all he'd done for me and how much I missed him. I might go home to watch Hank on the DVD. "You're right. I'll tell my bosses right away. Goodbye, job. Oh, by the way, I take my coffee plain black, and I'll take a bear claw to go with it. You know where the clinic is?"

"Seven-thirty, okay?"

"Perfect."

It was on the counter when I arrived at work the following morning—a fresh, moist bear claw. When I asked to talk to my bosses, I was ushered into their private office. Doug and Max glanced at something on the computer. Both crossed their arms and turned to me, expecting a request.

"I need to tell you something."

"No raises. You were warned."

"I wish it were as simple as that. It's somewhat more complicated. I assumed by the time I was working here, everything would be worked out, but it's not." I observed them as they suggested we all sit down. "I have a problem, but you might as well know it's actually two problems. It's all right to fire me. I should have disclosed this, but I was assured my situation would be resolved by now."

"Are you in trouble? State board? The law? Losing your license?"

"Yes, no, no, and no. I'm not in trouble, but I may be in danger." I went on to tell them about the corruption case and the stalker, who was harassing me and on bail for attempted murder. I had the two cards that came with the flowers. I watched them move from disbelief to, I hoped, concern.

"Lauren, are you in any immediate danger?"

I shook my head, but I don't think I convinced them.

"We'll need to think about this. Take a tech with you today, and we'll let you know how we want to proceed. Thanks for letting us know. Are the trial dates for both cases set now?"

"Yes, sir." Neither man corrected me this time. It was a 'yes sir' moment.

Chapter 25

Rebecca

How things can change! Mrs. Gardiner and her niece suddenly felt the need to move to a warmer climate. I'm sure Sam was lamenting not dancing once more with her. I told him it was perfectly acceptable to grieve the loss of a dance partner. Ow, the response was short and swift.

Who was going to be the thorn in my side now? I felt a void, but it didn't take long. The Parkers moved into Mrs. Gardiner's old house. Mrs. Parker was an interesting woman. She was in her mid-thirties, thin with a head of hair that would probably hit the ground, except she held it all in a tight bun on top of her head, making her appear taller than she was. Her severe, drawn facial features were intimidating. She had four children, ranging from fifteen to eight years old. She and her husband shared the house with her mother-in-law.

The elder Mrs. Parker was a wonderful woman with a wicked sense of humor. The younger Mrs. Parker was a hypochondriac. You name the disease, and she either had it, or one of her family members had it. She owned a copy of an old medical book, *A Dictionary of Medical Science*, but the one she referred to was *Dr. Watson's Guide to the Human Body*. I was familiar with the dictionary book, and our medical library included a copy of the book. The other book was probably a figment of her imagination. I asked several times to see the book, yet she declined.

I'd heard the term Munchausen syndrome and its associated term, Munchausen's by proxy. A caregiver, who is frequently the mother, either imagines an illness that does not actually exist or facilitates the creation of a condition to draw exceptional attention to oneself. I didn't name the term if it hadn't been discovered, but my associate John Harmon mentioned it during a brief meeting. He had already washed his hands of her and had passed her on to me. I could not thank John enough. I couldn't thank him at all, and I threatened to fire him. "Try all you want, Becky. Alf will side with me."

Alf nodded in the background. "You're the patron saint of all lost causes, Becky."

"And you are dirt under my toenail."

John shook his head. "Where do you get those phrases?"

"From the future, John."

"Don't you and I wish."

"You might wish for the future, John, but I'm content right here and now."

"Good luck with her. It's primarily female conditions, anyway."

"Remember that I won't be around next week. The cattle and horses will leave early for the drive. I'm in the process of preparing a few of the horses and will be conducting men's work next week on the Cattle Creek Ranch."

Sam and Dan still didn't officially approve of how Hanna and I finished off the horses bound for the cavalry. We didn't care since it was our time together. We helped each other and enjoyed each other's approach to horse-training problems. Her methods were derived from her time living with the Indians, and mine came from my father.

When I was young, my mother would threaten to send us back to the Indians if we didn't behave. I took her at her word until after her death. As I applied to college, my father helped me with the application. He wouldn't let me check the box for Native American ancestry. I was suspicious at the end of my mother's life when no Indians showed up for the funeral. I was disappointed. When I asked my dad if he had any Indian heritage, he simply smiled and shook his head.

Because his methods resembled those of Hanna, we worked well together. We trained nine horses above the cavalry's expected performance level. Since we had two weeks to go, I believed we could get a few more ready. "Hanna, why don't you ask Alexander for help? I'll bet the three of us could turn out several more before they have to go."

"Ma, he's a boy. He'll only get in the way."

"Hanna, he's a nice boy. You could do worse, you know. He's certainly going places."

"Sure, Ma." It was terribly disappointing to see her so blind to inner beauty. Sam kept smiling and counseled me to let them both be.

I was back at work at the hospital the following week. My new best friend, Mrs. Parker, was seated in the waiting room. "Hello, Mrs. Parker."

"Becky, I feel that we're going to be best friends, so call me Celia."

"I'm honored, but are you certain?"

"Yes, definitely."

Alf walked behind me, carrying a tray of washed towels for a pending birth. He grinned as he passed behind Mrs. Parker. I nodded toward him but gave him 'the look.' He scurried quickly into the next room. "What are we looking at today?"

"Do you prefer Becky or Bec?"

I wanted to reply, 'Dr. Buchanan.' Alas, I gritted my teeth and responded, "Becky." I was on a first-name basis with many clients, but the authorization came from me and vice versa with their first names. I would have preferred that this lady bow and kiss my wrist when she greeted me.

The litany of ailments was a lengthy one. Mrs. Parker had hers, and two of the children had theirs. The consult consisted of her describing her lumbago, chills, sweats, rashes, and headaches. Fortunately, she had already diagnosed everything from her two medical books. She recognized and had implemented the cures. She simply wanted to ensure she was on the most up-to-date remedy.

"And what would that be, Celia?"

"Why, Becky, I have come to you. Surely you know that brandy at night is the sole cure for this particular affliction."

"A single glass may do the trick. Any more than that could be more harmful than the ailments themselves."

"Yes, that's what Doc Watson advises, as well."

"So happy that great minds think alike." As she glanced out of the window, I rolled my eyes.

"You may someday become as famous as Dr. Watson, too, Becky."

"A girl can dream...."

"That might be possible. You never know, though, do you?" She shook her head as she responded.

"No, ma'am."

I observed the two girls with possible conditions ranging from acne to female issues. "Celia, they aren't old enough for female problems. In all probability, these issues won't be a concern for at least a year. She's too young, so it could be even longer. Let's deal with it then. I saw no acne, but the younger daughter had scabs from scratching."

Celia was clearly annoyed with my summation. "I had problems. I can't imagine they won't."

"Let's cross that bridge when we come to it."

"I'm so glad we had this chat. I'll be back tomorrow with the boys."

"What's the problem?"

"Nothing, really, but if we can get on top of it early, then we can stop it."

"What is it?"

She leaned in and said quietly, "You know what young boys do."

I was reasonably sure I knew what she was talking about. "You know, that's pretty normal too."

"No, it's not, Becky. It's a sin."

"Sin or not, it's not a medical problem. Maybe you should consult the minister."

"I'll bring them to you, anyway. What if it's worms?"

"See you tomorrow, Celia."

"I thought you could come for lunch. We live nearby. It's such a shame we don't spend more time together."

"I'm only in town occasionally. Sick people in the hospital often require my attention. If no patients need my attention, my daughter stays with me, anyway, at the boardinghouse. Sorry, but I should care for her."

"Maybe she could stay with us. We could assist her with her homework, and I would make sure she stays well. You realize I'm practically a doctor with my books and things."

"See you tomorrow." I left the room. Mrs. Parker made Mrs. Gardiner look like a saint.

This saga continued for the entire week. There wasn't one day she didn't present for an ailment or bring me homemade cookies or muffins. I threatened to quit if I didn't get some relief from this woman. John, Alf, and I brainstormed ways to get her to stop pestering us with her health issues. Most were imagined, but some were real. Her daughter began to show symptoms of something more than an invented illness. We feared it might be blood cancer or leukemia.

Thankfully, the symptoms were resolved, following which Celia returned to her usual irritating self. I was nearly ready to retire. *How could this woman hold my associates and me hostage?* We had to find a strategy for her to stop annoying us. I considered referring her to the hapless doctor in Carson City, who still practiced after my trial. That would be payback plus some. Oh, well, I was going home for two additional weeks. I would deal with her when I came back. After I bid adieu to my colleagues, Hanna and I headed home.

Because Hanna stayed with me in town for the week, she was anxious to go home. She wanted to show Cassie something and obtain her advice on some sewing. I was so proud of her. I was almost jealous of the relationship she and Cassie were building. While Alexander also rode home with us, he informed us about an entrance examination for an engineering college. Some money set aside from Pam Wilkins' estate would probably get him through the first year, after which he might earn a scholarship to complete his schooling.

Hanna stared at him. "I don't know why you would want to go to college when you could have a good job on the Cattle Creek Ranch."

"Hanna, he wants to better himself. Don't discourage him. You should support his efforts to further his education." Her lack of interest in encouraging him was disheartening. I wish she could simply get past his looks. Alexander was growing out of his gangly phase and had shot up to at least six feet tall. I wouldn't say handsome, but he would be a nice-looking young man with some muscle.

It was good to get home and away from Virginia City. I kissed both Sam and Gee Ling. After Hanna kissed her father, she went straight out to see Cassie. "Dinner will be in one hour. We're eating early, so we can work on the horses tonight. Hanna, are you listening to me?" She wasn't.

When we finished supper, Hanna and I went out to tend to the horses in the corral. The ranch hands had settled on four of them that were worthy of additional training. They were under orders from Sam not to let us work on rogues. I wasn't supposed to know this, but one of the hands let it slip. We each took one, saddled, and performed some groundwork. We mounted, did some arena work with a hackamore, and switched to bridles when they were supple and responsive. It typically required approximately three days to advance them to the stage that they were ready for further work.

The following night, I took the evening off because I didn't feel well. Sam went to Dan's to review plans for the cattle drive. Hanna still wanted to ride. I proposed she ask Alexander to come with her. That way, someone would be there to assist her if anything happened. I sat by the fire in the great room to read the book Sam had bought for me the previous week. Since I felt terrible that I was not helping and could not really settle, I decided to join Hanna to ride the current horse I was educating. I went into the tack room for my saddle. Hanna and Alexander were in there, and I could not deny what I saw.

They were kissing, and he had his hand on her in a place that no boy's hand should be at that age in the 1800s. Of course, it would have been commonplace in the 1900s. And then I said them—the exact words my mother said to me after one of many transgressions. "Go to your room. Wait until your father gets home, young lady." Hanna didn't say a word.

Alexander was red-faced. "It's my fault, ma'am. Don't punish her, please. I love her. We want to get married as soon as we can. I'm going to college to obtain a good job. We'll have a beautiful house and lots of children someday if

Mr. Buchanan says we can get married. Please don't tell her father. I promise nothing will happen until we're married."

Oh, man. I was the biggest fool ever. I was totally clueless. I realized even Sam suspected this. I glared at Alexander and shook my head. At fifteen years of age, I was not even interested in boys. By sixteen, I had been felt up by at least two boys. Did I educate and guide my daughter to help her decide what was appropriate for her age? I know her father said there would be no dating, but was this the kind of behavior he meant?

"Alexander, no more. I'm on your side. Perhaps in the future, Hanna will be ready for what you and she would like to do, but you are both too young to make those kinds of plans. Am I clear? I'm not threatening to send you back to the orphanage. You're too old, anyway. But if you do more than hold hands and kiss once per day, I am a woman of unique capabilities, which I won't hesitate to use." My fingers made a snip-snip motion.

"Yes, ma'am."

"Okay, go back home to the Littles."

"Sorry, ma'am. I still love her, though."

"Some things are worth waiting for." We both smiled. As I left the barn, Sam returned from Dan's.

"Sorry, I'm late."

"So late." I shook my head.

"Oh?" Sam cocked his head.

"Yes, oh."

"What happened? Are you alright, darling?"

"We need to talk. What do you know about baseball and sex?"

"Nothing." My Victorian husband blushed at the mention of the word sex.

"I told you about baseball when the batter hits the ball and runs around the bases."

"Maybe. I don't remember. How does this concern me?"

"Second base, Sam, second base."

"I think this might require alcohol." He went to the cabinet to pour two glasses of brandy.

"Where's Hanna? Jenny wants her to care for the children this weekend."

I pointed upstairs. "Restricted to her room until she turns eighteen."

"Oh?"

I took a pen, ink, and paper to draw the bases on a field. I pointed to first base.

"First base is kissing." I pointed to second base, took Sam's hand, and placed it on my breast. "This is second base." Sam's magnificent dark eyebrows went up as he gazed toward the stairs.

"Both parties understand they have crossed a line. Perhaps you could talk with Alexander to reinforce what I told him. I need to talk more with Hanna. Did you realize any of this was going on?"

I thought Sam would be furious, but he seemed somewhat amused. "Only the first-base stuff, as you say."

"How come you didn't tell me?"

"Becky, how old were you when you arrived at second base?"

"Those were different times."

"I'll talk to both. Best to wait until tomorrow. Let her worry a little tonight."

"I'll tell her to go to bed." I started for the stairs. She and I would have a severe talk the next day. Sam might be amused, but I was upset.

"Is fourth base what I think it is?" Sam smiled.

"It's called a home run. That's the desired result for the batter."

"Any chance we can try for a home run tonight?"

I threw up my hands. "Men," I exclaimed in an exasperated tone.

"I raised three boys. I somehow managed to get it all done without knowing anything about baseball!"

Lauren

I was called into the office at the end of the day. Max, Doug, the tech Sara, and practice manager Dot were all in the room. I tried to look confident and fearless. I assumed they would ask me to leave. I'd prepared my exit speech. The best I could hope for was, "Maybe when this is over, we'd love to have you back...."

Doug started, "Lauren, we are a family here. We take care of each other. If one of us is having problems, we all attempt to assist in some way. But, and this is a big but, if we don't know, we can't help. We did a little digging without contacting anyone from the agencies. We have a few connections, and we feel you are worth the risk. We're going to keep you on, but you must be extremely careful about what you do. We have assigned Sara to work with you. She's aware of the story, and we believe the risk is minimal. We're going to limit your after-hours to horses. You'll be on call more days, but it will only be for large animals. I hear one of your roommates always goes with you. Is that true? If they can't accompany you, you should call me when you go and when you return."

I was so relieved, and I could have kissed them all. I was incredibly appreciative that Sara agreed to ride shotgun with me all day. I thanked them and completed my daily medical records and billing. I noticed I would see Liz and Megan the following day. This visit would be their first time for the new clinic. I high-fived Sara as she walked out the door.

"Sara, thanks for taking me on."

"No, thank you. I listen to old people's music when I ride with Doug. I like your music much more."

"Bring your CDs and anything else. I'll listen to anything to make you happy."

I told the guys at home how the new clinic reacted to my dramas. It was late, but I called my family, and Mom answered. I told her what had happened without anything scary, after which my dad took the phone. I almost cried when I heard his voice. I hadn't informed him about the rock that came through the window or the flowers, but I did say I saw the stalker. Dad wanted me to return home, and, of course, I declined. Dad claimed he might retire in the summer, and he and Mom would be out for a visit. I added that maybe Jim would be back by then.

Sara and I went to see Liz and Megan the next day. I told Sara about Megan riding along with me for a day when I was still at Rocky's. Sara noted this clinic rarely permitted such a practice. Still, these vets occasionally hired high-school students for the small animal weekend work.

"They'd pass up free labor? They're missing out."

"Hey, Harper, that's my job you're talking about."

"Oops, there is that side, as well."

Megan was waiting in the barn, eager to help. Sara, who was impressed, later admitted she had potential. "Okay, if your stalker knocks me off, you can take her on calls, but until then, no way."

"Yes, ma'am." I saluted her. Riling a vet technician was a sure way to doom your early career in practice, especially a tech who was guarding your life.

I quietly explained to Liz that no one could ride along with me now. I told her I was on probation. Maybe later, but guests were not permitted for the short term. "Got it. Your one day with Megan really made a difference. She is one determined girl now. Her grades and attitude have improved dramatically."

"Happy to help."

We finished the call, and Liz suggested that we should get together socially. "Sounds good. I'm working straight through the next three weeks, but possibly after that." The first trial for the stalker would begin, then she would hopefully be jailed, and I could relax. When I arrived home, there was a letter from Jim. I waited to open it until after dinner. I was so nervous. At least he was alive.

Dear Lauren,

I still can't tell you what I am doing or where I am, but rest assured, all is well. In fact, I have been given my

marching orders. I will finish sooner than expected. I should be

back Stateside in early May. I will have two weeks of debriefing, and so I should be free by June. I hope

you still want to get married as soon as possible and isn't a June wedding every bride's dream? Please let me know your thoughts and send them to the same address as last time. Please, please, please say YES.
Love,
Jim

I screamed. Rich didn't even knock. He ran into the room, with Dirk in close pursuit. I handed them the letter and then rang my parents. It was late enough they were in bed. My dad answered, and I shouted, "How about a June wedding?"

"What? Nope. Your mom and I are going away. We won't be back until August. Sorry, darling." He hung up. What the hell? I was shocked. No, I was furious. He didn't even ask what prompted me to call. I started to dial Lisa's number when my parents phoned back.

It was my mom this time. She was laughing. "Your dad has been waiting to do that to you ever since you returned from your mysterious trip. Yes, June is fine. The dress you selected is still available unless it's been sold in the last few weeks. Do you want me to get it?" I could hear Dad prompt her. He told her that a civil ceremony was so much less expensive, and we could have a lovely honeymoon on what we would save.

"Jeff, shush. My daughter is having whatever kind of wedding I want. It has nothing to do with her or your needs. Live with it."

"Thanks, Mom, I guess. Yes, if you don't mind, the dress would be nice. I can pay you back."

"Lauren, don't ever, and I mean ever, discuss money and this wedding again with me. I'll call the church tomorrow."

"Thanks again, Mom. I love you." I have two mothers whom I love. How lucky am I? I wish I could have both mothers at my wedding. "I can't believe he's getting out early. I can hardly wait. Sorry to call so late. Tell Dad I love him, too, even if he's a bastard."

"Lauren, don't swear. Sweet dreams."

My next call was to Lisa. Since she didn't answer, I left a message to choose a bridesmaid dress for June and call me the next day. Now work, work, work to get through the next few months.

Dirk returned to Arizona, much to both Rich's and my dismay. Things had gone well, and he was going to make a permanent transfer. It was back to my pseudo-husband and me once again. Our neighbor thought things were interesting when Dirk was here with us. Helen thought I had two boyfriends and wondered how that worked. Because I hated to ruin that illusion, I didn't deny it.

I was collecting the newspaper when she stepped out simultaneously. We had almost become friends and were happy to see each other. "Hi, Helen. It's finally starting to warm up."

"I'm still cold, but at least the days are getting longer. Want to come in for some coffee or hot chocolate?"

I was in my bathrobe, and Rich wasn't going to be up for a while. "Fine. Sounds good." Always best to have a neighbor on the same side. She poured me a cup, and we conversed about the news and life in general. I was convinced she had some information or wanted to know about the stalker.

"So, Lauren, you're kind of a legend in the neighborhood."

"Oh, really? Is it my friend who was trying to make my life hell?"

"Uh, no. Don't get me wrong, but I'm not the only one to notice this. To each his own, but how do you juggle two men? I mean, my hat is off to you, and I am totally on your side. If those Mormons can have those sister wives, I don't see why we can't have two men."

"Helen," I started to say, but she cut me off.

"I am in awe."

"No, seriously," but again, she kept on.

"Aren't you tired? One night you're out with one and the next another. Don't tell me what goes on in the house. I don't want the details. It's just that I can't get a date, and you have two gorgeous men at your beck and call."

I was trying to stifle a laugh and barely could reply. "Well, it isn't all fun and games as you can imagine."

"No, I bet not."

"They were constantly fighting over who cooked or cleaned for me and who got to go out on vet calls. At least Dirk is gone again. I only have to worry about one man now."

"All I can say is that you're phenomenal. You go, girl. If you ever need a stand-in, I'm available."

"I'll keep it in mind. It's never-ending. Work, work, work. Speaking of which, Rich will be up soon, and that man's appetite is enormous." I winked at Helen, and she smiled back.

Back in the house, I could hardly conceal my mirth. I wanted Rich to get up early to tell him, but he had the blues. I knew he would sleep for a long time. Rather than burning the pancakes, I thought I would go down to the Coffee Café and maybe catch some friends. Ted went skiing for sure, but maybe Mel or Cary was there. If not, I would get Rich's favs and come right home.

On the way, I received a call from a new client who had a horse with food and saliva coming out of its nose. "Sounds like a choke."

"I don't care what you call it. I really need someone to fix it. I'll pay if that's your problem. I've got the cash."

"No problem at all, sir. I'll be right there." He provided me with his name and address.

I turned away from the café and headed to the property where the horse was kept. It was dark and musty. The barn was dilapidated, and daylight streamed through various cracks. The emaciated mare was now down in urine-soaked, muddy soil. Ulcers were prominent on her hips and the sides of her head by her eyes. She couldn't stand, which she attempted when I entered the stall, but slipped and fell back into the mud. She regained her footing only to fall again.

I smelled rotting flesh, which almost made me dry retch. There was a massive tumor on her leg, which seemed like a giant wart. It was probably a sarcoid tumor attached to the front of her hock. Without saying anything, I just stared at the horse. I was appalled on every level at this abuse. How could the man let this happen? I had witnessed neglect cases before, but nothing like this.

"What can we do to save her? My daughter will never come to see me again if her horse isn't here."

"When was your daughter last here?" How could anyone not see and report this?

"It's been a while. She won't come anymore. I haven't seen my grandchildren in several years, ever since my wife died." He didn't finish his sentence.

The man was probably in his eighties. While he appeared fit and could move around the stall and barn quickly, I thought he most likely suffered mild dementia. I probably should call someone for support. This poor horse needed to die. "Mr. Davidson, do you have a friend or someone I could call to help me?" I purposely didn't say to help him.

"I have my daughter's number, but she won't answer." He handed me his phone. He had the presence of mind to call our clinic, and he was able to hit the correct number to get the large animal division number. There were several numbers on his phone. One number had been called frequently, and I could tell the length of the call was longer than a hang-up.

I read the number off, and he said that it was his daughter's number. I rang it from my own phone. Someone with a young voice answered. He sounded like a teenager who had just come into puberty. I asked to speak to his mother. "She's dead. Do you want to speak to my dad?" Thankfully, Mr. Davidson had gone for some hay.

A man's voice came on, and I quickly explained the situation and who I was before the owner returned. Mr. Davidson's son-in-law explained that his father-in-law had mild dementia and called the house regularly to speak to his daughter. The woman had been dead for three years. They visited the old man several times a year, but they lived in Salt Lake City and hadn't come down for several months.

The son-in-law had asked the man to move up to Salt Lake City, so they could care for him, but the man refused to leave the horse. The last time he saw the horse, she was fine except for an immense growth on the leg. The horse had belonged to his wife as a child, and the old man kept it alive as he thought it would entice his daughter to visit. The horse must be in its thirties. "I guess he just can't accept Ally's dead. I'm sorry that I can't be there. You know, he was a brilliant physicist who worked on the Manhattan project. You should go into the house to see a collection of memorabilia that would blow your mind."

I explained how bad the horse was and that if Mr. Davidson didn't give me permission to euthanize the poor mare. I would have to call the authorities. The son-in-law suggested that I phone his friend, Mary Knox, who was friends with Mrs. Davidson until she'd passed a year before their daughter died. I thanked him and hung up. I immediately called Mary about the situation. She didn't live far away, and I said I would get back to her in a few minutes.

The mare was now paddling, and I realized the next few hours or minutes would be unbearable to watch. He stood in front of her in an area where her front legs could hit him as she paddled.

"Mr. Davidson, I am young, and perhaps I lack the experience you seek, but we have a mutual friend. Mary Knox is your friend, too, isn't she?" He nodded. "How about if I go over to get Mary, and will you let me relieve your mare of her pain if she says it's time?"

That was the key. It was as though Mr. Davidson woke up and saw the situation for what it was. He stared at the mare. "No, it's time to do what you must do. How am I going to bury her, though?"

"Don't worry about that, sir. I'll work it out. Do you want to be here, or do you want to go inside? You know, Mary would love to see you. I could take you down there, and I could get everything done while you and Mary have a nice chat."

He agreed. I took him down to Mary's, where she greeted him like an old friend. I told Mary what was going to happen and left them. On the way back to Mr. Davidson's property, I called Rich. "Want to go to a funeral today?"

"Where the hell are you? AWOL, Harper. Not acceptable."

"Yeah, but I am doing a good deed, and I need you to help, cowboy." I explained I'd need a backhoe. Rich said he would be there within the hour and to stay put. "Yes, sir."

"Don't think doing a good deed absolves you of an unauthorized reconnaissance, Harper. You are in serious trouble, young lady."

I went straight back into the barn, and the mare was still alive. I quickly euthanized her, and the mare's battle was over. I can't explain why some animals get to me, and others don't. This was one of those tearjerkers. Maybe it was the attachment and history. I didn't know this man, and I had no record to go by, but I cried for the mare's loss and for what she endured over the last few weeks. I didn't blame the owner, who had his own demons. I just hoped that I was never alone and in a similar situation without family nearby to help me when I was old.

Rich showed up. With great effort, we winched the now-dead mare out of the stall and through several gates to the only area suitable for burial. The ground was thawed, and he was able to dig a nice hole. Digging down, we identified several farming tools. We even discovered a branding iron that appeared similar to the Cattle Creek Ranch brand. Rich didn't pick up on it and simply tossed it to me. I threw it in my truck. He brought LB, who was having a great time running around. We hadn't walked her much, and I could tell how much she enjoyed her time out. I would figure a way to get her more exercise.

We buried the mare, after which Rich returned the backhoe to the construction site from where he'd borrowed it. We had to pay the backhoe owner, and Rich gave me an amount that was far too cheap. I handed him twice the amount.

"Nope. My guess is he won't even take the money. Lots of people knew the Davidsons. He was a Nevada legend in his time. No one is supposed to know about his work, and he may have changed his name. The house is still supposedly filled with books and papers about fission or fusion physics."

"Rich, he really needs help. He believes his daughter has abandoned him. Apparently, she's been dead for quite some time."

"Let me call Cary to see what she thinks. She would know whom we should call."

"Thanks again, Rich. I promise to be careful."

"Lauren, you have no choice. I promised Jim to watch out for you. I take my promises seriously."

"All right. I'll go to Mary's, bring Mr. Davidson home, and then come straight back."

"See that you do, young lady." We both laughed, but he pointed at me and wagged his finger in a not-so-friendly way.

I went back to Mary's, where she and Mr. Davidson were engrossed in recollections of times past. He was much calmer, and I could tell he needed companionship. I proposed that the three of us get together for dinner the following week. Mary was pleased. Neither could drive anymore. I offered to bring Mr. Davidson over on Wednesday night, and Mary would cook.

I returned Mr. Davidson to his property and took him to the horse's burial site. He thanked me for my assistance. He paid me and paid for the burial. He was looking forward to dinner on Wednesday but had a favor to ask.

"Dr. Harper, do you mind if it's just Mary and me? I'm sure you are a nice young lady, and you remind me of my daughter, but I want to talk to her about things that wouldn't interest you."

"Okay, I'll still pick you up, though." You old fox. This was going to be fun.

I received a call from Mary an hour later. "Lauren, thanks for bringing him over. I have a favor. On Wednesday night, can you maybe have an emergency? Come for a few minutes, drop him off, and return about nine. Is that possible?"

"Jeez, Mary. I don't know. Will you have a plate of food and some pie ready for me to take on the emergency? I'm not just a taxi, you know. Can I trust you two to be alone? This is asking a lot. I don't want any hanky-panky while I'm gone."

"Lauren Harper. You need a good..." but I interrupted her.

"A good what?"

"A good, you know. Do we have a deal?"

"Two pieces of pie, and I'm your girl."

"You drive a hard bargain."

When I arrived home, Rich was waiting for me. "I talked with Cary. According to her, it's difficult to get anything done unless someone is in imminent danger to someone or themselves."

"Crisis aborted. We may have a solution." I mentioned the Wednesday date night and the way each called and wanted me to take a hike, so they could be alone together. Rich thought it was hysterical.

"Oh, by the way, Jasmine has eaten breakfast at the Coffee Café every day since the party, so that is a no-go zone, Harper." So much for taking back my life.

"Yes, sir."

Capter 26

Rebecca

My new nemesis, Mrs. Celia Parker, began to take away some of our business. She created concoctions for several different ailments. Because laws didn't exist against quackery in Nevada, she was free to sell her potions to whomever she wanted. Many people were curious to try her wares for aches and pains. We smelled a few bottles from clients who were bold enough to bring them in when the remedies failed to cure a specific illness. As a result, we knew she had a generous quantity of alcohol in all her potions.

My associate, John Harmon, was getting particularly mad about her trade. "Becky, we've got to stop her."

"How would you advocate we do this, John? It's perfectly legal. Even the apothecary is selling her medicinal remedies in his store."

"If you can't beat them, join them."

"She's a nuisance."

"Becky, would you talk to her?"

"Why me?"

"She respects you."

"That's the problem. Celia Parker doesn't. She's a law unto herself. I miss Mrs. Gardiner. At least, I could reason with her."

"Well, let's vote on who talks to her."

"Yes, let's vote. I want a record that I was forced to endure this woman."

Both Alf and John raised their hands. *Bastards*, I thought. Ever since I was incarcerated and tried for murder, I noticed my vocabulary had taken a turn to my pre- 1800s life. So far, I could just think it and not say it except under dire circumstances. I still had a self-preservation thing going on. My attitudes had changed over the years, but it was still a man's world, and I had to live with the idea of men controlling the lives of women.

I took our hospital manager, Maggie Clayton, with me due to safety in numbers.

"Becky, you owe me for this."

"Maggie, whatever your heart desires. I totally agree. Want a raise? No problemo."

"Becky, you and these darn sayings."

We walked over to the Parkers. Old Mrs. Parker was sitting in the front room. It was raining, and she was lamenting the cold. When I asked if Celia was in, she pointed to a room off the parlor. We knocked on the door, to which there was no response. I turned to the elder Mrs. Parker, who waved her wrist. "Go on in, dear."

The room was in a shocking state of disarray. Broken bottles were scattered on the ground. The smell of ether, alcohol, and camphor—along with some spices—permeated the room. Celia was on the floor in a stupor. She was drunk, but I suspected she was an ether sniffer, as well. Maggie and I picked her up to help her out of the room, which was dangerously close to exploding. We took her out on the porch and yelled for assistance from two men walking down the boardwalk.

Several men came to get everyone out of the house, including old Mrs. Parker. We could not find anything that would ignite the room, but we couldn't take a chance. The two Mrs. Parkers were taken over to the hospital. The entire area was cordoned off. How or why things happened is a mystery. Late in the evening, when we thought all was safe, a massive explosion occurred. The house went up in flames in seconds. Mr. Parker, who had returned from Placerville the following day, was confident there was no danger. When he heard what had happened, he was furious with his wife. The children were all safe, and only a cat was missing in the end.

Glenn Frasier walked through the remains a day later. The rain drowned out any embers long before daylight. In what would have been the basement were the piping and pots for a still. Glenn arrested Mr. Parker, who claimed ignorance of the still and his innocence. He was adamant that it was not his fault, and he only came home for a day or two in a month.

When Celia Parker was presented with the news that her house had burned down and her husband was in jail, she smiled. Her mother-in-law confessed. She and Celia had a clandestine enterprise making whisky, which went into her concoctions. The ether was purchased from Carson City, and the doctor who testified against me was the supplier. Mr. Parker was released from jail, and both the elder Mrs. Parker and Celia were sent to a women's prison. The children and their father moved to Placerville. I hoped they would escape from their psychotic mother, whom I knew they still loved despite her faults.

At the end of the week, when I was due to return home, John, Alf, Maggie, and I were having coffee together. We all agreed this solution was somewhat more than planned, but our medical enterprise was back on track, at least for now. "You can thank Maggie and me. I think I may have promised Maggie a reward, gentleman."

Alf groaned, "Not another raise?"

"Done." John was so pleased to be rid of the Parkers that he was happy to grant her a raise.

The final cattle-drive preparations were made. Gee Ling's cousin was going along as the cook. He and Gee Ling furiously readied a cook wagon. Sam and Dan moved cattle to the corrals before the start of the drive with Alexander. Sam had assigned Alexander many chores since the baseball encounter. Poor Alexander had no idle time these days.

Cassie remarked that Hanna rarely came to visit. I hadn't had time to clue her in on what I had discovered that fateful night in the barn. When Cassie heard about it, though, she was upset she had not known what was happening. "I knew they were sweet on each other, but I had no idea they were going to the lengths that you observed. Alexander will be on a short rope from now on. He took the exam last week and passed with high marks. He'll go to college in a year if Sam or Merv doesn't kill him first."

"I think my precocious daughter may be more to blame than Alexander."

"What did you say to her when you found out?"

"That was difficult. Sam and I talked with her separately. I told her she was blowing her chances for the long term by acting on her impulses for short-term pleasure. Sam warned he would thrash her within an inch of her life if he even thought anything was going on. They were not to be in the barn alone again. Who knows which one worked and whether it will hold?"

"Blowing her chances? Becky, where do you get these terms? Do the people back East say those kinds of things?"

"Sure do. I learned so many modern expressions back there." *Oops.*

Lauren

The first trial was due in one week. Jasmine MacArthur was being tried for the attempted murder of Frank Lash on the trail leading to Miner's Meadow. No known motive existed, and the details were sketchy when reported in the press. Her name and picture had been suppressed. Jasmine's family arrived in town and spared nothing to get her free of these charges. A team of lawyers was already assembling in town. The prosecutors were up against a herculean force of experienced men.

I was called into the district attorney's office. Realizing they must present a more robust picture to the jury, they decided to use my experiences with the defendant.

Frank and I sat in the waiting room of the federal court. "Lauren, I'm really sorry to do this to you." Frank reluctantly told them I was the primary target.

"So why was I there?"

"Fishing. You were teaching me to fish. You ran away with the pole when she fired at me."

"And why have I not come forward before?"

"Scared shitless." We both laughed.

"Actually, that's pretty much the truth."

"I tried to protect you by saying I was the target."

"It might work. I guess we'll see what the prosecutors claim. There is one more thing. How do we know each other?"

"Well, we can't deny we knew each other. We were spotted eating at Meg's. I guess the truth could be applied here. You were looking up information about your mother, who went missing many years ago, and we became friends in the process."

A small, older woman with a severe bun came in to sit down next to Frank. It was Frank's wife, and she didn't look pleased to meet me. Introductions were made, and she sat stiffly, holding Frank's hand. He kept whispering to her. She began to relax and even smiled at me. I smiled back as we were called into the prosecutor's office.

The story was told to the attorney. "Well, at least we have a motive. Is it the truth?"

"Yes, sir. I have many witnesses if you need them." I listed Lisa, Ted, Rich, and even Rich's neighbor Helen. The prosecutor was furious we hadn't provided all this information before. It created a great deal of work to obtain subpoenas and inform the defendant's team about this late twist in the charges. I furnished them with the phone numbers of everyone except Helen. Someone from the FBI has my old phone with her voice-mail messages. I told the lawyer about the report to the local sheriff's office about the recent rock-throwing incident and my rented cabin, which had burned to the ground. I explained that my fiancé, who was overseas in the military, had been her target for several years. Still, I couldn't contact him. I mentioned restraining orders in two other states where Jim had worked.

"Your fiancé is overseas in the military, and you don't know how to find him right now?"

"Yes, sir."

"What branch of the military is he in?"

I explained what I knew. Jim was on a mission and was contactable only by mail to a base in Georgia. The attorney, who recorded the details, had a few more questions before he let us all go.

I had to testify now, but the actual date and time were not set. I told my bosses about this development. They had a few questions, but the hairiest one was the reason I was up at the scene of the crime, and how did I know this Professor Lash? Since it would come out at the trial, I told them he'd contacted me about my mother's disappearance many years ago. Yes, my mother was the young veterinarian who went missing in the rockslide, yet her body was never recovered.

"Anything else you want to tell us?"

"Nope, not that I'm admitting to, anyway. Oh, wait. I forgot. May I have a week off in June?"

Doug appeared exasperated. "Why then?"

"I'm getting married. My fiancé will return from deployment."

"We'll see what we can do. Have you taken any days off yet?"

"No, sir."

"By then, because we'll owe you some time off, you can have a week."

"Okay. My mom might call you about only a week, but simply ignore her."

"At our peril? All right, we'll keep your schedule open for the next week. We'll make sure we can change appointments to accommodate any court appearances."

"Thank you. I'm so sorry to do this to you all."

"Lauren, we're more than happy with your work. Things come up for all of us from time to time. Just be safe."

"Certainly, doing my best."

The trial started on Monday. There was a suppression order on names and witnesses. I was called to present testimony on Tuesday afternoon. I wasn't allowed to come to court until I testified, so I didn't know what was said. I was told to answer only precisely what was asked. The best answer was a short one. I was full of bravado when I walked into the court. After I took one look at Jasmine, however, I was a wet noodle. A bevy of smart-looking lawyers in fancy suits surrounded her. The prosecutor was a small woman and had only one other lawyer assisting her. I was not informed about the switch in the prosecution team.

Frank, who had already given his evidence, was seated behind the prosecutor. He smiled at me, and I weakly smiled back. I was asked questions about myself, which became more challenging. At last, I was asked about many events of which I really had no firsthand knowledge. The rock through the window could have been anyone. The arsonist who burned the cabin was never found. The birthday flowers at work were curious, and it was difficult to tell how anyone else might have sent them. The only thing was my eyewitness account of the shooting. I was asked to read something from across the room, and it looked for once as if I might be able to identify her from a great distance. The cross-examination was brutal. In the end, I wasn't a great witness.

One aspect was evident to me and, hopefully, to the jury. Jasmine stared daggers at me the entire time I was on the witness stand. As I was led out, I heard the prosecution had arranged for a secret witness at the last minute. I hoped it was someone who knew her better.

Members of the press were in the courtroom, as well as reporters in the corridor outside the courtroom. I was surrounded. I commented that I was not allowed to say anything until the trial was over. They understood they couldn't publish it, anyway. During the mayhem, the police gathered around someone who had just left a room next to the courtroom. I didn't see his face, but he wore military clothes. *Was this someone who was also hunted by this woman?* I wished I could go back in. Because the prosecution might want to question me again, I was not allowed to enter the court. I waited for an hour, but finally, I was told I was permitted to leave the court. The current witness would be examined for the rest of the day and possibly even the following day.

I was recalled to court the following day. The dozens of text messages and voice-mail messages that I had received constituted the prosecutors' final submissions. I was asked to verify that I had received them, which I did. I glanced around the courtroom to determine whether I could identify the mysterious man who testified for the prosecution. He was not in court. I stared directly at Jasmine, hoping she would do or say something out of fury that would alert the jury of her intention to kill me, but she didn't look at me today.

I was again dismissed and taken out of the courtroom. This time, I was escorted to a side room with a round table and cushioned chairs, where attorneys could confer with their clients. I waited there for what seemed like hours. No one came in to tell me what was happening. I dozed off after an hour or more because I did not have anything to look at or read.

When I heard a click of the door opening, I glanced up to see a distraught Jim standing in the doorway. I jumped up and went straight to him when I realized it was not a dream. Jim kept saying he was sorry he hadn't known about any of this until the previous week. He was afforded special leave to fly back to the States to testify. Jim was here for only two nights. Following this, he would return to finish the previous months of his assignment. We hugged, and both cried. His testimony had hopefully put her in jail, and we would be free of her for years to come.

After an hour, a clerk came in, and said we could leave the court. Jim had to fly out at nine the following morning. I had sixteen hours to be with him. I had to return to work, and the entire staff applauded when I came in. They knew

Jim was my fiancé. My boss, Doug, handed me a long list of appointments. He said I could go home if I completed them early. I showed it to Jim, who said, "Let's ride, cowgirl."

As we headed to the truck, everyone shouted, "April Fools'." It was April 1. I was told to go home and report for duty the next day after dropping Jim at the airport. Doug and Max both shook Jim's hand and were more than gracious to us both. I introduced him to everyone, and we left for home. Since Rich was still at school, we had the place to ourselves. Need I say more?

LB was beside herself when we opened the door. She wouldn't leave Jim alone. He was jet-lagged and promptly fell asleep after welcoming festivities. I lay next to him and watched him sleep. He'd lost more weight and probably more hair too. Jim appeared like a skinny Hank Buchanan. Both my mothers would be pleased. When he woke, I made him some lunch. The fishing season was open, but the creek behind my old, burned cabin was still raging from the snow runoff in the mountains. A for-sale sign was on the property where the cabin no longer stood. We decided to go to the realty office to find out the price.

Jim realized I may have had a connection to the property and was interested in it before the fire. I didn't tell him about what I had been doing since he left. All I said was I didn't go to Honduras. I promised him I would explain it when he returned for good.

"As long as you're safe, Lauren. I don't care what you did."

We discovered that the property went farther back into the woods than I had thought it did. It was ten acres, and some problems existed with the water rights, which is common nowadays. The price was quite reasonable. We would think about it. There'd been no interest in the property, and the agent didn't press us for a commitment. That reminded me of the gold nugget Sam had given me.

We weren't going to commit to anything immediately, but Jim was considering living in the area. I had contracted for one year to work at the veterinary clinic, which I genuinely enjoyed. I liked the staff and bosses. Since the two other owners were gone, I knew only half the team. When we went back to the house, Rich was home from school. He was as surprised as I had been. He and Jim greeted each other warmly. Helen from next door waved. I smiled and shook my head, wondering what she would think now.

Rich and Jim had a men's talk while I took a shower. First, we needed to call our parents. I phoned my family first. My mom answered.

"Hey, Mom, it's me."

"Hey, honey. How are you? How's the trial going? Did you testify?"

"Yes. I don't know if we will win, but the prosecutors provided a special witness who might have swung the jury our way. I want you to talk to him."

"Hello, Mrs. Harper. Nice to talk to you again."

I heard my mother yelling at my father. "Jeff, get on the phone. It's Lauren's Jim. What are you doing there? Are you done?"

"Not yet, but I'm a free man after two more months."

"Jim, it's me, Jeff, Lauren's dad."

"Hello, Dr. Harper. Nice to talk with you again."

"Jim, did I hear you're going to be free in June?"

"Yes, sir."

"Son, you're marrying my daughter. There is no freedom. Ball and chain, son, ball and chain. Ouch. Sherry's hitting me."

"Mom, may we set the date? Can we hire the church on the third Saturday or not? I think we should wait until the end of June in case he isn't done with his deployment when he says he is."

"I have set aside the first three Saturdays in June. If we can't have our church, there's a new one, which is even nicer." We discussed the details for a few minutes and hung up. We could only leave a message for Jim's mom, as she hadn't answered.

We decided to go out to dinner to celebrate. It took some convincing, but we persuaded Rich to accompany us. We discussed the wedding, for which Jim asked Rich to serve as his best man. Rich was honored. He inquired if he could bring Dirk, and we laughed. Of course, he could bring whomever he wanted. Dinner was delicious, and we all had too much to drink. A couple was sitting near us who knew Rich. They offered to take us home. It was a wonderful evening—my two favorite men.

I checked my phone when we arrived home. I had missed a call from the prosecuting attorney. The jury members had made up their minds, and the verdict would be read in court in the morning. I had to take Jim to the airport, and I doubted whether I would be back in time to be there.

I called Frank Lash, who was happy about the way it ended. He believed we were in with a chance. I thanked him and hung up. Poor Jim was asleep on the bed by the time I was ready. We slept fitfully, and we had time only to shower and leave for the airport in the morning. Jim stopped at a gas station to purchase some carnations for me. It was hard to say goodbye after such a brief visit.

"Lauren, I love you and can't wait until we're married. I can tell something's bothering you, and I hope it isn't me."

"No, that's for sure. I have some things to tell you when you return. It's all good. Really good. It's just too much for this short time we have."

"No secrets, darling."

"Nope, definitely no secrets, Jim Bob." He was called to board as we reached the end of the terminal. We kissed but letting go was so difficult. I watched him walk onto the tarmac and climb the stairs on the back of the plane. He waved again and was gone.

Chapter 27

Rebecca

One of the broncs kicked Merv Little, our head stockman, a few days before the drive. I quickly set the fractured leg he sustained and knew it would heal, but he could not go on the cattle drive. Sam decided to take his place. I was disappointed they didn't want women on the cattle drive.

Alexander had no choice in the matter. He was going on the drive, and his studies would have to wait. He was so far ahead of everyone that time away would not matter. A little enforced separation was what the doctor ordered. They would be gone for several weeks.

Sam insisted that he and I take time off from work. We were going to spend the entire month of July in Hank Heaven. I thought it was somewhat extravagant, but he claimed we both worked hard, and it was time to enjoy a vacation, doing some fishing and relaxing.

Jenny was now showing her advancing pregnancy. Dan and Sam would return in plenty of time for the delivery. When Hanna wasn't at school, she helped Jenny with the children. Little Hank had become a handful. He was into everything and was giving his mother no end of trouble trying to contain him.

We all decided to go on a picnic. I was going to teach little Lizzie to fish. The best place to go was the spot where a rattlesnake bit my dear mule, Spit, several years ago. Hanna was present when the snake bit him, and she has never liked the place. However, it was grassy, and the water that flowed into and out of the pond was slow and gentle—perfect for fishing. We set out with a buckboard midmorning on a warm spring day.

When we arrived, I walked around, searched for snakes or other dangerous areas, and declared the site safe. Hanna and Lizzie explored the edges of the pool and gathered wood for a campfire, on which we would fry some fresh fish. Jenny kept Little Hank busy until he fell asleep. I brought fly rods and a simple rod with a line and cork, so Lizzie could see when a fish took the worm I placed on the hook. I tossed it out, after which we sat together, watching the cork bob up and down. Hanna went to the other end of the pond and cast flies where the water flowed into the large pool. It wasn't long before the cork started to bob, indicating a fish was grabbing the worm.

I held the rod, with Lizzie sitting in my lap. We both jerked the line, and immediately we hooked the fish. The rod had no reel, and we simply had to stand and back up while the fish fought the process of being caught. Lizzie had her first fish. She was so pleased with herself—oh, for a camera. Jenny took the fish, which Lizzie only reluctantly gave up, to prepare it for lunch. We caught two more, while Hanna caught a single large trout. That was plenty for lunch. We would resume fishing later for dinner.

We ate a tasty lunch of trout, apple, and bread. The children played in the grass while Hanna and I caught enough trout for dinner. Gee Ling had ridden to town for several days, which left us on our own at the Cattle Creek Ranch. We returned to the ranch in the late afternoon. Since it was easier for Hanna and me to go to Jenny's house for dinner, we headed there after cooking everything. Little Hank had been fed and was asleep. Lizzy practiced fishing with a button at the end of her line. A kitten swatted the button. Life was good.

Hanna and I went home and to bed following supper. A loud knock at the door awakened me. When Bushy, an old ranch hand, had made a final pass on the mares due to foal, he noticed that Sam's horse, Cash, had not eaten his dinner and was drooling. Sam left him at the Cattle Creek Ranch because of his fractured coffin bone. It had healed, but weeks on the trail were too much to expect of his beloved horse.

I pulled on a robe and went out to look at him. He seemed okay, but I felt he had a fever when I looked at his gums. I'm not good at judging horses' temperatures by feel, but this situation was an exception. He was hot. His gums were all right, but he had a modest, firm swelling near his throatlatch, which was most likely painful for the gelding. I placed my hands on either side of the throat right behind his jowls and pressed. The reaction was strong and abrupt since it hurt. He was an older horse, and the two diseases that came to mind were a grass-seed abscess or strangles.

"Bushy, are any of the other horses sick?"

"No, ma'am."

"It's probably simply a grass seed. I'll hot-pack it for a while and see if it gives Cash some relief."

"Doc, I'll do that. Why don't you go to bed?"

"Thank you, Bushy. Since it might be contagious, wash your hands before touching any other horses. Also, don't stick your fingers in your mouth without washing them. I'll put the kettle on in the house and prepare some hot water for you. Make sure it's not too hot, Bushy. If you can hold the rag in your hand, it won't burn Cash. Sam would kill us both if Cash was scalded."

"Sure thing, Doc." Bushy was about the only person around who called me Doc. I didn't mind either way. The oven in the kitchen still had embers, and I quickly heated water and returned. I left strict instructions for Bushy and everyone to keep Cash isolated until I was confident it wasn't the dreaded, highly contagious strangles. We would know soon enough. Strangles is caused by a bacterium that spreads from horse to horse but can be transmitted by shared water troughs.

I remembered Sam had ridden Cash into town two days before leaving on the cattle drive. Because our hay was clean and had few grass seeds that would penetrate the mouth and cause problems, I had to think that strangles would be a possibility. The day before leaving on the drive, Sam had ridden Cash to see the mares and look at the foals that had been born several weeks earlier. I'd never experienced a strangles outbreak on the Cattle Creek Ranch, but I had encountered it back East. I was worried. The next day, my fears were realized. Twenty or more horses showed signs of the dreaded disease.

"Ma, why do they call it strangles?"

How I would like to tell Hanna about the specific bacteria, the vaccine, and penicillin. "Sadly, I think you'll see the reason in a few days, darling. It causes large abscesses under and around the throatlatch. The abscesses are sometimes so big that a horse can't breathe."

"Can we catch it?"

"It is possible, but it is extremely rare. Be sure to wash your hands if you touch any pus and wash your hands in between touching any horses."

"May I stay home from school to help this week?" The thought of Hanna riding one of the sick horses into town and unknowingly infecting the other children's horses was a consideration.

"Hanna, let's put a few horses that don't seem sick up in the corrals on the other side of the west bunkhouses. Get your horse, Penny, and any others. We'll set up clean buckets, and you can oversee watering and feeding the horses that aren't sick. You cannot go near the other horses. Do you understand?"

"Yes, Mom." The 'mom' had come from Lauren. I realized Hanna had heard Lauren call me 'mom' on rare occasions when she forgot about what time my older daughter was in. I liked it and didn't correct Hanna.

We had a skeleton crew due to the cattle drive. Merv, our foreman, was no help due to his broken leg, which had taken a toll on him. He could get up and move around, but standing on the crutches, was difficult since he had put on weight over the years.

I brought all the men together to explain how we would isolate the sick horses from the healthy ones. We couldn't hot-pack all the horses, so we would wait until the abscesses were close to bursting, run the horses into corrals, and snub them. I would lance the abscesses with a knife that I had honed to the size of an oversized scalpel. The horses would either live or die.

Oh, for some sedation, local anesthesia, and penicillin. Kill me now because this was going to be horrible. I understood we would have losses. The worst part was that while many of the horses would have long-term immunity, the bacteria would be in the soil, and this scenario would be repeated yearly. I had the men make up lye solutions to saturate the areas where we kept the horses and opened the abscesses. Soil contamination was a long-term problem.

Cash's abscess grew, but it burst within a week. I didn't have to lance it. Once it burst, he was much better. The older horses usually suffered from a milder case than the young horses did. Several horses didn't have an abscess. They merely had fevers, stopped eating for a few days, and drooled.

One consequence of the outbreak was a condition called bastard strangles, when an abscess forms in one of the lymph glands in the abdomen or chest. This ailment was evident in a few horses that either wouldn't improve after the external abscess burst or from horses that were still sick without any apparent abscess. When I noticed the first one and termed it "bastard strangles," the two men who assisted me appeared shocked. I then just called this condition internal strangles. *Sheesh, these prudish Victorian men were painful.*

After two weeks of care, we'd lost more than twenty horses, many of which were foals or weanlings. We expected more deaths. We all worked feverishly to try to stop the spread and help the horses survive.

One of the yearlings struck me when I was opening an abscess one day. He reared up, hit my forearm, somehow opened the gate latch, and knocked me over before anyone could stop him. The poor men who were handling him felt horrible. They helped me up and asked whether I was all right. I realized my arm might be broken, but I believed it was only a crack, and I carried on for several more hours.

At home that night, I crafted a splint from a small, smooth piece of wood and rags. The swelling had increased in my forearm the following day, but the pain was less. I sent Hanna into town with Cassie for some plaster of Paris for a cast. I resumed my abscess-bursting ways and counted more than a hundred sick horses on the Cattle Creek Ranch. The death count went up to over thirty, which was a sad and painful time for us all. Several men had horses they had ridden for many years that succumbed to the bacteria.

With the aid of Hanna and Cassie, I made a cast using gauze and powdered plaster that evening. It was sturdy and yet not too heavy. I wrapped it in several layers of paper when I worked on the horses. It might do to keep it clean—fail. The second abscess was so large that the purulent material went down under my cast. I was almost dry retching, knowing what was sitting next to my skin. I went down to the stream closest to the house that afternoon to wash the cast and arm until they were as clean as possible.

The smell from under the cast was putrid by morning. I needed to take it off. I had to saw it, and there were no cast cutters to save me from an accidental cut or puncture. Because the bacteria were residing under the cast, any perforation of my skin would most likely cause infection. One of the men began the sawing procedure. Eventually, it came off without causing any damage to my arm. Thankfully, I was able to implement the original cast to make an impression mold. We constructed a second cast and sawed it down the length of the cast, resulting in a half-splint. I could splint my arm as needed. This approach slowed down the healing process, but I wasn't going to ruin another cast with streptococcus bacterium. Even if it was solely a horse disease, it could potentially infect me.

Bushy's riding companion never got a visible abscess, but he stopped eating and began to lose weight. I realized what was coming. Bushy wouldn't give up. He tried all kinds of home remedies, including onions and garlic. In the end, his horse became so weak that Bushy shot him. Poor Bushy was so upset he just started to walk to town. I offered him one of the better, healthy horses, but he refused.

Ray Thompson came out the following day. He tied up his horse several yards from our horses and walked to the house. Ray reported that Bushy was drowning his sorrows at the Bucket o' Blood. He inquired how things were going. The outbreak had peaked in town. Many of the livery-stable horses had died. Apparently, onions weren't working, and neither did the leftover bottles of Celia's brew. I shared the idea of getting the abscesses to head up quickly, opening them, and disinfecting the area. Ray was impressed.

"Becky, you're a marvel. You know so much more than anyone I know."

"We've had losses, too, Ray."

"Nothing like in town, though."

"It won't end anytime soon. If people don't disinfect the areas that horses congregate, and the nasal discharges and pus are left, it will come back next year."

"I'll tell anyone I see. Have you heard from Sam and Dan?"

"Not yet. The drovers should be getting close. Maybe another week or two."

"I'll be glad when Sam gets back. Our friends are dropping like flies these days."

"Be glad that you get to see them out. It could be you, although I doubt either you or Sam will croak anytime soon."

"Croak?"

"Eastern expression, Ray." *Oops again.*

"Becky, you need some rest. You look exhausted."

"Yes, I should. I'll get right on that suggestion, Ray."

"Sure, you will. When I grow wings."

We kissed, and he left—still a fox.

It took three more weeks before I did rest. In the end, the Cattle Creek Ranch lost several young horses. I doubted we could meet the numbers for next year if we continued the contract for the cavalry. I figured Sam and Dan would have to go on a buying spree. I hope to hear from them soon. It was getting warmer every day, but I expected a regular bed warmer when I signed on for this life. I didn't envy him. I may have spent one of the worst periods of my veterinary life, but sleeping on the trail was tough.

The new Penny never got strangles, and Cash recovered fully. There were several lingering cases. One of the complications of a severe bacterial infection is laminitis or founder. Numerous theories exist about the cause of this condition. I wished I'd asked Lauren for any new ideas about the pathophysiology of laminitis. Gosh, all the cool words I understood from my days in vet school are nearly gone from my brain. I was going to spring that on Sam when he returned. I'll be interested in his reaction. He is a well-read, intelligent man, but he doesn't like people who flaunt their education with big words. Dare I use the term 'cool?'

Whether the blood is shunted away from the feet or toxic chemicals penetrate the foot is questionable. The result is tearing the lamina, or the fingerlike projections of the live foot, and the similar ones from the horny hoof. It's like putting one's fingers together, from one hand to the other, and then breaking them apart.

It's the same mechanism that keeps people's fingernails from falling off their fingers, except horses must walk on them. The result is termed rotation of the third phalanx, or coffin bone. It's probably best not to use that phrase too frequently around Sam, either. In this time, we call it founder. Anyway, several of our horses survived the infection, but some foundered after an overwhelming infection.

The other complication is a disease named purpura, which is an allergic reaction to some infective agents, such as the strangles bacteria. The symptoms are generalized swelling of the face and legs and sometimes of the lower chest and abdomen. The treatment constitutes steroids and penicillin. Once again, we were up a creek without a paddle. Tragically, another eleven horses had to be shot, leaving

Hanna beside herself. I was informed the men drew straws to choose who had to check the stock for new cases or complications. We were now down to seventy-five percent of our original herd.

Abscess-lancing duties were completed, and most of the horses were recovering. When I returned to my hospital responsibilities, I was grateful for the relief. In town, circumstances had been just as dire. Horses everywhere exhibited signs of post-strangles issues—from weight loss to continued small abscesses. I attempted to talk to the livery-stable men, but my recommendations continued to fall on deaf ears. I forbade anyone from riding into town with horses that had managed to evade strangles, at least currently. New foals were born, many of which did not get sick. The foals which received colostrum would carry the protective antibodies for several months.

A telegraph from Sam reported the successful end of the cattle drive. He signed the same contract for the following year. He and Dan wouldn't be home for a month. I dreaded telling him what had happened. I sent one in return, congratulating Sam and Dan and stating they might want to acquire some breeding stock on the way back.

Lauren

After dropping Jim at the airport, I drove to the courthouse, where there was a delay for the court proceedings recommencement. I tried to call Frank, but he didn't answer. I observed a crowd of onlookers and sheriff's deputies on the courthouse steps. I quietly spoke to one deputy to inquire what was happening.

"Jasmine MacArthur hasn't shown up for her verdict. We're out looking for her." The deputy, who recognized me, escorted me inside, where the press and attorneys were standing around. I saw Frank and approached him. He looked relieved that I was there.

"I can't believe this has happened." I was nervous and watching the doors in case Jasmine returned with a weapon.

Frank shook his head. "Can you believe this?"

"Sadly, I can. This place needs cleaning out. The level of incompetence is amazing."

A prosecuting attorney escorted us into a side room. We were notified that Jasmine stayed in a hotel with her family. She didn't answer when they knocked on her motel-room door in the morning. It was feared she might have taken her life, and the maid was summoned to open the door. She was gone, and her bed had not been slept in.

A manhunt was conducted. Frank and I were asked to stay in the building until further notice. When I called my coworkers at the clinic to explain what had happened, they had already heard the news. My calls were rescheduled. Dot took the phone from the receptionist and told me not to even come close to the clinic. The FBI agents were stationed in the courthouse, while some were directed to unmarked cars in the parking lot.

I called Rich to leave a message, but he was teaching and didn't answer. Fearing Jasmine might go to my house, I called our neighbor Helen, and she didn't answer, either. I left a message on her phone. I thought that was a little odd. She was retired and always answered when I called. I told the attorneys that it might be worth checking her out, but Rich's house was already staked out. The deputies had knocked on the neighboring doors. The information was passed on to individuals in the area, and Helen was again contacted. Helen answered this time, stating that she was alone and everything was fine. Helen informed the deputy she had company and was getting tired of them bothering her. I was not made aware of this until later. Had I known, I would have thought that her response was highly unusual.

We were safeguarded in the room next to the court for an hour. Frank was confident he was no longer a target and wanted to leave. The FBI agents were not as sure about me. They discussed the possibility that she had fled the state, which seemed like the most probable scenario. They were all fighting and blaming one another. I was caught in the middle, and they were taking no chances. It was bad enough that she had not been guarded, but it would put more than egg on their faces if she escaped and harmed the key witness.

I was taken to a hotel for the evening, and Rich returned my call at last. His phone had been turned off all day, and he had just received the message. He wanted to know where I was and whether I was all right.

"Too all right. I'm fine, but the police won't let me come home. I'm under guard. I can't tell you where I am, in case she has an accomplice, and someone gives her any information. They believe she fled the state."

"No, shit?"

"Yep, no shit. Hey, will you feed LB for me?"

"You're on the news. Did the court lift the suppression order?"

"Must have."

"Law-enforcement officials are all over the area."

"Will you check on our neighbor Helen for me?"

"Of course. Take care, Lauren."

"You, as well, big bro. She may be armed and dangerous."

Employing his best and yet pathetic John Wayne accent, he replied, "Okay, pilgrim. I'll be heading to the west forty to do doggy patrol."

"Thanks, John." I hung up and turned to the woman guarding me. She shrugged. "Are you going to feed me, or will I starve?"

"I'll call my boss. I can't leave you."

The police lady brought me a Hank burger and fries an hour later. She consumed a Comstock special. She asked me if I watched Comstock. "Funny, not until recently. How about you?"

"All the time as a kid. Who's your favorite?"

"Well, I like Hank. He kind of looks like my fiancé. How about you?"

"Clint, he was a dreamboat."

"He is good-looking, isn't he?"

My phone rang. It was Rich. Helen hadn't come to the door when he knocked. The agents were investigating.

"Make sure LB is protected. If she were around, I know Jasmine would try to hurt LB to get back at me."

"I think Helen is more important."

"Oh, of course." No, LB is my best dog ever, I thought. "What am I saying?" Like hell. "Call me back and let me know."

As I hung up the phone, my guard received a call, and she went out on the balcony. Surprise, surprise! The FBI was convinced that Jasmine was holding Helen captive.

They would start negotiations as soon as they had access to a phone. Neither Jasmine nor Helen would answer. The FBI wanted me to leave a message on Helen's phone. The FBI hoped that hearing my voice on the answering machine might prompt Jasmine to allow Helen to pick up the phone. She did.

"Where in the world have you been, Lauren? Jazz and I are becoming acquainted. She wants to give you a piece of her mind. Frankly, I'm on her side. You've been a bit of a harlot in the man department. Did you think I was so stupid that I thought you were sleeping with two guys and yet engaged to another? You don't deserve any of them."

"Helen, I can explain." I was cut off.

"You certainly can. You're nothing but a two-faced liar. Lauren, I need you to do what Jazz says. You already have two men on a string. You should let the other one go."

"Helen, tell her I'm ready to negotiate about Jim. Some things aren't worth the effort."

I could hear Helen repeating what I said to Jasmine. There was a pause, and the phone was muffled as though Helen had her hand over the receiver.

"Jazz wants proof."

"What kind of proof?"

"You've got to come over to talk to her directly."

The guard made circles with her hand to indicate I needed to keep the conversation going. "I'm willing to talk to her, but I have to have assurance she won't hurt you or me."

Again, there was muffled talking. "Jazz will let me go if you come to the house."

"Does she have a gun?"

"No."

"Helen, would you say no either way?"
"I don't understand what you're asking."
"Never mind."
"She's unarmed."

I stared at the agent, who was now flanked by two others who were shaking their heads. "Tell Jasmine I'm on my way, but she must allow you to leave the house before I enter. I'm going to get into a car to come over. Helen, stay on the line and talk to my friend here, and I'll drive over. I'll be there in twenty minutes or so. You have to be out of the house before I come in." I read what I was told to say from a script an agent handed to me. I was not coming. There was no way the FBI would let me go.

They had an agent who was my height and weight, but her hair was short. They gave her a wig, along with a bulletproof vest. Helen had all but admitted Jasmine had a gun. Apparently, Jasmine's family was now in contact with her. They were begging her to give herself up. The authorities were working on her from many angles.

While I was in protective custody, poor Helen was the one in danger. The agent assigned to me offered a rundown about what another agent at the scene reported. It felt like hours before I was informed that it was over, and Jasmine was in custody.

Helen also provided me with her side of the ordeal later. Her rendition was more descriptive. "Lauren, I stood at the window and told Jasmine when I saw your double coming toward the house. Someone knocked on the door. Jasmine was exhausted, made a mistake, and let me out while your double tackled her. I ran behind a tree. Jasmine didn't shoot. She realized the game was up, and she sat down in the living room and began to cry. She was tackled to the floor and taken into custody."

I was returned to the courthouse, where I was debriefed. I was not allowed to discuss these events with anyone and not allowed to talk to the police. Jasmine's identity had been made public for a short period due to the need for public safety. However, her lawyers were quick to have that stopped. Her trial for attempted murder would be postponed, and all parties were considering a plea bargain. I was advised this approach was the best-case scenario. She would get fifteen years and maybe serve seven.

"What kind of prison? I would hate to think she could escape." No one could say for sure, which made me wish there was another solution. I wondered how many stalkers gave up after a prison sentence. I saw both Frank and Helen at the courthouse. Helen, Frank, and I all hugged one another. Helen was in her element because she was being interviewed and feted by everyone, especially the FBI agents. I could tell she was eyeing one agent off. I laughed to myself, watching her work the crowd.

"How does it feel to be a hero?"

"Darn good, sister. Really, I never want that scenario again. I was scared shitless."

"I was scared for you, as well. I'm really sorry to bring this to you."

"There may be a silver lining to this situation." She pointed to the agent, who had paid somewhat more attention to her than had the rest of them. They would be of similar age. I noticed no ring, and he kept glancing her way and smiling. "Lauren, I hope you realize I didn't mean what I said to you on the phone."

"I know you didn't. Maybe it's time for us to have a talk. I know you're a good person and wouldn't betray the trust Rich and I have in you now. We must be careful, but it will be out in the open in the next few weeks, anyway, so you might as well be the first to know. Sadly, I'm not the woman you think I am." I quietly told her about Rich, Dirk, and Jim. "Yep, I'm a one-man woman. One is more than enough."

"Oh, there goes that dream. How the mighty fall."

PART 3

DESPERATE TIMES

Chapter 28

Rebecca

Sam finally returned. After the shock of learning what happened, he accepted we did what we could to minimize the damage. I explained all I knew about strangles and the cause, as well as modern-day preventions and treatments. I even carefully introduced the term pathophysiology. Sam laughed as he searched for the derivation of the word in our dictionary.

"'Patho' pertains to disease, while 'physiology' concerns normal function," he declared. Sam didn't require a dictionary, but he was glad to add the word to his vocabulary. However, he would never use it in front of anyone, except for me. I showed him some microscopic slides I had made, on which he could see the chains of small cocci, or spheres, under the microscope.

Enough of the bacteriology lesson. This one was not Sam's first outbreak. He understood the need to isolate the healthy from the sick. Until further notice, no horses were going to share the water troughs in town. He and Dan would buy stock as soon as possible.

I'd written to the Merritts, and I planned to travel down to Woodland with either Dan or Sam to visit and see the horses they had to offer. Sam realized that the Merritts were my biological great-great-grandparents. He had not met them, so it was decided that he and I would go down and take some of the men to bring back the horses we might purchase.

Alexander had to stay home this time in preparation for his further education. We would allow Hanna to come with us. I wanted her to meet the Merritts and their children. The boys would be getting older. She was excited to be able to finally do some traveling. The entire family would be together at least for a month. Since spring was mild, Sam and I went up to Hank Heaven alone one day while Hanna stayed with Dan and Jenny. Because they both knew about Alexander and Hanna, they were on guard for any transgressions.

Hanna was on her best behavior. Cassie and Merv were on the alert, as well. They had Alexander either working or studying day and night. I prayed we would get Alexander to the mining college before anything happened. Sam spent quite some time with him on the trail. He had grown to like and respect Alexander. Sam mentioned if the two lovebirds ended up together, he would think he'd done well by Hanna. Sam only wanted to ensure they were mature enough and had the skills and means to care for each other and raise their own family. He hoped that would be when Alexander returned from college. We both recognized the risk that he would find someone else when Hanna wasn't around.

On our way up to Hank Heaven, we stared down at the portal pool. It must have made Sam nervous to consider a place where I could go and never come back. Nothing would make him leave his time and life. He understood, though, that I had another life. Granted, it was a life I had chosen to abandon, but I had reasons to contemplate the options.

"Bec, do you think about going back anymore?"

"I'd be lying to you if I said no. The only thing that would make me do it would be if I learned Lauren was in trouble or ill, and I was the only person in the world who could save her. Other than that, no, I don't."

Sam realized I had made sacrifices to be with him in his time with his family. Never a day passed that I didn't experience his gratitude. Were life and marriage perfect? No, but they were much more than I could have ever dreamed of. I could trade them, yet I opted not to. I hoped my affirmation would never be tested.

We descended into a verdant valley with two waterfalls and rivulets crossing the valley floor. The sky was blue with large billowy clouds, which occasionally darkened the grass. When the sun quickly emerged, the light warmed our backs as we made our way to Sam's cabin.

We expected to stay merely one night. Consequently, we immediately made a fire to begin to heat the room. Sam went to Hank's grave to clean it from the winter ravages and sat down to visit with his deceased son. I stayed with him for a few minutes, after which I went out to the lake to catch our dinner.

The fishing was not easy. The water temperature was still quite cold, and no insect hatch lured the trout to the surface. I changed my fly to a streamer and waded farther into the water, closer to where the fish were hiding. I removed my pants and was naked from the waist down. Sam was always shocked by my lack of modesty. I wasn't going to walk around in wet clothes all day, and we both knew he was the sole person to see me. He came down to the lake and watched without comment.

The previous year, Sam had given me a woven wicker creel, which he had seen in a magazine. I wouldn't hurt his feelings and not use it, so it was over my shoulder, and I placed the first trout in the creel. When I had enough for a good dinner, I turned, and Sam had left. I returned to get my pants, which were gone. A few choice words were considered. He was smiling when I arrived at the cabin.

"Avert your eyes, Mr. Buchanan. The sight of a naked old lady may scar you for life."

"A risk I'm willing to take, my dear wife. You seem cold. Let me help you get warm." We both smiled like teenagers.

We got back to the Cattle Creek Ranch with more fish the following day. Our family ate a meal down at Jenny and Dan's house. Little Hank was walking and talking. He loved Sam, and the feeling was returned. Lizzy was in love with Hanna, who did her best to ignore Lizzy, which annoyed us all. We all realized she was thinking about Alexander and still in her intolerable teenage years. Dan teased her unmercifully.

I quietly whispered to Jenny, "Just wait. You'll have this on your hands in a few years."

"No. I'll go away and send them to their grandparents."

I turned to Sam, who was oblivious to the entire scene. "We should get new locks on the doors, darling." He seemed perplexed, and I said I would explain it later. This dinner was our celebration for a successful culmination of the cattle and horse drive.

The Cattle Creek Ranch was thriving. It would be difficult to imagine that it would not go on forever. I was the sole person to realize it wouldn't. I simply hoped it was a happy ending. In such a patriarchal society, the burden would be on Little Hank alone unless Jenny carried a boy or Clint returned from Australia with his children. I would never say anything, but I guessed Sam figured that his family reign would end because I never mentioned the Cattle Creek Ranch in modern times.

We journeyed down to Sacramento and Woodland by stagecoach. We thought we would ride some of the stock we planned to purchase back to Nevada. The ranch hands would come in a fortnight to bring the broodmares and young stock. Our immediate needs were for healthy, rideable geldings up to six years of age. The Merritts owned livestock all over the West, but they arranged to have several at their main home in Woodland. Gee Ling accompanied us to visit cousins in Sacramento while we traveled across the Sacramento River and rode to Woodland.

It was like coming home. The house had assumed the maturity that I remembered from my grandmother and mother's pictures. The Merritts resembled the Buchanans at the peak of their dynasty. The children, who were becoming young adults, readily took Hanna into their domain. We hardly saw her. She was invited to a dance. Sam took her aside to give her the rules of deportment. If any infractions occurred, she was doomed to live inside her room at the Cattle Creek Ranch.

Sam was in awe of Dr. Merritt. Of course, they were on a first-name basis. The Merritt house was far more extravagant than our home was. While Hiram's holdings were vast, the Cattle Creek Ranch—with its timber, mining, and grazing land—was probably worth twice the value of the Merritt holdings. The Merritt mansion did not intimidate Sam. I understood that it eventually burned down, and I'd heard that my grandmother was probably the last child to be born in the house after her father died. Of course, I didn't tell anyone.

"Becky, you come from good stock." We were dressing for dinner after a successful day of horse-trading. I adjusted Sam's tie.

"I think so. The best part is the Merritts have no idea about me, yet they have been extremely kind over the years." Jeannette and I regularly corresponded. We knew what the other was doing and the ways our lives had changed over the years.

After dinner, the men went to the porch to smoke cigars. Jeannette and I sat in the parlor to discuss our families and our aspirations for the children. I told her all about Dan and his family and that we were expecting a new grandchild soon. I described my work at the Virginia City clinic, as well. Hiram had mostly relinquished medical practice for farming and land acquisition, which were much more lucrative endeavors. I think he was in awe of my continuing to work as I approached sixty years of age. We all understood my work wasn't for the money.

Hanna, who returned from the social, was the belle of the ball. She danced with several young men and made friends with other young women. Jeannette and Hiram suggested that we let her stay for the summer. She would meet many people, and they could introduce her to society. I was against it, but Hanna and Sam wore me down. She would stay for only two months. The time away from Alexander would most likely cure her of lovesickness. It would allow him time to prepare for his college courses, as well.

After a few more days, we left Hanna with the Merritts. Sam and I traveled back to the Cattle Creek Ranch. I wanted to buy another mule, but one stare from Sam closed that subject. Most people are lucky to have one great horse in their life. I had three so far—Penny I and Penny II and Spit, my beautiful mule. My horse Jack was a challenge from my first ride on my wedding day to the final ride last summer when he almost tipped me off. He was always around the barn, and I occasionally rode him, but I had to outride the buck first. Because Sam worried that I would fall off and be injured, I only rode him when I was desperate—really desperate.

We returned home with the start of the new horses. I rode a gelding we named Bingo that was quick and soft in the mouth. By the time we arrived home, he was as broke as I needed. Penny II was in foal, and I would have to locate another mount the following year when she foaled. The horses had all recovered from the strangles outbreak. We still required additional stock, but the horses we purchased from the Merritts would arrive here in several weeks. Since we would put our young stallion over a few open mares, we hopefully would have more foals for our future needs.

Jenny would be ready to deliver in several weeks. We weren't sure of her exact due date, but I guessed the babysitting we did last autumn wasn't the event that led to her impending delivery. I figured she might have conceived a few weeks earlier after I examined her.

Dan decided to get a puppy for Lizzy and Little Hank in the meantime. A bitch that died unexpectedly left six puppies. They were ready to wean, anyway. Two puppies went to a family just out of town, while the rest were still with the farmer who had the mother. The puppy was a cute little mongrel that Little Hank wouldn't let anyone else hold because he was in the 'mine' phase. None of us was permitted to touch the puppy, and Little Hank would scream if Lizzy even came close.

My associate John mentioned the farmer, who had visited the clinic a few days previously. The vague symptoms the farmer displayed puzzled John. He presented with a rash and fever. When his wife called us out to their property two days later, the man exhibited severe neurological symptoms, worsening by the hour. I was paralyzed by fear when I saw him. He was uncontrollable, spitting at his wife and children.

"Mrs. Jenkins, what killed the bitch?" I dug my fingernails into my palms, waiting for her reply.

"I don't rightly know, Dr. Buchanan. She crawled under the house. We've had problems with skunks lately, and I know she was fighting with one. She killed it, though, after which I never saw anything else until she died."

"May I see the puppies you have left?"

"The last two died, and we sent one to the McCabes."

"Mrs. Jenkins, who else has had contact with the bitch or the puppies? Have you fed them?"

"No, ma'am. My husband did all that."

John realized what I suspected. He opened the door where Mr. Jenkins lay writhing, spitting, and wetting himself.

John was in shock, as was I. "Where did the puppies go, Mrs. Jenkins?"

"Of course, Dan took one, while two of them went to the traveling tinker man. He offered me a pot in trade."

"Mrs. Jenkins, I need for you to remember who else held or played with the puppies. Did any other friends or children handle the pups?" I was frantic. I was afraid Mr. Jenkins had rabies. Others probably required urgent medical attention.

All I could think about was Little Hank, whom the puppy had licked for hours. I wasn't sure about Lizzy and the rest of the family, but Little Hank would undoubtedly have been infected. I realized Mr. Jenkins had no chance of survival. Whether anyone else had been affected would be known soon, but I had to get home to Little Hank. I could hardly direct my horse. I jumped on, took off for the ranch, and did not even check the girth on the saddle. I went down when my saddle came loose. My arm, which had been healing well, took the brunt of the fall. I presumed I refractured the bone, which I could barely feel. My only thoughts were for Little Hank and Lizzy.

I went straight to Dan and Jenny's house. The puppy was outside and appeared healthy and playful. Jenny was lying down on the bed, where Lizzy was seated with her mother. I said I was just stopping by to see how Jenny was. She wanted me to take Lizzy while she grabbed a few minutes of sleep. I didn't want to alarm anyone until I examined the children. When I checked out Lizzy, I discovered no punctures. I sneaked into the baby's room, where Little Hank lay in his crib, holding his blanket. I identified two puncture wounds on his hands, which appeared to be from the puppy.

Dan was surprised I was there when he arrived home. I didn't want to scare him, but he had to be informed about what was happening. I hated to tell him some of the puppies from the litter had died possibly from a disease that could be contagious to people. Dan understood in an instant what I meant. He started to cry, picked up Little Hank, and held him. He saw the two punctures, as well.

I'd written a report on the history of Louis Pasteur for an assignment in high school. Rabies treatment was only a few years away from reality. Only a miracle would save Little Hank. I was paralyzed with fear and dread. My tears said it all.

Jenny came staggering out of their room. Observing Dan and me, without recognizing the reason, she began crying. Since this set off Lizzy, which awakened Little Hank, soon we were all crying. Dan was going to kill the puppy. I asked him not to do anything. Little Hank might not have rabies, and the puppy was the best indicator of the chances for Little Hank to survive. We put the dog in their barn and offered him food and water. He seemed healthy in every way. I left strict instructions to not let anyone near the puppy.

I rode back to the Jenkins farm, where several people were attending. Mr. Jenkins responded somewhat to commands and was not as wild as when I had been there earlier in the day. This period of behavior might last a week or more. He might be violent, sleep, and then repeat his irrational and unexpected behavior. Mrs. Jenkins understood he was going to die. She left him at the farm and took the children into town to stay with her sister for protection. She would not return to the farm, and Mr. Jenkins was left on his own. John and I attempted to get some drugs into his system for sedation.

He couldn't swallow anymore. We started to employ syringes, and we injected him with a strong sedative that barely touched him. John threw a blanket over him, and we tied his hands and legs to the bed. I wanted to end the poor man's life. It was agony to watch him suffer as he strained against the ropes, and it was utter terror to consider he could break free. I would be helpless if he did, but both Alf and John were strong enough to restrain him, hopefully. I'd been vaccinated against rabies as a vet student. My immunization had been excellent, and my postvaccine titers had been high. If challenged by the virus, I might mount a response and not contract rabies, but I couldn't count on it because that was more than twenty years ago.

It made me think. I recognized human-to-human transmission was rare, and I wasn't too worried about myself. The men who arrived began to systematically kill the skunks under the house. Such gunshots set off Mr. Jenkins, who would writhe and experience spasms from the gunfire sounds. Only the tinker, who took the two puppies, and Little Hank were in danger to my knowledge.

I had to act on this. Following my prior visit to the future, I swore there would be no reason for me to leave this time.

I doubted I would do it for myself alone. My chances of contracting rabies from my exposure to Mr. Jenkins were small. However, I believed the prospect of Little Hank contracting rabies was almost inevitable from his two small punctures. I had to act. I realized I could most likely save him.

Lauren

My boss from the clinic called. Doug was elated that Jasmine was in custody. I would not be needed for some time, and my short period of notoriety had been good for business—exceptionally good! I was asked to see several clients who had not wanted to see me earlier. They wanted a peek at the minor celebrity. Several individuals asked me to vaccinate their horses or treat them for minor ailments. Megan, her mother, and Mary called specifically to inquire whether I was okay. Mary had a date with her dinner partner, Mr. Davidson. They wanted me to stay for dinner and not serve only as a convenient chauffeur this time around. Helen was invited too, but she had a date.

"Might I inquire with whom?" I smirked as I observed her. I could see she was thrilled.

"Lauren, you know that FBI agent who was staring at me?"

"Get out of town, Helen."

"I'd like to, but it seems we are only going to the Thai place. It's a beginning."

When Rich and I picked up Mr. Davidson, I noticed his barn had been demolished. The property was looking much better. The gardens were weeded, the lawn was mowed, and the house had a new coat of paint. I jokingly asked him if he was selling up. "Yes, as a matter of fact. I may be moving."

"That's great. I'll bet your family will be pleased to have you closer."

"They would be pleased if that were the case. Mary and I have considered joining our forces."

"What?" I glanced at Rich, who smiled and nodded. "Am I out of the loop?"

Rich wagged his finger in my direction. "Dr. Harper, Henry, and I have been working on a few projects. It appears you have been so preoccupied with your own small problems that you haven't realized the rest of us also have lives. The place didn't get this spiffy on its own. Some of us have friends who have friends...."

"You don't say."

"I do." Rich and Henry Davidson high-fived.

We arrived at Mary's, who wanted a report about my little adventure. I embellished the story to make it seem as if I had taken Jasmine down single-handedly until Rich told the actual story. Mr. Davidson—or Henry, as I was requested to call him—had moved over to put his arm around Mary. I was jealous. Jim would be back in about a month, and I would soon walk down the aisle, but they had each other right now. After dinner and the traditional pie, we were told to leave. Henry was spending the night!

Rich laughed. "Mary, what if your mother finds out?"

"Rich, I already broke that barrier with my husband. The kids are currently the problem, and there will be hell to pay if they find out!"

"Okay, mum's the word."

"Damn straight. You whippersnappers get the hell out of here, so Henry and I can have some adult time."

Oh, did we laugh on the way home! How things had changed at this time. I longed for the freedom that old age gave them. It reminded me I was not free.

I still had one more trial to go. Even Lisa was being flown in to testify. At least, I could look forward to that. I could hardly wait to see Lisa. She and my sister were going to be bridesmaids, and Lisa bought the dress my mother had selected. I prayed it wasn't too awful. My sister was with her when she picked it out, and that was my salvation. Jane would never wear anything that wasn't flattering. Lisa said she liked her dress. All systems go.

The district attorney called the next week to ask me to come in for some pretrial discussions. There was still the possibility of a plea bargain, but no one was counting on it. I was instructed to go over my story to ensure my testimony was consistent with my statement. I was not shown the original declaration, but they were happy that my memory had not changed.

There'd been no further developments, and the corruption appeared to be isolated to those two men. The trial would begin the following week. I was told to be careful. It was not clear who was buying the marijuana grown in the cave behind my old cabin. Since it could be coordinated by a sophisticated cartel, I still might be in danger from the cartel people.

At least, I could go to breakfast at the Coffee Café to see my friends again. I arrived the morning after the dinner with Henry and Mary. Ted was there, and we hugged each other and sat together. He was back at work full time. He missed me, and I missed him. The clinic was going well. The previous week, he had talked with Rosa, who was still in love. "She finally kissed her boyfriend. She found out that it wasn't the home that forbade her to kiss but her own family members. She told them she would be careful. Rosa understands how babies are made, she is not going to get pregnant from kissing, and she told them to mind their own business."

"Isn't she in her late fifties?"

"Try the sixties."

"Yeah, I can see the concern about birth control."

"I heard you saw Jim."

"Yep, still alive and ready to tie the knot."

"Well, I have a bit of a surprise. I must make a lifestyle adjustment."

"You're coming out?"

"We're expecting."

"Oh, Ted, that's fantastic. No more ski bum?"

"We've decided to limit it to just one month. Because the new clinic pays me as much as I can make as an instructor, I might want to hang around home a little more."

"That's great news. Is it out? May I tell people?"

"Yep. It's in the public domain. Hey, I'm going to be late. See you later."

We hugged, and Ted left for work. I glanced at Mel, sitting next to her new girlfriend. They waved as I greeted them. "Free at last. Free at last."

"We thought you'd never come back."

"My friend was here most days since someone blabbed. I came here in the morning, Mel."

"Ouch, is that me or my roomie?"

"I don't remember, but it certainly did alert her. Anyway, hopefully, she'll be gone for a few years. Maybe she'll finally move on when she gets out."

"How's work?"

"Been off for a few days. How about you?"

"Making the transition into the summer dramas. The orthopedic docs went home because the skiing has stopped."

"Who and what do you treat mainly?"

"Old people, cardiac issues, the rare fractures, sprains, bee stings, alcohol-related issues, and lots of morning-after needs."

"Do you ever take a vacation?"

"Cary is on hers now. I'll start mine next week when she gets back."

"I don't suppose you can make it to my wedding in late June?"

"Never say never, but I doubt it."

"Well, consider yourself invited."

"Why don't you throw a party when you get back?"

"That's kind of the plan. I'll pull double duty then. The big boss is leaving right after I get back, but who knows?"

"Hey, gotta rumble, baby sister."

I went to the office, where I received a mile-long call list. Sara was locked and loaded when I arrived.

"Only another week or two of riding shotgun for me. The psycho bitch is out of the way at last. Now, all we have to worry about is the mob."

"Pfft, compared with Jasmine, I'll take the mob any day. At least with them, it's just business."

"That's comforting. Who should drive?" I hoped Sara would drive.

"You. I'm doing my nails while we go. I have a date tonight."

"Get out, with whom?"

"No one special. Just the lead singer of the local group at the Star Sign Bar."

"They have a name?"

"Nope."

"No name? How do they become famous?"

"The name is Nope."

"Weird. Is Nope any good?"

"Nope." Sara laughed. "It's like 'Who's on First.'"

"I get it. Where are we headed, Kemosabe?"

"Take Hutchins and then go right on Hancock."

It was a great day. You name it, we did it. I love my job. I believe I need to explore surrogacy. Taking time off to have kids wasn't looking like that much fun anymore. When we returned to the office, I worked on my case reports. The small animal nurses finished up and discharged the surgical cases. It was quiet, and everyone was in a good mood.

Max wanted me to join him for a beer in his office. I was unsure about drinking with the boss, but he told me to lighten up and enjoy some downtime. We discussed the clinic, and the way business was going overall. He was more of the number cruncher than Doug was. "Harper, how are things?"

"Great, sir. I may even survive this first year."

"Yes, I guess it's been a hell of a year for you."

"To say the least." We laughed.

"It'll get better."

"It is better. You're not thinking of falling off the perch, are you?" *What was Max getting to?*

"You never know. I hear your fiancé is somewhat of a whiz with numbers."

"I reckon he is. He's fairly good at a lot of things, actually."

"Lauren, do you think he would be interested in taking over for me?"

"Oh, my God. Max, are you ill?"

"No. Not at all, but my wife is, and I might have my hands full with her this next year. She has advanced breast cancer and will require all available support."

"Max, I'm sincerely sorry."

"Yeah, life can be a bitch, really. Fortunately, our girls are married. However, unfortunately, they both have small children and live interstate. Consequently, either I hire someone or do it myself."

"I'll ask him when he gets back. It won't be for about another month, and then we have our wedding. Since he's helped vets in need for quite a while, you fit his preferred customer profile."

"What are our chances of snagging him?"

"Before you give me a raise or after that?"

"Before. Man, you are one brazen woman."

"Ninety-nine percent, Max. A hundred percent following the raise."

"I'll risk that one percent. Ask your fiancé as soon as you make contact, will you? No raise. Remember, I'm the number cruncher."

I received a call from the FBI agent in charge of the corruption case the following morning. All three men took a plea and would be sentenced the following week—finally, some good news. Lisa was called, and she canceled her trip out, which was annoying. Lisa needed to be at her new clinic, and she was not keen to see Tahoe anytime soon. I would have to wait to see her in her bridesmaid's dress. She promised to continue to hold her weight even though it was killing her.

The sole obstacle in my life was that Jasmine had not agreed to a plea deal. The attorneys, her family, and the judge were trying to make her come to the table. The new charges would undoubtedly increase her sentence. If she took the deal, she might receive three years, yet Jasmine might receive up to twenty-five years if she did not take the deal. I wanted to tell her not to plead, but I had no access to her.

Rebecca

Sam was up, waiting for me when I returned to the Cattle Creek Ranch late at night. He'd seen Dan, and he wanted to hear about what I might be able to do. Sam understood this was going to be a pivotal moment in our lives. Sam took me in his arms and said he would accept whatever I suggested. He was my rock and my strength. I cried and nodded. He had saved some food and poured me a glass of milk and then brandy. I simply sat staring.

Finally, I shared with Sam what I had learned about rabies. I described the transmission and the sequence of signs in humans, as well as animals. I explained that in the early stages in many animals, the symptoms mimic other conditions, which is how veterinarians are particularly vulnerable. Hence, we received vaccines in vet school, which provided us with long-term immunity, like smallpox. We were told to expect protection for ten years.

I then explained that rabies treatment, once the symptoms were showing in humans, was far too late. The key is getting antibodies into the patient early—before the virus takes hold. I'd previously informed him about tetanus and tetanus antitoxin in the treatment of human beings and animals. In rabies, there were two ways to prevent the virus from taking hold. One was vaccinating the person with the rabies vaccine before experiencing any exposure to the virus. The second was postexposure prophylactic treatment. Rabies antitoxin, or immunoglobulin, was a well-known treatment.

I remember that our local vet operated on a cow that was subsequently diagnosed with rabies when I was a child. He and two men assisting him with the cow had to receive a series of painful injections of the rabies antitoxin. I thought it was thirteen weekly injections, but I wasn't sure. I realized the number of injections had significantly been reduced since then. I didn't know what the current treatment involved, but I guessed it was improved and not as painful.

The solution to our worries was obvious. Sam immediately recognized my strategy. He and I moved from the dining table to the divan and gazed into the fireplace. It was warm enough that he had not lit it. On the last visit to Hank Heaven, we both examined the water level at the portal pool. It was easily survivable for an adult, but the other side was questionable, and we didn't know if Little Hank would drown in the process.

"Do we tell Dan and Jenny about your plans, or do we just kidnap him and take our chances that they will forgive us?" Sam was alarmed and appeared shocked.

"You aren't suggesting that you go, too, are you?"

"He's my grandson." Sam used his take command tone of voice.

"Sam, you can't go." There was no way this man could arrive in the future and not cause total chaos with the world and virtually all belief systems.

"Why not?"

"I can do this much easier than you can and way easier without you." I wasn't going to argue about this, but I pretended to consider his objections.

"Do you care to expand on this?"

"Not now, but I will if it's a cause for divorce. You must trust me on this. I've never failed before, and I will die trying to save my grandson. Please believe me."

"What do we tell Dan and Jenny?"

"The truth this time, but only if it's a deal breaker." I had hoped this day would never come. This might be the end of all our relationships.

"When will you leave?"

"Tomorrow. We need to act quickly."

"I guess we can tell them in the morning. Becky, what if they find you over there and try to keep you? What if they won't let you come back, or if you can't come back?"

"Who are *they*, Sam?"

"I don't know. The sheriff or your husband? I don't know."

"Sam, if we don't try, my guess is Little Hank will be dead in less than a month. It will be a gruesome, painful death."

We held each other in bed that night, and I cried. I could feel Sam wiping away tears. We barely slept. In the morning, I woke to the smell of coffee that Sam brought to our room. He had toast and obviously had been up most of the night, thinking about what I had planned.

"I'm going to ask one more time to go, but I'll respect your decision to decline, and I won't ask the reason. I doubt either Dan or Jenny will allow you to take Little Hank without more information. I think it's time they realized the truth about you and about us."

"Yes, I agree. Let me return to town for any information regarding the tinker and the pups he took. I'll check on Mr. Jenkins and notify Alf and John that I'll be gone for a while."

"How long do you think?"

"I'm hoping for a month, but it could be longer. I don't know how long it will take to complete the treatment. Once the treatment is finished, I'll head straight back. I promise. If the treatment doesn't work, it doesn't matter where Little Hank is. I'll obtain medication to ease his pain and passage while I'm there."

"I love you, Rebecca Buchanan."

"I love you, too, Sam." We held each other for a few precious minutes.

When I arrived at the Jenkins house, Alf was in the process of leaving. The rabies disease was progressing swiftly in this man. He was in a full-blown coma. The word from the tinker was that the other pups died quickly, and he hadn't been bitten. He'd done nothing to expose himself to puppy saliva. I informed Alf that I was certain Dan's son, Little Hank, was exposed. I claimed I heard about a treatment back East, and I was headed there to keep Little Hank from contracting rabies. Alf was interested in learning about this and wanted me to acquire any possible information on the topic. He and John would both be glad to cover the hospital duties while I was gone. We hugged, and Alf wished me well.

Dan was holding Little Hank when I arrived. They'd been up all night. Sam was in the house. He and Jenny were trying to comfort Lizzy, who was aware that her parents were upset, and the poor, confused child was trying to make sense of it all.

I hoped Lizzy would not comprehend what I planned to tell Dan and Jenny. Lizzy settled in Sam's lap. He was her port in a storm these days. Thankfully, she was asleep in a minute.

Sam started the explanation. "Dan, Jenny, there's something we need to tell you. You'll find this unbelievable, but it's the truth. When I first heard it, I didn't believe it, either. It took over ten years for me to come to terms with this fact, but what we will tell you might just save Little Hank's life. Believe us or not, I'm begging you to consider it." Sam stared at me and nodded.

I took a deep breath. "Dan, you inquired how old I was many, many years ago. Do you remember? Your father commented it was impolite to ask my age. I responded I was so young that I wasn't even born yet."

"Yes, I asked when your birthday was after you and Pa were married."

"He was protecting me for another reason. My true birth year is 1949. Not 1849, but it's 1949. I come from the future. I am what they call a time traveler. I know this is hard to believe, but it's true. I was married, and Lauren is my daughter. She learned to time travel too. I experienced a rock slide and ended up back in time. I think it was 1857. Your father, Lauren, and I are the few living people who know about these circumstances. But do you remember the piano player? He went missing when I went away, a few days before your father and I were supposed to be married. I think you and others thought I left your father for him." Jenny simply stared openmouthed, and Dan sat forward, cradling Little Hank.

"Go on." Dan's look was one of complete disbelief.

"I really am a veterinarian. I graduated from veterinary school in 1981. I was near Tahoe, seeking a veterinary position when I rode with a woman, and we were caught in a rockslide. She was killed, and I ended up in Virginia City and met your brothers. After a few days at your ranch, I traveled to Sacramento and San Francisco to seek a way back to my time, my husband, and, of course, Lauren."

"How does this concern our son?"

"I understand there are treatments and chemicals to prevent those who have been exposed to rabies from dying. They were invented in the future to stop the virus from taking hold in the body."

"What's a virus?" Jenny seemed to be taking it in, and I thought she might believe me.

"It is a small particle that invades the body, replicates itself, and causes such diseases as influenza, smallpox, and chickenpox."

Dan was dubious. "What about the strangles?"

"No, that is a slightly larger particle called a bacterium. You can't currently detect viruses in the microscope, but you can see them in the future. I learned through the piano player the way to travel back and forth from the present to the future. Lauren met him in the future, which is how she came to visit us. I need to, well, want to, take Little Hank to the future for the treatment. I must leave today or tomorrow at the latest. I can go to Lauren, who will be able to help me get what we require."

"How do you know where Lauren is? Isn't she back East in Virginia?"

"No, as far as I know, she's a vet in the 2000s, in Virginia City."

"She's also a vet?"

"Yes. Lauren's father, who raised her, is also a vet. She decided to become a vet, which is the reason she knows so much. I hate to cut this short, but I should leave soon. If I leave mid-afternoon, I'll be able to get to a safe place to stay tomorrow night. If not, I must leave tomorrow morning. I'm so sorry to spring this on you. I'm sorry I never told you, yet I think you can understand much more about me now."

Dan gazed at his father. Sam smiled, reached over, and patted my arm, which was still in the splint. "Dan, Becky's telling you the truth. I waited a long time to remarry following your mother's death. I chose a modern woman, and I've wondered what the deuces I was doing several times. However, she is the love of my life and a genuine marvel. She went back once and returned with medicine that saved my life. I am begging you to trust her."

Dan and Jenny glanced at each other, and Jenny began to cry.

"Becky, are you certain you need to do this?"

"No, not sure, but I would advise you to take this chance. By the time the puppy in the barn dies, it might be too late."

Dan and Jenny stared at me and Sam, who held a sleeping Lizzy. Dan had tears in his eyes. "Okay, what should we do, Becky?"

"I'll need a change of clothes for Little Hank and some diapers. It's preferable to wrap them in something that's either waterproof or dries quickly."

I knew babies would automatically hold their breath underwater. I'd seen it many times in my old life. He was still going to be wet and cold. Logistically, I had to get him off the mountain trail before the night chill. I also didn't know where anything was situated as far as Frank or Lauren was concerned. I had no way of contacting anyone. I would simply have to hitch a ride from the parking lot to town and locate the vet clinic. I decided to start out that night. I had the means to start a fire if necessary and keep Little Hank warm. I planned to take plenty of food and even a canteen filled with cow's milk, which he now drank.

When Sam and I went home, I changed into light clothes that would dry quickly and, more importantly, might nearly appear modern. Sam had the perfect idea to put clothes for Little Hank and me, along with a gun and some gold, in an airtight box. He realized paper money would not be worth anything, but one could always sell gold.

Saying goodbye to Dan and Jenny and taking their son with me was one of the hardest things I've ever done. I doubted I would be back in time for the pending birth. I insisted that Jenny go to the hospital when her time was near. She would benefit from Alf and John's skills to ensure the next Buchanan was born safely and without complications.

Sam and I took Little Hank up to the portal pool. Sam buried a metal box next to a large tree. It should last over time. He'd placed the clothes and diapers, as well as the gun, in the box. I would dig it up when I arrived in more than a hundred years. He left a metal digging spade, which was hidden near the same tree. It was nearly four in the afternoon. We fed Little Hank and dressed him in an outfit that would dry quickly. The pool was deep, and the water level was perfect. We prayed for a minute, and Sam held and kissed me. "Godspeed, Rebecca."

I laughed. "It could only be his speed. I love you." After I jumped in, I surfaced at an even lower water level. I quickly glanced toward the ridge. Luckily, no one was around. Little Hank howled. He was alive and cold from the wet. I immediately stripped him and went to the tree where Sam had buried the clothes. I had the canteen and some food that had been wrapped to stay dry. The tree was much larger, but we had counted on that. I couldn't find the digging tool, and poor Little Hank was crying because he was wet and cold. It was too late in the day to expect his clothes to dry. I was chilly and wet, as well. I gave him some milk by dripping it through my shirt and letting him suck on the milky shirt like a teat.

I dug the ground around the tree by hand. After about an hour, I hit the edge of the box. It required around another half hour to uncover the box, and only with great effort was I able to remove the metal box from the soil. Since the lid had rusted, I had to use a big rock to open the cover. Inside were just partially damaged clothes, which smelled moldy, but they were warm and dry. When I dressed Little Hank, I quickly checked his vitals. He still seemed healthy in all respects. A note in the box was not there when we buried it.

My Dearest Wife,
It has been only a week, but I miss you terribly.
I have bad news. The puppy became ill during the next
few days and died. Godspeed to the people who
can help Little Hank. I love you. You will be my
lasting love for eternity.
Sam

I took the letter. Holding Little Hank, I climbed up out of the creek and onto the trail that led to the parking lot. Little Hank was sleepy, and he didn't resist me holding him while walking. When we came to the car park, he woke up, and his eyes widened. Several cars were parked in the lot. It was now dusk, and the chances of getting a ride home were small. I rested for a minute, picked up the baby, and headed for town. If I walked all night, I would make it by dawn's light to Virginia City. The walk reminded me of my initial trip to Virginia City and Dr. and Mrs. Sullivan's medical office in the 1850s. I was convinced it was a television or movie set. Oh, how I'm glad it wasn't, although it took me years to accept my second life.

While I walked along the road, I detected headlights. I was nervous about whether I should signal the driver or not. When it went past, I could tell it was a forest-service truck. I could have kicked myself for not taking the chance. Approximately thirty minutes later, I hailed down the same truck when it passed me again. The man stopped his vehicle and rolled down his window. "Ma'am, you lost?"

"No, sir, but I'm somewhat stranded. Could you tell me how to get to the local vet clinic in Virginia City? My daughter works there, and I need to take her son home to his mamma."

"Where's your car?"

"That's a long story. My daughter took it, and my husband was supposed to pick us up, but there's been a mix-up. I suspect he thinks she was coming, and she thinks he's coming."

"Do you have a number where I can call him or her?"

"I don't have their numbers because I left my telephone in the car. I usually hit their names on my phone."

"I know how it is, ma'am. What's your grandson's name?"

"Lit..." I corrected myself. "Henry. Henry Harper."

"He isn't Dr. Harper's son, is he?"

Think fast. "Yes, kind of, well, yes, Henry is, but he lives mostly with me because of Lauren's job."

"I see. I know her. Lauren eats breakfast at my father's café most mornings. I know where she lives too. How about if I take you there?"

"I would be forever thankful. That would be wonderful."

He pulled up to a house that had two separate living areas. No lights were on, and no cars were visible.

"I don't think she's home. Do you want me to take you to the clinic?"

"No, I'll wait for her to return home. Thank you. You have been ever so kind."

"Are you certain? What if she's out?"

"We'll be fine. I know where the key is." I didn't, but I didn't want him to think I didn't know my way around. I waited until he drove off. Poor Little Hank was sleeping. I had all the clothes wrapped around him to keep him warm.

I sat on the porch after ringing the doorbell. *What if she's in Kentucky and getting married?* If she wasn't here by morning, I'd hitch a ride to the local hospital.

A woman came out of the house next door and asked me who I was and who I was looking for. I claimed I was a distant relative looking for Lauren Harper. She stated her neighbor and Lauren would be back any minute. They weren't. After a while, she returned, invited me into her house, and offered me a cup of coffee or tea. She was suspicious, and I didn't blame her. I realized it seemed strange. She questioned me to no end.

"You might have heard that we've had problems with a stalker and some police, and poor Lauren has been through the wringer these last few months. At least I sorted the stalker, though. She's waiting for a trial and is finally in jail. The others are awaiting their sentence. I don't know how she survived. That lady is crazy, with a capital C."

"I hadn't heard about this. I must ask Lauren." I had a feeling Sam knew about it. There was always something between them that was hidden from me. I guessed that Lauren may have told Sam, but he asked her not to discuss it for fear of worrying me. That would be like my husband. Total chauvinist, God love him. I would talk to him about it when I returned—if I got back and if I had a healthy child when I returned. *Where in the world was Lauren?* Helen and I waited until quite late when someone pulled into the driveway in a big pickup truck. Little Hank was asleep on the couch in Helen's house.

Helen met Lauren and whoever was accompanying her and told them I was in the house with a small boy. Lauren ran over and immediately recognized it was an emergency.

She didn't call me by name in front of the woman and the man with her. Lauren had described Jim. This was probably not him. He was supposed to be overseas in the army. How was this going to work?

After hugging an extremely shocked Lauren, I extended my hand to the young man. I introduced myself as "Linda," her second cousin on her father's side, and the little boy with me as "Henry." I explained that I lived with my husband in a commune in Idaho. "I've run into some trouble healthwise and need some assistance. I know Lauren's gone to vet school and thought she might be able to help."

The silence from them all was deafening. "Oh, please. If I'm not welcome, I can leave."

"Oh, no. Not at all. Do I call you Aunt Linda, or simply Linda?"

Helen was still suspicious. "You aren't his mother, are you?"

"No. Henry's mother is religious and won't seek aid. I came alone."

Rich stared at the sleeping little baby and picked him up. "Let's get him into a proper bed. How sick is he?" Rich motioned for Lauren and me to leave.

"I'm not sure. Henry was bitten by a bat that died. Since a bunch of animals died, I think he might have rabies."

They all gasped. Lauren understood at once the reason I was there. I was confident she was well-trained in human-rabies treatment and prevention protocols. Lauren remarked that she'd been vaccinated and had an excellent immune response like mine. She thanked Helen, who went into overdrive with her suggestions and questions.

"By the way, I'm Rich, Lauren's housemate. Come in, and let's get you settled." He carried Little Hank to his house and handed the key to Lauren, who still seemed in a state of shock. She reached for her phone by the time we entered the house, dialed a number, and left a message for someone to call her right away. It was midnight. She took Little Hank from Rich and set him down in what must be her bedroom.

"Aunt Linda, have you had anything to eat?"

"No, but I'm not worried about myself. I should get the baby to a doctor urgently. I know there's something to be done, and I want to get the medicine to save his life. He doesn't show any symptoms so far. I don't have access to anything where I live."

A yellow dog came over to sniff me. "This is my dog, Ladybug. Don't worry. She's very friendly." I patted her, and she stared at the baby and me with a kind eye. Lauren had told me the story about her. The trust-fund dog wagged her tail. I liked her immediately, and I think the feeling was returned. I heard Lauren in the main room, talking to Rich as her phone rang. After Lauren spoke at length to someone, she returned to us.

I was exhausted and becoming frantic. Lauren shut the door and hugged me. "Mom, I'm so sorry. It's rabies for sure?"

"We assume so. A man near Virginia City is dying from it. He had puppies, and Dan got one for Little Hank and Lizzy, but Little Hank wouldn't let anyone play with the puppy. We believe that two puncture wounds on his fingers are from the puppy. Since the puppy died, I must quickly get some treatment into Little Hank."

"I just talked with a friend who's an emergency doctor. She's driving to Las Vegas for what we need. I offered to go, but it is a little tricky with dispensing the drugs we require. She'll be back by morning."

"No one knows who I am, do they?"

"Not yet. How'd you get here?"

"The usual, after which I walked out of the forest and caught a ride from a ranger who said you eat at his dad's place for breakfast. Oh God, Lauren, I'm so sorry to burden you. If there was another way, you know, I didn't plan to travel like this anymore. I really couldn't let this child die without trying. I couldn't live with myself."

"What did you say to Dan and Jenny?"

"The truth. I don't know whether Dan and Jenny believed me, but I had to try, and they realized he was going to die without some type of treatment."

"Mom, I'm so glad to see you. I never thought I was going to see you again."

"Me, either. I simply wish it could be under different circumstances."

"Me too. I guess I can tell you a little about what's been going on. I figure Helen related some of it to you?"

I nodded, and Lauren began to tell me all the problems she had since before she left for the 1800s and after returning to the present. "I'm sorry I didn't tell you there, but Sam wanted to protect you."

"I will strangle him when I get back."

"Yeah, right." Lauren smiled. She went out to inform Rich that the rabies drugs were coming in the morning. We would stay in her room tonight. He shook his head and said he was available to help. "They can have my room, and I'll sleep on the couch."

I heard Lauren decline the offer because she didn't want to cause a problem.

Then I heard, "As if you haven't been one the whole time, Harper. I'll have more to celebrate when you are hitched and leave me and my amour to our boring lives."

She returned to my room. "Mom, he's leaving in the morning to visit his boyfriend in Arizona. They're moving his partner, Dirk, up here. I'm leaving in about three weeks to get married. Jim is due back anytime now. We set a date for June 25th."

I hugged Lauren and told her how happy I was. I wished I could attend, but that was obviously out of the question. We climbed into bed, and I slept for a few hours before Little Hank stirred. I went into the kitchen, warmed the canteen of milk, and poured some into a cup. He'd drunk from a cup before, and I held him while he drank it and settled again until light.

I woke in a panic. Lauren was gone. *How did she leave, and I didn't even wake up?* I was a mess. I had only my handmade clothes, in which I had slept. I guessed I probably reeked. Little Hank was awake, calling for his mother. I went into the kitchen. Rich left his room, took one look, and pointed to the bathroom. "Ladies first."

I laughed. "These clothes are all I have right now. Lauren is gone. I can wait until she comes back. I don't even know what day it is."

"It's Sunday, Linda. She probably went to get us all coffee and sweet rolls. She should be back soon. I'll go first then."

While he was in the shower and Lauren was out getting breakfast, there was a hard knock at the door. I hesitated but finally decided to open it. There stood a big man—with a slightly receding hairline and a kind, broad face—who resembled Hank. He was carrying flowers.

"I've come to claim my bride." He peered at me and stepped back. He didn't say anything, but he just kept staring. He glanced over my shoulder. "Lauren?" he shouted. He looked at me again and smiled. He must have seen a picture of me when Lauren was a baby. He recognized me immediately. I put my finger to my lips, as did he.

Chapter 29

Lauren

The phone rang at five in the morning. Thankfully, it was on vibration mode. I jumped out of bed and went to the bathroom to answer it. My mother and Little Hank were so out of it they didn't even notice. The call was from a regular client with a colicky pony. I sneaked back into the room and took some clothes and my keys. I was able to get away without anyone stirring. Even LB didn't get up.

As I left my room, I gazed back at Little Hank when a wave of nostalgia washed over me. He'd grown and was looking a great deal like his father. His dark, curly hair was getting long and thick. The sleeping gown was so 1800s! I should get him some more modern clothes today. He couldn't go out in public looking like that.

Cary would be on her way back with the rabies vaccine and immunoglobulin treatment. I would take Little Hank in by myself. My mother couldn't risk detection. I wondered whether Little Hank would recognize me and be happy to go with me. He'd been such a friendly child when I was with him last, which was several months ago. I would soon find out.

I drove to the property where the pony was boarded near a modern house with a clean and contemporary barn. An older couple had owned the pony for more than twenty years. This pony had been their daughter's pride and joy. The daughter strayed off the tracks and has been missing for the last five years. She became mixed up with the wrong crowd and became an addict to some form of methamphetamine. In case she returned, her parents kept the pony. The daughter might find a reason to stay if the pony was still with the family.

The pony was a stocky bay, with a wide blaze and white stockings on the hind legs. He was nearly obese but didn't exhibit signs of his advanced age. He was thirty years old and had abdominal distension, a high heart rate, and pale gums. I couldn't auscultate any intestinal sounds when I listened to his abdomen. I performed a rectal exam and could easily palpate an impaction about the size of a softball in his small colon. I felt some distended loops of the bowel, which were the result of a complete blockage.

I treated him with an analgesic and a combination of oral electrolytes, stool softeners, water, and a little oil. I realized the oil would not be of much use, and I gave enough only to show the passage of the impaction when and if the obstruction would be relieved. After cleaning up the stomach tube and bucket, I listened to the abdomen again. I still heard nothing but a high ping, indicating the increased distention of the large colon.

The owners were desperate to keep the pony alive. I offered them several options, including surgery and intravenous fluids. The woman was a nurse. She thought if I could insert a jugular catheter, she could maintain the intravenous fluids. It was agonizing. I wanted to go home, but I wanted to save the pony, as well. This kind of situation was going to be my life. I would always struggle with my family's needs and my clients' requirements. My dad opted out of general practice shortly after my mother went missing. I laughed to myself that I used to say, "after my mother died," but I certainly wouldn't say that now. My dad believed he had to be there for me, so he accepted a nine-to-five job.

It was only six o'clock in the morning. I figured that Cary wouldn't be back until after eight. I knew my mother would cope until I came back. I conducted a quick surgical prep and put in a long, intravenous jugular catheter. I superglued it to the pony's neck and wrapped it with Elastoplast, a cloth-like sticky bandage. In the meantime, some intravenous fluids had been warmed in their microwave. I gave two liters and demonstrated to the owners how to continue the administration, discontinue the fluids, and cap the extension to prevent blood from going retrograde and clotting in the catheter. The woman was so well-versed that, in truth, she could have taught me a thing or two.

I returned to the clinic to obtain more fluids for later. I gave them more pain meds to be administered later in the day if needed. The nurse had a stethoscope and monitored the decreased heart rate and increased intestinal sounds, indicating that the pony responded to the rehydration. I felt for these people. They hadn't seen their daughter for five years, and they weren't even sure she was alive. They just had to pray their daughter was alive and maybe even receiving necessary help.

I headed to the Coffee Café to get coffee for my mom and Rich. I purchased some sweet rolls and stopped at the grocery store for some baby food and milk. Cary called when I was at the checkout to say she was an hour away and for me to bring the baby to the hospital at nine-thirty. She would be set up and ready for us by that time.

I decided to take a punt and go by the Goodwill drop-off depot. People often left bags of clothes outside the receptacles, where maybe I could find some children's clothes. A sheriff's deputy who showed up recognized me while I was going through some shopping bags. We both knew what I was doing was illegal. He gave me a stern talking and asked what I precisely needed. I explained a distant relative from a commune had come into town with a toddler with only one set of clothes. Until the stores opened, I was searching for an outfit, so I could bathe him and get him ready to see a doctor.

"Get in your truck and follow me." He pointed to his car. I followed him to the sheriff's department, where he instructed me to join him inside. Jeez, I guess he would arrest me or at least fine me for what I had done. I was embarrassed and annoyed with myself. He told me to wait on a bench until he returned. Two more deputies who walked past stared at me since they knew who I was. I sat there for about five minutes, regretting my venture into the criminal world. *What in the world is going to happen to me?* A few minutes later, the sheriff himself walked into the building with some bags in his hands. He acknowledged me as he walked past.

After another few minutes, they all came out and handed me a box of clothes. "Dr. Harper, we want to thank you for what you did for us. We had a feeling that we had problems with some of our, let's say, former employees. Your courage in sticking to your guns, so to speak," and they all laughed, "helped us do a bit of well-needed housecleaning."

"These are some clothes from our staff that might fit the child. We all have relatives from less-than-perfect families. Good luck."

"Total itinerant, but you can't choose your family, can you? Thank you so much. I promise not to stray from the straight and narrow too often."

My heart was full. I would call Lisa to tell her what happened when I had things sorted out. The coffee was cold, but we could reheat it in the microwave when I got home. I raced home, and I probably broke the speed limit, already coming back on the wrong side of the law. The pony owners called and reported the gelding had passed some gas and was seeking food. "Nope. No food until he passes five motions. It's the law." I laughed.

I parked in front of the house, where a rental car was parked in the driveway. *Could my mother have rented one?* I grabbed the food and would have to return for the clothes. As I approached the door, it opened. I handed my mother some of the bags and went back to the truck for the clothes. When I turned around, Jim was standing behind me. I dropped the bag and jumped up into his arms, wrapping my legs around his waist. We had a short, laughing cry and kissed through the tears.

Rich came out to collect the clothes. "Harper, I hope you have some extra donuts."

"I can go back." Rich and I shared a foolish grin.

"Not on your life. I only want you." Jim swung me up into his arms and carried me into the house. "I met your relative, Linda, and little Henry." He set me down. "I thought the bride was supposed to go on a diet before the wedding."

I had to kick him, but I couldn't stop gazing at both him and my mother. I was convinced he recognized my mother. I'd shown him the photograph Frank had given me, but I hadn't told him about my journey through time.

"Did Linda explain the reason she's here?"

"Yes. I assume you're getting the necessary medicine ready?"

"We are due at the hospital by nine-thirty." I glanced at the clock. "That gives us only twenty minutes."

Little Hank took one look at me and ran to me and put his arms around my legs. "Yoran."

"Hey, baby cakes, let's get you cleaned up and dressed." My mother and I took him into the bathroom for a quick sponge bath and dressed him in modern clothes. I told my mom it was best if I took him on my own to the hospital. "Jim can hold him in the car. We'll get a car seat later." She understood. My heart was racing, thinking that my life partner was here to help. We headed to the car, but I ran back into the house. Rich was packed and ready to go. I kissed him and told him to behave himself. "If I get a bad report from Dirk, I won't be impressed. Hopefully, I'll be out of here when you return."

"No hurry, baby sister. I can't imagine life without you."

"Oh, yes, you can. Less chaos, more order, and totally boring."

"Take those damn *Comstock* DVDs with you. If I hear that music again... He does kind of look like Hank, doesn't he?"

"No more *Comstock* because I have the real deal now. Safe travels, my friend."

He bent down to give LB a hug and kiss. "They're evil, LB. You're better off living with me."

"Maybe we can time-share." We were both chopped liver in LB's eyes, though, since Jim had returned. She went right back to sit down at his feet. Little Hank wanted to play with Ladybug. The baby showed no clinical signs consistent with rabies. I scooped him up and handed him to Jim, and we left for the hospital. My mother seemed upset that she was unable to go with us but understood it was too risky.

Jim drove while I held Little Hank. "I guess you have some explaining to do."

"I do."

"I do what?" he asked in a false irritated voice.

"Have some explaining to do."

"Linda isn't Linda, is she?"

"Nope. She certainly isn't Linda."

"I figure her real name is Rebecca."

"That would be a good guess. How about we get through the next few hours? When you and I take a drive alone. I'll tell you everything. I planned to do it when you came back. My mother turning up was unexpected, but I'm certain you'll understand when you hear the entire story."

"Just tell me she's been living in a commune."

"I wish I could." We climbed out of my truck in the hospital parking lot and walked toward the emergency entrance. Jim held Little Hank. Cary and two other doctors were waiting for us. Cary appeared surprised to see Jim. She hugged him, glanced at me, and shook her head. "I guess you have a story for us?"

"Yeah, well."

"Any history of vaccine for tetanus or anything?"

"No. For sure, no vaccines."

"Some people." Cary led us to a small examination room.

"I know."

"When was your nephew bitten? Or is he your cousin?"

"Distant cousin. Maybe three or four days ago. I'm not certain. No more than that." I almost laughed when I thought about my reply. *Try one hundred years ago.*

She handed me an admission sheet. "Okay, fill in the name and info of this kiddo while I take him into the back. This is brutal. You won't want to be there. His name is Henry?"

"Yes, Henry," and I paused.

"Kennedy," Jim piped up. "Henry Kennedy. He's really my nephew. My sister has been in the commune. We think she may be hiding from someone, and she's afraid to come out, but he really was bitten."

I took Jim's hand and squeezed it. I leaned against his shoulder, and he put his arm around me. "It had better be interesting, Harper. I just hope you're worth my committing a felony."

"Totally worth it."

Cary came back in a few minutes. "We decided to give him a little ketamine. Why don't you both rob a bank and return in three hours?"

"I'm happy to assist."

"You know the rules. We charge more if you watch. Do you realize you have blood all down your arm?"

"Oh, colicky pony and an IV catheter. Thanks. May I use the sink?"

She pointed to the sink. "Vamoose."

Jim thanked her as I washed off the blood. After we left, I drove to a Kmart store to get my mom some clothes and a child's car seat. I wasn't sure what would happen, but I was confident Little Hank was in good hands. I realized it would involve more than one hospital visit. My assumption was he would be here for at least a week.

I purchased some clothes to fit my mother. Mom was still physically fit and trim, but she was six inches smaller than I was. When we arrived home, the house was cleaned, and the bed in which we slept the previous night had clean sheets. My mother prepared my bedroom for Jim and me. Rich had suggested that she and 'Henry' sleep in his bedroom tonight.

"Mom, I guess we need to reintroduce you to Jim. Jim, her name, as you guessed, is Rebecca, but she's remarried. Her last name is Buchanan."

"Like the Buchanans on the *Comstock* series?" Jim extended his hand to my mother.

"Kind of. I figure the best place to start is from the beginning." I turned to my mom.

"Lauren, may I start?"

Jim turned from my mother toward me. "Let me interrupt here. Lauren, when I met you, you hadn't seen your mother in more than twenty years, but now you seem to know each other fairly well. I'm somewhat confused."

"Jim, I wish this wasn't happening so fast. I'll understand if this is the deal-breaker but remember that you want no secrets in our relationship. I hated seeing you the last time and not telling you, but I swear this is the truth." I gazed at Mom and nodded.

Mom began her story. "I think you probably know I've been missing for some time. According to Lauren, you and even Rich checked into my disappearance." Jim nodded, but I could tell he was distancing himself from this conversation. My heart was sinking.

"I don't know any other way to explain it, but I'm not dead, as you can tell. I've been living in another part of the world—you might say in a different world. Jim, I've been living in the 1800s. I more or less fell through time and landed in the same spot, but it was in the 1850s rather than in 1981."

"Go on." Jim's posture changed. He became more erect. He took his arm from around me and moved away a millimeter or a mile. I'm not sure which. If I have ever seen a person shut down without moving a muscle, it was right then. I could touch the mental barrier he established in front of my mother and me.

"That's it. I attempted to return. For about twenty years, I tried to discover the portal to get back to this time. I finally gave up, after which I reconnected with an extremely generous, kindhearted rancher with whom I decided to stay. At that point, I had no choice. Since I didn't know how I could return, I decided to marry this man whom I had grown to love."

"You both know this is ridiculous. I'd love to drink the Kool-Aid you are drinking, but I have my normal life to live." Jim's demeanor showed his repulsion for what he was hearing.

"Jim," I pleaded. "Do you remember Frank Lash, the college man whom I met?"

Jim shook his head yet nodded too. "He is the one who realized how to time travel. He showed me. That's when Jasmine shot at me. Well, while you were gone, I went to see Frank, and he took me to the portal. We're not the only ones. We met a woman who also traveled back. We don't understand the way she did it, but we know how we did it."

"I was gone for several months while you were deployed. I meant to go for simply a week or two, but I kind of got stuck."

"What's with the Buchanan name? That's not really history. The Buchanans do not exist. They act for a made-up television series." Jim shook his head.

I had no answer to this question, but Mom did. "Lauren, even you are not aware of this fact. It turns out a frequent visitor to Virginia City came, went, and was acquainted with both Sam and Ray. This was all before I arrived in that time."

"Who's Ray?"

My mother continued, "Jim, he was the sheriff of Virginia City. He appears on *Comstock*, as well. The thing is that this man was probably also a time traveler. His name is Alex Conrad, who is the creator and producer of *Comstock*. He met my family and modeled them for the television program. He recreated the Buchanans even down to our cook, Gee Ling."

Jim stood up and stared at me. The pity on his face said it all. He was engaged to a lunatic, and it was familial. I was crazy, as was my mother. Jim walked out the door and drove off in his rented car. I could tell he was crying. I turned to my mother, who advised me to give him some time. "I've been through this once before."

"Huh?"

"Did I tell you how Sam reacted when I told him?"

"Maybe. I don't remember. How long did it take before Sam accepted you?"

Mom glanced up. "About fifteen years. Give him time."

I gazed out through the window into the backyard. A light rain had begun. I checked my watch. It was almost time to pick up Little Hank. I went into my bedroom and lay down on my bed. LB jumped up and put her head on my waist. She sensed the profound sadness that had enveloped me. I'd stupidly scared the one man in the world whom I loved more than anyone else. I was sure I had seen the last of him. He did not leave anything in the house. *And did I blame him?*

I decided to see the pony that had colic earlier. The owners were walking him and allowing him to have a pick of grass. He'd passed three motions, was hungry, and was nearly back to himself. I left more intravenous-fluid bags and showed the nurse how to remove the catheter the next day if he continued to progress. I then went to the hospital. Cary seemed surprised. "I thought it was only Jim here. Did you decide to come too?"

"What's Jim doing here?"

"Making the financial arrangements and retrieving his nephew. Do you guys communicate?"

"I thought we were." *Was he stealing Little Hank from his strange relatives?* "May I see him?"

"They're in Room four, down the first hall on your left. You'd better be nice to this guy. I could go for him."

"I think he's up for adoption."

"You mean Henry?"

"No, I mean Jim." I was confused.

"How many uncles will pay that kind of money and not even inquire about the cost?"

"I don't know." I was perplexed. Cary pointed down the hallway, and I walked down and turned into the room. Jim was holding Little Hank, who was sleeping in his arms.

We stared at each other. It was a long time before Jim spoke. I was determined not to be the first to talk. He smiled weakly. "I've had the opportunity to marry some mighty awesome women in my time. They were beautiful, intelligent, and clever at what they did. Not one was bat-shit crazy. Why did I fall in love with a loony tune like you? And the worst part is that it's genetic. Your mother is the same." He paused and patted Little Hank's sweaty forehead. "Well, for richer or poorer, mental illness or health, you're stuck with me, Lauren Harper."

I began to weep. "When's the last time you did any fishing?"

Little Hank was irritable, his hand was bandaged, and he was feverish. They decided it was best if he stayed the night. Jim took the first shift. I went home to tell my mother what had happened. She was happy that Jim was quicker than Sam had been, but these were different times. I'd left my laptop on and instructed my mother about how to navigate the World Wide Web. She located the general news and major current affairs. She also researched the corruption case and my stalker case, set for a second trial in November. Jasmine had not accepted the plea deal. Fortunately, she didn't make bail this time.

I told her about what occurred at the hospital and why they decided to keep Little Hank overnight. Jim was going to stay until midnight, and then I would take over. Little Hank was fine, but his hand was very painful as they attempted to inject some of the rabies anti-toxin into the area. Most of the serum was injected into other sites, and he was given a human rabies vaccine. More vaccines were planned to follow this injection in about a week.

"Thank God you're able to help, Lauren. I don't know what I would do without you."

"Well, we must enlist a few others. If Little Hank is required to stay for a month, I have a wedding to attend. I wish you could come, but that isn't possible. I think you know that, don't you?"

"Oh, darling, of course. Maybe you could send me some pictures by computer, and I could see them the next day. I wouldn't spoil your day for anything. How are your father and my sister?"

"They're pretty upset about me going AWOL and not telling them where I was last year, but they eventually accepted me back into the fold. Mom, how is it with you and your family?"

"He and Dan took the large herd to New Mexico, which went well. While they were gone, though, we had an outbreak of strangles and lost about a quarter of the herd. They're trying to buy stock to fill next year's contract."

"That's terrible, but is everyone all right health wise?"

Mom laughed. There was one minor incident. She proceeded to tell me about the murder trial and Mrs. Gardiner.

"Mom, shouldn't that have been the second thing you told me about after Little Hank? You act as if it was no big deal. You were almost hung. Are you certain you want to go back there?"

"Lauren, what would you risk being with Jim?"

"Not sure it would be my life. Knowing Jim, he would have broken me out of jail."

"Exactly." My mom smiled and looked skyward.

"Really?"

"Do you think Sam would have let me hang?"

"Where would you have gone?"

Mom stared at me and smiled.

"Oh, yeah, there is that. Do you think Sam would cope in the 2000s?" I could imagine a man resembling Colin Chandler showing up in current times.

"Sam would survive anywhere."

The clothes I bought for my mother fit well. She appeared like any modern woman, yet I wasn't ready to risk it. I left to get some food for her and Jim. I picked up hamburgers and stopped at the hospital.

"One Hank burger and the works."

"Oh, you shouldn't have." Jim reached for the food.

"After that performance this afternoon, you're right. I'm giving you a second chance."

"Well, some evidence aside, I may give you one too." Little Hank was asleep in a cot, from which he couldn't tumble out. I shut the door to his room and sat in Jim's lap.

"May I eat first?" I could see Jim was hungry.

"No. Okay, but hurry. I need some lovin', cowboy."

"No lovin' in the hospital, Harper. I have my limits."

"We could go into the bathroom."

"Not gonna happen. Get home to your mom, and I'll see you at midnight. Who the hell am I marrying, anyway?"

"A very horny vet. Oh, that reminds me. Want a job?" I let Jim know that my new clinic had an opening for a vet who could do the numbers and some geeking. "I actually like them. They have given me two weeks off for the wedding, and I haven't even been there a year." I explained about Max and his dying wife. "Just what the vet ordered. It smacks of you all over."

"It sounds interesting. Hey, do you have to work tomorrow?"

"Yep. Want to come over to meet everyone?"

As I asked him, a nurse carrying a tray walked in with her back to me. When she turned around, I recognized the owner of the pony.

"Dr. Harper, what are you doing here?"

Thankfully, she wore a badge. "Julie, I go by Lauren. This is my fiancé, Jim Kennedy, and his nephew, Henry."

"I heard about him. Such a sad case."

Jim bristled. "He's loved and well cared for. It's not as if the general population is vaccinated for rabies."

"Jim's a vet, as well. We both have been vaccinated, but I'll bet you haven't?"

"Sprung. You all got me there. I'm sorry for judging. God knows this could be my grandson."

"How's your pony?"

"I think he's cured. I'll take out the catheter tomorrow when I come off shift. Thanks again. I really am the last person to judge families."

"We all have skeletons in our closets." Jim finished his Hank burger and left the room for a few minutes while we swapped the diaper, and Julie conducted observations on him.

Jim returned, after which Julie left us. "I should take the other burger to my mom."

"Aren't you having one?"

"After that comment about my weight? The *bride's diet*? Are you kidding?"

"Lauren, you could gain fifty pounds, and I'll still love you as long as you keep fishing."

"I already ate a Danny meal. Get ready because I may gain fifty when I'm preggers!"

"Lauren Harper, have I told you how much I love you lately?"

I gazed at him and smiled. He was going to watch Little Hank while I tended to my mother and work. "You don't have to. Your actions say it all. I love you too."

Chapter 30

Rebecca

Waiting for Little Hank to return from the hospital was torture. The Hank burger was cold, but I hadn't eaten fries in a long time. Coke! I was a Pepsi girl, but I couldn't complain. I was so spoiled. Having my own personal cook for so many years was a luxury that few would have. It was a struggle to stay fit and trim with an angry Chinaman, continuously trying to make me eat more. I was winning, but it was a daily battle. It was easy to slip half the hamburger to a waiting yellow dog.

Lauren described the hospital and what she knew about the treatment. Apparently, they gave ketamine to Little Hank and injected the antitoxin around the puncture wounds. He didn't have a large enough area, and more injections were administered up the arm and his torso. In addition, he received a vaccine. More injections would be administered in a day or so. For now, Little Hank had to get over the reaction to the volume and immunological response and resultant malaise and fever.

He would be home in the morning. Lauren told me to go to bed and prepare to do the bulk of the caring and nursing tomorrow. She had to work and was taking Jim in for an interview. It was a promising start to their early post-wedding careers.

I would give anything to be a fly on the wall at their wedding, but we both understood that wouldn't happen. Jeff and Sherry raised her, and they deserved to see their daughter get married unencumbered with a former wife, who mysteriously appeared at the time of the wedding. I had to live with my choices. I was fortunate that she didn't seem to resent me for choosing to stay in the nineteenth century.

Lauren traded places with Jim around midnight. He came to the house, and I made him a cup of hot chocolate before he went to bed.

"He isn't your biological grandson, is he?"

"No. I don't have any biological grandchildren. I'm counting on you."

We smiled. "I don't know what Lauren told you about my other family, but I have an adopted daughter who is almost sixteen. If you don't get going, and Hanna doesn't slow down, she's going to give me my first grandchild."

"Sixteen?"

"Hanna's not that young for the 1800s, but much too young for us, according to her father and me."

Jim didn't say anything else. He smiled and went into Lauren's room. In the morning, he emerged and retrieved the paper that was delivered every day to the house. Jim immediately found the real-estate section. He didn't eat and went straight to the café where he got his special coffee and to the hospital to relieve Lauren. She had to get to work. Little Hank was ready for release. Lauren came home, showered, and changed for work. Jim waited for the doctors to say it was safe for Little Hank to leave. He was home around ten. Jim went to see Lauren's clinic and find out about the job.

Lauren left Frank Lash's number for me. I waited until later in the morning when Little Hank was asleep to call him. Lauren suspected I would reach his message machine, but he answered right away.

"Hi, Frank. This is somewhat of a voice out of your past. It's Becky."

"Who?"

"Rebecca. Becky Harper, or Buchanan."

A long pause ensued. "May I call you back?"

"Of course. Do you want the number? I don't know it. I think it's unlisted."

"Give me five and call me back. Only five minutes. Don't wait any longer than that."

He hung up quickly, and I waited for five minutes to return the call.

"Frank Lash."

"Hi, it's me again."

"Where are you?"

"I'm at Lauren's place near Lake Tahoe. I don't want to bother you. I'm sure you're busy, but I just want to thank you for all you did to encourage Lauren to visit me."

"Yeah, that was a bit of a struggle. Lauren said she was glad she went. I'm sorry. You caught me at an inconvenient time." There was another long pause when I could hear he was talking to someone. His hand must have been resting on the receiver. "Nice talking to you. Take care." Before I could respond, he hung up. He was with someone, but I realized he had Lauren's number. If Frank wanted to talk, he could find me.

Little Hank was fussing. He'd finally begun to react to his surroundings. He wanted to hug and pet Lauren's dog. LB was a kind soul who tolerated the strangulating hold and ear twisting of an aggressive, two-year-old child. No wonder the puppy had bitten him!

It was a glorious summer day. The rain had cleared during the night, and the smell of the pines and grass made me homesick for the Cattle Creek Ranch. When I considered it, I recognized the Cattle Creek Ranch's location. I thought I might get Lauren to drive me around, so I could witness how it had changed. Little Hank felt better, and I was so grateful it seemed that he might survive this disease. I would be glad I did this for Dan and Jenny even if I never arrived back home.

As I was sitting on the porch outside, I heard a knock on the front door. I wasn't sure I should answer it, but I heard Frank's voice, asking whether anyone was home. I picked up Little Hank and went to the door just as he was walking away.

"Frank." I was aware that the neighbor might be watching. He turned and smiled. I was inside the door where she couldn't see me, but I thought I saw the curtain move. I signaled for him to come in.

Frank was older and had put on weight, but there was no mistaking him. "How's the piano playing?"

"Great. I'm not playing professionally any longer, but I can entertain my wife and friends. How's the medical profession?"

"Not curing cancer, but I do what I can."

Frank eyed Little Hank and cocked his head.

"Grandson. He belongs to my stepson, Dan."

"What brings you to this century, Becky?"

"Rabies. A rabid puppy bit my grandson. I realized he could be saved if I could get him here fast enough. He received his first treatment yesterday." I held up his bandaged arm.

"Ouch. Really, how are you?"

"Much better, now that I know we have a chance to save this little man. I truly have a great life. Thanks to you, I got to know my daughter, and I hear you saved her life from the crazy stalker lady."

"Lauren said you got married. Still the queen of the Cattle Creek Ranch?"

"Ha! I'd like to think so, but really I'm just an old married woman."

"I think you're more than that. According to Lauren, you have a wonderful life."

"Frank, I have information that will sort a few things out for us. Would you like a cup of coffee?"

"I have an hour at most. I leave tomorrow for Sacramento. My wife is reuniting with her college friends, then we head to Hawaii to relive our honeymoon. What do you know that will make our experience anything close to normal?"

"Other time travelers. Know any?" I suspected he did. I always thought there must be others.

"I'm convinced there are some, but I never talk to any others."

"Do you remember when you took me to the restaurant near Reno, where we saw the *Comstock* producer? His name was Alex Conrad."

"Yes, and he thought he knew you or had worked with you."

"He's a time traveler. You know how most of Virginia City burned down, and many of the official records of deeds, taxes, and papers like that were destroyed in the fire? The Buchanans actually existed. Both Ray and Sam remembered him, and he was there. He recreated what he saw and experienced, and he identified actors who looked like the Buchanans. They were all replicas. The Buchanans did exist, Frank."

"Becky, I can't say you are right or wrong, but why did he think he knew you?"

"I can't explain that. Maybe Mr. Conrad was there in my early days, and the men just forgot, or maybe he was mistaken. At least, it makes my life somewhat more believable."

"Of course, it does. And mine too. Fortunately, they don't have too many delusional people locked up anymore. We're pretty much free to live on the outside with our fantasies. I must go. How long will you be here?"

"I don't know yet. When you are back, call Lauren. Possibly we can get together for a barbecue."

Frank laughed. "Yep, I'll introduce you to my wife. That would go over well (not)."

"Never told her?"

"Never." We hugged, and he left.

After he'd gone, the neighbor Helen came over. Little Hank, who had woken up, was not feeling well again. His reaction had returned, and he required anti-inflammatories. I explained that 'Henry' might be coming down with chickenpox, and I tried to isolate him. Luckily, that cured her of wanting to visit.

Lauren

It was chaotic at work. Doug was sick, as were two nurses. Sara and I had three colicky horses, and there was an outbreak of parvo. We had four vomiting, dehydrated, circling-the-drain dogs. Kill me now if I must deal with those. Even the worst diarrhea in horses was nothing, compared with the smell of parvo diarrhea. We took off as soon as we could to escape from the sick small animal cases.

After attending to the three colicky horses, I stopped in to see the pony from yesterday as a courtesy. Julie was sleeping, and we examined the pony. He was fine. We removed the catheter and took back the remaining unopened bags of intravenous fluids.

"Call the clinic to see if there is anything else we can do to avoid the 'diarrhea-thon.'" Sara contacted the clinic to say we were coming in to help unless we had received another call.

Dot, the practice manager, answered. "To help with what?"

"The parvo dogs."

"All resolved. A relief vet came in. You can return. The coast is clear." She was kind of kidding, and kind of not.

I called home but realized my mother probably wouldn't pick up the phone. I tried Jim, and he didn't answer. When we arrived back at the clinic, Jim's car was in the parking lot. He must be interviewing. I wondered who the relief vet was. I parked in the back to empty the trash and restock, which Sara covered. I took the money and receipts inside and planned to do the case reports. As I walked in the back door, I detected the isolation-ward parvo smell. I glanced in the window, and Jim was writing on a clipboard.

When I knocked on the window, he signaled me with a thumbs-up gesture. I smiled right back and headed to the reception and an accessible computer. I hadn't eaten any lunch, but the smell of the parvo dogs made eating not as much of a priority as it had been before.

Max approached me. "He is a geek, isn't he?"

"Through and through. Could you satisfy Jim's demands?"

"He drives a tough bargain, but I think we can meet them. Heard you had a rough time last night. If you're done, you can leave early."

"Boy, is anything a secret around here?"

"Jim told us about his nephew. We all have crosses to bear. I just hope the treatment is successful. Those darn communes are dragging society down."

"Tell me about it."

I left the clinic after I finished my reports. I called my mom and dad in Kentucky. "I have good news. The Messiah has arrived. All good to go on the planned date. Have you talked with his parents?"

"Yes. Jim's parents are rather different, aren't they?"

"You know, I've talked with them only one time. Jim describes them as sort of aloof. He says they reside in the same house, but not really in the same space and time."

I headed to the store for more supplies, including disposable diapers. We would have spaghetti. I even got Oreos for my mother and returned to Rich's house with all the food. I'd picked up some orange popsicles and handed one to Little Hank. Of course, he had never seen or tasted such a thing. He bit into it, puckered his lips, and had a hilarious, painful look. That lasted for approximately a second. I took my own and showed him how to lick it.

My mother was into the Oreos in a heartbeat—a shopping success. The newspaper was on the kitchen table, open to a rental property section, with a realtor's number circled. I called to explain I was looking for a home in the local area, I had a dog, and I was planning to keep a horse. The woman stated a place was open for inspection with notice to the owner. It was a fixer-upper at a reasonable price. She had someone coming out that afternoon. I could come the next day if he did not take it.

"Would you tell me where it's located?"

"No, the owner is quite private. I'll take your number, and I'll call you this evening."

She took down my number, which reminded me my mom needed a way to answer the phone. We decided that

I would let it ring twice, hang up, and call again. We did it once, and it worked well. An hour later, when I was making spaghetti, Jim came home.

"You left in a hurry."

"Dinner will be ready in thirty minutes. Want to shower? Actually, that's not optional."

"Showered at work. That place is amazing. Looks as though we'll be working together."

He did smell good. He put his arms around me and glanced over his shoulder. Noticing my mother and Little Hank out on the patio, he brought his hands up into a zone that could make me want to take him right then and there.

"You realize you're done like a dinner tonight, mister."

"Can you put that on hold? We have an appointment to see a rental property."

"Is it with the company circled in the paper?"

"Yes. Did you make an appointment, as well?"

"No, but not for lack of trying. I'll get my mom to take over. Now get your hands in a more respectable area, Jim Bob. Wait, maybe just one more minute." We heard the door open, and he was quick to let go.

As my mother entered the kitchen, Jim smiled sheepishly. "What would you like me to call you, Dr. Buchanan?"

"My friends call me Becky."

"Mom, we have an appointment to check out a rental property. Can you finish dinner, and we'll be back within the hour?"

"Does it require advanced cooking skills?"

"Becky, can you boil water?" Gazed over my shoulder at my mother.

"Get out, you two. I'm not hopeless."

We met the realtor to head out of town. As we turned up a side road, I recognized where we were going. "That old fox."

"Huh?"

"It's the Davidson place. I'm already familiar with it. I'm his chauffeur. I take him to Mary Knox's house twice a week for dinner with Mary. I pretend to come for dinner, but they expect me to leave until after dinner most of the time."

The realtor found this hysterical. Jim also was amused. We pulled in, where he was sitting outside, smoking a pipe. He greeted me like his long-lost daughter. The interior was a surprise. It was built when he moved there many years ago. The detail and the woodwork were so elaborate. He had a magnificent, large fireplace, which reminded me of the Cattle Creek Ranch. I was in love.

"Yes, we'll take it."

"Lauren, are you going to let me hold any negotiations here?"

"Nope. It's everything I want."

Jim shrugged. "If the lady wants it, the lady gets it. You're not ever going car shopping with me."

"I doubt you'll even get me out of the house."

"What about all this?" Jim examined the stacks of papers and mementos.

"That's the problem. I don't think there's enough room at Mary's."

I nodded. "Not nearly."

"You haven't seen the basement. It will hold all this, and there will still be enough room for a pool table."

"Done."

"Lauren, will you please?" Jim was exasperated. "When will we have time to move all this?"

"That's what mothers-in-law are for, darling." We understood whose mother I meant, but they didn't.

We would move Mr. Davidson in with Mary as soon as I received the okay from her. We'd start moving in our belongings right after that. I asked the realtor to call Mr. Davidson's son-in-law to make sure all parties were happy.

We returned to Rich's, where the dinner was hot and delicious. When my phone rang, I recognized the number. "Hi, Mary."

My mom and Jim looked up expectantly. "Yes, tomorrow? Well, I'm not certain. Are you sure this is what you want? Aren't you a little old for this? All right. Yes, ma'am. Tomorrow. No, I haven't been spanked in many years. I'm not planning on it, either. Yes, ma'am. I will. Immediately after work." I hung up. "Boy, you don't want to rile her up too much. She wants Mr. Davidson to be at her house tomorrow. We can have the house this weekend."

Jim squeezed my hand under the table. Little Hank was falling asleep in my mother's arms. My mother seemed pleased. "How many bedrooms?"

Jim and I glanced at each other and shrugged. We hadn't moved past the front room. "Anyone want any dessert? Jim, do you work tomorrow?"

"No, I don't start until next week, and I have time off for the wedding. I figure I'll set up two oldies to live in sin. I'll take Little Hank back for his second round, which is simply a vaccine this time. The worst of it is over."

My mother said she had performed some research on the internet. "Several protocols exist. Most of them have prevented rabies if the treatment starts before the onset of signs. He's going to be okay. I know he is."

I poured us all a glass of Rich's brandy. "To modern science."

Jim made a toast to "oldies falling in love."

I added, "To the end of deployment and a night off from work."

Why did I say that? What in the world was I thinking? My phone rang as we chinked our glasses together. "Lauren, it's Max. My wife is quite sick tonight. Could you treat a vomiting dog? Sounds like parvo."

Jim went with me to examine the dog. The dog was not a local, where most of the cases came from, and he'd been vaccinated. *There is a God.* His temperature was normal, and he vomited up a large piece of a horse's hoof as he sat on the examination table. "Do you have horses?"

A sheepish client admitted the farrier had been out, and the dog liked to eat the trimmings. We suggested he would be okay, and we would be happy to keep him, but there was probably no danger unless some of what he ate got stuck in the bowel. Because that was unlikely, I recommended they take him home. We would take him in for further workup in the morning if he continued to vomit.

When we returned, my mother had gone to bed. Jim and I gazed at each other like a couple of kids. I was nervous, and I wanted this night to be perfect. We were both exhausted, and we just held each other forever.

"Do you mind telling me what type of deal you made with Max about your employment?"

"I'm not sure I should tell you."

"No secrets?"

"You'll know soon enough."

"Tell me."

"I'm not telling you everything, but I will tell you one thing. I've extended your honeymoon."

"What do you mean?"

"You and I will have an extra week after the wedding. You can be off from work ten days before the wedding, and we both will be off for three weeks after the wedding."

"Max went for that?"

"Instead of a significant salary. Yep, he did."

"Oh, that reminds me. We received an early wedding gift."

"What? From whom?"

"Sam Buchanan and my mom. Close your eyes. No peeking."

"You expect me to believe this?"

"Yep. Are your eyes closed?"

"Sealed."

"Hold out your hands."

He did, and I placed the gold nugget into his hands, which dropped down from the weight.

"Don't peek. What does it feel like?"

"A lead weight."

"Open them." He did, and his eyes widened.

"Is it gold?"

"Probably."

"My mom and I found it in the creek after the flood. Sam believed if it was known to have been discovered on the Cattle Creek Ranch, he would spend years keeping a torrent of miners off the land."

"It must weigh more than a pound. How much is it worth?"

"I don't know. We can verify that this week if you have time."

"I'll make time. Let's put that away because I need a refresher on my fishing lessons."

"Let the instructions begin."

Chapter 31

Rebecca

What a difference a good night's sleep made, at least for Little Hank and me. I'm not sure the other two could say that. Lauren was up and gone before I even got up. Jim went straight to the shower and emerged with wet hair and a smile on his face. Little Hank went straight to him and climbed in his lap.

"Becky, I'll bet you're getting cabin fever. How about you and I do some retail therapy?"

"I don't think I've heard that expression before."

"It's a female expression. Today, instead of hunting and gathering, women acquire things and experience satisfaction from shopping."

"I get it. My idea of a good time is learning about some medical information that will help me when I return. I can do that on the computer, thanks to Dr. Google, as Lauren calls it."

"Well, a woman doesn't live by work alone. Let's buy a truck."

"I'm not sure I should be going out. Last time I was here, I got caught red-handed, so to speak."

"We'll head to Reno. You should be safe there. I can tell Little Hank is better. Lauren gave me the okay."

I was impressed Jim had already learned the rules of significant purchases. "Buy nothing more substantial than a bread box without the wife's permission," I suggested as he laughed.

"Lesson learned long ago. I'll get us some proper coffee and the car seat, and we can go."

I tidied the house and dressed Little Hank and myself in modern-day clothes. I was anxious to discover what had changed. Several years had now passed since my extended visit when my dad was dying. I hadn't really done much surveying and comparing the terrain with the 1800s.

I was ready when Jim returned with his rental car and child seat. Society had become so obsessed with safety. As kids, we used to ride in the back of the truck and stand up behind the cab while dad drove well above the speed limit. That wasn't going to happen today. Little Hank put on a turn when he was strapped into the child-safety seat. Jim laid down the law, and the tearful child finally accepted his relegation as a second-rate citizen in the backseat.

Jim turned on the radio to find a country-music channel, which fascinated Little Hank. I wondered what he would remember when he went back to his family and the 1800s. I thought about it and silently prayed that we could return.

I was amazed at the amount of development that had taken place. There were automobile sale lots for a mile. Jim pulled into a lot that sold used cars. He wanted us to stay in the car while he spoke to the man who directed him toward a lot further down the road. Little Hank was captivated by the cars, and he watched them as they circled around the lot and then out onto the street. He would have no sense of danger, and either Jim or I tightly held his hand or picked him up while we examined various trucks.

Jim observed that Little Hank was quite taken with the color red. We decided to use his Christian name in public. "Henry, you are a man with a vision. How did you know that red trucks are faster than all the other trucks? I think we'll concentrate on that color."

"Red," repeated Little Hank several times. Jim now carried him around the lot and even let him sit in the driver's seat and play with the steering wheel. I could leave Sam for this man. I was so happy Lauren had seen past all the other people she might have chosen and how he had the making of a wonderful spouse.

Jim settled on a green truck, despite the protestation of Little Hank. Jim pulled out a card and paid for it upfront. It was only a few months old, but the price had been reduced by several thousand dollars as it had been repossessed. I was asked to drive it to the car-rental place, where Jim dropped off his rental car. Because I hadn't driven a car in years, all the new features intimidated me. I couldn't even see over the steering wheel. The salesman shook his head. He showed me the lever to raise the seat. I was slightly embarrassed but impressed that everything was electrical.

I followed Jim over to the rental place and parked out on the road. I didn't have a driver's license, so Jim decided it was best to drive from now on if we were stopped. We drove past the restaurant where I'd eaten with Frank and met the producer of the *Comstock* television series. "Have you eaten there?"

"Yes, once. The chicken is good." I considered telling Jim about my experience, but it was complicated. I wanted to get Little Hank back for a nap. We returned to the house, where I put Little Hank in the bed and made some lunch for Jim. He was going up to the Davidson property to take Mr. Davidson to his new home. He would return to pick up Little Hank and me to show off the house and maybe do some cleaning in preparation for the move. Tomorrow was going to be another hospital visit for Little Hank. There might not be an opportunity to work on the house, and I was anxious to see it. I had a feeling it was close to where my house was in the 1800s.

The phone rang two times, and it rang again a few seconds later. "Hi, Mom. How's it going? Did you look for a truck yet?"

"We have one, and sadly it's not the truck that Little Hank wanted. Still, it's quite nice. I think Jim got a bargain, however, and he seems pleased."

"We want to do as much as possible. If Jim gets back from moving Mr. Davidson, will you tell him that I'll get dinner and meet you all up there?"

"How's work?"

"Busy, but good. I saw a horse with a fractured splint bone. My boss is back. He'll remove the distal fragment tomorrow. He is something else. He's doing it standing."

"Oh, interesting. I wish I could watch."

"Me too. How's the baby?"

"No fever and bright as a button. Little Hank loves Jim and LB. I think you've picked a winner there."

"Don't I know it. Jim must be compared with Dad and now Sam. I think he measures up nicely, though.

"I can't think of any better men to emulate."

"All right, back to work. I already talked with Jim. Boy, is Doug happy Jim is going to work here! I'll probably get the shaft."

"He doesn't like horses, does he?"

"Nope, my saving grace."

"Jim's coming back to pick me up, and we'll tackle the house this afternoon. I'm excited to see it."

"Yeah, the fireplace is amazing. It reminds me of your fireplace on the Cattle Creek Ranch. I can't wait for you to see the house, either. Mom, don't let Little Hank run around too much. The barn was torn down recently, and my guess is there are tons of nails lying around."

"He was vaccinated for tetanus, wasn't he?"

"That immunity won't kick in for a few weeks."

"Lauren Harper, I didn't roll off a turnip truck. My doctor's degree was not printed in an old newspaper. I'll be careful."

"Sorry, Mom. I guess I'm getting maternal."

"In spades. Here's Jim. Gotta go."

We loaded the vacuum cleaner and some cleaning products in the truck and placed a screaming child in the backseat. He wanted his mother. I felt awful, but he got over it as soon as the car started to move. As we drove, I attempted to get my bearings. I was convinced we were close to the Cattle

Creek Ranch homestead, but this property was located on a hill.

We climbed out of the car. I would never have guessed what was inside by observing the exterior. The walls were built with beautiful timber. The windows were old-fashioned but possessed the double glaze that kept the cold and heat out. When I turned the corner, there stood the fireplace Lauren had mentioned. By studying it, I tried to see how it differed from ours at home on the Cattle Creek Ranch. I recognized which rocks went where and the feel and contour of the stones that made the remarkable symbol of my family's existence. It was not a pretend fireplace with a gas-burning fire on the *Comstock* set. It was a genuine fireplace like the one in my home.

Could it have survived when my family did not? Might it have been moved from where it was constructed before I was involved with the Buchanan family? I realized the way to tell. When Danny was a boy, he carved his initials into stone inside the rock flume. Sam showed me one summer. I searched for a flashlight or torch. Jim wanted to know what I was looking for. When I responded I wished to examine the inner shaft of the fireplace, he handed me his phone. It was such an innovative device, with a small flashlight inside. Jim pressed a button igniting a powerful beam. I stepped up and into the large cavern. Along the inside, at about my height, was the area that Sam had shown me. I couldn't detect the initials and chuckled to myself. Of course, there were none. I explained to Jim, and he shrugged. "As if they could move something that big and not have it fall apart."

"It definitely appears real."

"I suspect there are many replicas from the television show."

"I guess that may be true. Well, there's much to do, and it certainly makes me feel good to help you both." We worked for three hours, moving papers, and washing the curtains and bed linen. Lauren provided us with store-bought food again. We worked for another hour, but it was time to get Little Hank to bed. After Jim drove us home, he returned to assist Lauren at their new place for an hour or more. I was exhausted, and both Little Hank and I went to sleep early.

Jim took Little Hank into the clinic for his second vaccine. Two more would follow. Jim mentioned he cried a little, kissed Cary, and thanked her. I was so proud that he showed gratitude and seemed to understand that we were trying to help him. Well, that's what I hoped Little Hank was doing. His father was a total flirt until he met Jenny. Maybe he was simply flirting.

Once again, he had a mild fever and was cranky. I stayed home while Jim worked on their new house. I fried chicken for dinner. It was Gee Ling's recipe. Lauren and Jim came home to eat, and they returned to their new house.

Mr. Davidson requested that a few items be brought to Mary's home. When Lauren took them to him, she asked Mr. Davidson about the house. He told her when he retired, his wife wanted to build a place near Lake Tahoe. He drew up his own architectural plans to create the home of her dreams. Lauren inquired about the fireplace. He claimed his wife had been a *Comstock* fan, who wanted the same fireplace featured in the television series. She found a replica left on a site where a house had burned more than fifty years before that time. He disassembled and reassembled it and built the house around it.

"Mom, I asked him where the fireplace was located, but he couldn't remember. He and Mary are so cute together. It is as though they have lost ten years of age. They walk, do the gardening, and wash the dishes together." Lauren glanced over at Jim, who had come back.

I realized how kind Sam was to me by allowing me to work during a time in history when a working wife was considered scandalous. I hoped Lauren was marrying a man who was comfortable in his shoes and would not try to restrict her ambitions. I wondered about their upcoming wedding. I noticed Lauren started to receive several calls a day, which she took away from me. It was probably my sister, Sherry, or Jeff. I didn't ask. Lauren lived her life in the twenty-first century, while mine was in the past.

Chapter 32

Lauren

The wedding plans took a toll on my other mother, who planned the event without my help or input. I didn't care. Just get me to the altar, and I would be happy. Jim would begin work in several days. I had a month off in total, and he had about three weeks. I was scheduled to leave for Kentucky the following week.

My bio-mom expected to stay a bit longer after I left for Kentucky so poor Little Hank could receive his last rabies vaccine. Jim would take them to the trailhead as my mother requested, and she would walk to the portal pool with Little Hank. I took several pictures and had them printed and sealed. I was able to order antibiotics and some local anesthetic for her to take back. We made waterproof bags for her travel through the water.

This time, we understood we would not see each other again. Our time together was precious. Mom was content to help prepare the new house. She would know where I lived and where I was going to work. I took her to the clinic one night when I realized everyone was not around. She was amazed at the technological advances. "You treat animals as if they are human. We should be so lucky."

"You know, you could always bring your family for a vacation here." She knew I was joking, but the thought was out there.

"You never know."

Jim and I moved to our new house over the weekend. I was on call, but we personally had so few belongings that moving from Rich's place to our house was the easiest part. We had assumed most of Mr. Davidson's personal possessions. We moved them down to the basement, replaced the sheets and towels, and bought a new microwave. My mom gave us the gold Sam had given her to pay for Little Hank's treatment. Jim didn't want to take it, but my mother explained that she was wealthy beyond her dreams compared to us. She insisted that she contribute to some of her stay. We took a photo of her and me together. If anyone ever saw it, some complicated explanations would be required. Mr. Davidson remarked that we were welcome to put whatever we wanted in a built-in safe in the basement, which had been empty for years. He recalled the combination, which I recorded.

On Sunday, as we were setting up the kitchen, I remembered the safe. I believed it would be best to start putting away photographs of my mother in case someone came around. I tried to open the safe, but the combination didn't work. I yelled up to Jim, who was replacing a faucet in the bathroom. He came down, carrying Little Hank, and tried various ways to make the digits work.

"Apparently, he doesn't recall the numbers correctly. Let's ask him again when we see them."

My mother came down to examine the safe. She did a double-take and asked for the combination. Her eyes went wider as she studied the sizable solid cabinet next to the safe. It took her one attempt to open the safe. Jim and I stared at her. She smiled.

"They did exist, you know. The Buchanans were real. We may all be dead now, but we were real." Neither Jim nor I replied. She examined the paper, noted the second number as twenty-one instead of twenty-two, and walked away carrying Little Hank.

Jim took me in his arms and hugged me. I thought about the graves in Miner's Meadow. "Let's go up there for part of our honeymoon."

"I'd like that."

"Should we take your mom up there before she returns?"

"We could ask. You understand that my mother can go there and never see anyone since she owns it. I'm not convinced she would like to see how the cabin and valley are so full of strangers."

"We could inquire. I could take your mother up there after you leave."

This made me realize how close it was to the time of my departure and when I would be saying goodbye, probably for the last time. Jim sensed my melancholy and held me.

We took the last of our possessions from Rich's house and loaded them in the new truck to head up to our new home. Helen emerged with a casserole and cake. "I'm going to miss you guys."

"Helen, we'll have you up as soon as we get back from the wedding. We're kind of crazy right now, but God knows that we owe you big-time."

She hugged me and whispered to me my secret was safe with her. I observed her quizzically. "I know who your cousin or aunt is."

"You do?"

"Don't tell me now, but someday tell me where she's been hiding all these years."

"You wouldn't believe me if I told you."

"You never know. Enjoy the food. No rush about returning the dishes. I was a bride once too. I know how difficult it is to combine visiting with family, working, and wedding planning."

I gazed at her and realized I had a true friend. "By the way, what's going on with the FBI dude?"

"All systems go, Lauren. All systems go. Yours isn't the only new romance on the block." She hugged me one more time, and I handed her the keys. Rich would be back either later that night or the following day.

I almost forgot. The branding iron was behind the house. I retrieved it and threw it in the back of the truck. I planned to show it to my mother. I turned back toward the place that protected me for many weeks. I called Rich to tell him where the keys were and let me know if I had left anything.

"If I can do anything for you or Dirk, call me. I'm sure I'll see you before I leave for the wedding, but you'll always have a home with me just in case."

"Hey, in all the drama with your aunt, I forgot to tell you. I'm out and proud."

"Congrats, big brother. So happy for you both."

LB wagged her tail while we ascended the hill toward the new house. Little Hank ran naked on the small patch of lawn and held a hose with running water. He tried to get LB to join him, but she stayed back. My mother sat in a chair, watching him. She was so tiny but so strong. She held her own in a man's world. I would never be able to match her in her presence on earth. I loved and respected her so much, and yet she made me feel as though I was an equal. Aside from a handful of people, she would be remembered as the woman who disappeared. Only a plaque would commemorate her existence on earth. She was quite at home and content sitting here at this minute, caring for her husband's grandson.

Mom glanced up and smiled. It was as if she could read my thoughts. My mother was happy. In a week, she would be back with her second family, where she felt she belonged. She would know I was married, but she would be long dead. Her body rests in Miner's Meadow or her beloved Hank Heaven. I had this moment to learn from her and show that her genes would survive. I wiped a tear from my eye. I realized my mom saw it, and she turned to Little Hank, who was getting cold in the breeze.

"Let's get you ready to eat dinner, little man."

He squealed and kicked as she picked him up and interrupted his play. He turned to me and shouted, "Yoran."

"I'm coming. Mind your grandmother."

Jim came out of the house. "Shall we eat?"

"Coming. Have you washed?"

He splayed his hands—wet and clean—snatched me up, threw me over his shoulder, and took me into the house. I observed my family and their interactions for maybe fifteen minutes. This probably would soon be the last time I'd be with my mother, which was one more time than I anticipated. *Never say never.*

Rebecca

Little Hank had received his last vaccine the day before Lauren was to leave to prepare for her wedding. We celebrated by going to Reno for dinner, but I wore a disguise to the restaurant. Jim went to bed and left us after our supper.

"Lauren, how can I thank you?"

"Mom, you don't need to thank Jim or me. Little Hank is family."

"You saved his life. You realize you did." I hoped Lauren would remember her role in extending my family's existence.

"What will you do when you get back?" I wanted to think of my mother in her cabin fishing and enjoying herself. Sam had already told me of his plans for July.

"Sam insists we will spend the entire month of July in Hank Heaven. We'll see. I can't imagine him taking that much time off."

"Maybe he's finally letting go somewhat. How will you cope? You're the workaholic in your family."

"Hmm, true enough. I like that term. Is it new?"

"I don't know when it happened. I may have inherited that gene from you, though."

"You could do worse."

"Yeah, I could have inherited the short gene."

I had to swat her for that remark. "How are your father and Sherry doing?"

"Mom, you know dad is older, and I believe he is even older than Sam is. He retires this month. It'll be interesting to see what happens next. He claims he has several projects. I hope he will come to stay with us for a while. Mom, I mean Aunt Sherry, is doing well. She has her life, friends, and golf. I guess she'll live forever, sort of like you."

"I'd like for you to say 'hi' from me, but don't. It's best that they think I'm dead. You're a lucky girl to have that man."

"And Hanna is lucky to have you."

"I don't know about that. I caught Hanna with Alexander at second base."

Lauren laughed. "I warned her."

"You knew?" *I must have been the only one who was clueless.*

"It was fairly obvious, Mom."

"When she returns from her summer adventure, Alexander will be in college."

It seemed as if Lauren knew something, but she arose to enter the house. "My future husband awaits. Sweet dreams, Mom."

"Pleasant dreams to you too."

When Jim drove Lauren to the airport, I went along but remained with Little Hank in the car as Jim went in with her. It was early, but Jim had to get back to work. It was a bittersweet farewell. I gave her a locket I had kept until the last minute. Sam had it made for me a while ago. "Something borrowed."

"Something blue. It could fit under the *old* category, too, Mom."

We hugged, and we both cried. Little Hank was confused and wanted to go with "Yoran." It was hot, and we kept the car running. The air conditioner could cool him off since he had once again reacted to the vaccine. Little Hank was nearly becoming accustomed to vehicles and was more interested in the airplanes taking off and landing. *How was this going to work when he returned?* He wasn't two yet. Hopefully, his memory would fade. Possibly he would become an inventor and make modern-day things from his subconscious.

Jim took us home, after which he went to work. I spent my last day cleaning and preparing for our return to my time. Because it was hot, thinking of the cold water was pleasant. I prayed it would be the same on the other side. Jim and I discussed his upcoming marriage. He admitted his uncertainty about the time-travel concept, as well as the *Comstock* aspect.

"Why don't you visit us?"

Jim stared at Little Hank. "You never know." He continued eating and assisted Little Hank with his dinner. We washed the dishes together. He was quiet, and I assumed he missed Lauren.

When his phone rang, he ran to it. It was an emergency. He was not working in the morning to take Little Hank and me to the parking lot. I didn't want him to go all the way to the portal pool, and he concurred with me. Some things are better imagined than they are visualized.

Jim left for the clinic while I put Little Hank to bed. Little Hank had become obsessed with the Dolly Parton song, "I

Will Always Love You." I sang it until he fell asleep. I sat on the couch, facing the fireplace. Boy, this was an excellent replica of my fireplace at home.

I searched inside the flue one more time, but of course, no initials were there. Because the internet had not been turned on here, my research tool was cut off. I had learned a great deal about herbal medicine and other topics, which would help me in the 1800s without raising any alarms. I had to decide how to explain the rabies treatment to my associates. I figured the best way was to claim that the infected puppy had not bitten Little Hank after all.

In the early morning, I rose and changed into clothes that would dry quickly. Sam said he would leave a change of clothes for us, starting a month from when I left. However, a month had not passed yet. Jim took Little Hank to see the deer that regularly ate the oats growing near the old horse pen, which had been demolished when Mr. Davidson's horse died. I wasn't allowed to meet Mary, which was understandable. She would have recognized me from my pictures in an instant.

Jim positioned Little Hank in his car seat, and we said goodbye to Lauren's dog. LB was going to stay with Mary when Jim went to Kentucky for the wedding. As I climbed into the car, Jim handed me a package, which was a sealed plastic box. "Lauren and I want you to have a few items when you get home. Since an ice pack is in there, be sure to follow the instructions."

When we arrived at the parking lot at daybreak, Jim got out of the car and helped little Hank out of his seat. He carried him to the back of the truck, and he sat down on the tailgate. He kissed us both goodbye and promised to love and care for Lauren until death.

"Becky, I actually want to believe you, and I understand something happens. Whatever it is, and however things turn out for you, please realize you can always come back. Lauren and I plan to give you more grandchildren, but that must be when she's ready. It might not be for a while. Your DNA will live on."

"Jim, it's not my DNA I care about. It's my values and spirit. I have no worries about that. Take care of my beautiful daughter. She means the world to me. If there's any way to thank her father without...." I paused.

"I've got it. Don't worry. 'Her mother would be so proud...'"

"Yep, that'll do." I inhaled deeply. Another vehicle joined the three cars in the lot. I decided to wait until the occupants were on the trail for a while. Little Hank wanted to walk. I hoped that would last for a while. Jim pulled out, and Little Hank yelled goodbye until he couldn't see the truck anymore. We sat on a log for nearly twenty minutes.

We began our walk, which would take about an hour. It was still cool and shady. Little Hank was a trouper, but he finally grew tired. The climb up to the rock-slide area took longer with a small child. Lauren had mentioned a plaque along the trail. I wanted to examine it.

I hid the box behind a tree. The couple who had come before my arrival were long gone. It would be a mere fifteen minutes out of my way. Instead of scaling down to the creek, I continued to locate the plaque. Well, maybe I would be remembered somewhat longer. As we were about to turn around, a couple rounded the corner and encountered

Little Hank and me looking down on the plaque. They inquired whether we were going to Miner's Meadow.

"Not today, but isn't this a beautiful place?"

"Do you know all the stories about it and the cabin?"

"Yes, I've heard them."

"Did you hear about the two women who were killed?"

"Yes." I kept my face turned down and pretended to search for trout in the pool below.

"We feel the one they never found is hiding in the mountains."

"Really. That could be what happened."

"What do you think?"

What the heck! "I believe she traveled to another time." When I laughed, they joined in.

"That's as good an explanation as any. How far are you heading?"

The trip with a toddler to Miner's Meadow was improbable. "I guess reaching the meadow will be difficult with my grandson. Henry, let's go a little farther before we turn around."

"Good luck."

"You too."

I picked up Little Hank, went around the corner, and waited. After a few minutes, I headed back to where I knew I could safely descend to the creek. The water was low and slow. I saw no trout, picked up the box Jim had given me, and slid down the embankment to the edge of the stream. I stared at the trail, waited, heard nothing, and considered all my options. I knew there was only one. I stripped Little Hank and took the plunge. He screamed when his naked body hit the cold water. I hoped it would take his breath away.

When we surfaced, the water level was higher. I prayed it was the correct year. We climbed out quickly, and I searched for clothes Sam may have left for us, yet I did not see any. I waited near the creek for our clothes to dry. The box survived the trip and still appeared sealed. *Why hadn't I laid the garments in such a box?* The polyester clothes dried sufficiently after about an hour on such a warm day. Getting Little Hank up the embankment was a challenge, but at last, I was up on the trail that led to Hank Heaven or home. I turned the other way and was relieved that I would be home in a few hours.

I was tired and hungry, and Little Hank was irritable. Not bringing food along was a huge mistake with a toddler. *What was I thinking?* Approximately an hour from home, I heard hoofbeats. Little Hank and I hid behind a tree. I was on the main road now, where I spied Dan pulling a wagon. I stepped out and yelled. He stared hard, realized it was us, halted the wagon, and jumped off. He ran to his son and picked him up. Dan observed his modern clothes, hugged him, and cried. Little Hank kept saying, "Daddy, Daddy."

"I'm your Pa." We laughed, and Dan hugged me and held Little Hank until he cried and pushed away. He held out his hand, which Dan kissed. "Let's get you home to your mother and sisters."

"Sisters?"

"Elaine Rebecca Buchanan is nine days old today."

"All good?"

"Perfect, Becky." I climbed on the wagon, and Dan lifted Little Hank up to me.

"Car, daddy, car."

"Tell me about it."

I rolled my eyes. "You don't want to know. You'll go there and never return."

We arrived at Dan's, where he took Little Hank in to see his mother and baby sister. "I'll take the wagon back to the main house, Dan. I'll let you have your reunion and be down later."

It took me a few minutes to reach the main house. After one of the ranch hands retrieved the horses and wagon, I went inside. I saw Gee Ling and placed my finger on my lips. He smiled and pointed to Sam's desk. I rounded the corner and, without looking, Sam shouted for more coffee. I walked up to the desk, and he glanced up before I could even reach for the coffee pot. Several years' worth of lines and tension were erased in an instant. He stood up, took me in his arms, and held me. The smell of an 1800s man, plus pipe tobacco, told me I really was home. It was no dream.

"He's fine. No rabies."

"And you?"

"Lauren's getting married next week. I gave her the gold locket you gave me two years ago. I hope you don't mind. I said something borrowed."

"Thinking she might return it?"

"Something like that."

"I'll have another one made for you."

"Her fiancé is a wonderful man. He reminds me of Hank in looks and of you in manner. I'll tell you more later."

We held each other, and Gee Ling finally came around the corner.

"So happy, missy home. Gee Ling make special dinner tonight."

I hugged him and straightened his queue. "Anything will do, Gee Ling. I'm so glad to be back home with the most important men in my life."

Sam and I walked down to Dan's house. Jenny had dressed Little Hank in his traditional 1800s clothes. Jenny ran across the room, hugged me, and thanked me. We both cried, and the men politely watched us. Little Hank ran to Sam and held up his arms to be picked up. The image of Sam holding his grandson at that moment would be burned in my mind forever. *Where did the chain break? Did Little Hank have only daughters? Would there be any more heirs?* I didn't care. I had my family, and I was at peace, even though I missed and loved my natural-born daughter.

Chapter 33

Lauren

I had to sit on the plane for several minutes. I'd forgotten how hot and humid the Kentucky weather could be. I finally retrieved my bag, called my mother, and waited by the curb because she ran late. I helped an elderly man with his bags. His children, who picked him up, thanked me.

My mom pulled in behind me and waved as I stood with the gentleman and greeted his children. He was familiar. After I placed my bags in our car, I realized he was a retired vet who had started the largest equine clinic in Kentucky. He was a God among horse vets. *I am not worthy*.

"Well? I see you keep good company."

"Do you know who that was?"

"Of course, your father and I have been to his house many times."

My mom wanted details of my new practice and Jim. I played dumb. Leaving my other mother was too raw. I closed my eyes and feigned exhaustion.

"What's on the agenda for today?"

"We're headed to the bridal shop for a fitting. A special exception was made for two seamstresses to fix the dress, which must be ready next Saturday. We have a high tea at the country club tomorrow and about fifty other things to do."

"Will I have any time to sleep?

"Nope."

"All right, fearless leader. I am at your service."

The gown was beyond gorgeous. I was thrilled with it. The required alterations were minimal, which lowered my mother's anxiety about three notches.

Lisa and Janie were all set. I still hadn't met anyone from Jim's family. His sister, my final bridesmaid, was flying in the following day.

The groomsmen were my brother, Andy, Rich, and Jim's classmate, Roger. I knew nothing about him except he and Jim lived together during vet school. Rich was due on Thursday, but Roger wouldn't arrive until Friday. Jim was driving in late Wednesday.

"What if he can't get here? This is all so risky. All we need is bad weather, and someone won't make it on time."

"Mom, it will be fine. I'm getting married, and we'll have a great reception. Did I tell you we have an extra week off for our honeymoon?"

"Will you ever inform us about where you're going on this honeymoon?"

"We'll head to Jackson Hole and the Grand Tetons, but then we'll hike to Miner's Meadow and the Sierras."

"Got your licenses?"

"Yep, all sorted."

"If the wedding is a bust, at least your dad will be glad you can fish."

"Where is dad?"

"Gosh, Lauren, he's back at work."

"What happened?"

"You know your father. The new conglomerate boss called him. The heir apparent is lost. He has no idea how to do the research. Your dad is assisting them."

I smiled. I assumed maybe I inherited the working gene from both sides of my family. "I hope he's happy."

"Pig in mud, and he's getting paid a bucket of money. It'll help with the cost of this wedding."

"I told you I could have done it at city hall."

"Nope. Remember that weddings are not for the bride in Kentucky. They're for the mother of the bride."

I gazed down at my engagement ring. "If you say so."

When we arrived home, my brother and I wrestled. He pinned me, and Jane told me the bathroom was hers until further notice. My mother tickled my back while we watched a *Comstock* episode. Dad arrived home immediately before dinner. He appeared tan and happy. We went out together to examine the last of our horses.

I could sense he wanted to talk to me. "Okay, Dad, what gives?"

"Your mom has gone to much expense and effort to plan this wedding and ceremony for you. Will you simply go along with it all? Don't argue. This is truly a big deal. She never had a big wedding. If she wants you to do something, will you do it?"

"Sure, Dad. Jim and I get it. How about you, though? Any special requests?"

"Yes." Dad pulled a bracelet from his pocket. "This piece of jewelry once belonged to your mother. I mean Becky. I know she would want you to have it. Something old. Something new. It's yours now."

I examined it and put it on. It coordinated well with my locket. I hugged my father and thanked him.

"She would be so proud of you, darling. So proud. Now tell me about your stalker."

I reported that she would not accept a plea bargain, and her trial wouldn't recommence until November. The district attorney believed she would receive twice the time, but nothing was certain. She didn't make bail this time around. I also shared with him about our rental house and how the owner and my friend Mary lived in sin. If Jim and I were asked to stay, we might try to buy the place. I described the location and the architecture, along with what was in the house.

"Lucky you."

"Don't we know it?"

Mom yelled that dinner was served. I quietly observed my family. We would eat together as a nuclear family this week for the last time. The first electron was going out of orbit. The others would follow. It would have been so easy to say I had a wicked stepmother, but that just wasn't the case. I had a great stepmom. I had no complaints. It would be nice to feel allegiance to one or the other, but I loved them both. It wasn't equal. For each, it was different. I wished my other mother could come to the wedding, but this was the way it was.

The first of the glitches began Wednesday night. Jim, who was late, called to say he would not arrive until lunchtime on Friday due to mechanical problems with the new car. His parents weren't coming until after the rehearsal, but before the dinner they were hosting. They had not contacted the restaurant.

Lisa was good, but Jim's sister did not respond to phone calls or text messages. My mom got a migraine, and my brother would not be able to do anything except stand with the groomsmen since he sprained his ankle. The flowers were not doing well in the heat. Furthermore, the caterers experienced a conflict and would deliver the food but not serve as promised.

Other than that, everything was great. By lunchtime on Friday, not even Jim had arrived. He was so sorry that he was still not there. He was about to abandon the truck and hop on a bus. It was so past ridiculous that my sister and I got the giggles. We kept coming up with scenarios in which more things could go wrong.

Jane added to the possible problems. "The church could burn down."

I continued, "A thunderstorm washed out the reception and knocked out the tent."

"The minister forgot to come." And on it went.

My father attempted not to laugh. He consoled my mother, who was now teetering on the edge of a second full-blown migraine. A loud knock on the door made us all sit up.

"Delivery," shouted Andy from upstairs, where he was icing his ankle. Jane ran to the door, where there was a commotion. She squealed, "Run, you idiot. Run before it's too late."

My dad and I raced to the front door. It was Jim, who was totally shocked.

"Jane Harper, you stop that now."

"I'm trying to save him from a fate worse than death."

I came up behind her and put her in a headlock. She screamed, and we pretended to fight to the death. Jim and my father peered at us as though we had recently come out of the Ozarks.

We stopped at the same time, and Jane calmly commented, "All right, big sister. He doesn't scare easily. He might be okay."

Andrew descended the steps on crutches. He had applied makeup to make it appear he had suffered an accident and was sporting a very black eye. Jim stared at him and shook his head.

"You should have seen the other guy." Andrew spit into his hands and made fists, pretending to box. I rolled my eyes, and the three Harper kids broke down in hysterics. My poor father had no idea we had planned all this. Jane was literally on the ground, laughing.

"Jim, I swear I did not father these kids. They're changelings who merely live here and drain blood from us on a regular basis." In his best Hungarian accent, he asked, "Vwont you come in?"

"Wrong house. Sorry to bother you." He turned around and walked to his truck. We kids were shocked. I ran up to him, and he grabbed me and threw me over his shoulder.

"You know, in twenty-four hours, I will be the man of the house, and all forms of punishment are on the table." As he walked through the door, he high-fived my dad.

"It's about time we had a little discipline in this house."

"Dr. Harper, I'm here to help restore order. What needs doing?"

"I'd say put her down, but I'll let you decide if that's wise."

My mother came downstairs. The groom's arrival was reassuring to her, even if carrying the bride on his shoulders was unorthodox.

"Jim, I'm Sherry. These are not our children. The real ones will be here later." She stared at us all and shook her head. "Your mom just called. They arrived early, and we are all headed to the church in an hour for the rehearsal and on to the dinner at Chez Michael's."

"Anyone heard from Rich or your sister?"

"We're all here, staying at the Holiday Inn." Jim reassured my mother that everyone had arrived.

I could tell my mother was starting to recover. While my dad and Jim were drinking a whisky, Andrew tried to persuade Dad to let him have some 'for medicinal purposes.' My mother shook her head, but this time Dad overruled her. I went upstairs to put on a summer dress, which mom purchased for the occasion. Jane had a new dress, as well.

Jim and I headed out in the truck, and my family followed in the van. We all met outside the church. Rich and Dirk were already there. Lisa came with yet another new companion. Finally, Jim's parents arrived. They seemed like ordinary people. His sister was shy, but she soon opened up when Rich and Dirk took her under their wings.

I was nervous about meeting Jim's family, but they were friendly, and I liked his sister. The rehearsal went well. Things seemed to fall into place. I was concerned about the level of alcohol consumption, *but how can you tell your parents not to drink?* Of course, my friends were socially responsible (not).

Jim and the guys left, allowing Andrew to drive them. He returned home around midnight and confessed there would be somewhat more partying at the Holiday Inn. My mother's migraine was transferred to me. Lisa slept over, so Janie took Lisa to the hotel to retrieve her dress. They brought Jim's sister, after which the four of us dressed for the wedding at the house. A photographer arrived at our home in the late morning for the standard, pre-wedding photographs. My parents were so hungover that they sent Andy for headache medication. It might have been Bloody Mary ingredients. Lisa was under the weather, and I worried she would not make it down the aisle. I was not hungover, but I certainly wasn't hungry, either. I drank straight from the faucet every few minutes for rehydration purposes.

Next up was attempting to pee while wearing a wedding dress. The process required three people, and we broke several barriers that day. We finally coaxed Jim's sister out of her shell. I don't think we all laughed so much as when we negotiated bodily functions in our dresses. Finally, we were ready. A limo came to pick up everyone, except my father and me.

Dad sat, and I stood in the foyer for several minutes. He glanced over at me and smiled. "Where did you get the locket?"

"Borrowed." I would have killed to tell him it was from his Becky. I didn't.

"What's blue?"

"Want to see my undies?"

"No, thank you."

"The garter, Dad."

"Becky would be so proud to see you now."

I glimpsed at his watering eyes. "Thanks, Daddy." Mine were watering, as well.

We heard another car pull up. I gripped his hand to pull him up off the bench. He seemed a bit unsteady. I hoped it was from the alcohol last night. I thought, *please don't get old; please don't get old*.

"I swear, I'm giving up alcohol."

"Me too." We stared at one another and laughed—fat chance saloon on that promise.

"I love you, Dad."

"You too, Lauren. You too."

I understood he was thinking about his life and my mom. I grasped his hand to squeeze it. "Let's rock, old man."

"Let's rock, little girl."

The wedding was perfect—even Janie and Andy behaved. Jim was standing at the altar when my father and I made our entrance. The flowers appeared a little wilted, but I don't think anyone noticed that. The minister was Mom's old friend, who had to be prompted to proceed from one thing to the next. A ripple of laughter could be detected when he almost skipped the vows.

My parents were both teary. Mrs. Mason, Dad's longtime secretary—who was seated beside them—was outright silently bawling. She was taking over for the caterers, who had bailed on us for the party. The food was there, but there were no servers. Masey, as my dad called her, organized the serving.

Jim was so handsome in his tuxedo. He smiled as he firmly took my hand. That was the moment I was confident I had made the correct choice. My hand in his felt as if I had put on my old softball glove—familiar yet protective. My hand fit perfectly. I thought, *Let's play ball*. I laughed, considering it, and Jim gazed at me with a quizzical look, which returned me to my senses.

When the time came to exchange rings, I turned to Lisa, who stared blankly at me. I glared at her, cocked my head to the side, and pointed to my finger. She was supposed to give me Jim's ring. Lisa shook her head as she patted her dress. I glanced around and back at her. She reached under her bouquet to pull out a piece of paper, which read, "This is for scaring the shit out of me twice. Never go AWOL again, big sister."

I read the note and chuckled. Lisa winked at my parents, who were obviously in on the conspiracy. She reached back to take the ring from my sister, who was now spasming with laughter.

"I now pronounce you man and wife." The entire wedding party was involved in the prank, and everyone, except for Jim and me, was laughing.

The reception was a success. There were no thunderstorms, and the food was delicious. My mom was in her element. She could relax because her social obligations had been fulfilled. She beamed, watching Jim and me during our wedding dance. I requested the traditional father-daughter dance, which was bittersweet. He represented the old, worn, softball glove, which I had set aside. He was still available if I needed him, but he and I realized my father was relegated to a minor role in my life. He smelled like Old Spice. He'd been the perfect role model for the ways I would both live and parent. "Thanks, Dad."

"I'm not finished, you know. I have to instruct a few grandkids how to fly fish."

"I'll get right on that."

"You'd better because I'm not getting any younger."

While the reception was winding down, I went over to thank my mother. She was not feeling any pain, hugged me, and thanked me for accepting her as my mom and allowing her to share my dad. She mentioned Becky would be proud of me.

"You couldn't have done any better. I will always think of you as my mother. Thanks for such a lovely wedding."

Jim and I left for an undisclosed location in the truck, which Andrew and his friends had decorated. We spent the wedding night in town but headed off for Jackson Hole early the following day. We hiked and even did some fishing. My parents presented Jim with a beautiful rod and reel. We applied for and acquired single-day licenses and discovered a spot on the Snake River, in which we both caught fish. We determined we were better off closer to civilization when we saw a bear. The following day, we headed back to Virginia City. Jim and I had dinner plans with Rich and Dirk when we returned. We picked up LB from Mary's. I showed her a few wedding pictures. She quietly told me there was going to be another wedding in a month. I congratulated her and inquired how I could help. "Will you be a bridesmaid?"

"I would be honored."

Our next stop was the clinic. Thankfully, all was good. We were set to start our real honeymoon. We weren't taking horses, so we packed our backpacks. While I was worried about my recent decline in fitness, I figured I would be ready to tackle the hiking after a few days. We planned to go to Miner's Meadow for two nights, then head up another trail for some serious backcountry hiking and fishing.

We headed over to Rich's house for dinner. I called ahead and wanted to know whether they needed anything. "Nope, I've got it all covered. Simply get your sorry *ahem* over here by six."

We did, and about fifty people were gathered when Rich opened the door. I glanced at Jim, who was as surprised as I was. Ted walked up and asked to kiss the bride.

Jim smiled. "Of course, Ted, but I want one first." Ted kissed Jim, who was taken aback, before planting a good one on me. A succession of men and women followed, including Mary, Mr. Davidson, Dan and Grace Hughes, Phoebe, Brad, and most of the vet- clinic staff. Cary, Mel, and many of the softball team members attended. They recruited me once again, but I was permitted to miss the initial practices. Lois arrived and told me how nice it was to work at the clinic under the new management.

I was sent to the backyard, where several old clients, including Liz and Megan, surrounded something. They separated to reveal Rosa, sitting in a chair. She looked the same, smiled, and got up. Rosa had difficulty walking, and I noticed her oxygen tank. A man was helping her, whom I assumed was the new boyfriend. They both sported rings. LB ran to her and nearly knocked her down.

"No hugging, Lauren. I'm married now." She introduced her husband, Malcolm. I shook her hand and his. "We had a wedding night," she whispered in my ear. My eyebrows shot up.

"Really."

"We kissed under the covers. I don't let him touch me, except for hugging. I told him to sleep in his own bed since he wiggled all night long. We have two beds in the same room."

"You old married woman. We should talk more often to advise each other."

"My sister told me to just set limits. It works."

"Excellent idea. I'll set some beginning tonight. Thanks, Rosa."

I went over to Rich and Dirk, who grinned like two Cheshire cats. I wagged my finger at them. Helen came in with several food trays, which Dirk took from her. A man followed her, who must have been the agent she was trying to snag. I'd met him, but I didn't recognize him in his civvies. She winked at me and wanted to know whether I'd heard from anyone, meaning my mother.

"Nope, that's a once in twenty years' experience."

"When will you leave?"

"We're headed out tomorrow. LB is staying here while we're gone."

"Behave yourself."

"Yes, ma'am."

The party didn't end until early in the morning. We were exhausted, so we decided to not even sleep. We were packed and ready to go. Rich came by to pick us up for a drop-off at the trailhead. The fact that there were quite a few cars in the parking lot alarmed us. Rich kissed me, shook Jim's hand, and left us.

We hiked for an hour along the trail that followed the stream. The smell of the pines and the dark, clear-blue sky was intoxicating. I didn't even glimpse the creek as we passed by the portal pool. We stopped to look at the plaque with my mother's name etched into the brass. We sighed. After another hour, we had nearly reached the top of the pass when Jim asked me how I felt.

I thought about my first year following graduation. It felt like one hundred years. I laughed inwardly, thinking of my experiences with time. "Exhausted, how about you?"

"Yep, but I'm also ready for our future."

We held hands as we crossed the ridge, where we looked down into Miner's Meadow. Neither one of us said a word. This was not the way I imagined my honeymoon. Tents dotted the meadow. We saw children running and could hear their laughter. A couple walked up the trail toward us.

"How was it?" I awaited a reply. The couple looked back and sighed.

"Crowded and noisy. A Boy Scout troop is holding some type of summer camp there. The fishing was terrible."

They continued, and Jim gazed down. Shading his eyes, he simply stared. "Well?"

"Well, what?" I hoped Jim had an acceptable alternative.

"I was counting on this as the start. What do you want to do?"

I had a lump in my throat. "I'm open to suggestions."

"Do you believe backpacks would survive time travel?" Jim searched my face and grinned.

"What are you talking about?"

"What if we traveled to your mother's time? Who would be there?"

I considered it. "Maybe my mother and a few others, but that would be all."

"And the fishing?"

Yep, I definitely married the right man. "Let's go, cowboy. Are you sure?"

"It will tell me whether I married a nut job or the most amazing woman ever."

"Buckle up. This isn't for sissies."

Three hours later, we were back precisely at the spot where we had changed our honeymoon plans. We gazed down on a pristine valley, with a single, tiny trickle of smoke coming from the trees where the cabin resided.

"I guess you'll meet the rest of my family."

"Lead the way."

Rebecca

"What are you searching for?" I observed Sam. For some reason, he continually watched the horizon and trail down to Hank Heaven every day while I skinny-dipped.

"Just making sure you aren't being watched, Bec."

"Dan knows to fire his gun if he's coming down. There's no one else except for a possible stray Indian. You should relax."

"You never know. I wish you would wear at least those… What do you call them?"

"Shorts, darling." Sam kept looking, but from down in the warm, muddy, shallow water, I could not tell what he was watching.

"I'm ready, anyway. Avert your eyes, my prudish Victorian husband. I'm coming out."

Sam stared over at me and then back at the trail. Sam brought a sheet and wrapped me in it. "Your timing is fortuitous, my wanton, modern wife." He kissed me and turned me toward the trail. "We have company."

The End

Acknowledgments

Once again, I would like to thank my family, coworkers, and my friends who read the first drafts of this book. A special thanks go to my primary readers, Jane Gropp, Jeanie Olson, Julie Laughton, Jodee O'Leary, Sandra Fletcher, Dr. Sharon Spiers, and Denise Piggott. Thank you to my editor, Marilyn Anderson, and cover designer, David Blake. Also, thanks to Emma Moulds and Jodie Vaughan for technical assistance.

I would like to thank all the creators and producers of television Westerns who gave me a love of a very sanitized and probably unrealistic version of the past. I still loved watching these series. Are you sure that time travel isn't possible? I regularly travel back to the 1800s in my mind.

ABOUT THE AUTHOR

Elizabeth grew up in postwar California. Sure she was the daughter of Roy Rogers, she spent her youth emulating him. Sadly, DNA evidence has proved her wrong. Thus, she followed in her other father's footsteps into  equine veterinary practice. She subsequently migrated to Australia, where she practiced equine veterinary medicine near Adelaide, South Australia, until her retirement in December 2020. She began writing about her experiences as a horse vet and published her first book, Horse Doctor An American Vet's Life Down Under in 2005. A few years before her father's death, she discovered a treasure trove of personal and historically significant letters. She knew this would make a great book not only for her family but also for WWII enthusiasts. She published Jack's War, Letters to Home from an American WII Navigator in 2015.

While veterinary medicine has been her passion, fly-fishing, horseback riding, and writing occupy her leisure time. Her new books include stories about women in equine practice. Small Town Secrets: Horse Doctor Adventures 2021 is her latest book. She now resides in North Georgia, where she follows her passions.

She loves to hear from readers! ewoolseydvm@gmail.com

https://www.facebook.com/elizabeth.woolseydvm

https://elizabethwoolsey.com/

https://amzn.to/3dPAoGc

BOOKS BY ELIZABETH

Horse Doctor Adventure Books:

Horse Doctor Adventures Small Town Secrets

The Travels of Dr. Rebecca Harper Series
Book 1 A Matter of Time
Book 2 Troubled Waters
Book 3 Lauren's Story
Book 4 Past and Present
https://amzn.to/3fwXDoG

A new series
Catch and Release
Catch and Keep
https://amzn.to/3CdUraI

Amazon Catch and Release Series

Also by Elizabeth Woolsey (Herbert)
Horse Doctor: An American Vet's Life Down Under
Jack's War: Letters Home from an American WII Navigator

PREVIEW

CATCH AND RELEASE

Chapter 1

"Mum, they're crazy over there. They all have guns, and they have murders every day." There was an endless list of reasons my children didn't support my return to America. They didn't want me to leave them. My three children all lived in different states, and I was only flavor of the month in December. Not one of the kids came home for Christmas last year. They had their own families and had moved on. I left them in Australia to return to my native country—God bless America, I hoped. I was starting over.

Old age is not for the faint-hearted, but what's old? Starting my new life in a rural community far from friends and family was scary. My sister and brother thought I was crazy, which I think we'd already established when I upped and moved to Australia to follow my future and now ex-husband.

My kids were furious, and they had every reason to be. Admittedly, I was abandoning them. It was alright and preferential that they moved out and started their own families. Still, parents are expected to stay and be the nuclear family's anchor. I failed my kids and bailed on them. Sorry—not.

I was restarting my life back in the States after twenty-seven years of living in Australia. I pulled into the long driveway to make my way up to my new home. I'd purchased a log cabin on forty-eight acres last year. I told my family I lived in a gated community. An old Powder River gate with a lock protected me from the gun-toting heathens who my children had envisioned. The gate had seen better days and had a large indentation from a vehicle or a bison. I don't think there are any buffalo here, but I could dream. The gate was well off the road, allowing someone with a truck and trailer to pull into the driveway and be safe when the gate with its chain and ancient lock needed to be opened.

The property looked like a desert with rocks and sage as the only prominent features visible from the road. It fooled me when I came last year looking for retirement properties. I could not imagine wanting to buy this place as I looked up the hill from the road. My realtor, Carol Carter, and I drove over the hill and descended into a small, lush valley with a log home, barn, and fenced paddocks next to a year-round creek abutting a dense forest.

Carol turned to me. "Proceed?"

"Maybe. So, what are the issues? There must be a catch. This place has been on the market for six years. How come?"

"Let's just look before I say any more." Carol pointed to a white speck in a tree. "See her?"

"Is that a bald eagle?"

"Maggie, we can leave, but I think it's worth a look." I observed Carol smiling to herself.

"No, let's at least look around. Any fish in the creek?"

"Some. There's a story, but I think you may just be the one person who can get over a few details." Carol lied. The word detail implied a small obstacle; it was not. Despite knowing the true story, which was far more than a tiny issue, I purchased the property, and now, nine months later, here I was, ready to move in and start the next ten years of my life. I planned to live like this for at least ten years before I went to live in 'the home,' as my children called it.

A bottle of Barossa Valley wine, flowers, and house keys sat on a table on the deck, which faced the surrounding forest. My spectacular view was worth every penny. I sat down on the chair next to the table and pulled out my small book of contacts and reminders. Most of my essential details were on my phone. My to-do list was usually written out so I could get the pleasure of ticking the items off. I added a reminder to send a thank you note to Carol. The rocky gravel road would need to be graded and smoothed out. I would add that to a long list of things that would need to be done to make this place livable year-round.

There was an envelope with a list of tradesmen and contact numbers for the utilities and a state fishing license—go Carol! There was a second smaller envelope that contained an invitation to an annual picnic for the locals. Carol mentioned her brother-in-law had an event every year. Attendance was mandatory if I wanted to meet the who's who of the area. I was told not to bring anything but my appetite. The theme was western casual, and it was in two weeks.

Here was my haven from my past life—no more work. No more being on call and no more worries about sick or dying horses. Veterinary medicine had been good to me. I was lucky that I loved what I did, but that life was over.

I left my country of residence, my children, and my profession for a rural life of solitude and recreational fly-fishing. My clients, family, and friends said I would fail at retirement. No one, including me, could imagine I could find joy outside of my professional life. My coworkers were incredibly doubtful. I'd devoted the last fifty years of my existence to veterinary medicine, and to the exclusion of anything else. It was inconceivable that I could find joy in other activities.

They didn't know. I had a secret plan. I was approaching my late sixties when three years ago, I noticed that the joy in my work had finally waned. I no longer looked forward to saving the lives of horses. Most of my contemporaries had retired long before me and found joy in cruises, grandchildren, and hobbies. They encouraged me to do the same. "You can't be a horse vet forever. It's dangerous, and you're vulnerable. Your reaction time is not what it used to be. Remember Larry Childers? You don't want to end up like him."

I never met Larry, but he was a legend in equine veterinary medicine. Larry had been killed when a stallion struck him in the head. He was a good horseman, but Larry took risks. He didn't have my staff. Their number one job was to keep me safe. I'd given up the dangerous stuff years ago. I no longer collected semen from stallions or stuck the first needle into an unbroken colt to be castrated. Still, it was often the most unexpected occurrence that did many vets in.

The reason for my decision to retire was not fear of injury. It was not the midnight calls for help or even the continuous being on call for emergencies. I just had lost interest. I simply found no joy in veterinary medicine. I was at the top of my game, and I didn't want to play anymore. I wanted a new life, and while I was leaving many friends, I wanted new ones.

Living in another country was the best decision I'd ever made. The reason for the original relocation overseas, my ex, did not turn out like I had planned. Still, thankfully it gave me children and a great professional life. I used to say, "Pinch me. They're paying me to do this." Now I have changed the verb to "paid." Sadly, my Australian friends had either died, moved away, or had families and responsibilities that superseded me. We had different interests and, more importantly, different values. I wanted to get back to my people. I had no problems making friends. I thought I might find like-minded people here in rural America. So, I sold up and moved back home to my people and heritage.

Before entering the house, I decided to walk down to the creek. There was an old fence on the other side of the stream. The barricade was damaged in many places. A bear could walk onto the property, and a horse could escape—more for the to-do list. I was aware that bears and mountain lions were known in the area. I saw scat down on the bank and considered adding gun procurement on my to-do list. I left my dogs with my children until I was ready to have them sent over. This might have been a mistake. I was told the dogs were being held for ransom until I came to my senses.

I checked my phone. Only one bar, would that be enough? "Help, I've fallen, and I can't get up." I wasn't that old, and one month ago, I was still wrangling horses. My last call before retirement was a horse with a grass awn in its eye. She was not impressed with me and vice versa. She thought the prick of a needle was a cue to rear. Better living through chemistry, a good vet nurse, and she was on her way home drunk and medicated—good luck on the follow-up. That was my past, and this is my future.

I returned to the cabin and picked up the keys. The door was solid with a heavy-duty lock. I unlocked and opened the door. Phew. The smell of death permeated the great room. I immediately remembered the 'detail' that Carol had explained, which stopped sales for several years. Oh my God, what had I done?

Chapter 2

The smell was overpowering. I stepped back and closed the door. Six years ago, there was a murder-suicide in this house. It was an older couple. The Calhoun's bodies had not been discovered for several weeks. Despite many attempts at removing the smell, bodily fluids had soaked into the floorboards, and the scent of death continued to fill the house. The son of the couple had finally replaced the flooring. Still, knowing the history, buyers shunned the property, and it sat empty.

There was a fire that may have been arson to collect the insurance, so the couple's son might get some of his inheritance. He was interstate at the time and was never charged. If he hired someone, no trace of an arsonist was established.

The fire failed anyway, and the damage was minor and easily repaired.

Carol explained the reason for the murder-suicide was never confirmed. Still, the husband had Alzheimer's, and it appeared the wife killed him and then herself. They had only been in the home for two years and were not social. He was an artist, and they moved there so he could paint the scenery.

I negotiated a significant price drop and bought the place well under the estimated value. When I first visited the house, there was no lingering smell. The windows were opened, airing the house for my inspection. But that was a year ago.

Carol promised to have the electricity on, a satellite for cable television, and an internet connection ready. When I picked up the key to the property, the secretary explained the cable guy was unable to come until I was onsite. I needed to explain where the modem and television cables were to be installed.

So, what was the smell? It had to be from something big. Really big. I retrieved a kerchief from the car and covered my mouth and nose. I re-entered the house and immediately began to open the windows. I searched around and discovered a dead snake in the kitchen. I thought of my two cats, which I left at my veterinary clinic. Add cat procurement to my list. I removed the snake. How did it get in? I turned on the fan and opened the doors, but the smell lingered.

There were a few cleaning products under the sink and a spray can of Oust. It was empty. I cleaned the floor, and the smell began to retreat. I didn't have any furniture, and I planned to buy everything new. I had a sleeping bag, and I would sleep on the floor until I had a bed delivered. My sister was arriving tomorrow, and we were going to do major retail therapy as soon as she got here.

The thought of sleeping on the floor where a snake could crawl was scary. I had many friends and colleagues who had died in their first few months of retirement. I was determined to live for at least ten more years. My plan did not include passing anytime soon, and it didn't really include retirement. I was starting my new profession as an author. I'd started it two years ago, but I kept this redirection in my life to myself. I was excited like I had been when I began my veterinary career. Even if I failed, I was getting so much joy out of my new career that I didn't care if I was successful or not.

I checked my phone, which said, 'no service.' I already knew this from my initial visit. The house had a landline, but my plan was for a satellite booster for everything. I considered getting a motel for the night. I wasn't poor. I could afford it, but I decided to tough it out. My sister, Christy, was coming tomorrow and bringing two camping mattresses. We were heading to the big smoke to look at furniture and fixtures for the cabin. I walked up to the top of the hill between my house and the road. My phone immediately dinged, signaling a missed call and message.

"Maggot, I'm ahead of schedule. Be at your place in two hours and I'll be expecting dinner and alcohol. My decorating services aren't free. See you about five-ish."

Crap, I had left the milk and tonic in the car. I walked back down to the cabin, unloaded three bags of groceries, and put it all in the cabinets and fridge. The refrigerator was new and enormous. It was on and cold. There was an inbuilt ice machine, and I decided to try out the ice and water. The initial water was horrible. I had the water tested before I bought the place, and it was clean and filtered. I let it run for a minute and was rewarded with sweet, clean well water. I checked the ice, and it smelled fine. I was ready for gin-o'clock.

I brought my clothes and fishing rod out of the car. The new SUVs had tons of space. My overseas belongings were on their way, but it would be weeks before they arrived. I surveyed the house and walked through each room. I purposely bought a house with three guestrooms and a large sleeping room upstairs for my extended family and friends. I didn't live close to anyone, but this place was ideal, and I would attract visitors who would use my house as a vacation spot.

My immediate plans were to purchase enough utensils and kitchenware and get two bedrooms ready. Christy was on her way to visit her in-laws and was only staying a couple of nights. She and her husband Miles would be back later in the summer for some hiking and exploring. My brother and his wife would come later in the summer. At least one of my children would cross the pond—as we referred to the Pacific Ocean—next year for a few weeks of berating me for leaving the family home.

Most of the house had a timber interior, but the bathrooms, basement, and one room used as an office had walls that needed new paint. The other task was to fix the fences and barn and find a safe horse to ride. I walked around and added to the list. I had so much to do and all the time in the world to do it. When had I ever felt like that?

I went into my bedroom, which faced the mountains and creek. There was a balcony off my room. It was high enough I was safe to leave the doors open. If there were ghosts, then I was happy to share the space. I might even sleep out on the balcony and get a feel for the outdoors. I could hardly wait for my sister to arrive., and I didn't have to wait long. She arrived in less time than she guessed.

Christy looked around and smiled. "Maggot, I could almost be jealous."

"Thanks. I was hoping you would see what I see too."

"Miles and I get saves on the first two weeks in August next year and then the following year."

"Maybe Bill and Lonnie will come too, and you could bring the grandkids."

Lonnie was our sister-in-law. She was tons of fun, which compensated for our brother, who inherited our long-dead father's inability to see the humor in anything. Hey, want to walk down to the creek?"

"Nope. I'm starving, and I need some dinner."

"No prob. I bought steaks, and we can have a salad. Ready for a G &T?"

My sister was smaller than me and had brown hair in contrast to Bill and me. Of course, Bill had let himself go gray while Christy and I kept our "natural" color. We dared each other to let nature take its course, but neither of us was ready to allow the outside world to see us as anything but middle-aged women.

"Where are the pots and pans?" Christy was looking through the cupboards. "Hey, is there a dead mouse in here?"

There was no way in hell that I was telling her about the snake. "Yep. Mickey bit the dust and then the dustpan. I swear there was a frying pan here. I don't even see a tray to catch the drips off the oven grill. Shall we go check out the natives?"

"Is there a place to eat in town?"

"Mabel's. It isn't bad either. I ate there last year."

"Should I dress?"

"Yeah, they don't do naked."

"Do we need to call ahead?" Christy was probably joking. The town was so small.

"Hopefully, not." I wasn't kidding, but we didn't. The café was half full, and the food and smells were delightful. I explained to my sister that, for a short time, I didn't want people to know I had been a vet. I was happy to fly under the radar. Christy thought it was a good idea too. She'd been plagued by people calling for advice and wanting her to come back to work when she retired. We ate and left without notice from the locals.

We returned to the property. As dusk approached, we climbed over the hill, and there was my new home. There was a light on over the garage. I hadn't been in there or the room above the garage since I'd arrived. I still had two boxes of clothes to bring in from the car.

Christy said she wanted to see what was in the room upstairs. She took the key, entered the garage, and headed up to the small room upstairs. She returned and asked if I had been there on my previous visit last year.

"Yes, it could be used for another bedroom if I was desperate, but it was empty when I last saw it."

"You better come up. Someone's been in there."

I went up, and there in the room was a table, chair, and a sleeping bag. There was a notebook with drawings and legends explaining the illustrations. They appeared to be the work of a child.

"What the?" I was at a loss to explain this.

"Goldilocks?" Christy thumbed through the pages.

"Bears?" I joked.

"No, these drawings are more sophisticated than your average bear."

"Some kid has been up here playing house. Maggie, you better call your realtor in the morning."

"Yeah, good idea. Are you sure the door was locked before you tried to get in?"

"No, not one hundred percent. I just automatically used the key to open the door."

"These drawings are pretty advanced, and with cars, houses, and a dog, it's definitely a boy's work."

"Well, Maggot, let's go over and have a drink and maybe watch the stars. Do you know who your neighbors are?"

"Just one, but he hasn't been up here in years. Do you remember the actor, Colin Chandler?"

"Get out! That old geezer? Is he still alive? Maggot, you're holding back."

"He supposedly keeps staff, and his children occasionally visit. He used to have a massive horse facility, but Carol said it was now down to just a few horses and a few stable hands."

"He was a fox in his day. Wasn't he America's sexiest man in the 1800s?" She laughed at her pathetic joke. "He's got to be at least eighty now. You never hear anything about him.

Maybe the kid belongs to one of the staff members who live next door on his property."

Chapter 3

Christy set down her wine glass. I had my usual gin and tonic. "Barossa wine, can I take some back with me?"

"It was a gift from my realtor."

"So, what are you going to do to keep yourself busy?" Christy poured a second glass.

"Oh yeah. Well, tomorrow it will be in the news, so you might as well be the first." I went to my suitcase and retrieved the first product of my plan. I came back to the porch, and in the candlelight, I handed my sister a book.

"My new life."

Christy examined the book while I waited with anticipation. She opened the book and saw the dedication. To my children, sister, and brother.... It went on to describe how they helped me in ways they never would have guessed. The book was about the outback men I met during my professional career. I used my maiden name, Margaret Kincaid. The book had been picked up by an Australian publisher, and it was due out next week on Amazon.

What I didn't tell my sister or anyone was that I had a contract for five more books, of which three had been written and edited. They were fiction and were a series about a woman veterinarian who solved crimes. The Australian book was not a big financial deal and was destined for the Australian market. An international publishing company paid me in advance for the fiction series. I was advised to hire a good investment planner. The first book in the series would be out in a month or two. I was contracted to do interviews and book signings if the sales were as expected.

"Maggot, I love the idea. Can I see the other books? Are they in print?"

"I have a reviewer's copy of the first fiction book. It's my only one. You can see it, but I need it back." I went to a box still in the foyer and retrieved the book. "Read this to get to sleep."

The following morning, Christy reported she loved the book and could hardly wait to get her own copy. "Mom and Dad would have been so proud, Maggot."

"Thanks. Want a cinnamon roll for breakfast? I want to get going. It's a long drive to the city."

"Coffee, and let's rock and roll."

"Pun intended on the roll?"

"Yep." Christy had showered and was ready to leave.

My sister was fit and still looked like a woman fifteen years younger than her actual age. She was a year older than me, and she was my role model. She'd taught chemistry at the local college and ran a private tutoring school for disadvantaged kids on the side. She'd won awards for her work with underprivileged kids. Miles had a large construction firm that renovated old buildings in San Francisco. Their children had all married and had kids of their own.

Christy tried to set me up with her single male friends, but I didn't want to meet anyone for fear of being tied to a place that didn't suit my recreational needs. I'd spent the last two years on the internet looking for waterfront properties all over the country. This area suited me for several reasons. While I hadn't met anyone yet, I was advised the population was a mix of people who liked the outdoors and had rural ranching backgrounds.

There was a small group of artists and writers and the occasional ultra-wealthy landowner who jetted in and out but only rarely visited. I hoped to meet both men and women who had similar interests. Still, they would have their own lives, so I could enjoy occasional companionship with a heavy dose of privacy.

As we got into my sister's car, the cable guy, Ralph Childers, arrived. I quickly explained what I needed and where I wanted all the outlets and modem to go. He said he would have it done by the afternoon. I had to arrange to get the system turned on and pay for the service, and he gave me the number to call with my details to start getting the internet. Sweet, I was anxious to Zoom with my kids.

"Ma'am, I'm sure glad you're taking such a chance on the place, given the history. Not many people are willing to live alone and especially in this place with its past."

"You mean the murder-suicide?"

"Well, that's one theory. Most of us locals think it was a double murder, and the sheriff's department didn't investigate it properly."

"Really? This is the first I heard about it." I turned to my sister while she pretended to gaze out the window toward the mountains.

"There are reports there is money still hidden, and the son was still visiting the property just a few months ago."

"I've owned the property for the last six months. Maybe I should change the lock on the gate."

"That's for sure. I'll lock it when I leave, but a new lock would be a good idea." Ralph returned to his truck to retrieve his tools.

We thanked him for the information and drove out. We looked at one another, and my sister said, "Where do you want your ashes placed?"

"Here. Yeah, I better get a new will."

To purchase the first book in this series https://amzn.to/3CdUraI

Catch and Release

CPSIA information can be obtained
at www.ICGtesting.com
Printed in the USA
BVHW052134170323
660681BV00011B/151